Midway on the Waves

by the same author

Another Self
Ancestral Voices
Prophesying Peace
Caves of Ice

Midway on the Waves

JAMES LEES-MILNE

faber and faber

LONDON · BOSTON

First published in 1985
by Faber and Faber Limited
3 Queen Square London WC1N 3AU

Phototypeset by Wilmaset
Birkenhead, Merseyside
Printed in Great Britain by
Redwood Burn Ltd Trowbridge Wiltshire
All rights reserved

British Library Cataloguing in Publication Data

Lees-Milne, James
Midway on the waves.
1. Great Britain—Social life and customs—1945–
I. Title
941.085′092′4   DA589.4

ISBN 0–571–13723–7

Library of Congress Cataloging-in-Publication Data

Lees-Milne, James.
Midway on the waves.

1. Lees-Milne, James. 2. Architectural historians—
Great Britain—Biography. I. Title
NA2599.8.L43A2   1985   828′.91403 [B] 85–10238
ISBN 0–571–13723–7

In Memoriam
Fratris Dilecti Mei
R.C. L.-M.

The shadow of the dome of pleasure
Floated midway on the waves;
                    Samuel Taylor Coleridge
                        'Kubla Khan'

Contents

Foreword   *page* 11
1948   13
1949   139
Index   231

Foreword

This fourth volume of diaries finishes off the hungry forties. I left the fifties to look after themselves. And as for the sixties they are to me as yesterday, and not yet history. Thenceforth I no longer kept a day-to-day diary, which is the only sort dealing with a trivial life to be readable. Fragmentary jottings, known to academics as *disjecta membra*, are only acceptable from very powerful minds. I doubt whether Parson Wood-forde's reflections upon Michelangelo's status among Renaissance artists or even man's place in the Universe would have proved very stimulating – except to himself.

During 1948 and 1949 I lived in a flat on the ground floor of no. 20 Thurloe Square, South Kensington. My parents' home and my birthplace was Wickhamford Manor between Broadway and Evesham in Worcestershire.

The principal persons referred to in the following pages are given their proper names and designations in the index. Those places mentioned which are now National Trust properties are printed in capital letters.

'Sunt lacrimae rerum et mentem mortalia tangunt.'

J.L.-M.
19 Lansdown Crescent
Bath, 1985

1948

Saw Lord Bearsted today. He assures me the catalogue of pictures at Upton is nearly ready. I fear this poor man will not last long, for he is very tired, slow and shaky. He is of my father's generation (the Kaiser's War and all) and they seem to age badly.

After 6 o'clock went, at their invitation, to see the Wyndham Clarks' house, 44 Berkeley Square, and the way Shearsby has repaired the painted ceiling of the great room. I introduced him to them and had forgotten I did so. What a wonderful house it is, but the Clarks, who seem to have money but no servants, keep it like a vast jumble heap, which, servants or no, is not necessary, I think.

Friday, 2nd January

To the British Museum. Soane Jenyns introduced me to Collins of the Manuscripts Department, to whom I showed some Charlecote mss. I brought up. He liked the Cromwell writ of summons and the Edmund Waller passport, but was not so keen on Sir Thomas Lucy's Wages Book. I am. I consider it romantic that here in his own writing are Justice Shallow's detailed accounts kept over the precise years when the Shakespeare incident is supposed to have taken place.

Saturday, 3rd January

Paul Hyslop lunched. He explained to me that the word 'rag' was coined by Eddy [Sackville-West] to mean a cagey queer, the opposite of a 'tearing' queer, the term rag applying to pages of children's books made of that material. A 'billiard ball' is the smart, dandified, smooth, City type of queer, who tries to appear otherwise. Well, one lives and learns.

Sunday, 4th January

Met Eddie Marsh in the bus, both of us bound for Brooks's and luncheon. He said he was busy correcting Winston Churchill's page proofs of the famous War History.

I gave a dinner party, without meaning to, for Riette Lamington, Lady George Cholmondeley, a banker friend of hers, and Jamesey [Pope-Hennessey]. After dinner we tried table-turning. Nothing stirred.

Drove down to Long Crichel. Lunched excellently at my favourite eating place, the Wheatsheaf Inn, and stopped at Winchester. In the Cathedral choir were one old man reading the New Testament to himself, very loudly in an affected voice, and two ladies discussing hats, each party oblivious of the other. I enjoyed this odd little scene on a dull afternoon in January. The three had evidently sought refuge in the warmth rather than spiritual consolation. At the bookshop I was lucky to buy the architectural book I saw there last July and always meant to go back for – 'Some Designs of Mr Inigo Jones and Mr William Kent, by John Vardy 1744'.

Each day Eardley [Knollys] and I went to Stourhead, arriving at 10 every morning. We worked like blacks. There is hardly one piece of furniture in the state rooms that we have not shifted ourselves. At last we broke the back of our difficulties and assembled all the furniture in the rooms allotted to them. It is astonishing the amount of stuff left over which we cannot place. Nearly every day it has rained and the rooms are pitch dark. But we have enjoyed ourselves.

Raymond Mortimer is staying at Long Crichel. A wise man. He warned Eardley and me against looking up all the words we did not know in the dictionary when reading French books, advising us to look up only a word that recurs frequently. Talking about some silly-billy, he observed that most of us have our own censor that prevents our uttering all the foolish thoughts that tumble into our minds. I returned to London on Friday afternoon. All the inmates at Long C., Eddy, Raymond, Desmond [Shawe-Taylor] and Eardley are angelic to me and this house has become a sort of second home.

On my return I dined at B.S.'s. There was present another man, Archie Colquhoun, whom I had met years back. B.S. terribly tied up and adolescent. At 10.15 Harold Nicolson arrived and ate a sandwich supper. He had come from Croydon where he was adopted as Labour candidate. He was rather silly and bumble-beeish. *Memo.* Not to be bumble-beeish with younger persons in twenty-five years' time.

[16]

Tonight I went, cursing, in the rain, to dine with the Barry Craigs. She was Theodosia Cropper whom I came to know and like well – she has a dreamy, abstracted manner which appeals to me – when I was on sick leave in 1941. There was a sweetness in her welcome and spontaneity that won my heart instantly. I liked him too; a good-looking, friendly and competent artist.

At 6 went to Doreen [Colston-Baynes] in Ovington Square. She was very kind about my book, but has not read it, which shows that her appetite has not been whetted. Says her brother has taken and is reading it. I told her of Sachie Sitwell's charming letter of congratulation I received this morning. It was unsolicited for I had not sent him a copy. Evenings at Doreen's are a bit of a strain at times for she can be goosey, dear thing that she is. She has been introduced to Chips Channon by Peter Coats, and is thrilled to the marrow. Theirs seems to be no more her *monde* than the Bing Boys' or the Crazy Gang's would be Queen Mary's. Then I went to the Dorchester Ordinary. I had thought dinner was to be at Sibyl's [Colefax] house, but this is a habit she has of inviting one and then at the last moment letting on that dinner is at the Dorchester, for which one pays. But I felt sorry and my heart melted, because she was just out of a sick-bed, looking bent, crumpled, ill and so old. I sat next to Harold and Mrs [Eny] Strutt, whom I found rather formidable. She talked of class and breeding and the necessity for both. After the Ordinary I walked away with Harold, Ben [Nicolson] and Noel Annan to Brooks's. The last very affable and, though young, coot bald, a don at Cambridge who reviews for the *Statesman*. He was modest and polite which is rare in a don and an intellectual. I liked him. He spoke admiringly of James's writing and forecast that his *Lord Houghton* would be *the* book of the decade. We drank whisky upstairs in the Subscription Room. Harold in excellent form. He reminded us of Croker drinking at Brooks's with Colonel Stanhope who was decrying the Duke of Wellington at the moment when the mob poured past the windows with the news of the victory of Waterloo. Sir Edmund Gosse related to H. the following story: Lord John Manners told Gosse that he remembered attending a Belvoir Hunt dinner at Belvoir Castle. A footman handed the Duke of Rutland a letter. The Duke broke the seal, read and exclaimed, 'Oh, how terrible!' Rose to his feet, and said: 'Gentlemen, I think we must discontinue our festivities. I have received bad news. Lord Byron is dead.'

Doreen confessed to me this evening that she preferred the company of stupid, well-bred people to that of intelligent, ill-bred or common people. I think I do too, on the whole. Certainly I would on a desert island. She complained how dirty were the hands of the bus conductors – worse than those of the conductresses – so that she tries to avoid their touching her gloved hand when they give her change. In consequence she is apt to drop her coins on the floor of the bus. I said it would be surprising if at the end of a long day their hands were clean, poor things.

Tuesday, 13th January

Went to see Sibyl Colefax in bed today and brought her my book as a present. Anything to give the kind old woman slight pleasure; this sounds horribly condescending. Lady Anderson came in before I left in such a cloud of scent that I smelt it on me all the way back in the tube to South Kensington. Bowler-hatted commuters sniffed me suspiciously.

Thursday, 15th January

Dined with Helen Dashwood who had asked Nancy [Mitford]. Just the three of us, very agreeable, until Francis [Dashwood] and friend arrived from Switzerland which interrupted the intimate flow. Nancy looking very beautiful indeed in lovely black dress, flounced and long, about one foot above the ankles, small waist, padded hips, and thick black petticoat of silk, and muff. As she says, never have women's fashions been prettier.

Friday, 16th January

I have seen a good deal of Michael [Rosse] these few days, he being very important and taking the chair at numerous meetings. A trifle too gracious. I was pleased to be able to reprove him for ordering Anthony Martineau [National Trust solicitor] to get in touch with the Princess Royal's solicitor without her authority. 'How could *you* do such a thing? Such an unwonted lapse by you of all correct people.' M. was for the first time in his life abashed, and actually blushed.

Saturday, 17th January

Quite a profitable day. Spent the morning at the National Portrait Gallery looking at the pre-Restoration portraits, of which at present there are only two rooms shown, so it does not take long. There ought

[18]

to be more of these earlier people. I don't think the Gallery is very well hung. All this weekend I have worked on French Renaissance architecture.

At breakfast this morning it snowed heavily and I wondered whether to put off my visit to Gunby. Decided to persevere. Luckily I did so for it stopped snowing by 10 o'clock. I motored off and passing by Wrest Park, drove up to the house, now under requisition. Rather an attractive big house of *c.* 1830, but I could see nothing of the famous gardens; the days are so short that there is no time for loitering. Then to Houghton, Bunyan's place, superbly situated on a hill, now a complete ruin. It is of red brick with stone dressings; in shape and general style Jacobean. Can just see how it might be by Inigo Jones. The windows are mullioned and pedimented and the over-lights are oval; the doorways are classical and on one front between the wings is a classical screen. Bunyan called it the House Beautiful, I believe, and Walpole, 'picturesque . . . but bad and inconvenient within'.

At Peterborough had a quick walk round the Cathedral to refresh my memory of the glorious Perpendicular ambulatory with fan roof. The cast-iron stoves in the Cathedral I always admire for their Early English Gothic design. There are no mural monuments in this Cathedral. Then I called at the Red Hall, Bourne, which the LNER have offered to the Trust. It is a nice Jacobean house, seductive from a distance, but unfortunately at the very edge of the railroad and indeed part of the station. It is divided into two tenements, inhabited by a railway labourer and a tailor. Both these people were very kind in showing me over. I was astonished at the deplorable condition of the insides and the friendliness of the inhabitants. The wife of the railwayman inveighed against the LNER for never improving, but the tailor was cheerful and made allowance for his landlords. The wallpapers in both houses were hanging in festoons; damp everywhere; many square panes missing and the holes stuffed with rags. Red Hall is square, of red brick and stone quoins, pointed gables, a central projecting porch with Orders. In one dwelling is the original oak staircase, balustered, and newels bearing obelisks. Upstairs under the roof one large room with gypsum floor called the ballroom; exposed braced timbers overhead.

I arrived after tea at Gunby, the car having gone very well. Lady Massingberd, only recently widowed after fifty years' bliss, was extremely cheerful and just like her old self. I do admire her. No complaints and she is making the best of her situation. She says that so long as the Whartons stay, she can remain at Gunby. The Field Marshal's pension of £1,700 p.a. is now gone and there is a big drop. She tells me that he died quietly, having had his first seizure nine months before. A tired heart finished him off. Wharton gave me some more particulars with the relish servants always indulge in. He confirmed that the FM suffered no pain, just declined; ate nothing towards the end, adding that 'not a drop came out of his body anywhere, after his death'. The Whartons were much moved and are erecting an iron gate, chosen by Lady M., with an inscription 'To the memory of our beloved Field Marshal', which is touching. Lady M. worried a bit who would live at Gunby when she was gone. She said the FM's last wish was that the Trust should give back the two portraits by Oswald Birley, for he did not want himself and his wife to go down to posterity as portrayed by this artist. During the visit I read one volume of Peregrine Massingberd's diary, enjoying it immensely. I told Lady M. that it ought to be edited and published.

Saturday, 24th January

Tonight I went at 4.30 to Wayland Hilton Young's wedding at St George's, Hanover Square where my parents were married in 1904. Keith Miller-Jones persuaded me to go in act of friendship. Dosia Cropper was in the church and walked away with me to the reception with her left hand clasped in mine in my topcoat pocket. I love her spontaneous affection. She acts and speaks what is in her mind without forethought or afterthought. I knew no one else at the reception.

Had Nancy [Mitford], Bridget Parsons and Tony Gandarillas to dinner. Emily gave us a lovely spread, with partridges. I did not much enjoy it for Nancy's scintillations dry me up, and talk – which she hogged – was mainly Parisian scandal, which means nothing to me. She also mentioned Gerald Berners's stroke, a slight one. He is very depressed. This highly sophisticated man is unhappy because he cannot find God, according to N., and doesn't know where to begin looking for him. She gave us an outline of her new book, a funny story ending with the uncle, who had married his deceased wife's niece, greatly to the rage of the niece's parents, falling in love with a young man. N. longs to *épater* the public.

Monday, 26th January

Motored to Montacute arriving in time to lunch with the Yateses (pouring rain all day). Eardley already there. We spent a long afternoon rearranging the parlour, putting out the needlework furniture, and hanging Michael Peto's tapestry. Then to Long Crichel for the night.

Tuesday, 27th January

In pouring rain still E. and I in my car motored to Higher Bockhampton. Looked at Hardy's birthplace. The little house and surroundings are just as Hardy must have known them; the rising heath behind the property surely unchanged. The cottage of brick and thatch is of the simplest. The two nice elderly lady tenants are very anxious to stay on and willing to show visitors round. Educated women yet content to live without a bath and with oil lamps. We lunched at Exeter. Called at Bradley Manor and saw Mrs Woolner. The place tidied up since our last visit, the lodge painted and the neat NT notice board in place. Outside of house newly harled.

We stayed with Patrick Kinross at Easton Court Hotel, Chagford. Charming and friendly; greatly improved in health and looks since I saw him on his first return from Egypt – less gross and yellow. We were shown photographs of all of us, Patrick, Christopher Hobhouse, Alan Pryce-Jones and me – all quite nice-looking too – when we were here in 1932.

Wednesday, 28th January

Again in pouring rain motored to Cotehele, losing our way as usual down deep and narrow lanes. We started arranging the show rooms. Cook, ingenious man, clerk-of-works acting for us on the estate, most helpful, eager to clean the armour in the great hall and do anything we want. A sort of super-*bricoleur*. We made strides and felt quite pleased with ourselves.

Thursday, 29th January

Again poured heavily the entire day. I worried about my car standing in the rain lest water got into some vital parts of its anatomy. Cotehele has a peculiar melancholy and beauty of its own, especially at this season, for the state rooms are heated by large wood fires that fill the stuffy air with blue smoke. Eardley and I finished our arrangements. Every room is hung with tapestry treated like wallpaper over the plaster walls. No regard was had for the merit of the panels which were cut ruthlessly to fit over doorways, beds and cupboards.

On our return to Tavistock we combed the antique dealers. I bought a glass candlestick for the centre of my marble table, a strip of red and blue matting and a pink case lined with tortoiseshell and covered with leather. Very pretty and cost 3s. What it is exactly I don't know. The dealer and his son were 'characters'. The son said to the father in front of us, 'What are they?' and the father answered, 'Artists or something', and turning to us, 'What are you really?' 'Did you get any money out of them?' asked the son. Then the father became friendly and showed us everything he had. E. and I went to the cinema last night and tonight.

Friday, 30th January

Off we went this morning, glad to leave the gloomy Bedford Hotel. It was pouring again and I was in ill humour until the sun came out at Tintagel; but E. is patient and sweet, and helps dispel my ill humours. There is no one in the world with whom I have shared more cherished moments of giggling, *vide* yesterday carrying the grandfather clock down the stairs at Cotehele, clankings coming from the mechanism. I thought I would have a stroke we laughed so much, and yet could not put it down. This morning we looked at the Old Post Office, Tintagel, a dreadful Hans Andersen gingerbread witch's house. It was streaming with damp. I hated it. Such a sweet old caretaker took us round, a toothless hag with a beautiful voice and the manners of Lady Desborough. I warmed to her at once. A poor sad old thing. We wanted to embrace her. We lunched at Okehampton – no *antiquaires* here; an anti-*anti* town in fact. Then looked at Burrow Mump, a good new property, a landmark in the middle of Athelney on a mound. The ruined church late eighteenth century, very pretty. Tea at Wincanton. E. left my map behind in the Antelope. We found muff Raymond at Crichel, still with a cold, and Eddy back from broadcasting a record of his *Le Grand Meaulnes* for tomorrow night.

Saturday 31st January

I left Crichel this morning, collecting my map at Wincanton. (Olde-worlde Eddy pronounces it *Win*canton, with accent on first syllable.) Then called at Stourhead to make a few more notes for the guide book. Lunched at Amesbury very badly after passing through a vehement hail storm by Stonehenge. On my return B.S. telephoned and dined with me at Brooks's. He is a strange, unbalanced youth, with whom the world should be careful for he is sensitive and neurotic, torn between religious mysticism and the usual lusts of the flesh which he sublimates to his own unhappiness. Since he is handsome and engaging and intelligent I am tempted to advise him to make discreet hay while the sun of youth still smiles upon him, yet I don't want to influence him. He left at midnight, then early Sunday morning dropped a note through the letter-box at breakfast time. Note conveyed that he did not wish to 'hurt' me who am anyway unhurtable nowadays. I gathered from the strange effusion that he meant he could not fall in love with me who have not the slightest inclination to fall in love with him. How puerile, and pathetic, and vain.

Sunday, 1st February

Listened to a Covent Garden concert this afternoon, of contemporary English composers, Vaughan Williams and Walton. Enjoyed the first moderately, and the last's symphony a lot. What two years ago would have been cacophony was today melody. One must be prepared to undergo persistent torture to arrive at this blessed state of receptiveness. But were the *gondalieri* faced with this intellectual exercise before they positively enjoyed singing arias from Verdi, I ask myself? At 6 heard Eddy's excellent broadcast on *Le Grand Meaulnes*, and then B.S. called to explain away his note, poor youth. So I tackled his problem at once and counselled him thus – remain celibate provided you lead a truly saintly life and can maintain it: otherwise, live life to the full without restraint. The first path is undoubtedly preferable if you really mean to enter the priesthood. And please let me hear no more about it.

Had a dinner party of Viva King, Janet Leeper and Burnet Pavitt. Janet L. is in a wild sort of way intelligent and earnest. Viva so different, is more intelligent, not at all earnest. On the contrary is wicked and amusing. I prefer the latter's intelligence. I thought they would never go. They left at 11.40 but B. stayed on for half an hour. He confided that he could have done without either lady, I having invited them for his benefit. B. a very sympathetic man, extremely musical. Tells me he plays duets with Joan Moore who is a great friend.

Tuesday, 3rd February

Refreshed, I take the two brass horns from Cotehele to the British Museum and hand them over to the eminent expert, Kendrick, a dusty, vigorous man with a wooden leg and grey hair. I tell him that all the experts have given conflicting pronouncements, and he only can now judge whether the horns are genuine. He answers: 'Balls!' Then, 'Of course they are; value £50 a piece.' I say aghast, 'Is that all?' Anyway they are hideous things. I dine in and work but at 11 pm go to a party Hamish [St Clair-Erskine] and Jennifer Heber-Percy give in the next street to mine. In spite of the number of 'old friends' I hate it. I believe my generation to be, for the most part, 'unreal'; cliquey, dated, prejudiced, out of touch with the new world and preposterously exclusive –

[23]

arrogant, arrogant, with few redeeming qualities of any kind. They have nothing original to impart. At any rate nothing to me. I do have one conversation with Roy Harrod and Sachie Sitwell on Roy's broadcast about Keynes. Roy says he has been all through Lytton Strachey's correspondence with his brother James written before 1914; a lot of it is purely – I don't know why I write 'purely' – 'about pieces of human organs!' I return home, not depressed, for Burnet rings me up and we have a jolly chat, but intensely irritated by pretence. I don't truly care if I never see these people again. They are only tolerable singly or in very small groups. In a mass they are detestable and contemptible. Am I one of them?

Wednesday, 4th February

Accompanied Admiral Bevir to the Public Records Office. We lunched with Colonel Malet, Keeper of the Archives, and Atkinson, and made liaison. They promised to give us the names of all local and county archivists to whom we might transfer deeds and papers that the National Trust inherits. They took us to the Rolls Museum afterwards and I saw Dr Young's tomb from the Rolls Chapel. I must say the figure, presumably not by Torrigiano (indeed it is Gothic) is far finer than the monument, and the heads of Christ and two angels in the lunette quite conventional and insipid. I was glad to see this tomb; also an illuminated portrait of the young red-headed Henry VIII, positively looking pretty.

This evening took John Fowler to a box lent to Grace Davenport in Covent Garden for the *Meistersinger*. English performance. What a cock-teasing opera. Only the prize song is moving. Too many repeats. Bad voices except that of Frank Sale as Walter von Stolzing. John and I, seated at the back, being men, could see nothing. Thence we took Grace D. and Mrs de Freville to the Savoy. John was angelic and lent me money. The whole evening cost us about £4.10s each. Agreed later, as we sat here after midnight, what *hell* affected, rich, smart, spoilt society women could be. Asked each other why we ever did these things? He is a kind, cosy, good-natured man to have put up with the evening I landed him in.

Thursday, 5th February

In rather good form today, and for once genial in the office in spite of a late night, for John talked till 2 a.m. In the afternoon came home and began upon my guidebook to Cotehele. Received from poor B.S. a long letter of a very compromising nature about himself, complaining of his hopeless effeminacy, and confessing that he wanted love to be made to him the other night; that his Sunday letter was all nonsense – which I suspected. There is nothing I can do to help him for he is ineducable.

An old retired craftsman from the Wallace Collection called on me. He told me that very few young were attracted to his profession because they got bigger wages for mechanical, unskilled work in factories; that although he needed no extra money he regarded it as his sacred duty to impart his craft to those younger men and women who were anxious to learn it. I told him he was a noble man.

Tonight I dined at Mrs Carnegie's in Lennox Gardens. She has been ill but is now recovered, and as upright and sprightly as ever. The party was to meet the American Ambassadress, a good-looking, charming woman. There were three old butlers waiting in the hall in evening dress as I arrived five minutes late – the last to come – rather off-hand, but if one arrived on the dot to dine with one's contemporaries there would be no servants, hostess or guests assembled. At dinner I sat next to Frances Peto's sister, Cathleen, whom I mistook for Frances, and Diane Maxwell, Austen Chamberlain's daughter. She is not handsome but very agreeable. The large dining-table covered with a huge snow-white cloth and sprinkled with silver candlesticks, cups and bric-à-brac. A substantial sight. Dinner meagre compared with those of the old days here; a little fish, a little hot ham, deemed a luxury and American no doubt, a tiny savoury, and desert of one tangerine; a little red wine and a little port. Yet I had no appetite and ate sparingly of this sparse fare. During port I talked to old Lord Courtauld-Thomson who expressed a wish to read my book. I said there was nothing to prevent him. After dinner I talked to an American woman accompanying the Ambassadress. She spoke in that low Boston voice which I find the loveliest of the English-speaking voices. I could easily become enamoured of her. She said thousands of Americans will visit England this summer and she hoped they would not stay in the smart hotels but the lesser ones, in order to see how little the English still have to eat today.

A profitable day reading morning and afternoon in the British Museum library. Called on Francis Dashwood who told me he quite definitely intended to live at West Wycombe in no matter how small a way, and blamed his father for giving up the contest. Had an early supper with

Bridget and went to the Anna Karenina film. The best photography I have seen and the clothes designed by Cecil Beaton. Vivien Leigh reminded Bridget and me of Anne [Rosse]. She has the same proud little way of walking, tossing the head and pouting. An exquisite creature.

Work at home all day while listening this afternoon to a concert of Bloch and, more interesting, the Brazilian composer, Villalabos. Fate, or the god of Love, is extraordinarily mercurial. It is as though he has turned his back on me. I am loveless.

Sarah [Churchill] to whom I spoke yesterday on the telephone attracts me much. The sound of her voice again, mocking, independent and gay, quite made my heart jump to hear. I am to see her this week. I have only one trouble just now – money – or, like love, lack of it. Bills fly in and I have nothing with which to meet them. I suppose I am extravagant, yet I consider I live very simply, and have so little to show for it. And I work very hard. I just don't earn enough. It is all very sad.

Diane Abdy had a party before dinner. B.N. was there, sitting starchly upright, nagging about the NT. How tiresome and dislikeable she is on social occasions. Maureen Dufferin I talked to about Ava and how well I knew him at our private school, less well at Eton, and hardly at all at Oxford. When I spoke of him her eyes, hitherto listless, sparkled and her whole body tautened with interest. She vibrated with memories. She said her son, Sheridan, is just like Basil. Freddie Birkenhead intends to edit a book of essays by different friends of Ava. Would I be a contributor? Could I write? I said I didn't know. She was wearing a dress bare above the breasts and elbows with no straps over the shoulders, and the effect was *inquiétant*. In talking to her I found myself stammering out of nerves. Burnet dined at Brooks's.

Had a hangover this morning. Burnet feels just as I do about parties. We telephone nearly every day. Young Lord Lothian lunched with me at Brooks's. He is very shy and blinks and twitches. But he is very charming and handsome. Has three children already and is a passionate Papist. Professor Richardson telephoned me this morning and we arranged to meet at 2.30 at Brooks's. He said, 'I have read your book. It is superb. It is an important work.' All of which was very kind and heartfelt, but utter nonsense. I saw Doreen and she complained that she dreads James's visits nowadays. He sits drinking her sherry and never utters, looking bored to death. This must be very noticeable for she speaks ill of no one. We talked of highbrows. Agreed we were middlebrows and not intellectuals. She consoled herself by believing that what she wrote was sometimes thought well of by highbrows.

Friday, 13th February

Sarah dined with me alone and brought me one of Mr Churchill's Havana cigars as a present. Alas, I do not smoke cigars. We talked and talked. She told me that to leave Vic Oliver she had to adopt a sudden, cruel course – and just bolt. There was no other way. She is curiously ignorant of books and painting and music. Just not interested. Only knows about the stage. This is odd for she is bright, quick with an answer, and naturally intelligent. I like her very much.

Saturday, 14th February

At 12 I went to see Grandy Jersey and meet his new Italian wife, Bianca, not a beauty but attractive. Grandy said that Mr Aneurin Bevan had told him he wanted to nationalize the N. Trust because he thought the old families enjoyed too many privileges; that I must take cognizance of this attitude among the left-wing members of the Cabinet – damn them. I shall tell Lord Esher.

Harold chucked our Blickling tour as I expected because of his beastly by-election impending. So I asked Burnet to come instead, and he accepted. Burnet and Ben lunched at Brooks's and we set off. We had tea at the Rutland Arms, Newmarket, and found Eardley at the Royal Hotel – a commercial, vulgar hotel·– Norwich. We had the greatest fun nevertheless and went to *The Ideal Husband*, an excellent film.

Sunday, 15th February

The four of us motored to Blickling and spent the happiest day: weather sunny and mild. Miss O'Sullivan, the late Lord Lothian's old secretary, lunched with us at the Blickling Arms. Ben selected the best pictures to hang in the South Drawing-room. Burnet found a piano and played for an hour. We were all occupied. We hated the Norwich hotel, large, ugly, grim, no cheer, indifferent food. After dinner we walked round the town looking for drink or life. Found only coffee, like mud.

[27]

Dropped Burnet at his factory in Welwyn and cast a quick eye over it. A pre-war building, light, cheerful and in parts beautiful. Clinically clean; drugs and pills being made by people in white overalls like dispensers; I thought how agreeable to work there.

At luncheon at Brooks's Woodbine Parish came up and said, 'You know I have decided to stay on at Batemans after all?' 'Why, yes,' I replied, for he had already announced that he was breaking his lease. 'It was because you told me how sorry you were to hear it the other day and said such kind things.' Ben, who was with me and overheard, said that one could be paid no greater compliment than that. Yes, but I don't know how pleased my colleagues will be about the 'kind things' I said.

Tuesday, 17th February

Lunched with Margaret [Jourdain] and Ivy [Compton-Burnett]. The latter in a malaprop mood; referred to Vita having been made a CB and to a Cona coffee machine as a 'costermonger' machine. Margaret read me a transcription of letters from the Adam brothers to Lord Dalkeith in 1751, at which early date they apparently designed Dalkeith House.

Wednesday, 18th February

Had an excellent luncheon at Baldwin's with John Wilton, then drove to Merton where with Robin Fedden we looked at the Abbey wall which the NT owns, a ridiculous bit of flint wall in the middle of a paper factory yard, and quite pointless. Then drove to tea with Sibyl Colefax. Talked to Lady Anderson who told me Sir Stafford Cripps was devoted to the arts, yet had only once been to the opera, and that was in Russia. So she took him to Sadler's Wells. He hates private ownership of anything and gives all his possessions away.

Thursday, 19th February

Mrs Esdaile lunched at the Allies Club. Poor old thing, she looked very wild and odd and complained that she could not work as she used. She must have had a stroke. She asked eagerly to come to Stourhead and Charlecote and I told Eardley, who was there, that we must get all the information we can from her without delay. She told us there was a bust at Stourhead of Alderman Beckford. She was looking like an old rag-and-bone woman with the blackest handkerchief you ever saw; yet was so grateful for a nasty meal. She is a very great woman.

A Reports Committee this morning. Lord Esher, back from America, in the chair, wearing his fur coat, and bright as a button. He teased Hubert Smith and the agriculturists who, he said, were wishing to hold agricultural estates within a ring fence inalienably, and pounced upon the immorality of this. Of course he was right and I found myself in entire agreement with him. So it was that as usual we were fighting together against the others.

I lunched with Alan Pryce-Jones at the Caprice restaurant to meet Princess Marthe Bibesco. Lys Connolly was the fourth. Princess B. in black with a toque slipping off her head, first this side, then the other after she adjusted it too vehemently. She told stories in English but spoke to Alan in French. She wanted us to meet in the near future to discuss George Lloyd and his Catholicism. She is quite unpolitical and got into trouble in both wars for entertaining the enemy. Personalities, not principles, are her concern.

I went out this morning; otherwise at home, huddled by the fireside, perished. The grip of winter has descended and the snow is thick outside. My pipes are frozen and I cannot have a bath. Heywood Hill told me my book is now his best seller.

Called on Bill Astor at 12. He is always very friendly. I persuaded him to write and ask his father to agree to Cliveden house being opened at least one afternoon this season. I stressed that the public could not be expected to understand how Lord Astor found it impossible. Then I lunched with Lord Braybrooke who is most kind and thanked me for what the N. Trust had done in persuading the Government to buy Audley End from him. I *am* sorry that the NT has not got it all the same, because I am convinced that they will present houses better than the tasteless Ministry of Works. Alec Penrose called at my office to offer St George's Hall at King's Lynn.

Dined tonight at Dick Girouard's. The Eshers were there. We talked about the seven deadly sins which Lord Esher thinks are mostly misnamed. Gluttony and sloth he called 'perfectly divine sins'. He said that class feeling today is infinitely less strong than during the eighties. He remembers how as a child he, and the grown-ups, were in living terror of the East End marching to the West End. His mother could not drive to Buckingham Palace with the windows of her carriage down for fear of the 'mob' spitting into it. He said the poverty and rags were deplorable and terrifying. 'Things get better every day,' he finally said – and he meant it too.

Finished my Cotehele guidebook this morning. Lunched with the Admiral at the United Services Club. It is a fine building – by Burton? – with a beautiful and vast stairwell, the single first flight spreading into two.

Lord Esher at Brooks's said the Admiral never failed to write a letter that caused offence. He said, 'I know I worry you at meetings by always agreeing with you, to your embarrassment vis-à-vis the agents.'

Alex Moulton has come to stay with me. He tells me he has invented a new steam-, paraffin-driven motor car and hopes to have the first model on the road this year. He is certain it will be a success, but says he can make no money out of it, such a thing these days being impossible. It is his means of creation. He is earnest and intelligent, with a forceful, positive and inquiring mind. No philistine, and a reader of poetry and highbrow books. Human beings never fail to surprise me. Hitherto scientists and inventors have been enigmas to me. We drank wine and talked till midnight.

Oh, the dreariness of society with a large S. Went to a cocktail party given by Diane in her 'twee' little flat as Anne would call it. He! he! he! and giggles and preciousness. Would I sign my book and would I put 'from the author', for how could posterity know who Jim was? How indeed? But I would not, and that was the end of it. I hadn't *given* it.

Resold two tyres, the tractor ones, to the garage at Mortlake. Then went to the Chagall exhibition at the Tate which I was prepared to hate. On the contrary found the surrealist pictures gay, inspiriting and dreamlike. Jamesey dined with me here, and we had a gossip. He says that when he finds himself in bed with someone incompatible he prays all the time to St Teresa, who sympathizes. Harold is very shocking about his by-election. In the coldest weather he fears to wear his fur-lined coat. He dissuades Ben from visiting the constituency because his voice sounds too patrician; expresses the hope that the Communists, and not De Gaulle, will get to power in France. James had a row with him and told him he was unprincipled and defeatist.

Worked in the British Museum reading-room morning and afternoon. This vast domed room with galleries of bookshelves ought to be a national monument, if it isn't already. In the evening I had B.S. to dine and insisted on going to a film, *Cry Havoc*. Very bad film but I could not face an evening alone with this young man who bores me, with his unhealthy odour of sanctity and bottled-up lechery. I am trying to get him a job with *Country Life*.

Mass at the Oratory and work at home. After luncheon walked to the Tate to see the Chagalls for the last time; but this time far less impressed. I tire of the nursery bathroom fantasies and babyishness, and absence of all form and dignity. Certainly some of the silly fantasies are pretty, but they are pre-adolescent.

Lunched at the Dorchester with Sibyl Colefax in a very overheated little room on the top floor overlooking the park, the sun shining directly upon us. A curious party and one wonders why it was given. There were the Hartingtons, T. S. Eliot, Ava Anderson, Georgia Sitwell, Peter Quennell, Alan Pryce-Jones. I sat between Alan and Lady Anderson. T. S. Eliot dark, swarthy, professorial, retiring, quizzical, diffident – a medical practitioner or undertaker's clerk. Alas, I had no chance of talking with him. Lady Anderson, rather blowzy, resembled the Hayter portrait of Queen Caroline at Battersea House. She said she could hardly bear to look at her reflection in the glass. I made no comment. Very pleased to see Debo H. again. She said she would ask me to stay at Chatsworth in June. Wants to take me round the big house, now empty. She was pale, with no make-up at all. Beautiful and melancholy-merry.

Office in the morning, and after a quick luncheon drove to Olney, Bucks. Called at Lord Denham's house in Weston Underwood village. It was indeed Diana and Greville Worthington's house where I so often stayed before the war, and which the Denhams bought after the tragedy of their deaths. Lord D. was away but Lady Denham, a very pretty woman with grey hair, blue eyes and pink complexion, accompanied me in the car to Cowper's Alcove. She is a sister of Lord Redesdale and aunt of Tom and Nancy, etc., but my reference to them was unfortunate. I do not think she cares for the Mitfords. This will make Nancy chortle with wicked glee. She is a friendly, but stupid, philistine woman. The Alcove stands on a mound at the end of a field overlooking Olney, and is just as Cowper knew it, save for the wooden struts under the arches and the lime trees in the foreground which have now gone. I also saw the Gothic temple in the Wilderness and the urns and monuments to the poet's hare and the Throckmortons' dogs. The Denham boy showed me the blue ceiling of the Gothic temple painted by poor little Diana. They have removed all her pretty wallpapers from the house and substituted boring distemper, saying what awful taste the Worthingtons had.

Motored to Wickhamford in time for dinner.

Thursday, 4th March

Took Mama to Packwood today. We lunched adequately at the Swan's Nest in Stratford. Darling Mama has an increasingly tiresome habit of not listening to what I say, and repeating the same question three or four times during one meal. This cannot be age so much as lack of concentration. She now confuses everyone's names. We walked around Packwood, she being very sweet and friendly with the gardener Weaver and his wife, both old friends, and enjoying herself no end. Joshua [Rowley] has got an excellent couple who, by strenuous polishing, have made the rooms and furniture shine and sparkle. I think the place will be a success when opened.

Friday, 5th March

This morning left early for Charlecote, meeting Hollyoak (agent) and the Lucys. Alice is suffering from heart trouble, or nerves. Like Packwood, Charlecote is beautifully kept, and I approve of the introduction of the bed into the Morning room. All here seemed well. I continued to Worcester and met John Wilton, returned from Croome, and motored him back to London. We dined at Henley. John very companionable, gay and gossipy. Much laughter.

[32]

Very fuggy and foggy. Burnet, back from staying with the Bowes-Lyons, lunched, and we set off for Slough. Had a look at Gray's monument at Stoke Poges, and entered the church. The monument is a singularly pleasing piece of classical architecture, or sculpture, not however in accord with Gray's sombre Gothic ethos. Then we walked round Eton. I was cross that we couldn't get into the Chapel at 4.45. The same denial at Windsor; St George's Chapel closed. We reached Englefield Green at teatime to stay with Garrett and Joan [Moore]. Carmen Gandarillas, also staying, has scarcely altered. Drank and ate too much. Burnet and Joan are closely united by a bubbling humour as well as great piano-playing proficiency. I have never heard two people enjoy playing duets with such gusto and giggling.

Tuesday, 9th March

An awful meeting at the Ministry of Works on the subject of Ham House. The Admiral presiding over a baker's dozen (I being the vantage loaf) of dreary subfusc civil servants and attorneys. How I hate their guts. Little achieved owing to huffing, puffing, um-ing and er-ing. Left at midday and met Eardley and the Curator of the Ashmolean who very kindly has offered to help us improve the museum at Chedworth Roman Villa. Lunched with Aunt Puss [Milnes-Gaskell], then rejoined Eardley in hunting for fabrics for the William Kent chairs at Stourhead. Suicidally depressed by the international situation and my own.

Thursday, 11th March

To the Albert Hall in Bridget's box to hear Furtwängler conducting. His movements are sharp, jagged, sure and Gothic, and he conducts with his long legs as well as arms. But a dull programme and the Sibelius very irritating. Bridget came back to dine. She has just returned from France. Brought me a black bow tie for a present. She has asked me to go to Monk Hopton for a week at Easter, to begin my new book, if I do not go to Belgium, which I now think I shall not do.

Friday, 12th March

Had a drink with Sheila Plunkett. Lady Coke said that she and her husband are moving into one wing of Holkham. Lord Bridport, who is younger than me, has not even *one* hair on his pate, which is smooth as a boiled suet pudding. He thinks Communism will not come to Italy in April, by a pip. He owns 30,000 acres in Sicily, he tells me.

Ted Lister, round as a ball, spectacles on the tip of his nose, dined with me alone and stayed till nearly midnight, knitting and gossiping. When he gave these two recreations a rest he practised on an imaginary harp, twanging non-existent strings with stumpy fingers, and humming execrably.

Went to the theatre with Ted Lister – *The Hidden Years* – all about a romantic schoolboy friendship and its implications. Very bad, sentimental, toshy play, in the *Young Woodley* tradition, only the subject even today rather bold. Ted brought a pair of old-fashioned mother-of-pearl opera glasses through which to quiz the young ladies and gentlemen, much to my embarrassment, so that I was constrained to prevent him using them. He carefully put under the seat his square, semi-bowler, semi-tall hat. Theatre practically empty but for a sprinkling of old queens. A horrifying experience really.

Went this afternoon with the Admiral and Lord Esher to the Treasury for a meeting with the permanent official, Sir Bernard Gilbert, and the Ministry of Works official, Sir Eric de Normann, two smug, obstinate, unimaginative civil servants. The meeting was about Harewood House. In spite of Esher's ably presented case these men implied that they might advise the Chancellor to let the Government hold the house and estate, if they were asked to take them in part payment of death duties, and not hand them on to the NT. A dangerous precedent indeed. Nothing we could say would convince them that we were the qualified body to hold and run country houses inhabited by their previous owners. Esher and I were distinctly depressed by the interview. The two brushed aside our argument that in an imperfect and disintegrating world country house owners disliked the NT far less than the Government.

Burnet and I met for tea at Brooks's and then went to the Opera at Covent Garden – *Tristan and Isolde*. We cut the second act, and dined at Rules. Both of us terribly tired. I could hardly speak for fatigue. I find the whole Wagner sentiment, the Heine-Nazi ethic most unappetizing. Yet I am glad I heard Madame Flagstad as Isolde, for she is one of the great singers of our time. Her massive mastery of her theme, and her discipline beyond criticism.

Wednesday, 17th March

Esher telephoned me this morning very depressed about yesterday's meeting, and came to the office at 12.15. We walked to Brooks's and discussed how best to bring pressure upon the Princess Royal's agent. I am to go up there and explain matters to her, if permitted, and the implications of the estate falling into the Government's maw.

Dined at 7 with Rick [Stewart-Jones] for John Summerson's lecture on eighteenth-century London architects.

Thursday, 18th March

Lunched with the Aspinall-Oglanders in their flat in Carrington House. Mrs Fleming, Ian and Peter's mother, once a great beauty, and the Eshers present. Lord E. took me into the passage the moment I arrived and said, 'I sat next to Sir Stafford Cripps last night at dinner and he remarked, "You are taking a long time to spend the £50m we have put aside for the Nat. Trust." ' Esher replied that he had had a set-back, describing the sour fruits of our recent Treasury meeting. Cripps brushed it aside and went on, 'You can spend as much of the reserve as you like so long as it is spent on the NT and not on the previous owners.' Esher feels that the two officials we saw were talking through their hats, and we must go over their heads (what a funny juxtaposition of similes). This is encouraging. I drove away with him to the SPAB [Society for the Protection of Ancient Buildings] meeting and he remarked, 'How Joan does talk. One cannot get a word in edgeways.' What a silly-billy of a woman she is, but good-hearted. During luncheon E. said rather acidly to Antoinette, 'Are you telling this story, or am I? For it is a mistake that we should both be telling the same story at the same time.'

Went to see Mr Harry Batsford who rather depressed me about my new book and seemed to want me to tackle another subject altogether, the Palladians. I said I had always wanted to write about them but Charles [Fry] had counselled me not to; that after one year's reading on the Renaissance I really could not throw over all the work so far done. I am always being depressed by something or other, and must stop it.

[35]

Yesterday motored to Cliveden, met Bill Astor and measured up the rooms for the ropes and drugget we shall need. Today motored to Woolbeding and lunched with the Edward Lascelleses and daughter, nice people who own this house. It is a disappointing house after the tantalizing photographs of it in last year's *Country Life*. It is near Midhurst in lush, wooded country off the downs. It belonged to Lord Robert Spencer whose great friend, C. J. Fox, frequently stayed there. In 1875 Lord Lannerton spoilt it by converting the centre courtyard into a wretched stairwell and adding a wing in unsuitable style. None of the old rooms has any quality, but all the books, many pictures and some excellent inlaid furniture belonged to Lord Robert. The Lascelleses are hard up and the house is rather forlorn. They consider asking the Treasury to take it in lieu of death duties on Mr Lascelles's death and hand over to us.

This afternoon I also looked at the Cowdray ruins, and in particular for Renaissance detail, viz. the cherubs' heads in the spandrels of the fan vaulting of the hall porch. Then to Chichester Cathedral to see Bishop Sherbourne's monument which to my surprise turned out to be completely Gothic, not Renaissance at all – coloured alabaster.

Sunday, 21st March

Dined with Diana Selby-Lowndes who told me that she married two months ago a man called Charlton because she was starting a baby, that he has already left her, her father has washed his hands of her, she has no money and is selling her clothes to live on the proceeds. I am extremely sorry for her; but what a hash she has made. I wrote to Patrick [Kinross] to suggest that he should see her father, whom he knows, and tell him he must provide for her. Patrick is the best friend she has and is always ready to help those of us in distress.

Monday, 22nd March

Went to a lecture at the SPAB. this evening by Sir Sydney Cockerell on William Morris, whose secretary he was and whom he knew intimately. He did not disclose anything new about Morris, but to listen to Sir S. talking of him, Ruskin, Burne-Jones, Philip Webb as his close companions conjured up the past vividly. Morris had fits of violent rage, once tearing his own clothes to ribbons; then immediately subsided and was penitent like a spoilt child.

The first meeting of the National Trust Gardens Committee. Vita, whom I had persuaded to sit on it, attended. She asked me to lunch and it was sad I could not go for I had Martyn Beckett lunching at Brooks's. The small committee are enthusiastic and not dampened by the silly Admiral's misgivings about inadequate funds. Sir M. Beckett a nice young man who turns out to have been Diana Worthington's half-brother. He cannot act for us as architect in Yorkshire, he says, because he is so seldom there.

Trained to Leeds and back today. Lunched at Harewood with the agent, Mr FitzRoy, then after a talk went to the big house. HRH was opening something, but young Lord Harewood received us, and we talked for an hour in the library. He is shy and bashful. Has a head shaped like his father's, but a large Hanoverian mouth, and the same resonant, deep voice as his mother's. Looks away from one while speaking, like HRH, but when he warms up and smiles, is engaging. Is hopelessly defeatist about the future of Harewood. Nevertheless is definitely opposed to the Government holding it and practically insisted that if not held by the NT then it must be held by no other body.

Being semi-royal must be tormenting, for one is neither fish, flesh nor good red herring, and to have one's mother in one's own house, with two ladies-in-waiting at every meal, curtseying and Ma'aming, yet oneself to be an ordinary human subject to the kicks and pricks of this mortal life, most unsatisfactory. In the train at dinner on my way home a seedy, black frock-coated individual sat opposite me. He looked the typical civil servant of an unimportant sort, with ill-fitting false teeth and a starched winged collar. He ate and drank little, choosing precisely different courses to mine. Yet I was struck by his intelligent face and his extraordinary courtesy to the waiters. When he got up and left, the attendant told me he was Sir Norman Birkett. I got home at 10 o'clock, rather tired but not exhausted, having had a satisfactory day.

Rather a rushed morning, packing, getting the car out and going to the office where I was bad-tempered. At noon called for Bridget [Parsons] and motored to Shropshire – glorious, clear, sunny day and the hedges bursting with shoots, life and spring. We lunched at Amersham, called at

Charlecote, where the brew-house with its new labels looked very smart indeed. We reached Monk Hopton at 6 where we stay over Easter with Lord and Lady de Vesci. House very well 'appointed' and comfortable; delicious plain English food with yellow butter, home-made bread, eggs and everything the hungry but not over-fastidious stomach requires.

Friday (Good), 26th March

A gorgeous day. I already feel better. Sit in a summer-house reading books for my review in the *Spectator*. This afternoon we motor with the dogs to Wilderhope Manor, I informing Bridget and Lade de V. that it is a model of what a youth hostel should be. Indeed it used to be before the war. To my horror the place was untidy, filthy and unkempt; a positive disgrace and discredit. My companions, naturally hostile to the NT, were tacitly cock-a-hoop. I wrote a strongly worded protest which I shall circulate on my return to the office. We also called at Lutwyche Hall, now empty, but soon to be a school. Once a good Jacobean house, I guess about 1615, it was altered in 1861. All the windowpanes taken out and plate glass substituted. Nasty additions made. But the Queen Anne staircase is very good with twisted balusters sharply cut. The hall is a remarkable room with ceiling divided by thick plastered ribs and walls of Rococo stucco. The small library has early eighteenth-century carved Corinthian pilasters. The front of the house of the Bramshill type, only in miniature, but spoilt in Victorian times.

Saturday, 27th March

The sore place I have mysteriously developed on my leg will not heal. I cover it with boric acid but the constant rubbing through walking irritates it so that no scab will form. Interesting. Today we motored to Attingham and there met George Trevelyan and a grim-visaged companion. He is a self-confident man, talking of the wonderful things he is going to achieve at Attingham as curator of the Adult College. A little folk-dancing, some social economy and Fabianism for the miners and their wives. We felt quite sick from the nonsense of it all. At a time when this country is supposed to be bankrupt they spend (our) money on semi-education of the lower classes who will merely learn from it to be dissatisfied. The house looked very forlorn and down at heel which worried me a good deal. Then we visited Buildwas Abbey, well cared for by the Ministry of Works, I am bound to admit – Norman and Early English remains, and nearly the whole body of the church intact. We had tea at Wenlock Priory with the Motleys. Mary is a dear and very domesticated with her four sons whom conversation can barely range beyond.

Easter Sunday, 28th March

Beautiful sunny day, but still a cold wind. I drove the two little Irish maids two miles to Mass at the top of an old farmhouse, where a family called Bell have a chapel, decked with forsythia and daffodils. It was under the roof and might have been a recusants' place of worship in the bad times. From far and near about thirty people assembled. This was at 9 o'clock. We waited ages while they all went to confession, including myself. A romantic and bucolic little ceremony, miles away in Shropshire for a small community of proud and devout people. After Mass they offered the congregation tea. I gave ten shillings to the priest's collection.

Monday, 29th March

I left Monk Hopton after luncheon today, Bridget staying on for a week. As usual I was glad to leave, although I have enjoyed myself and am grateful for the kindness received. I suffer from *gêne* in other people's houses and from guilt in that I do not pull my weight, i.e. don't garden, which is always a welcome assistance from guests these days. The other three gardened all the time. Not once did I offer to do so. I hate it. Stooping makes me giddy. Yet the delicious food, deep sleep and the long lies in the mornings did me good. In spite of the nearly complete relaxation was obliged to take one Epanutin pill per day. Back in London shall be obliged to take three a day. One admitted drawback here is the dreadful, inescapable proximity of Lord de Vesci, with whom I repeatedly find myself alone, being the only other male. He is an arch-bore, who never stops talking and grumbling about the decline of the country, the incompetence of the Government, and the menace of Communism – what I am fairly apt to do myself. In another it is intolerable. He is the most reactionary man, bar none, I have ever met. On the other hand there is something rather likeable about him – that truculent bewilderment as of a spavined horse. And it cannot be agreeable to be despised by both your wife and stepdaughter.

On the way home I stopped at Harvington Hall and Coughton where I had tea with that angelic Lady Throckmorton, who looked thinner and not too well. She is all alone in this house, and has a struggle to keep going and make both ends meet. She is a noble and splendid woman.

[39]

At the Connaught Hotel this evening met Archie Gordon and Blewitt of the Television BBC who are organizing a broadcast – if that is what it is termed – on the television about the National Trust. They invited me to cooperate in finding suitable performers and to attend the performance, which I certainly shall do on the 16th. I declined to play a part on the screen because I cannot speak impromptu. Lord Vansittart talked to us – a nice, genial man, with smooth face and simple manners, about sixty-eight.

Friday, 2nd April

This week has been very bad. Terrible depression. Pierre Lansel says I am to go away and stop my pills and take others in their place. Michael and Anne have pressed me to go to Birr, which is noble and sweet of them.

Wednesday, 7th April

Flew this morning to Jersey. Left Victoria at 11 o'clock – departure was scheduled for 10.30 – and reached Jersey at 1.15. Grandy and his wife Bianca there to meet me. She is very appealing, pretty and vivacious. Elegant legs and feet. Pregnant. Has lovely dark brown hair, which she wears in a tail knot drawn across the nape of her neck and partly over one shoulder. Very smartly dressed with much gold and some good jewellery, which I like. But I don't like Jersey – the island. It is over-built with villas, over-cultivated, over-prosperous and middle-class, with puny little coombes and slopes. There is always a wind. The Jerseys' house, Radier Manor, is a plain farmhouse Georgianized: all fresh painted, for here labour is abundant. Grandy has some few pieces of furniture from Osterley, one very 'Louis Seize' piece from the library, which he says is by Robert Adam, and several French Impressionists.

After luncheon we had a long talk of three hours, and again next morning. At first he told me he was making arrangements to sell Osterley, house and contents, in the open market. I almost fell on my knees and begged him to reconsider this lamentable decision. Eventually we reached the following arrangement. He definitely withdraws his unconditional offer of the complete property to the National Trust (a) because he is incensed with the Middlesex County Council going back on the settlement of 1944 and has no confidence in them at all, and (b) because as a landowner he feels the country persecutes him, and the

Budget capital levy of yesterday has determined him to *give* nothing away to the Government. Instead he now agrees that if the Council will *buy* that part of the estate which they were to have rented from the Trust free of payment, and if the Government will buy the furniture and keep it in the house, then he will give the house and pleasure grounds to the Trust. Beyond this he will not go and, even so, he is removing all the pictures, including the Rubenses, to Jersey where he will build a gallery for them. I cannot blame him.

Thursday, 8th April

We lunched at St Helier and I was glad to get away. It was very windy indeed, so we flew high, 10,000 feet, and this affected my ears. It took 1¼ hours from Jersey to Northolt. I noticed that from the air the fields of pasture showed distinct brown streaks of the old medieval strip system.

Grandy looks very young still, has all his straight brown hair and very fair complexion: has a small, nervous mouth.

I dined with the Eshers alone at a club they belong to on the Chelsea Embankment and we returned to drink coffee at their house, and talk. I told them about Osterley, and Lord E. did not think Grandy's attitude blameworthy. Also discussed the NT generally, and the Admiral. I told E. that although I did not dislike the Admiral, he was a disastrous secretary, and left it at that.

Friday, 9th April

Lord Crawford came to the office at 5 and stayed till 6 talking about his tour, and I was late getting away to St Paul's, Waldenbury. Arrived at 7.30 to stay with Burnet whose fortieth birthday it is. He has taken a little red brick farmhouse next door to the Bowes-Lyons, called Bury Farm, and just moved in. It is not yet furnished; only the small dining-room in commission. We lived in the kitchen; cooked our own dinner, or rather heated what had been prepared for us by the daily char-woman. Bedrooms with no carpets down, etc. B. is rather depressed by the whole business, the loneliness, the expense of the move, but he will make it pretty and comfortable. He is not really a countryman. The house is on a corner of one of the finest landscape gardens of England. On Saturday we whitewashed the ceiling of the servants' hall and distempered the walls, as we thought, beautifully, but the following day revealed a very indifferent performance.

[41]

I left B. at 10.30 for London. After luncheon at Brooks's I drove – a glorious day – to Faringdon for the night. Arrived teatime. Was disconcerted to find Eddy S.-W. sitting at the table but later was glad he was there. Compton Mackenzie at tea, middle-aged, stout and undistinguished. Boisterous and verbose.

I enjoyed this visit. Faringdon is one of the most elegant country houses on the small scale, yet with large, grand rooms on the *piano nobile*. Wide horizoned views from one front, the town upon the other; as perfect a house as can be. I liked Gerald Berners more than I had done before. He was wearing a knitted green skull-cap. He is chronically depressed ever since his illness a year ago. For an ageing man he ought to be contented: possessor of the most coveted house in England, Robert Heber-Percy as it were, a son, with Robert's daughter Victoria, aged eight, living with him; art, music, books, beauty, civilization, excellent food and wine, and friends circumambulating.

Before dinner I wandered round the garden and lake with Eddy and Hugh Cruddas; then talked to Gerald and Robert about the place. Robert will not allow G. to make over any land, only the gardens, but suggests an endowment in cash to bring in £1,000 p.a. The NT ought to accept this even if the endowment is not enough on account of the lettableness (or is it 'lettability'?) of the house. They ask for opening days to be for two fortnights on end, spring and summer. After dinner talk of Catholicism. Gerald would like to become a Papist if only he could believe. A very amusing and not unedifying conversation ensued. Eddy said even he might be a convert one day. Robert too has inclinations. Penelope Betjeman has become one and worries Berners with proselytizing letters, taking the ecstatic's line of persuasion.

After breakfast I motored Eddy to Salisbury and then, parting with him regretfully, continued to Wilton. Picked up Mrs Esdaile waiting for me on a bench in the sun, and drove her to Stourhead. Never have I been in closer contact with a more unkempt female; yet she is an old pet. Her stockings hang in folds, covered with stains; her face and fingers are yellow from cigarettes which she inhales. Her clothes are a nightmare of cobwebs and must. She is rather vague now and walks with difficulty. Yet at Stourhead she plodded gallantly round the house and told us what she knew about each piece of sculpture, which was everything. I took notes as we went round. Eardley was there for the day, and Bob Gathorne-Hardy came for tea to start cataloguing the books in the library. Mrs Esdaile kept prattling about a monument she wished to see in a .church three miles from Stourton, at Silton. 'A stunner,' she called it. It was by Van Nost, she assured me, of a Windham. We took a look at it. I admit it was a splendid affair, dated 1684, full-blooded Charles II Baroque, standing in face of the open door. We got to London at 9.15.

Wednesday, 14th April

This morning called for Mrs Esdaile and motored her to Charlecote. A somewhat muggy day and, my goodness, the old lady and her chain-smoking in the car. I have never met any expert at a science (tombs) so dense about practical things. She cannot recognize a street, or a car. She could not even use the lighter in my car even after I had worked it ten times for her. At Wroxton she took me into the church. In the chancel is a magnificent Jacobean monument to Lord Downe, and she showed me how it was obviously by the same mason who executed the Sandys monument at Wickhamford; one by Wilton; one by Flaxman; and another, she positively avers, by Grinling Gibbons. An interesting lesson. At Charlecote she explained at once how Queen Elizabeth's bust was a cast of Colt's effigy of the Queen in the Abbey; the busts of the Lucys were plaster casts of the effigies in Charlecote church. Joshua Rowley met us and Kaines-Smith who talked volubly about the portraits.

I dropped the old lady at Oxford and dined late with John Fowler in his King's Road house.

Thursday, 15th April

George Howard of Castle Howard lunched at Brooks's: an odd, portly figure very like his cousin Carlisle, sweating although the day was cold. Exceedingly intelligent. He is willing to act as our representative in Yorkshire. He is knowledgeable about buildings, knows every land-owner within the area and beyond, and would, I fancy, be a great help to the Trust.

Tonight I had a dinner party of Burnet Pavitt, Harold Nicolson and Malcolm Bullock. Party would have been better without Malcolm who all dinner kept up a running commentary about politics and mutual friends. This did not however dam Harold's flow except when H. went to the lavatory which he did three times after dinner. Once there was a crash. I rushed to see what had happened, mindful of Gerry's lament that Harold always broke works of art. He had knocked down my Ethel Walker picture, smashing the glass to smithereens. Without Malcolm he would have talked more about Byron, for M. is bored by literary talk at which H. excels. H. told us he was convinced the reason for the Byron separation was not the incest – for Lady B. had been told of this before she married – but B. trying tricks on her. She complained that he was mad. Gosse told Harold that he had advised Polidori's niece to destroy Polidori's diary, which she did. Silly old prudish Gosse.

Saturday, 17th April

In the Abbey this morning. How I adore this fane. The Henry III tomb and Confessor's shrine are the earliest classical revival (or proto-Classical) work in England, I suppose, thirteenth century. I thought I might have made a discovery in supposing the weeping figures round the D. of Buckingham's tomb to be by Le Sueur, the dragon helmet of the nearest one resembling Le Sueur's helmet of Charles I at Stourhead. After luncheon drove to South Mimms church. It was locked. I was nettled, and rang the rectory bell. A head appeared at a window and asked gruffly: 'Who are you?' I replied: 'Just an ordinary person. I want to see the tombs please,' crossly. Then was filled with remorse for the old clergyman, whose head it was, was pathetic, longing for someone to talk to, and offering me tea. He wasted my time all right showing me things I had not come to see – a window and font by Comper, very good – but I saw the Frowyk monument, curiously classical for 1527, if the Roy. Hist. Monuments book for Middlesex is correct, which I doubt.

Arrived in time for tea at Clouds Hill with Blanche Lloyd who was so sweet, kind and pleased to see me. She is greatly mellowed, madly keen on Christianity, and against the Government and Communism of course. Also always losing her spectacles, her thimbles as of old, and terrified of having no money to live on. Still speaks of George with tears in her eyes and pride in her heart. I worshipped her.

Lord Lloyd called this house – which I think was the Rectory – after his friend T. E. Lawrence's cottage in Dorset.

Sunday, 18th April

Sat about, sometimes indoors under the sun through glass, sometimes out when warm enough, and agreeably wasting time, till 6 o'clock when I left. Stopped at St Ippolitt's church on the hill and saw the memorial to George Lloyd by Hugh Easton, tiny but pleasing. I liked the inscription: 'Remember George 1st Baron Lloyd of Dolobran', but not the Esmond Burton altar so much. Also liked George's tombstone

[44]

in the churchyard, with the Eric Gill lettering and coat of arms with supporters and coronet. Stayed the night with Burnet at Bury Farm.

Ran slap into a car in front of me in London, injuring one of my springs. The other car, having a buffer, was quite unharmed. Today had an interview with Sir Henry Hake and C. J. Adams at the National Portrait Gallery. Sir Henry, rather pompous, indicated that the Gallery must not be quoted in any advice it gives the Trust about pictures. He is an unattractive old man – vindictive, Ben Nicolson tells me. He quite sensibly suggested Ellis Waterhouse joining the Historic Buildings Committee. He would, I imagine, be an asset. After luncheon went to my first meeting as a member of the National Buildings Record, of which Sir Eric Maclagan is chairman. Not very interesting perhaps, but I am proud to be on the Council for I approve of what it is doing and make much use of its photographs.

I am garaging my motor at a new place for 30s a week – fearfully expensive but it includes service. It is just behind the V & A Museum. I shall try it out. The man motored me in my own car to the Air Terminus which was rather nice, at 9 o'clock, half an hour too early actually. At the airport I met Alan Lennox-Boyd, also going to Dublin for a Guinness Brewery ball tonight. We took off at 11.15 but when in sight of the Irish Sea turned back because we were told we could not land at Dublin owing to ground mist. Went back to London again, and at the Service's expense ate an excellent cold luncheon. I was glad to be with Alan whom I like. We set off again at 3.30 and landed safely at Dublin, seeing little en route because of the clouds. We were in a 4-engine Constellation and sat in the navigator's cabin. These very large planes alarm me for they are so heavy I cannot understand how they leave the ground. It was too late to catch the last train to Roscrea, so I went with Alan to Farmleigh and stayed the night with the Iveaghs, his in-laws. Patsy and the three children were there and Chips Channon's son, Paul, a curiously sophisticated, plump little boy, perhaps cunning. There was a ball in the house and, had I not had a lot to drink, I should have been most unhappy. Farmleigh is a large Georgian house, the inside ugly and Edwardianized, but luxurious. Lord and Lady Iveagh paid little attention, but seemed not the least surprised to see me. Late at night Alan said what a tiresome necessity of life dissimulation was. He kept saying, 'Isn't Patsy a wonderful wife?' I

[45]

could not deny it. Lady Iveagh once complained to Alan, 'Can't you change your friends a little more often?'

Wednesday, 21st April

Left Farmleigh at 8 with Alan, from whom I parted at Dublin airport, one of the best modern buildings I know. Its horizontal lines and tower give it a Picturesque quality. From Kingsbridge station to Roscrea the journey quiet and uneventful, through low-lying fields without a labourer in sight and stations with no one on the platform. A dead landscape, all the trees looking as though they were part of the earth and a thousand years old in spite of the green buds. The faces of the inhabitants express no surprise and, as they stare, are utterly vacant. When they are animated they are the faces of demons. Arrived Birr Castle in time for luncheon. Alan [Pryce-Jones] and Poppy staying for the night. She talks a lot and to the point; and has greatly improved in looks. In the afternoon Michael had us driven (he cannot drive himself) to see the Jacobean ruin that belongs to the Harewoods: very melancholy but complete. I feel terribly tired.

Sunday, 25th April

So far I have not done a stroke of work. I have breakfast in bed, rise at 10.30 and am down at 11.30. I read a certain amount, eat a lot, but carefully, wander into the town and buy handkerchiefs and shoes. The weather is superb and the air scented with peat. The shop assistants are polite and send whatever one buys round to the Castle; this never happens in England now. In the Castle are a butler, footman, four housemaids, besides a cook and kitchenmaids. Michael and Anne leave tomorrow but are allowing me to stay on for a week; and I have simply *got* to make a beginning of my new book. They are angels of generosity and understanding.

Sunday, 2nd May

Michael and Anne left on Monday last – I miss them – on which day I felt deathlike. I immediately drank at St Brendan's Well in the garden and wished that I might be enabled to begin my book. In the afternoon I could do nothing but lie in the sun feeling wretched. That evening the rector and his wife dined with Susan [Armstrong-Jones] and me. But I could eat nothing at all. Suddenly after dessert I made a bolt from the

[46]

room and was sick with greater vehemence than I ever remember. It gushed with the propulsion of an engine rather than of a human stomach. I felt better, and ashamed.

All this week however I have not felt well. Have been without appetite and pursued by attacks of nausea. What is it, if not just Ireland? I do not like Ireland. I do not like the country here. It is horizonless and dead. One cannot see further than one's hand. I wish I could define precisely what it is I do not like about the climate, the people and the scenery. My dislike is almost intuitive; certainly temperamental and racial. I fear the native hostility under the mask of deceit. At Mass the church here is so crowded that one cannot worship. Irish Catholicism is like a vice, crushing the congregation like nuts. The Irish God is not loving. He is a tyrant. The people are tight within his grasp. Unlike Latins they are subdued by their Church, not elevated by it. They derive from it no inspiration, recreation or romance. Here it is grey and puritanical. In the church the men herd on the Epistle side, the women on the Gospel side like battery hens. One senses that their appalling mendacity and untrustworthiness are the consequence of their age-long abortive attempts to escape the clutch of the priests. Oh, I do hate the whole island.

Things here strike me forcibly: a cart gallops through Birr town, with a line of three horses, unbridled, following at a trot obediently behind, in and out of the traffic through the streets. Why do they follow obediently without a rein? The lodge-keeper never fails to open the big double gates to the drive just at the very moment when the car comes into sight, as though by magic, the chauffeur not having hooted this time, Creepy! On other days, when many people are about the chauffeur keeps his hand on the horn, winnowing them aside, in warning. The family are treated like royalty and Michael is indeed a small king; or like a German princeling. One must realize this before understanding him. The town take the greatest interest in his coming and going, and Anne knows this and plays up to it. She is respected in consequence. There is too a sanctity about Desmond's memory. If you mention his name there is no respectful hush, but eyes sparkle and he is referred to as though still alive. The Irish are all eyes, and nothing else. No compassion, and I doubt whether there is any love, except for the dead. Much hate for the living.

Since the Rosses left I have got down to my new book – The Classical Revival shall I call it? – and worked about seven hours a day with short intervals for walking into the town and round the demesne. To this extent I have at any rate succeeded. I have begun the beginning. The plunge has been taken but I have hit, and shall hit again, my head against a few hard rocks.

Left Birr this morning at 9 o'clock; quite glad to get away though more grateful than any words can express to Michael and Anne who are my guardian angels. Travelled to Dublin in a first-class compartment, very old-fashioned and cosy, with an eccentric old peer wearing a scarf over his head under a homburg hat and a shawl over his knees. In Dublin met Morogh Barnard at the Shelburne Rooms. He gave me a solid luncheon at the Russell Hotel, entrecôte and strawberry ice adorned with young strawberries. Had no time to sight-see, and caught the afternoon aeroplane to London.

Cannot say I feel at all well; on the contrary in a highly nervous condition. I met Lord Esher at luncheon. He told me he had rented Iford from the Michael Petos on a fourteen-year lease; so this is the result of his abortive visit there to try and acquire the house for the Trust. He thought this a very funny joke and laughed heartily. This afternoon I went to the Annual Meeting of the SPAB held at the Apothecaries Hall, near Ludgate Circus, a charming late seventeenth- century building, which has happily survived the blitzes. Esher made an excellent and witty speech, Harold Nicolson, the chief speaker, a not so good one. I took Harold off to Brooks's afterwards where we had a long talk. He told me Vita was not at all cross, but amused, to find that I had forgotten I asked her to lunch last Thursday. Michael had told her not to be cross with me because I was in a bad way and tired after my last book! A curious reason for forgetfulness. Harold told me the story of a German friend, a long-distance runner, whom he met in Berlin and who pursued him for ten years with a hopeless passion which very much bored Harold. However, the story had a tragic ending for the young man was finally shot by his own countrymen in a concentration camp. Harold remembers urging him, as a good German, to oppose and resist the Nazis at all costs. Harold said he thought and hoped Ben was in love with a friend he had met at Oxford.

Went to the opening by Dr Trevelyan of K. Kennet's collected sculpture at Heal's shop. Trevelyan said K. was a woman whose life was dedicated, primarily, to the arts – which is true – that she hated fraud, sentiment and lack of courage; that she loved beauty and the young; and that it was not true she was among the dead.

Dined with the Chileans, Léon and Paz Subercaseaux. A very enjoyable party. Guests were the Aspinall-Oglanders, Barbara Moray, Riette

[48]

Lamington and Leigh Ashton. Leigh told us about the burglary at the V & A of two of Gerry Wellington's swords. The burglars were professionals. They climbed a 40-ft wall, cut the electric wires behind them; smashed a plate glass case, wrenched off the jewelled hilts, left the scabbards and escaped while the watchman's back was turned. Gerry heard the news on the wireless when in Spain and wrote Leigh a very pompous letter beginning: 'These swords have been safe for over a hundred years in my family.' I sat next to Joan Oglander and Barbara. Barbara told me that staying at Windsor Castle she found beside her bed my Adam book and Peter Cheyney; it was the room occupied by Mrs Roosevelt the weekend before. Joan Oglander was far less twitchy, jumpy and talkative, and consequently nicer. After dinner Paz spoke very understandingly of James's romanticism. She said he lived in a dream world and fabricated dream theories about people; that his romanticism was incorrigible and attractive; that he had enough curiosity to make a great novelist; and that his friends should overlook his tiresome behaviour.

Thursday, 6th May

Hubert Worthington, the architect, called to see me about the mill at Alderley [Cheshire] – a nice, intelligent, rather vague man. Hubert Smith and Christopher Gibbs lunched with me at Brooks's to discuss Harewood. At the Reports Committee only Lord Esher turned up. He told the Admiral as plainly as possible that he was a fool: a most embarrassing moment. It was over Buscot discussions and the old Admiral just did not know what he was talking about.

Tony Gandarillas took me and Daisy Fellowes to the Palladium. We had champagne in Daisy's flat at the Dorchester and drove in her huge black limousine. Her lifted face is beginning to assume the taut, mask-like grimace which is so frightening. We dined at the Ritz, with more champagne, and were joined by Lord Sherwood who got very drunk. He is a foolish little man who looks like a rat, which is what Daisy calls him behind his back. He is fifty, worships Daisy who is fifty-eight and clings to him nevertheless, being lucky to have a lover at all. She is still quick as lightning, sharp as a packet of needles and capable of seducing God. She is going to invite me to stay at Donnington, which I rather dread and much look forward to.

Tuesday, 11th May

Went to see Pierre Lansel who insists that I go next week to the medical clinic to have another blood test. Sugar content far below normal.

[49]

To a cocktail party given by Mrs Foley in Eaton Square to see the Stoke Edith needlework hangings in her drawing-room. Magnificent they are on first sight, because of the size of the panels. But the subjects being domestic and horticultural give them almost a cottagey flavour. Mr Hobson of Sotheby's told me that he was in favour of works of art being sold abroad, for art was international and, besides, the museums in England were overflowing. Dined with the Alfred Beits at the Savoy. I fainted at the beginning of dinner, but soon recovered. Maud Russell told me she was thinking of selling Mottisfont which was too big for her. Alfred and Clementine suggested my going to South Africa to help them influence the Boers preserve their seventeenth-century Dutch houses.

Thursday, 13th May

Helen Dashwood, Billa Harrod and Pam Chichester lunched at Thurloe Square. A curious little party. I sensed that all three hated each other. Yet they called each other 'darling' and behaved like good pussy cats that rub against a table leg, purring.

The Admiral and I had a talk with Lord Crawford at the Travellers. Lord C. told us of his interview with Sir Stafford Cripps who was quite ready to ask Parliament to buy the contents of both Harewood and Osterley, and indeed realized he would have to do this sort of thing increasingly in the future. He proposed having a list drawn up of the 100 greatest houses with collections. How often have similar lists not been drawn up? Cripps said he recognized the Trust to be the fitting body to hold them. This opens up a vast question as to how the Trust is to administer them. A limitation of great houses, with contents, to 100 is going to cause trouble in the future. What is considered bad architecture and bad art today may be considered good tomorrow. Besides, how many experts will agree on what is the best today?

Friday, 14th May

This glorious morning I motored to Rousham. On the way stopped at Quainton church near Waddesdon to look at two monuments, one to Winwood, husband and wife, erected by the wife in 1689; the figures very alive and Baroque, resting on their elbows. The second a strict Palladian affair with a broken pediment to Sir Richard Piggott of Doddershall, 1735, and signed 'I. Leoni'. I have written to ask Mrs Esdaile if this is the architect, Giacomo. Arrived Rousham at 1 o'clock and met by Mr Cottrell-Dormer, very gentle, intelligent, unassuming man. House itself disappointing, for it was added to and spoilt in the last century, and the Kent wings have been interfered with, or rather the connecting colonnades. There are only two rooms by Kent left, the dining-room with painted canvas ceiling in arabesques and great chimney-piece, gilded, and a surprisingly low ceiling; and the saloon, with ribbed ceiling and strikingly deep compartments. The stucco-work of picture frames and walls done by Roberts of Oxford about 1764. Some of the chairs are by Kent, but their quality is not outstanding.

The gardens are very important as the only Kent layout to survive, apart from the mess left by the urban authorities at Chiswick. There are statues, in a distressing condition, a seven-arched portico (Praeneste), grottoes, glades, a cascade, bath, pools, temples and straight and serpentine rides. The gardens are miraculously intact after 200 years. We had an *al fresco* luncheon below Praeneste, close to the Cherwell, and watched the mayfly hatching and flying off the river. Saw the kestrel.

At Banbury found the Reindeer Inn and called, only to discover that the fine ceiling and wainscot had been sold to America before the war. Arrived Upton at 5 o'clock and had tea alone with Lord Bearsted, she being ill upstairs. He informed me that on the Riviera Lady Kitty Lambton told him that Mrs Puleston left her some rare French medieval manuscripts; and that she had many other treasures from Emral. Lady Kitty had no idea who had inherited them. Lord B. showed not the least interest when I told him Mrs Puleston, wretched woman, was my aunt who on my uncle's death in 1936 informed me that she was leaving all these things to me as the rightful heir. I suppose it is boring for the very rich when the very poor lament their ill fortune. In any case I should remember that the rich at worst hate the poor and, at best, are embarrassed by them.

On my way to Wickhamford stopped at Weston-Sub-Edge church to see if there was any memorial to, or mention of William Latimer. Found nothing.

Monday, 17th May

Weather these holidays ideal – cloudless skies and a strong wind; even so sun too hot for sitting out of doors in the middle of the day. This evening after tea motored to Woollas Hall to talk to the Whitworths, but I knew before arrival that they would do nothing. She vaguely dallies with the idea; he is opposed to it since his son, he says, will not want to live there anyway. It is a most romantic house, perched on Bredon Hill. In the bad times the family of this Papist stronghold used to hang white sheets from the windows when Mass was to be said. The faithful from miles around would see the sheets and flock to Woollas. The Whitworths are upset by the new reservoir to supply Coventry with water which is to be made on their land. Their consent was never asked, nor have they been paid a penny in compensation. Is this sort of totalitarian measure what we fought the war for?

Visited Little Comberton, Great Comberton and Eckington churches, looking for other tombs by the mason of the Wickhamford ones, but in vain. At the last is a tomb to the Hanfords who built Woollas; his effigy exactly resembles his portrait at Woollas, of a thickset man with no neck. I dined at Overbury with the Holland-Martins. Old Mrs H.-M., Ruby and Christopher, all most friendly. To think how terrified I was, when a child, of the mother sitting on the top of a high step-ladder umpiring at tennis tournaments and shouting reprimands whenever I missed an easy shot, especially when partnering one of her sons. Rayner-Wood (and Julia, his wife) over from Colwall. I find this ex-Eton beak supercilious, snobbish and antipathetic. He complained about the condition of our old house at Tenby, as usual. Told us that the Provost of Eton now eats daily at a British restaurant. Horrors! That the Eton 'boys' maid' is extinct, and the boys make their own beds; and the housemaster's wife cooks for them. Times have indeed changed.

Tuesday, 18th May

Stopped at Burford church. What superb tombs; the Tanfields' might be by Epiphanius Evesham. A very good de Vries-type one, dated 1569. Then stopped at Christ Church, Oxford, to look at the Renaissance design under the oriel between the twin towers at the SW corner, and the hall which has no Gothic detail that I could find. Lunched at Henley. Stopped at Langley Marish and saw the Kederminster pew, but could not get into the library. The pew is a pretty example of painted Jacobean joinery. Went to a lecture at the Courtauld Institute given by Count Metternich on preservation of works of art and buildings in Germany.

Wednesday, 19th May

Enjoyable dinner at Barbara Moray's. I sat next to Elizabeth Glenconner. Conversation turned upon age and death. I suggested that the mere physical effort of attaining ripe years should entitle one to veneration, almost worship, as in the East. Agreed that of all the highbrows we knew John Pope-Hennessy was the least tolerant of silly people.

Thursday, 20th May

All morning sat in a clinic having a blood test. Had had no breakfast at all and nothing to drink until I got to the clinic, where I was given one glass of sugared water. At half-hourly intervals I had blood extracted and urinated into a tin can, making a pretty tinkle up the scale, and not down, which seemed strange. What with a little hangover from champagne last night and an empty stomach this morning I felt rotten.

To tea with Lady Mander. A Pre-Raphaelite tea party – Sir Sydney Cockerell with whom I had a long talk about Ruskin whom he knew intimately; Miss Lushington about Rossetti (she has his willow pattern dinner service to sell), Mrs Angeli, William Rossetti's daughter, and Mrs Joseph (Holman Hunt's daughter). It was fun. Sir Sydney is very spry and on the spot. He said the pity about Dr Trevelyan was that he had no sense of beauty and was totally ignorant of art. These disqualifications prevented him from being a really great historian. Of Kathleen Kennet, whom he had loved, he said she was no artist and knew that he was aware of it.

I told Sir Sydney that because I was more interested in the Classical than in the Gothic it did not make me despise the latter, whereas Ruskin who loved the latter denigrated the former. Why did he do this? He said Ruskin favoured the Gothic because it was the individual expression of man's creative ability, whereas Classical motifs were mechanical and expressive of nothing. 'There is no scope,' he said, 'for individual expression in a succession of egg and tongue.'

Friday, 21st May

Last night dined with the Eshers. The other guests were Lady Gosport and the Harold Bowens. I sat next to Vera Bowen and was overheard by Lord Esher, who, although deaf, never misses anything he wants to hear, telling her that I suffered from remorse. Esher joined in: 'Now that is a flagrant untruth. Young people *never* suffer from remorse. It is simply because he knows he can indulge in sentimental confidences with Vera who is an emotional Muscovite.' He told us that there were actually people who hated him. One was Princess Marie Louise who overheard him say to his hostess at a dinner party when told to take her into the dining-room, 'Must I?' He spent the whole of dinner explaining to the Princess that he meant it differently, for his card told him he was to take in somebody else. His protests were in vain. He said that the late Lord Willingdon felled all and sundry with his charm, which was the only quality he possessed.

Today went to Swakeleys. Met Carew Wallace and Walter Godfrey's architect son. Walked over this house and inspected the alterations the Foreign Office are making inside. The hall fireplace and Restoration screen are very interesting. The plaster ceiling of the Great Chamber is

[53]

coarse in execution, not in design. The floor over it had been taken out. We looked straight into the great hollow ribs of the plaster compartments which do not cover the beams as one might suppose. The exterior dressings of the house, instead of being in stone, are of composition. This gives a flimsy appearance.

At West Wycombe Carew and I visited all the temples. We punted over to the island and examined the Temple of Music. Then went to the house and met Helen, Johnnie and Francis [Dashwood], and the Eshers. Walked round outside and inside, listing all the improvements we would like to carry out, regardless of expense. Then had tea in the Brown Drawing-room. Lord E. and I teased Helen by observing that everything on the outside of the house was sham: imitation stone, wood, porphyry, etc. But we admitted that the interior had substantial, and exquisite, features, notably marble chimneypieces, ceilings, and the staircase of red mahogany with an inlaid star on each riser.

Saturday, 22nd May

To Westminster Abbey this morning. In spite of the perpetual crowds I never fail to be transported by aesthetic and historical emotions as soon as I set foot in this building. As for Henry VII's tomb the more I look at it the more moved I am by its abiding Tuscan beauty.

Caught a train to Denham at 2.10. Travelled with Dick Girouard and his daughter to visit Denham Place, open to the Georgian Group. A lovely William and Mary house of red brick overgrown with wistaria. House has a rich wooden cornice that gives a dignity and purpose, and relieves it from dullness. But the surroundings are dull, and indifferent. There should be a formal garden and a canal or some such feature. The interior is pretty good: two panelled rooms of the date, most richly carved. In the larger a great cupid suspended with bow from the ceiling. The plaster cove of fishing scenes in the Brown Tapestry Room is exceedingly bold and unusual; that of the next room, the colour of gingerbread, is astonishing in a peasant-like way, but too like a Walt Disney picture.

Got back for tea bringing Francis Watson, who was at Denham: a very entertaining, intelligent man, working at the Wallace Collection.

Monday, 24th May

Left by road to stay at Long Crichel. Stopped at Basingstoke. Enquired where was the Chapel of the Holy Ghost. No one knew. Finally a local antiquarian, proprietor of a jeweller's shop, told me the ruins of the

[54]

Chapel survived in the cemetery. But the Chapel had been ruinous since the Civil War. Went to have a look but could find none of the Renaissance woodwork that Gotch talks of. Then to Winchester. Saw the classical screen of delicately carved woodwork erected by Bishop Fox in St Cross church. Then to the Cathedral. Looked at cathedral screen and Bishop Gardiner's Chantry, and the Le Sueur effigies of James I and Charles I. Don't think Le Sueur can be called a great artist. These chantry chapels were often built by grand personages long before their deaths. Hence a difficulty in dating them. At Long Crichel Eardley, Eddy and Desmond ran around, greeting me like three big affectionate dogs.

Tuesday, 25th May

Eddy left this morning for Bristol. E.K. and I off to Stourhead which depressed us. The house is still in muddle and chaos. We could see no daylight.

Wednesday, 26th May

At Stourhead today we suddenly saw daylight, and made great strides. Bob Gathorne-Hardy joined us at luncheon in the pub and was encouraging and inspiring. E. spent hours hanging pictures, I arranging china, furniture, statuary and busts. I felt better. We listened to Verdi's *Otello* all evening; very loud for they have the wireless blaring at Long Crichel, Desmond, Bob and E.K. following the score throughout while I read Sydney Cockerell's correspondence with the great over sixty years. Desmond suggests our going to Rome together in September.

Later tonight Bob talked to me about Logan Pearsall Smith, whom he hated at the end. He has finished his Life of Logan. I cannot but think he has made a mistake in writing it, and in particular in setting out to prove Logan's insanity. It can only do Bob harm, for his readers will assume he is getting his own back on Logan for having cut him out of his will. Bob is a charming person with a thirst for all forms of knowledge and bald truth. He has quenchless curiosity, disarming frankness, and great volubility. He told me how before Logan died he slept in Logan's room on the sofa, kept awake by Logan's coughing; how two nights after his death he slept, no less unhappily, in Logan's bed, Logan lying on the sofa in his coffin. Bob is not exactly fastidious in mind or body.

Thursday, 27th May

Today we called for the Anthony Wests and motored them to Stourhead, Kitty intending to paint in the garden. Anthony West is the natural son

[55]

of H. G. Wells and Rebecca West. He has the profile of his father. His eyes and the lower part of his face are caricatures of his mother's. He has dark hair and eyes, sallow skin, a heavy, slack chin. Oafish. Is said to be clever; and is quirky, contradictory. He is a contributor to the *New Statesman*. Rennie Hoare greeted us at Stourhead with much gush which E. and I received without enthusiasm. In fact E. was very cold. I tried to appear warm but firm. Rennie made several preposterous suggestions regarding furniture arrangement that we could not adopt. I distrust him profoundly. This afternoon we finished arranging all the state rooms on the front. There are three behind which we have not yet tackled. They must wait for our next visit.

On our return the Wests took us to Fonthill. Of Beckford's Abbey there still remains one tower, into which we went. The complete Abbey must have been beautiful as well as striking. The quality of the surviving ashlar is good. Situation high and very remote. Tisbury church has good brasses and some stones to the Arundel family in the chancel. Then to Wardour Castle round which we walked. We were not allowed inside because there is to be a sale of all contents next week. Ted Lister once took me to luncheon before the war. The son and heir was present and told us how much he adored the place. He became a prisoner of war and, being a badly wounded case, was exchanged for a German prisoner. On his way from Liverpool to Wardour he died. The exterior is dignified and clean-cut; simple and severe. Much of the stonework now broken and the cornice of the front perished. The Jesuits have bought it. It is much neglected. I bet they won't repair it.

Friday, 28th May

Left on a lovely morning after breakfast, having much enjoyed this visit to Long Crichel, as usual. Drove to Wimborne. Looked inside the Norman minster; liked the Georgian painted grenadier outside the clock tower. Continued to Christchurch. Spent an hour in this minster which is singularly beautiful. Under the west tower is a 'Pietà' group of Mary Shelley holding the drowned poet in her arms, dated 1851 when I presume Mary died, though why it is here I don't understand. Carefully examined the Countess of Salisbury's chantry, Perpendicular with well-carved Classical arabesques. Observed the intersecting arcades of the north transept, a barbaric Classical. Drove on to Alresford, lunching there. To Miss Lushington's at Kingsley, near Bordon. She is a dear lady but a great talker. Her house is awful. Built by her aunts in 1870 as a school, it is huge, rambling, and of flimsiest material. She showed me all the pictures given to her father by the Pre-Raphaelites. Her mother originated the Rossetti neck. She has some oils by Lord Carlisle which are creditable. She offers to sell us her china. Mrs Gaunt, wife of William Gaunt, author of *The Pre-Raphaelite Tragedy* and one of her tenants, came to tea. Talk was about the interest of our age in the sexual lives of distinguished men. Miss Lushington expressed disapproval, but not too forcibly. I hedged because I knew she has inherited many papers relating to the Byron scandal and Queen Caroline's trial which she threatens to destroy. How to discourage her from carrying out the threat?

In London dined with John Macdonell, Australian, who is too dull for words. His other guest was Count Metternich whom I took to. Like most Germanic aristocrats he has an urbane cosmopolitan manner. Nothing provincial. A well-bred, cultivated man, with considerable knowledge of British art. His uncle was Ambassador in London before 1914. He remembers London in 1903, and says the streets were more congested with horse traffic, and noisier, then than they are with cars today. From a distance, say, in the middle of Hyde Park in 1903 there was a thunderous rumble of horse traffic that was unique to London.

Sunday, 30th May

After Mass motored to Cambridge. Entered King's Chapel. All scrubbed as to roof and walls and glistening with soapy cleanliness. The windows mostly reinstated. The sun shining through them like jewels. I gasped at the exquisite beauty of this building. Wandered in the sun to Caius gateways and the bridge over the Cam at Clare. Then continued to Ryston Hall for tea with Colonel Pratt and family. I had written asking if I might look at Ryston. You can barely discern the vestiges of Sir Roger Pratt's house which Soane altered by adding two wings, and cementing over brickwork, and which Colonel Pratt's father altered again fifty years ago. The Colonel has made the architect's library into a kitchen. The portrait of the first Roger Pratt by Lely survives. So do two chimneypieces of this date. The others are eighteenth-century like the staircase. Some of Pratt's books lie loose about the untidy house. On my way to Bradenham I stopped at Oxburgh. By some miracle the Renaissance terracotta Bedingfeld tombs survive, although when the tower fell the whole of the nave collapsed, and only the chancel escaped. How this fragile terracotta did not crumble I cannot imagine.

Alec Penrose's brother Beakers and his new wife staying at Bradenham [Hall]. At first I did not take to her but by the end of my visit succumbed to her extreme friendliness. I wish intelligent women were less affected and less familiar.

[57]

Monday, 31st May

Motored to Wisbech with Alec [Penrose] in the morning and went round
Bank House, deciding how we could divide it up, letting the large library
to the Wisbech Society, the basement to the Archivists, the balancing
1860 wing as a separate house, and keeping the main block for show. I
visited the Wisbech Museum and was taken round by Rudsdale. A
charming building of 1840 but hardly suitable for the Trust. We all
lunched at the Crown. Alec showed me Beaupré Hall (red brick, diaper
work, Elizabethan heraldic glass) which is in the most woeful state and
only fit for a ruin. To Wallington Hall for a drink with the Luddingtons.
A much restored house of the early fifteenth century. Best feature the
gate tower with terracotta panels and Gothic cusping. Luddington's
father took out many of the Georgian sash windows, substituting bad
casement lights.

Tuesday, 1st June

To Blickling where we had a fairly profitable day. Wyndham Ketton-
Cremer lunched at the Buckinghamshire Arms; also Lord Lothian whom
I allowed to take away some engraved glass, golf clubs, etc., I trust
acting correctly. Alec said of Wyndham he is the sort of man who has
found contentment of mind by cutting off all limbs that offended him.
Alec, I find, has aged mentally; is less elastic; slower, rather dogmatic,
almost pompous and, I suspect, selfish.* Frances seems to be on edge
with him. He is not very nice to his boys – very schoolmasterish. Yet he
is a dear man. I admire his taste and I am impressed by his profound
faith. He peers bewildered through owlish spectacles in the way, I
imagine, Edward Lear did.

I motored after tea to St Paul's, Waldenbury to stay with Burnet. We
discussed the cussedness of inclinations beyond one's control. Something
inside one may whisper futility, and caution against the inevitable
backfire of passion. Affairs of the heart mean not a fig more than the grip
of momentary drunkenness, rendering one rudderless and unreliable.
Civilized beings must rise above the distractions of lust. Pious thoughts
which tomorrow may wither beneath the sun of a new love.

Saturday, 5th June

Have seen no one these last few days. Refused a tempting invitation from
Joan Moore to a huge dinner party and then, too late, regretted refusal. I

*He was, I was to learn only too soon, already very ill.

[58]

have stayed in of an evening working very hard, and reading Osbert Sitwell's *Great Morning*. I wish my judgements were not so easily influenced. I recall Desmond [Shawe-Taylor]'s animadversions upon the man's style. He is right. It is not so pure as I thought. Perhaps this book falls short of its predecessors. They were surely magnificent. The style flowed like a clear river in spate.

Bobo Mitford has died which I find very sad. How Tom teased her the last time I – and I believe, he – saw her at Swinbrook like the big child she had become again.

Today Count Metternich and John Summerson lunched. The Count is a delightful man. He is as much at home in this country as in his own. John Summerson has a mildly deprecating, cynical manner, combined with disarming diffidence. He took us to the Soane Museum.

Sunday, 6th June

Stuart Preston comes to stay here for a week. How shall I find him?

Stuart has come. I met him at Victoria station. He looks well, is brown, not fat but stalwart, and has become very bald, with a tonsure. I invited the Cyril Connollys to meet him at dinner since Cyril expressed the wish. C. is a lumpish, bad-mannered man and was as bored with me as I was bored with him. His puny little wife is quite sweet and at any rate polite.

Monday, 7th June

Went to Covent Garden with Stuart – *Giselle* and *Les Patineurs*. I like Second Empire music. Stuart already in the opera house when I arrived. We dined late at the Ritz grill where Alvilde Chaplin joined us. Stuart said that she grumbled too much. I suspect that he thinks I do too. Grumbling is not at all a bad thing if, like literary criticism, it is constructive.

Tuesday, 8th June

Met Lord Gainsborough at 6 o'clock at the Marlborough Club and discussed Chipping Campden. He says he may offer his whole property including the Court House on condition that his family have a right of residence in perpetuity. He is a tubby little boy, very young, a sort of *Schoolboy's Annual* hero, with a distinct look of his handsome mother about the mouth. Very polite he is, earnest, Catholic, but physically a suet pudding.

I dined with the Harold Bowens in York Terrace and there met Midi [Gascoigne] whom I had not seen for nearly a year. She looks very thin, frail, delicate and beautiful. I have never seen her look more beautiful. But she is an invalid. At first I was shocked by her frailty and the smallness of her wrists. She has today seen a new doctor who says she has colon trouble, not ulcers, and has been starving herself for over nine months. She says her mother is now dying of cancer. She watched her mother come out of a coma and asked her if she had had nightmares. Her mother answered that they were not nightmares, but worrying dreams about little things she had neglected to do and others she ought not to have done. This is more frightening than sheer oblivion in the circumstances. Perhaps afterlife will be like this – worrying – for all eternity.

Thursday, 10th June

Lunched with Mr Harry Batsford and Sam Carr at the Connaught Hotel. This entertainment was intended as a kind assurance that they still wanted me to continue with my book. I asked if Batsford's would send me to Italy again this year and Mr B. said, 'Yes,' he thought so.

Dined at Dick Girouard's house with him and Alan Pryce-Jones alone. Very enjoyable. Alan very amusing in that sweet way he underestimates everything, including his own brilliance. Told us that he might become a Catholic one day. When a boy of seventeen he went to the Cathedral to be received. Had a formidable interview with several Fathers who sent him away with a flea in his ear.

Friday, 11th June

Stuart is staying till Monday. I have been nicer to him this visit. He and I dined with Bridget and Lady de Vesci who gave us champagne at the Ritz. We went to *Hamlet*; disappointing film. The play, an intellectual exchange between characters without action does not work on the film where action seems to be required. The producer was evidently aware of this phenomenon and made Hamlet walk continuously up and down stairs like a restless fly. Very irritating. Olivier gave a fine performance, yet he is not my idea of Hamlet. He made the part too straightforward and was actuated exclusively by revenge, and nothing else. He has dyed his hair yellow which makes him look older instead of younger.

Saturday, 12th June

To the Royal Academy this morning. The standard of indifference is undeviating. The standard of the architectural drawings plumbs the depths. Summerson warned me of this. This evening Alec [Clifton-Taylor], who had written most kindly giving me a long list of *errata* to *Adam*, called.

Vita [Sackville-West] and Doreen [Baynes] lunched. Vita was wearing the same old terracotta dress she wore every day last August on our tour, and smoking from her long holder. Doreen said after V. left that she had the most beautiful features and eyes D. had ever seen. Was much impressed too by V.'s 'kindliness'. Though V. was here little over a quarter of an hour, for she had a dentist's appointment, Doreen studied her appearance and manner intently. She sees so few people and goes about so little that she manages to absorb impressions that wash over the rest of us.

Lunched with the publisher Lindsay Drummond and his assistant, Miss Matheson, at the Escargot. They pumped me for information about the National Trust. I repeated that I did not wish to discourage them from issuing their series of books. Yet I did not encourage a venture which I believe to be incongruous. This evening Papa came to stay after his first day at Ascot. He looks well.

Today gave a luncheon party of five and was quite nervous beforehand, my table being very small and my guests rather grand. But it was a success. Guests were Michael Goodwin, editor of *The Nineteenth Century*, Diane Abdy, Sibyl Colefax and Gerry Wellington. Gerry had to come to London unexpectedly for a meeting called by Lord Esher to discuss the Blickling Tower alterations this afternoon. Excellent meal, lots of drink, ending with Cointreau and brandy. G. again rattled off the names of every marble inlay of my round table.

To Hatfield as a tourist. Escorted round the house. This palatial mass less fussy than I remembered it to be. The north front quite plain and more austere than Blickling. Brick darker. Few fanciful windows. Condition still a little dusty and unkempt from the hospital having been there all the war. It is not the architecture so much as the relics that interest me – Queen Elizabeth's garden hat and stockings, her jewel case, and those three astonishing portraits.

[61]

Stayed the night with Burnet at Bury Farm. After dinner David Bowes-Lyon walked round from St Paul's. He was alone, his wife being in London. He was wearing a blue collarless shirt under his coat, his neck bare, suede shoes and tight trousers. Has strong, crisp brown hair and regular white teeth. Very youthful; good complexion in spite of some sharp, haggard lines on one side of his face. He is a charmer. Took us round his garden in the twilight, and into the house.

Thursday, 17th June

Drove Bowes-Lyon up to London, leaving 8 o'clock. Pouring with rain and no windscreen wiper working. His conversation very strange. Did I not think women's thighs ugly? Men's figures more aesthetic? Did I like wearing shorts? He did not disapprove of any sexual practices – and so on. Trying not to be too distant, I did not commit myself to any opinions. He must have found me either a dolt or a prude.

Friday, 18th June

Went to Covent Garden. The Sadlers Wells Company dancing *Coppelia*. Pamela May in this role good but has common mannerisms and facial tricks that make one want to smack her. Hunter in the *Tricorne* in Massine's wonderful part as the miller was feeble. I am tired of this ballet and the thumping of de Falla.

Saturday, 19th June

Antique Dealers' Fair. There is too much to see. This is a fault of exhibitions these days. Some wonderful pieces of furniture, of course. Indeed I am amazed at the high-quality furniture still left in this country. Much must be faked. Prices exorbitant. I noticed six ordinary Chippendale chairs priced at £700.

After luncheon motored Dame Una Pope-Hennessy to Petersham. I had a down on this lady today. Her vanity is o'er-reaching. She talked of nothing but her successes in Paris and how much more intellectual she is than anyone else. Told me she has sold over 150,000 copies of her *Dickens*, which I can hardly believe, and this year had a capital levy on the earnings. Most gracious to me about the favourable reviews of my book by the ignorant, and pitying over the bad ones. When I said humbly that it made no pretensions to be a contribution to literature, 'Of course it isn't,' she snorted. Now she was quite right but she could have kept her views to herself, or snorted with less vehemence. We joined a party of

[62]

Richmond Georgian Groupers and went over Montrose House (very rich, very bad taste indeed), Rutland Lodge, Petersham Manor, and other houses, the names of which already escape me, as they say. Dame Una inquisitive and caustic. Would not allow me to have tea when offered – I was dying of thirst – because she wanted to return home for tea; and when I dropped her at 5.30 did not invite me in.

Sunday, 20th June

Patrick Kinross telephoned. He is back from Scotland, and came to dinner. Henry Reed, my American architectural historian, came too. Patrick very nice. He has finished his novel, which he has already rewritten once. It is about his wife, Angela, and is to be called *Ruthless Innocence* – not a good title. John Heygate is reading the manuscript.

Monday, 21st June

Drove to Stourhead, leaving at 9 o'clock. I stopped at the big church, St Michael's, Basingstoke and the verger told me all the glass from the Holy Ghost Chapel, moved to this church twenty years ago, was destroyed by bomb blast in the war. So that is that. Then called at Wilton. David Herbert not at home, but I saw the Holbein temple. Much of the detail resembles that on the gatehouse at Charlecote. An important textbook building. Reached Stourhead in time for luncheon and spent the afternoon with Eardley. At present the house is musty, dusty, drab and lacking charm. We made little headway and felt depressed. I fetched Eddy from Gillingham station. Both he and Desmond are at Long Crichel where I stay.

Tuesday, 22nd June

E. and I called on a Colonel Goodden at Compton near Yeovil. He owns a large Victorian version of Barrington Court built of Ham stone. The Gooddens have been here since the eighteenth century. In the church are many memorials to them. One excellent statue of Robert Goodden, *c.* 1822, a kind of Coke of Norfolk personage, robust and John Bullish. The house is now empty but was occupied all the war by Lord Aberconway's Air Company who messed it up and decline to give the old man proper compensation. The Colonel offered to lend us several things for Montacute. We agreed to take a sedan chair and much oriental porcelain looted by the aforesaid Robert Goodden from the imperial palace, Pekin. We fetched the Yateses and motored them to Dillington House to view the contents to be sold tomorrow by auction. E. and I both rashly made some bids for various objects and I am terrified lest I get some and can't afford to pay for them. Then tea at Montacute. Round the house with E., rearranging furniture in our usual way.

Muggy, sulky day, the sun somewhere, but not penetrating. E. and I motor to Crichel House and were received by the headmistress, Miss Galston. Napier Alington's daughter, the owner, has let the house as a girls' school. Wonderful too the school must be for hardly any of the Alington contents have been put away. They are used by the girls and not spoiled, even carpets and curtains. Pretty, sweet girls they seemed, all out of doors reading, walking or playing musical instruments. The house outside is stuccoed, a grey texture – some dull nineteenth-century additions. Only the south colonnade, imposed in 1774 upon a George II wing, is noteworthy on the outside. But the interior is very fine indeed with some rooms of high quality. Wyatt must have been the architect for I notice several of his tricks – fan pendentives, ellipses, etc. The dining-room ceiling beautiful, like the Heveningham one, blues and greens and plasterwork clear and not over-fussy, all white, the walls biscuit. The school tables are certainly not ornamental. I see no reason why they should not be so, yet simple. The drawing-room ceiling reminds me of Adam's at no. 20 St James's Square; green silk walls (modern), crimson upholstered gilt chairs. The mirrors throughout the house are fine. We walked round the grounds; lovely lake and woods.

Drove on to St Giles. Entered the church, too well kept up and over-restored. Every wall tablet to a member of the Ashley Cooper family. The exterior is early Georgian. Then tea at St Giles's House with Lady Shaftesbury. 'Shaftesbury', as she referred to him, was away. She is old, rather fat, bandy legs for she is lame, and *maquillée* in the Queen Alexandra fashion. Eyes very made up. Must once have been pretty, and has enchanting manners. Is a sister of the Duke of Westminster. Clips every 'g'. 'G-clippin'' has become a favourite joke at Long Crichel. After tea she showed us round the state rooms. They are *superb*; late seventeenth-century and early eighteenth-century. One drawing-room of greeny-gold silk, striped; all the frames of pictures and glasses of unbelievable delicacy and beauty. The dining-room perhaps the best room of all with Chippendale suite carved in finest detail. Library is Regency. A good terracotta bust of the 1st Earl, Dryden's Earl. A magnificent house. Pray God the contents are never dispersed. Lady Shaftesbury told us that, their son having died last year, they are faced

[64]

with £250,000 death duties. Presumably they had rashly made over the estate to him. Her exquisite personality impressed me strongly.

Thursday, 24th June

Eardley and I spent the day at Stourhead, again putting finishing touches to the state rooms. At last we completed all we had set out to do. There is still room for improvements of a lesser kind and some rehanging of pictures. This evening we discussed with Desmond plans for going to Italy, just the three of us, in September.

Friday, 25th June

Our great day at Stourhead. We met Paul Hyslop for luncheon at the Spread Eagle. Then the Eshers, Rennie Hoare and Paul Methuen joined us at the house. Rennie and Paul were somewhat in a camp apart. Lord E. cordially disliked R.H., thought him a bore and a philistine. He approved wholeheartedly Eardley's and my arrangements. He is the staunchest ally. He suggested a few minor alterations, really to appease Hoare and Methuen. We showed Esher the surplus furniture in the basement and attics. He decided that after Rennie Hoare had made a pick of what he wanted to rent from the Trust, we could take the rest to other houses, where needed, provided it was carefully catalogued as belonging to Stourhead, and sell the indifferent stuff. This will present a problem. We shall have to decide what may in the future be considered of interest to Stourhead that today we dismiss as rubbish.

After tea E., Simon Buxton [the N.T. agent] and I walked in the gardens along the lake. All the azaleas now over. Some of the old beeches have got to be felled for they are dangerous. It will be a tragic day when the great tulip trees by the water have to go. I motored home, dining at the King's Head, Cirencester en route. I was overcome by an attack of unaccountable melancholy in the dining-room. Life seemed to stand still. The room became claustrophobic. I could scarcely finish my meal for longing to get outside, and away. At Wickhamford I sat in Mama's bedroom, talking to her in bed. Told her of my strange experience at Cirencester. She explained to me that it was in the King's Head that her mother died in 1894 while waiting for the carriage to drive her home to Coates. Mama, a little girl at the time, was alone with her. My grandmother was driven nearly mad by the violent ringing of the Abbey church bells opposite. Ever since my mother has loathed church bells.

I called on Audrey at Prestbury and sat on a bench in her little garden under a rose tree and next to a mock orange of wonderful fragrance. In my imagination it seemed to conjure all the marvels of the East where I have never been.

Away at 9.30 to Hidcote. Walked round the garden with Lawrence Johnston who, apart from absent mindedness and some loss of memory, is otherwise sane and hale. He said he was incensed by a letter he had received from the Trust and had now decided no longer to 'give' us Hidcote. After much discussion and persuasion he agreed to leave it by will, if I would witness his codicil. The garden is a dream of beauty. The old-fashioned rose garden smelled as fragrant as I have always imagined a garden in a French Gothic tapestry might smell. Lawrie Johnston was very nice to me.

I stopped at Chipping Campden church to look at the Noel tombs. The two alabaster shrouded figures standing within their tomb are very moving. Then to Oxford. Left the car in the Roy Harrods' yard and joined my party of National Trust members in the charabanc. Drove to Ditchley. Mrs Tree received us smilingly and charmingly. She is handsome and natural and attractive. The butler came into the big hall and asked if I would go upstairs to Ronnie Tree, in bed with an injured back. He was very friendly and asked me to come again alone, and stay. While we were talking a tall, dark figure, a trifle bent, with long black hair, looking like the late Mr Winant, but more romantic, entered quietly. He was introduced to me as Peter Beatty. I said, 'You will not remember me. We were at school together and once swapped, you a beautiful pencil and I some trashy object. I got the better of the bargain and have ever since felt guilty. We must have been nine or ten at the time.' His reply was, 'I remember it well and I remember thinking I had got the better of you. You must excuse me for not having recognized you. I am quite blind at present; only temporarily of course.' But he will, I understand, never see again.

Ditchley inside is perfection. Exquisite furniture and fabrics, many original to the house. I have never seen better taste. Nothing jars. Nothing is too sumptuous, or new. The grounds, laid out by Ronnie Tree, are suitable to the house, the outside of which is a little austere, and I regret that the two cupolas and pediment were not carried out according to Gibbs's design. Our party had high tea at the Marlborough Arms, Woodstock. Only eleven members came, but we enjoyed ourselves. I talked to them all in turn and on parting we all shook hands and everyone thanked everyone else.

I fetched my car from the Harrods' house and motored to South Wraxall Manor to stay with Lady Glyn. She is the mother of David Long who was killed in the war and the grandmother of the heiress of this beautiful house.

[66]

David Long came to see me at the beginning of September 1939 in a great hurry for he was drafted abroad with his regiment. He begged me to devise some scheme whereby South Wraxall, which he loved, might be preserved by the National Trust. As far as I remember his solicitors raised difficulties and objections during his absence. The Eshers are staying here and they got me invited in order to talk over the future of the place. Lady G. is old now with a face like parchment, and painted parchment at that. Also staying Lady Marjorie Beckett, Diana Worthington's mother. She knew I was a friend of Diana and spoke sadly of her. Said she had no idea how desperate poor Diana was before her suicide. She was sweet to me because I loved Diana and asked me to stay with her in Yorkshire at any time. She must have been prettier than Diana who had a huge frog-like mouth that was, strangely enough, seductive. When smiling and lowering her eyes in the same poignant way she reminded me of Diana.

Sunday, 27th June

This house is not one I should care to live in. Lady Glyn has furnished it entirely by herself with what she bought from Thornton Smith's sale. The furniture is pretty, but not exactly good. All the floors are covered with rush matting. The various fireplaces of 1598 are interesting, particularly the gigantic Flemish one in the big room which gets uglier the longer you look at it: the loathsome caryatides with cruel boxes round their fat, shapeless bodies. Lord Esher is restless during weekends. Likes to talk. Never reads. Nevertheless is bubbling with fun and jokes; counting the cakes on the tea-table and calculating how many he may eat; and then gorging. Never walks a yard, saying we should hold Sir Edgar Bonham-Carter, who was a rugger blue and is now a cripple, as a warning not on any account to take exercise. Says he would rather remain in England and be atom-bombed into a jelly than emigrate to the colonies, blaze trails through the bushvelt and be eaten by scorpions.

In the morning I drove the party in the Eshers' Buick to Corsham. Paul and Norah [Methuen] showed us over the house which I must say they have arranged well. It has been cleaned and repainted under their direction with infinite care. I motored back to London in 3¼ hours, arriving 9 o'clock.

Tuesday, 29th June

Yesterday and today I have suffered from loss of voice, owing to tiredness, Miss Paterson says, but I have had a sore throat for several

[67]

days. I am distressed by Maud Mosley's death. She talked to me the last time I stayed with her in November about death and her indifference to it with cold detachment. I am indeed sorry for Aunt Dorothy. The two sisters wrote to each other every single day of the year, and had done so since my uncle's death in 1931.

Went to Shrewsbury for the day by train. To my surprise am not tired tonight, for I had a comfortable seat each way, good meals and read several things I needed to get through, on the journey. Walked home from Paddington. Keeble the decorator and I spent the day at Attingham. We went round the rooms estimating the work to be done in the state rooms. He means to start in a fortnight. This is satisfactory. The quality of the doors, friezes and ceilings of this house is pretty good.

Wednesday, 30th June

MacLeod Matheson lunched and gave some useful criticisms of National Trust properties he visited on a recent tour of Somerset. It is odd how an intelligent man can be an inverted snob – his consciousness of class distinctions is too acute for a left-winger.

Betty Hussey, whom I went to see this evening, urged me to ask David Bowes-Lyon to persuade the Queen to intimate that she would favour the surplus funds of the Queen's District Institute going to our Gardens Fund. This sentence reads like a minute from a subcommittee of an urban district council.

Thursday, 1st July

The Admiral picked me up at 8.25 with Ruby Holland-Martin and Colonel Vane, MP, of Hutton Vane. We drove to Fairford. I sat in the back with Vane, a nice man about my age. It is frightening how unfailingly disagreeable I am at this hour of the morning. Later I improved and kept the sombre party together, I like to think. I set out to be civil to Captain John Hill, the odious agent who was entertaining us. We got to Fairford before 11 o'clock and had time to look at the glass in the church. It is a medley of mellow colours, but lacks design. Dates from *c.* 1490. The handguides are most inadequate, giving descriptions of the subjects, i.e. Christ in the Temple, which one can make out for oneself (admittedly with difficulty), but no information about the workmanship or the artists. We inspected Fairford Park and estate. I was glad that Ruby H.-M. and Vane agreed with me that this property is unacceptable. We saw from Badbury Hill the Buscot and Coleshill estates. Drove to Great Coxwell and went inside the barn. It is really grand. I felt proud to be in it. Could any building be more serviceable, beautiful, robust, simple, religious and uplifting? It represents paganism and Christianity and is a shrine to Flora, Poma, Nature, what you will. Then to Boarstall Tower. Looked over the building. Then Hartwell House, where we had tea. This place greatly improved since I was last here, as regards the gardens. The interior is now being reconditioned, but all the walls still bare. The fake Jacobean staircase has been set in a new position so as to entail three flights instead of one central flight. It has involved some newly reproduced balusters, which do not matter. To think of Louis XVIII's court here, so densely packed that several members of the household were obliged to camp on the roof tiles.

Dined with Sibyl Colefax upstairs at the Dorchester. I sat between Cynthia Jebb and Mrs Hore-Belisha, who is outspoken. Both friendly, easy, rattling women. Left with Harold [Nicolson] who came home and drank brandy with me – to my distress next day – till midnight. Harold's affection for his old friends is demonstrated by a persistent desire to help them. Quite touching.

Friday, 2nd July

Dined at Kew with Mark Ogilvie-Grant, taking Malcolm Bullock and George Dix. A very hilarious, male, witty-smutty, funny party, at which disclosures and confidences poured out faster than the drink. Even Malcolm was embarrassed by certain idiosyncratic disclosures. The more outrageous they became the more harmless. Nearly choked with laughter. Oh, lust *is* a jest! How *would* we laugh without it?

Saturday, 3rd July

With courage opened Papa's letter in reply to mine telling him I was more than £600 overdrawn. He wrote kindly that we must have a financial talk next time I go home. No recriminations which was very unlike him.

Spent morning and afternoon at the Soane Museum, looking through du Cerceau's drawings of French châteaux, and talking to John Summerson and Dorothy Stroud. J.S. who is engaged upon Henry VIII is in despair. He is also about to edit Thorpe for the Walpole Society and confesses he cannot penetrate that mystery.

Sunday, 4th July

Dined alone with Puss Milnes-Gaskell in her flat. She talked of Queen Mary's astonishing activity. She said that Kenneth de Courcy actually sent Queen Mary a telegram inviting her to luncheon. Q.M. was furious. Aunt

[69]

Puss says that Princess Mary is a person of the greatest sweetness of character. Her one fault is talking far into the night. At Sandringham Aunt P. dragooned her to her bedroom where they discovered a bat on her bed. For one hour, amid giggles, they tried without avail to remove it. Instead they had to remove the Princess to another bedroom, the bat remaining asleep on the pillow.

Monday, 5th July

Dined at Barbara Moray's. I hope she likes me as much as I like her, but one never knows. Other guests were the Hugo Pitmans, he large, deaf, agreeable, and slightly tight; she, soft and inaudible: Lord Revelstoke who is distinguished and Lady Worsley, grey-haired and widowed in 1914. Barbara has struck up a warm friendship with this nice but ordinary woman who apparently asked to meet me. Strange I thought.

Wednesday, 7th July

Today had Sir Sydney Cockerell, Alan Pryce-Jones and Bob Gathorne-Hardy to luncheon. Bob thoroughly enjoyed himself, talking nineteen to the dozen. Sir Sydney, dear old man, very spry, not without a touch of – not malice – but impishness. He talked of Charlotte Mew as a great minor poet, whom Hardy admired. He seemed delighted that the three of us spoke with warmth of Ruskin, as though expecting a younger generation to decry that great man. He told us that Ruskin read aloud parts of *Praeterita* to him before publication. Ruskin spoke, as he wrote, in occasional passages of deep purple.

George Dix took me to Vanbrugh's *Relapse* with which I was deeply disappointed. Seventeenth-century bawdy unlike ours at Kew, not at all funny, and Colonel Blimp and his family crashing bores. Then went to a supper party given by the Eric Dugdales which was hellish.

At 4.30 (I have got my chronology wrong) Lord Crawford, Lord Esher, the Admiral and I went to the Treasury to discuss with Sir Edward Bridges, Sir Bernard Gilbert, and Proctor, arising from receipt of Treasury's letter announcing the Chancellor's intention to set up a Commission to deal with the problem of large country houses with collections. I am much concerned with this subject because my memorandum on the very problem was written before receipt of Bridges's letter, and is to be circulated to the Executive Committee. In it I have urged very strongly that the Trust ought to come to terms with the Government and indeed ask for, and accept, government subvention, in spite of our hitherto having set our faces against the risk of state interference. The alternative, I submit, is for the Trust to sink, for we cannot compete with Government competition and Treasury resources. I think I have convinced Crawford and Esher, both clever men, but the Admiral and Hubert Smith [Chief Agent] do not yet see the necessity. The Trust is at a critical juncture and I seem to be playing a backstair role in guiding its affairs. Backstair is the word.

Goodwin asked me to write an article on gardens for the *Nineteenth Century*. After due consideration I declined. I want, before going to Italy, to finish the synopsis of my book, and to begin writing it in the autumn.

Saturday, 10th July

Was to have gone to stay with the Oglanders at Nunwell in the Isle of Wight. All the week did not want to go. Braced myself to go and got to Waterloo at 9.15 this morning. Such an enormous queue on the platform that I could not even reach the ticket office. Returned home and telephoned Joan Oglander. Went to the Soane Museum in the afternoon and looked carefully through the Thorpe drawings, the whole book of them. John Summerson is baffled but he considers Thorpe immensely important, and undoubtedly a designer. Where Thorpe has written, 'perfected by me' or 'altered by me' John S. thinks he refers, not to the building, but to the design.

I went to tea with the Rosses in Stafford Terrace. This house is stifling, choc-à-bloc and pitch-dark with late-Victorian furniture and Linley Samborne *Punch* drawings. Interesting it undoubtedly is, but I could not myself live in it. I feel it would induce asthma or some allergy. It is not even comfortable. They told me that Emerald Cunard really is dying now, which is very depressing.

Sunday, 11th July

On my way to the bathroom saw Emily's [my housekeeper] *Sunday Express* with large headline: 'Fabulous Lady Cunard dies at 71'. This has indeed made me sad. My day quite overclouded by it. Cannot get the thought out of my head or concentrate on a book. I telephoned Tony Gandarillas to condole with him. He was in tears. Said he was with her while she died; she had no pain at the end, being kept under drugs. I met little Diane [Abdy] in Bennet Street after luncheon. She said Bertie also was with her when she died and feels as though he has lost his mother. Yesterday morning Emerald tried desperately to say something important but was unable to speak. This worries Bertie. Gordon, her maid, became a saint at the end, slept in her room, waited on her hand and foot, and never left her. Apparently it was cancer that killed her. I remarked to

[71]

Diane that in walking to Brooks's this morning I kept saying to myself, 'Why do all these people I pass, live? They are so ugly and so stupid, and yet Emerald dies.' She had been saying the same to herself.

My sorrow for Emerald is different to what I felt when Kathleen Kennet died. That was a dear friend going. Emerald's death means the end of an age, of a legend. I regret that I did not see her more often these past two years, but hers was a world not mine. I admired her more than I admired most women, for her lightning perception, her wide reading, her brilliant repartee, her sense of fun, and sparkling, delicious, wonderful nonsense. If only I could have attended her dinner parties like, say, a dumb servitor, the awkwardness of trying to contribute to the conversation and failing in the endeavour would not have arisen. I would have been content to listen to her, and watch her deft manipulation of the conversation until eternity. She seemed always to like me and was charming, but I knew I could never entertain her, and so I avoided her too often. That was the true reason. Yet I am glad I knew her for no one will ever take her place. No ordinary mortal can afford to be so detached from the chores of everyday life. Hers was entirely artificial, or rather unreal for these days, uncontaminated by worldly duties. What a loss she will be to society. It is hard to estimate it.

Monday, 12th July

John Summerson and I, by a process of slow and combined analysis, agreed that the ballroom at no. 4 St. James's Square was perhaps from Burlington's design as regards surviving ceiling and cornice, but the heraldic achievements upheld by *putti*, the chimneypiece and tapestry panels could be dated 1860. This decision was reached at the party Philip James gave in the Arts Council office for the exhibition of Lord Leicester's drawings from Holkham. Had a talk with Philip Hendy who said with a snarl that, when Lord Crawford ceased to be chairman of the National Gallery trustees, then he might lend pictures to Osterley. He is a rude, disagreeable man and I dislike him for disliking Crawford.

Tuesday, 13th July

Sisson lunched. He said the reason why he disliked modernistic architecture was that it was puritanical and eschewed all embellishment, in fact everything that might delight the eyes and senses.

Bridget and Tony Gandarillas dined. He talked of little else but Emerald's death, having this morning taken her to Golders Green for cremation. He described how, lying on her bed last night, her little hands manicured, pretty white hair brushed and curled, with no lines on her face, she looked sweet and ethereal. (I wonder why death gives back a person a fleeting youth which is of no use to him or her. It is a dirty trick.) Only Tony and Bertie Abdy were in the room when she died, which she did so peacefully that Tony did not realize she had ceased breathing. He said that Lady Diana Cooper looked in at 5.30 a.m. after a ball, glanced at Emerald, and left by air for Paris in the afternoon. E. died at 6 o'clock. Numbers of people, who were never great friends, pushed their way to front pews of the church for the service.

Thursday, 15th July

Motored after dinner last night to Polesden Lacey and stayed the night with the Feddens. This morning at 9.30 Midi came. I motored her and Robin to Brighton, to the Regency Exhibition. No one could honestly say, although most people pretend, that the Pavilion is not hideous. The outside is tawdry. Clifford Musgrave had arranged the Banqueting Room very well. Curtains drawn; candelabra lit with candles, table-cloth Nelson's, dinner service Derby, with gold knives and forks; fruits and sweetmeats in dishes, hock and port glasses, and so on. The Dolphin furniture from the Admiralty very magnificent. The Duchess of Kent paraded round. She is tall and upright, extremely chic. Effect altogether splendid. Lovely skin, her mouth curiously drawn to one side. Then we motored to Bramber Castle, much tidied since I was last there. Then to Amberley Castle where we were shown by the owner panels of the Nine Worthy Women by the Bernardi, mentioned by Walpole in his *Anecdotes*, on wood. By no means works of art. Their ground colour a lacquer-red, enriched with gold; all the women wearing armour like Amazons. This house is pretty and uncouth like most castles that aren't bogus ones. The gatehouse with Richard II towers circular and cylindrical. Then we called at Goodwood and were shown over by the housekeeper in a charming manner, as one would have been in the eighteenth century if one's carriage had been respectable. The house is not striking outside, the texture ugly. It is of unfinished octagonal plan, more strange than beautiful, with round towers at the angles, by Wyatt. The double portico resembles the one at Crichel. The inside is extremely plain and pleasing; 'chaste', Horace Walpole would have called it. The dining-room has a suite of rosewood furniture, inlaid with ebony. The sarcophagi chaste too. Several portraits of the Duchess of Portsmouth, progenitrix of the Dukes of Richmond. Not a pretty woman, and bad-tempered. Grey granite pillars from Guernsey in the hall. In the drawing-room the two famous Canaletti and a fine collection of Sèvres in wall cabinets.

Somewhat to my surprise my Memorandum passed through both Committees with hardly a dissentient voice raised. True, Lord Crawford added his account of the last meeting with the Treasury which thus made my Memo a little out of date. However, the Executive Committee agreed that if the Chairman were asked by the Chancellor of the Exchequer to accept a grant, it should be taken, provided it was attached to the maintenance of a specific building only, and was not a contribution to general funds.

Charles Fry back from America telephoned that he needed to see me at once. I called this evening. He is unchanged – detestable. I really dislike him unreservedly. He is utterly untrustworthy, without conscience, moral scruple, or decency. I shall have to see him once more as my publisher, and that is the end.

Sibyl made me take a friend of hers, assistant librarian to the hateful B.B., to Syon. Keith Miller-Jones very kindly gave us luncheon. The whole Georgian Group membership rallied there. It was like a royal garden party. It struck me during this visit, the last of so many, that after all the furniture was not up to much. But I was impressed by the early sixteenth-century portraits in the Fowler wing – a French picture of Protector Somerset with a red beard, a double portrait of Sir Philip Sidney and his sister Mary Pembroke.

This evening went to *Ambassador Extraordinary* with the Gandarillas and Bridget and dined at the Ritz. An indifferent play and the skit on atom bombs cuts too close to the bone to be in good taste. I suppose on that account it was hissed the first night. The Ambassador from Mars, a Frenchman, aged thirty-five, almost completely naked, a beautiful object.

Lunched with that fiend Charles Fry at the Ritz. He launched into paeans of praise of himself and his business successes, and when I asked if Batsford would send me to Italy this September, gave no encouragement and advised me to write to Mr Batsford. Conversation then lapsed into his drink and sex prowess, which disgusts and bores. During the hour and a half I was with him today he consumed five gins and tonic.

This morning the Admiral talked to Smith, Gibbs and L.-M. about the Memo on office reorganization, which we presented to him on Friday. As usual he was generous and grateful to us for our criticisms. A good but foolish man.

At 3.45 I motored homewards. Called at Bisham Abbey, now leased to a physical jerks college. Sweaty young men and women, black and white, doing exercises on the browned lawns. A gruesome spectacle. The whole placed looked horrible. The lady warden showed me the hall chimneypiece, on which I took notes. I suspect it may, after all, not be 1560 but Jacobean because of the cabochon ornament on the base of the capitals. Then called at West Wycombe to see how Shearsby has progressed with the colonnade. He has done it very well and Helen is well satisfied. She, her mother and aunt, were having tea in the colonnade. Very affectionate greetings. Continued straight to Broadway where I met the family at the Alexanders' golden wedding party. Lots of friendly old faces. Mama looking very bright and pretty, her complexion fresh and youthful. On seeing me her dear face lit up in its radiant manner as of old; suffused with childlike joy.

Lunched at Madresfield [Court]. Lord Beauchamp is fat, with a great paunch, looking like God knows what, wearing an old blue shirt, open at the frayed neck, and a tight pair of brown Army shorts, baby socks and sandshoes. Lady B. plump, but pretty. Both kind and welcoming. A lovely warm day. The house is not in my eyes beautiful. The situation, however, is made beautiful by the Malvern Hills looming over it. You approach it by a straight drive of more than a mile, but the actual estate is on flat and dull ground. The gardens (there are ten gardeners) are delicious, especially the long avenues and paths, and the arboretum. Busts of Roman Emperors under arches of yew close to the house which is moated. The contents are marvellous – pictures and sixteenth-century portraits. As for the miniatures, of which there are a great number, they are superlative. Also some good French furniture and many bibelots, snuff boxes, gold, silver, bejewelled, etc. One could spend hours here enjoying these things which by themselves make Madresfield worthy of preservation for all time.

We lunched in the great hall – again much altered eighty years ago. It faces a little central court, half-timbered in a Nürnberg manner. Lady Beauchamp is a Dane and her two stepdaughters and old mother, who does not speak and to whom one does not speak, were staying. Lord and

Lady B. spent all afternoon conducting and explaining. A picnic tea was had at the swimming pool. Then he took me to look at two half-timbered lesser houses on the estate, one Prior's Court on the Severn, round a square central court with seventeenth-century staircase and panelling. The rich tenants from the Black Country most obsequious and apologetic to the Earl for not being in their best clothes, whereas the Earl was dressed as I have described. Earls with sores on their legs and knees should not parade them exposed to their villeins. In spite of his fatness and unshaven porky face his manner is patrician and stiff.

Wednesday, 21st July

Took Deenie to Chedworth Roman Villa. Went round with the caretakers, Irvine and wife, a keen young couple, and suggested improvements.

Thursday, 22nd July

Left Wickhamford at 10 o'clock. I have not been a success this visit. To Charlecote and met Joshua Rowley there. On my return to London looked at the Dormer monument in Wing church, the largest purely classical monument of the mid-sixteenth century I have yet seen. Then to Chenies church where I was able only to glimpse through a window at the tomb of the 1st Duke or Earl of Bedford of the same style and period. A cocktail party at the Osbert Lancasters. Champagne to drink.

Sunday, 25th July

Very hot. Walked in the Park at 7 o'clock. Had an uneasy feeling that the proletariat, sunning themselves so happily, truly believe that all is well with the world and themselves just because they are richer than ever before and work less than ever before.

Margaret Jourdain, Ken Davison and Osbert Lancaster dined. Margaret quite overshadowed by Osbert who talked ceaselessly. He catalogued every British monarch from William the Conqueror down to the present in a few pungent words – Richard Coeur de Lion, the hearty Bullingdon bore, given to sodomy: Edward VII, the Jew-loving, lecherous philistine, etc. This doesn't sound as funny as it was.

Tuesday, 27th July

Dined at Sibyl's Ordinary and sat next to Godfrey Winn, who is more absurd than words can say. Still the eternal glamour boy and every mother's darling. He has snow-white hair where he is not totally bald and minces like a harlot. He has an inordinate opinion of himself. Notwithstanding all his follies there is something engaging about him. He is simple at heart, and wants everyone to be as happy and loved as he is himself. I went and had a drink with him in Ebury Street before he and his chauffeur drove off to his country house.

Gladwyn Jebb told me at the Ordinary that he saw a lot of George Mallaby who is the ideal secretary to a committee of Generals – a strange propensity.

Today as hot as ever I remember it in England. Leigh Ashton and I drove together to the aerodrome and flew to Jersey, arriving at 1.20. The heat of the plane on the sizzling tarmac when we entered it was so intense I thought I should die. I was wedged between Leigh and a stranger. Leigh started to melt like a monstrous lump of butter. On arrival we drove to Radier Manor. Grandy [Jersey] received us, dressed in a canary aertex shirt and khaki trousers; looking distinguished and handsome. Pompously Leigh produced a list of figures which the Treasury is prepared to offer for the contents of each room at Osterley, making a total of £120,000. Grandy, keeping perfect control, said he would take the list and compare the figures offered with what he hoped to receive from an antique dealer in two weeks' time, and then let us know. In other words the Treasury has made an ass of itself in not putting a value on each individual item. To lump all the contents of Osterley together under a round sum is unacceptable to an owner. I suspect that Grandy was disappointed with the Government offer, and felt insulted. I don't blame him, and I don't view the outcome with optimism. He is a good businessman and no fool. I think our journey was a complete waste of time and money.

Grandy's wife is very pretty and big with child. Leigh Ashton is companionable but slightly too pleased with himself now he is a knight. Everyone in the aeroplane on the return journey sweating and stinking. Oh, the smell of the English. I even notice it in the open Park.

Took Countess Borromeo and Mrs Vaughan to Knole. State rooms stiflingly hot. Nearly died. This evening Burnet took me to the Caribbean dancers. They dance barefooted, with great *élan*. Beautiful brown creatures with gay coloured clothes and turbans. But the music to my ears is monotonous, and the élan itself too barbaric to be endured patiently for three hours.

Lunched with Michael and Anne at Stafford Terrace. They are about to leave this afternoon for Womersley with all the children. The house consequently in some chaos. The Borromeos there too. They asked me to stay with them when I am in Milan. Countess B. complained to me yesterday that Susan, Anne's daughter, aged twenty, wrote to her as 'Darling Orietta', whereas Susan is no relation and she is a woman of sixty-one. She asked if all the young in England were so familiar. I said they were becoming so; and they meant no harm. All she said was 'Um!'

This evening I motored Malcolm Bullock to his house near Cambridge. Middlefield, it is called, built by Lutyens in 1910, on the grand scale in miniature. Of small, regular bricks very trimly laid. Nothing ingle-nooky about it. Perfect size for a widower. Pretty formal sweep of garden between yews. We had a delicious cold supper at 9.30 with pâté de foie gras and hock. Then sat till after midnight on the verandah drinking kümmel and gossiping about Edwardian society, a speciality of Malcolm's. It is so seldom one can sit out like this in England, and keep warm.

Lutyens evidently played a joke on the bachelor for whom he built this house. The staircase ceiling is supported by one stout twisted column, so fashioned to reproduce the outlines of the female bosom and buttocks, always there as you move round the newel post, either ascending or descending. Had palpitations during the night, presumably indigestion, or kümmel. Otherwise a perfect visit.

Left at 10 o'clock. Drove to Cambridge and looked at repairs in progress to roof of the Abbey House. Then to Stamford and had the filthiest lunch at the George I have ever eaten. Left the car at the drive gates of Burghley and walked to the house. Park open but house shut today unfortunately. Lord Exeter drove up and swept through to the forecourt where an old man wearing a bowler had been standing for half an hour to open the gate for him. So funny considering the Exeters have no indoor servants. Then I drove through Nottingham to Wollaton and spent an hour there. A thoroughly vulgar but well constructed palace. My conclusion today was that the *nouveaux riches* owners of these Tudor houses themselves designed them, Smythson at Wollaton being merely foreman of the workers; but I don't know. I looked at Smythson's mural monument in the church where the epitaph describes him as 'Architector and Surveyor unto the most worthy house of Wollaton, with divers others of great account'. This certainly suggests a status higher than a mere foreman's; but what exactly was an *architector* in Elizabethan times?

The interior of Wollaton is filled with glass cases of stuffed animals and fish. It doesn't much matter. The grounds are quite well kept up, but Nissen huts still cling like barnacles to one side of the house. Visited Winster to see the NT's little market house. Arrived Edensor House at 7 to stay with the Hartingtons. Their house built by Paxton as is the whole village of Edensor.

Sunday, 1st August

Debo and Andrew [Hartington] drove me to Chatsworth this morning. The site of house, the surroundings unsurpassed. The grass emerald green as in Ireland. The Derwent river, although so far below the house, which it reflects, seems to dominate it. Black and white cattle in great herds. All the hills have trees along their ridges. Neatness and order are the rule although, Andrew says, there are fourteen gardeners instead of forty before the last war. The inordinate length of the house undeniably impressive, and the 6th Duke's extensions do not make it lopsided, as I had been led to suppose. The limitless landscape can absorb it. The uniform yellow sandstone helps link old block to Wyattville's towered colonnade, which might be taken out of a Claude painting. We wandered through the gardens, the greyhounds streaming across the lawns. Andrew turned on the fountain from the willow tree. Water not only drips from the tree but jets from nozzles all round. The cascade not working this morning, but will be turned on for the public this afternoon. At present the great house is empty, under covers and dustsheets. Next year the state rooms are to be shown. We entered the house from the west door, let in by Mr Thompson, the librarian. The state rooms are all on the second floor, reminiscent of Hampton Court, one leading to the next without passages. All pictures taken off the walls. Interior terribly hot and stuffy. Andrew let me look through two volumes of Inigo Jones drawings of masque costumes. Henry VII's prayer book, with illuminations. Given by the King to his daughter who was asked to pray for him, as well she might. Inscription in his kingly hand.

The scale of Chatsworth is gigantic, beyond comprehension (like St Peter's, Rome) until experienced. The detail of outside stonework of high quality, notably the antlers over windows, frostwork in the central courtyard, the panels of trophies, by Watson presumably. The Tijou ironwork easily identifiable. The Hartingtons, eager to know their possessions, intend to spend several hours each day systematically looking through papers in the library – like schoolchildren at a holiday task.

This afternoon we drove to Haddon. The D. of Rutland does not live in the house at all. It is open most days to visitors. Thousands flock. Today it was shut, so we had it to ourselves. Very romantically situated upon the Wye river, with hills all round. Beautiful lichened grey walls. Yet I would not care to live in it. It is a haphazard, uncomfortable house. We were shown the late Duke and Duchess's bedrooms, approached by a spiral newel stair. Small bedroom windows which barely open. Garden filled with hollyhocks, rambler roses, and the courtyards recently planted with roses trained to climb the walls. The long gallery is the most spectacular room. Panelling of walnut fields, arcading of oak inlaid with bog oak in very elaborate designs. In the dining-room too are Henry VIII panels and a frieze of plasterwork.

When it comes to working on Inigo Jones Andrew says I may have full access to all the Chatsworth library papers. As a couple the H.s seem perfection – both young, handsome, and inspired to accomplish great things. He has a splendid war record and won the MC. Has contested one constituency and is now nursing Chesterfield, a very Socialist seat. All the more reason, he thinks, for contesting it. Believing it unlikely to win does not deter him. Both full of faith in themselves and their responsibilities. She has all the Mitford virtues and none of the profanity. I admire them very much.

Monday, 2nd August

Hardwick is a different affair altogether. We motored there this morning. The old Duchess received us amid a mass of grandchildren. She is tall, imposing, imperious, gracious and seventy-eight. The park is sombre and the trees are black and stag-headed. From a distance the house rises above the trees on its knoll like a fairy palace. How romantic and beautiful it is. Its pretty yellow stone is sooty and crumbling. It seems to be slowly disintegrating. The inside puts me in mind of Cotehele on the grand scale. There are few servants. Since the house is open to the public on two days a week the rooms are arranged for their benefit. Ropes tied from chair to chair and any old posts that are available. All floors covered with rush matting which being irreplaceable is today protected by old cloths and rugs where the public tread. All walls below the deep bold plaster friezes are lined with sixteenth-century

tapestries. Unlike Cotehele where the tapestries have been cut ruthlessly, here they fit exactly because, the Duchess asserts, the house was
built for them. The primary colours greens and blues, now faded, are
heraldic. I suppose the Elizabethan furniture here is the most splendid in
the world, inlaid and delicate, not coarse and clumsy. Not the usual old
oak stuff. The height of the great windows is stupendous. The cold in
the winter must be intense. The grandchildren say it is insupportable.
The Duchess showed us round. She is rather slow and talks a great
deal. Her knowledge is very wide but she muddles things up a good
deal. Hardwick has become her life task and she serves it faithfully. She
enjoys conducting the public round the house, so when I arrived, she
came to the front door and as she shook hands, said: 'I have always
wanted you to come here' – which, Andrew observed, was very flattering. When we left however she neglected to say goodbye to me
altogether, and I had to chase her in order to thank her and shake hands
again.

Tuesday, 3rd August

This morning it poured, but slackened a bit at 11 o'clock. Andrew had
to write letters, but Debo and I rode – the first time I have ridden for
quite ten years and probably more. We went through the great Wyattville entrance and into the gardens of Chatsworth below the terrace.
The wooden surrounds of the west front windows are still coloured
gold, now rather faint, but the sash-bars have not been gilded that one
can see. We went up the hill to look at the Cascade Temple and back
again, then across the main road to the far side of the valley to see the
Russian Lodge, built by the Bachelor Duke. His spirit at Chatsworth is
very prevalent.

I left after luncheon for Bolsover where I went round as a tourist.
Proudly set on its hill with far, misty, smoky views of open country
and a few mines. The little castle has some unusual Jacobean apartments, notably the panelled room with paintings by Francis Cleyn, the
tapestry weaver or designer, so the guide said. I carefully examined the
castle which marks a transition from Jacobean to Classical, of which the
doorways and some windows are absolutely pure. Yet the building as a
whole is Mannerist. Went to the church and transcribed the Hunting-
don Smythson tomb slab. It stands against the wall just outside the
Cavendish chapel. These Smythsons are far more real than the Thorpes,
it seems to me. The deserted houses hereabouts are rendered tragic by
their past glory and present decay. I stopped at Sutton Scarsdale again.
Am told that Osbert Sitwell has bought the ruin. Classical ruins in

England are not as satisfactory architecturally as Gothic ruins. They lack the picturesque gloomth of the northern medieval and the sunset pallor of their Mediterranean prototypes.

From here to Buxton the country is beautiful; luxuriant dales. Between Buxton and Macclesfield it is hard and cruel, the awful Peaks. I stay with Charlie Brocklehurst these two nights in his horrid little Lodge (Hare Hill), so uncomfortable. This little man is becoming pompous, conventional, buttoned up, and more and more snobbish. I think I do not like him, and therefore should not stay with him another time.

Wednesday, 4th August

Charles and I went early to Lyme [Park] which looks dried up and worn down. The impact of countless masses is telling on the place. It is also becoming slightly vulgarized – Walls' ice cream notices, etc. The furniture is too sparse and regimented and not, I find, very attractively arranged. The Hartingtons came over for two hours and were appreciative and encouraging. I introduced Charlie who was delighted to meet them. This afternoon he and I decided what colours to paint the chapel and dining-room. We walked up to the lantern tower for the first time. On our way back to Hare Hill looked at Alderley Mill, a wretched Trust acquisition.

Thursday, 5th August

Glad to leave this morning for Little Morton Hall which is looking very well. At Mow Cop saw Charlie's new stone to commemorate the Primitives, and reached Attingham for luncheon with Lady Berwick, one of whose eyes is very bad. I believe she is really suffering, poor thing. Met Keeble and George Trevelyan and settled some colours for the ante-library. Then drove to Wickhamford for supper with my mother, my poor father ill in bed with lumbago, which she likes to think is gallstones, and is worrying herself unnecessarily.

Friday, 6th August

This morning went to see Mr Wade at Snowshill to talk about the old carriages he offers the Trust. Also persuaded him to leave us his fine collection of clothes which he had suggested bequeathing to some museum. He is the weirdest little man, looking far older than when I saw him ten years ago. His thick dark hair parted in the middle almost reaches the shoulders. He was wearing knickerbockers, a Norfolk jacket

[82]

and stiff winged collar. He lives retired from the world, lamenting the old days when grass grew on the road to Snowshill and there were three gates to open between it and Broadway. I well remember these things and having to open the gates on my pony after leaving hounds at Spring Hill, an 8-mile hack home from hunting with the groom when I was about ten. Moreover the pony would invariably shy and make a scene on approaching the spinney at the foot of the hill. It was supposed to be haunted.

Sitting in Charlie Wade's bakehouse where he lives and sleeps is like being in an alchemist's cell, except that here all the implements, anvils, cogs, gyroscopes are spotlessly cleaned and brightly burnished.

At Oxford I looked at the portrait of old Bishop Fox at Corpus Christi in the hall. A kind scout showed me his gold chalice, beautifully chased, the earliest at Oxford, dating from the late fifteenth century.

I am forty today. The shock is not too great because during the past year I had been telling people that I was forty, in anticipation. But I am rather less good-looking and very bald now. My figure is as slender as ever. Only occasionally does my stomach swell, owing to the bad bread, but this is not serious. It soon flattens itself. I have lately found that the skin of my jaw and chest is slacker than formerly. It used to be tight and resilient. I am less stirred by desire than I used to be. It is the forms of physical falling-off that I most resent: the fact that the life-line only reaches an angle of 89.9 instead of 90 degrees. Oh dear, to say nothing of the decay of teeth, eyesight and hair. When in another twenty years I am too old to work I shall retire to a monastery and pray, for I shall presumably no longer see to read. This is my one consolation: that when my active life must cease I can still do good by praying. I am sure this should be the occupation of old age. One need never be idle. The prayer wheel when all else fails. At present my mental faculties, never first-rate, are better than they have ever been. All my life I have been a slow developer.

Sunday, 8th August

Worked very steadily this weekend. My notes swell to enormous proportions. Late this evening Rick [Stewart-Jones] and I walked in Battersea Park in the drizzling rain and looked at the open-air sculpture. The setting very beautiful in Lord Redesdale's lovely garden of umbrageous trees. This exhibition is an excellent idea and for England the only sort of outdoor show possible. The weather is hellish, cold and raining persistently. I told Rick I had hardly any true friends; but this was an untruth. He said I was too fickle to deserve any. I don't believe this is true either. I now think with affection of James Pope-Hennessy, Ben Nicolson, Mark Ogilvie-Grant, Patrick Kinross, Johnnie Churchill, Michael and Anne Rosse, Bridget Parsons, Harold and Vita, besides A, B and C. I have however no lovers and with folded hands await some devastating romance.

Tuesday, 10th August

Mrs James, widow of Henry James junior, the novelist's nephew, lately deceased, came to the office this morning all the way from America to offer us Henry James senior's house at Rye, which I am to go and inspect with her next week. A perfectly charming, elderly, sensible woman, with no affectations, and not rich. In the afternoon young Lord Rea came to suggest our asking the Treasury for his father's estate in Eskdale. The Treasury has now written that the Chancellor of the Exchequer is hesitating to let the Trust have Harewood. I take this gravely.

Wednesday, 11th August

Lunched with Ben Nicolson at Brooks's. He took me round St James's Palace afterwards. I wanted to see the so-called Holbein ceiling of the Chapel Royal. I find it too Italian for Holbein and prefer to think it may be by Rovezzano who left England in 1540. There are only two chimneypieces left of Henry VIII's reign – in the Tapestry Room and the one adjoining, which was redecorated by William Morris in the 1870s with sunflower patterns, very pretty and interesting, to Queen Victoria's express order. Patrick Kinross dined with me last night and he is really as confidential and engaging and as fun to talk to as ever before. I am glad we have returned to our old intimacy and mutual sympathy, only broken by his long absence abroad during the war.

Thursday, 12th August

Motored Florence Paterson this afternoon to Ham, Cliveden and Hughenden; a fine day too. At Ham saw two hideous brick pillboxes which the Ministry of Works have erected as fire appliance shelters, without informing us. We shall certainly insist upon their removal. I found Ralph Edwards seated on a sort of throne, hanging pictures, moving furniture (by proxy of course) and directing an army of slaves. With his beady eyes, raucous voice, little moustache he looked like a seedy sergeant-major, cane in hand instead of under the arm on the parade ground. At Cliveden went over the state rooms, since it was opening day and I wished to see the ropes and posts. They looked all right. I said 'state rooms' as though there was an enfilade. In this vast palace there are in fact about three to which the public are vouchsafed access. Miss P. very interested in the gardens. The herbaceous borders nearly over. At Hughenden the rooms have been arranged by Mr Langley-Taylor's mother-in-law, and I was surprised how many contents there were: several portraits of Victorian politicians and statesmen.

I then met James Pope-Hennessy at Heathrow aerodrome. He is ill and had to fly swiftly home, from somewhere or other. He has a slightly sinister smell and complains of fever, inability to pass water and spots that discharge. I suspect the worst and J. fears it may be, dirty little thing, but doesn't seem unduly worried.

Batsford's have given me some advance copies of my guidebook to Trust buildings, about to be issued in a fortnight. The cover is a hideous green; the jacket rather vulgar; the chapter headings inadequate. They never sent me proofs of the foreword or the format, which was annoying, for although there are no howlers I could have improved the appearance of the production.

Saturday, 14th August

Motored to stay the weekend with the Sitwells at Weston. It took me a little over two hours. Sachie is like a child in his enthusiasms and impulsiveness, his simple and direct humour and readiness to laugh like a sensitive trigger. Lord Hesketh and a lady he fancies, very common American, lunched. Lord H. is contorted with shyness and repressions, and drinks too much port wine. After they left the Sitwells persuaded me by sheer force of charm to motor them to Kimbolton. On arrival we could not get in but the reluctant agent gave his consent to our seeing the outside only. It was profoundly disappointing, grim and unsympathetic. Through the windows we spied furniture in heaps, untidy and in disarray. The place is to be sold as a school. It is sad. Then drove to Easton Neston, where the Heskeths gave us champagne on the lawn. The mother had had a seizure indoors, but is an imbecile in any case. I thought the house impressive and liked the late lord's improvements. His new forecourt and pool are excellent. The quality of the stucco-work indoors is very high. Staircase too narrow, with single returned flight. Like a large town house. The Hesketh family are ungainly to look upon.

Sunday, 15th August

Sachie is a voluble talker. His mind flits from houses, paintings, music, poetry, birds, nuns, flowers to jewellery and strawberries within one

[85]

breath. He is infinitely sympathetic and inspiriting. The sweetest of men. Yet he is outspoken and likes giving advice. He warned me (a) to have more self-confidence in my writing and set aside more time for it, (b) to take steps to save what hair I have left – he recommends some infallible lotion the Duke of Westminster uses – and (c) not to dwell upon cancer. We talked for hours about writing. He has written fifty books, has seven more coming out this year. Yet writing is a terrible effort for him and for weeks he cannot put pen to paper. Georgia is charming in her own home. She is also very pretty. So is her old mother who is staying with them. Reresby a nice, good-natured boy, lively and intelligent.

This afternoon we motored to Chicheley and went round the house. Sachie delighted with what he saw. It is sad that the Chesters have left their wonderful looking-glasses to be ruined by a boys' school. Then to Gayhurst and looked at the Roubiliac tomb to Sir Nathan Wright and his son in the Wren church. The stucco books, open and shut on the frieze, curious.

Tuesday, 17th August

Motored at 8.30 to Polesden, picking up Robin Fedden. On to Rye where we found Mrs James, her niece and solicitor at the Mermaid Inn. Walked round to Lamb House which she offers with the garden to the National Trust. A delightful George I house in a narrow back street, on a corner. A great tragedy is the complete destruction of the garden house wherein Henry James wrote from 1898–1916. It was a simple structure judging from photographs and I would have it rebuilt. E. F. Benson rented Lamb House after Henry James's death until he died in 1941 or thereabouts. All the windows remain blown out. Hardboard has been temporarily substituted, so the rooms are pitch dark. They are nearly all panelled. The stair balusters are twisted and the treads shallow and broad, beautiful to walk up and down. The house is in bad condition but can be repaired easily. It is fully furnished with much furniture that belonged to the novelist. His pictures still hanging on the walls. Mrs Henry James told me that the most intimate belongings, including writing-table and piano, were destroyed with the garden house. Much of the rest had been removed to America by the family on the novelist's death. She is unable to 'give' what furniture is left in the house but we have the option to buy it. So Robin is going to pick out what he thinks ought to remain, with the assistance of Henry James's old secretary who is still alive.

On return we visited Bletchingley church and the huge monument to the Claydons which is early eighteenth century, very fine. Sachie thinks highly of it. Jamesey dines with me. He is better, but has contracted distressing complaints and told me how he had caught them. Is penitent and determined to be positively good for ever more, so he says.

Drove to the south-west, lunching filthily again at the Cricketers' Inn, Bagshot, and reaching The Vyne at 3 o'clock. Mr and Mrs Chute received me most kindly for I had written asking if I might study the Renaissance windows in the Vyne chapel. This I did, and on hands and knees also took notes of the maiolica tiles on the floor in front of the altar. Mr C. kept interrupting by discussing the terms of his will. People adore reading one extracts from their wills, I notice, breathlessly and without pauses just as those idiots, solicitors, draft them without punctuation. I persuaded him to insert a clause whereby the National Trust might control the actual use to which the clergy tenants wish to put particular rooms. Otherwise we shall find abominable bad taste 'bon-dieuserie' disfiguring the Palladian staircase and the early Tudor gallery. Then he showed me a pile of books in the library which he had set aside for sale for, he said, the clergy would not want them. They were Wood's *Palmyra* and other eighteenth-century architectural volumes, the sort I would give my eyes for, and I can't think how to persuade him not to part with them. Damn the clergy! For a scholar, Oppidan head of Eton, who spouts Latin tags without cessation, Mr Chute is singularly unimaginative and philistine. He and his wife gave me tea and I left, arriving Long Crichel for dinner. Found Eardley there, very pleased to see me. Desmond at a concert.

Eardley and I motored to Montacute and did good work arranging Colonel Goodden's oriental china and some furniture brought from Stourhead, notably a new dining-room table and 1662 buffet inlaid with bone and mother-of-pearl. Crowds of visitors and everything here looking fine.

In the evening we motored to Cranborne Manor, taking Desmond. A dream house. Interior not very *commode*, but a number of large Jacobean chimneypieces *à la* Knole and Blickling, one with a wooden bust of a pope wearing triple tiara. Great Hall not good and stair up to great hall gallery bad. We were perplexed by the west wing, *c.* 1650, the windows of which on the outside looked renewed. Ancient grey walls very harmonious, notably colonnade of north side. Three stages of twin pilasters upon buttresses bizarre. Did not like grotesque gargoyle heads on colonnade, nor brick chimneystacks against grey stone walls. The green ride from the north front leading through iron gates between stone piers to a rise of ground, most effective. Enticing meadows beyond as though promising a world of the spirit somewhere out of sight. The garden simple and sweet with orchard trees amongst herbaceous borders. Many roses we noted and one François Juranville pink with a golden sunset sheen and an ineffably mellow smell. I had written asking Lord Salisbury if we might go over, and he called in to the office last week in a friendly way to say how glad he would be for me to see the house and that he had already written to his housekeeper notifying her to expect us. Altogether a dear, romantic, isolated English manor house. Church disappointing; a few pretentious and ugly monuments.

Friday, 20th August

A not so profitable day at Montacute for a meeting of the little Committee, consisting this afternoon of Sir Geoffrey [Hippisley-Cox] only. He brought his wife and the two of them had a few rather silly ideas of rearrangement to which E. and I listened politely, but acted not upon. After tea we left for Holnest Park on our way to Dorchester. Up the drive we encountered a tall, old-fashioned figure whom we took for the family butler hobbling with a stick. It was Mr Chafy, the owner, whom we had come to see. Poor man, he has a real grudge against fate. He complained that he is taxed out of existence and is obliged to sell the place, that he broke his leg fourteen months ago, that his wife died and that life for him is finished. And indeed it seems to be so. E. liked the house, but I did not. It is a dull early-Victorianized house of which there are so many. Grass is growing up to the windows. Dead flies lie in heaps within the windows. All is dirt, decay and desolation. House full of unsuitable furniture – mostly fake oak – some of which he offers to lend to Montacute. But we really have little room for more unless it be of extremely good quality.

Tonight stayed at the Bear, Wincanton, a pretty uncouth sort of inn. Wallpaper stained and peeling; but a kind welcome – which is a change – and excellent dinner of duck with Graves wine. After dinner we made friends with a nice young man called Michael Alvis, looking like Heywood Hill, with a sad voice. He is becoming a market gardener. Told us he was a navigator in the war and went out on sixty-eight operations. Pray to God he prospers.

Saturday, 21st August

Dear Uncle Robert's birthday. I looked at his mural plaque in Eton College chapel the other day – a joint one with William Leveson-Gower –

'and in their deaths they were not divided', it reads. Both were scholars and men of the utmost probity. This morning we motored to Longleat. The long straight avenue has been clear-felled. Miss Coates, Lord Bath's secretary-librarian, received us and conducted us round the house. I made several notes. Only the great hall, painted a healthy brown excrement colour, remains unchanged. The hall fireplace however is wholly Flemish. One cannot claim that this house is Italian. Indeed what sixteenth-century English country houses are? Grotesque terms and Persians linking arms, the free hands prinking their hair. I found upstairs in what may have been the long gallery a vast fireplace fairly classical, but earlier than the others, it may have been by Chapman. Otherwise the interior was much altered by Wyattville, and again in the 1860s by Italians in a very expensive manner. The library rooms are charming with inlaid doors of exquisite quality. Several interesting early portraits, notably of the Cobham family in the mid-sixteenth century, the children at table with apples, cherries, a marmozet and pet parrot. The orangery and stables by Wyattville we admired. Miss Coates has a flat being made for her in the stable clock tower.

At Stourton we found young Alvis had come on his Corghi to join us. We showed him the house. All day it has poured with rain. The inside of the house is now looking well. It merely needs flowers and small attentions to make it less lifeless.

Meant to stop at Taunton where I left my car at the garage, but the hotel looked so frightful we continued to Honiton, staying at the Dolphin. This inn pretty primitive too, dirty, but persons agreeable.

Sunday, 22nd August

At 11.30 to Sheafhayne House to meet Mr Meyrick, a young man about to be married. He told us that, subject to his trustees' consent, he would lend Drake's Drum to Buckland Abbey for the summer months only. We liked him much. He was as sympathetic as his house, an overgrown early seventeeth-century farmhouse with exquisite furniture, chiefly eighteenth century. Bowls full of flowers, Meissen china figures and elegant knickknacks found a surprisingly happy background in gloomy panelling. Meyrick is a descendant of Drake and possesses the navigator's ivory seal given him by Queen Elizabeth, and his pocket map of the world engraved on a round silver disk. He has a small Adam inlaid commode he wishes to sell.

Then we lunched with Carol and Eric Dugdale at Yarty Farm nearby. Very good food and claret. All their small children present.

[89]

Situated in a very luxuriant valley, Yarty is an enlarged farmhouse with John Fowler wallpapers and some pretty Regency furniture.

In Exeter Cathedral I saw a mural monument to Bishop Harvey, dated 1564, with much Renaissance decoration and candelabra. I don't greatly care for this cathedral. Liked the painter Northcote's monument, by Chantrey I presume – life-size, seated.

Then motored to Buckland Abbey which I had never penetrated before. The combe in which it is set is nostalgic. Brings back Ribbesford to me with its rooks cawing, its deep belt of trees. But *qua* house it is awful. A mess. Uneven floor levels, broken arches, and not one decent liveable room. The only passable room is the great hall with mid-Elizabethan plaster ceiling and pendants, grotesque figures supporting the cove; ornate panelling with arcades in top stages and frieze inlaid with holly strapwork; in the end lunettes over the panelling are plaster scenes, somewhat Hilliardish in conception, i.e. trophies hanging on trees and reclining figures. Overmantel has Grenville arms displayed. One chimneypiece upstairs displays the Drake coat in stucco. But the house is literally carved out of the medieval Abbey church, of which the central tower and parts of the transept survive. There is a pleasant early Georgian back staircase. A fire gutted one wing. It has been renovated. Three long, low rooms with iron girder supports. E. and I agreed we could think of no old house we would less like to live in.

Monday, 23rd August

Stay at the Bedford Hotel, Tavistock, which we are growing to like. The proprietor and staff all friendly. Today spent entirely at Cotehele with which we were well satisfied. It is beautifully kept by the angelic Mrs Downes. Two old craftsmen from Harris & Sons, the furniture repairers at Plymouth, met us. They were joyfully enthusiastic with craftsmen's true love of old furniture. Although totally ignorant of dates they knew instinctively what furniture was genuine, recognizing good workmanship when they saw it, appreciating that no nails had been used on one piece and certain dovetails on another. For years they have renewed broken pieces and reproduced others so expertly that they have become guileless fakers. I suppose this does not matter.

Tuesday, 24th August

We went to a silly film, *Uncle Silas*, last night in Tavistock, which gave me the creeps and frightened me. In the night I had a 'mare, but not about the subject of the film. I dreamt that an old woman was pulling out my toenails one by one. E. and I motored to Montacute and saw Bob [Gathorne-Hardy] there. He has practically finished arranging the library, and splendid it looks too. I trained back to London from Yeovil, first-class single, 42 shillings.

Carol Dugdale and I had an interview with the Ministry of Planning about Matson House [Glos]. To start with I was apprehensive and embarrassed. Carol swept in and was very curt and imperious. Relations began stickily. But I was immensely impressed by the very masterful way in which she handled the case. She never faltered or used a wrong word; held her ground and floored all counter-argument. In the end she got her way, much to my surprise. What confidence the woman has. She ought to be Prime Minister. She and Eric lunched with me at the Allies Club.

Dined with Alec Clifton-Taylor in Neville Terrace. He lives in a modernistic flat where everything is white. He is a gentle and intelligent man who knows his stuff, which is architecture, domestic and ecclesiastic. He says we are 'dedicants' to the arts.

At 4 Lord Esher came to the office. I motored him to Iford [Manor, Wilts], the Petos' house near Bradford-on-Avon which he has just rented. We called at Chelsea for innumerable parcels and oddments to take down. He is *par excellence* the ideal travelling companion, humorous and interested. He is however always a little too much in a fidget, anxious to stop, or move on; and of course in an emergency he would be less than useless, being totally unpractical and butter-fingered. Iford is romantic outside; indifferent within. I do not greatly admire the Eshers' furniture. He says he does not mind whether it is genuine or fake.

We set off at 10.30. A lovely day rinsed in autumnal melancholy, the early sun slanting through the Iford trees upon the dew and the tranquil doves' notes soothing. We drove without stop to Hidcote. Found Lawrence Johnston and lawyer, and Nancy Lindsay, Norah L.'s daughter. Lawrie J. signed the deed of gift like a lamb so, since he leaves for abroad in a fortnight, the place may be said to be saved. This has been a struggle but it is accomplished. We were conducted round the gardens by the usual route. How often must the old man have done this tour? I think it is a sad occasion for him and I wondered how far he understood that he was giving away his precious treasure of a garden. 'I have another Hidcote,' he murmured, presumably referring to his garden at Mentone. Miss Lindsay is like an old witch, very predatory and interfering. She maintains that she has been deputed by L.J. to supervise these gardens in his absence abroad. We were not overcome with gratitude. Anyway no mention of this condition was made either by L.J. or his solicitors before the signing. Sibyl Colefax will be delighted that the deed she worked so hard to bring about has been done. The Eshers always being in a hurry we did not linger at Hidcote. They kept buying things in antique shops at Broadway, and stopped for tea and cakes and jam at Winchcombe. Lord E. eats at tea with the relish of a child.

I enjoyed this visit and tour with the E.s immensely. I arrived 7.30 at the Dower House, Bradford-on-Avon, to stay the night with Alex Moulton. It is his mother's house. Mrs M. is a sweet and saintly lady.

Saturday, 28th August

Alex and I talked till after midnight, drinking whisky. In some respects he resembles the earnest, high-minded pre-1914 generation, for there is an Edwardian air about him. Yet he has more sense of humour and none of the aggressive superiority and chauvinism which one associates with that generation. In his particular line he is creative. He showed me the design of his steam car. This morning he took me round his factory, old and new buildings, and the gardens of The Hall which Mr Cook has interested himself in. Though a bit over-restored 100 years ago by Alex's great-grandfather, The Hall is a textbook Elizabethan house. The two downstairs rooms are fine of their kind, with massive double-tier chimneypieces. How much restored I can't decide. I motored back to London, arriving teatime.

B.S. dined. I gave him a tremendous talking to for being sanctimonious and dishonest. I told him that if he were genuinely ascetic and spiritual I would not reprimand him, but that he was, on his own admission, craving sexual pleasures. His strictures on the subject were therefore most unattractive. Having adopted this schoolmastery line I have now written to three different people asking for a job for the poor youth. If I could be bothered – and knew how to set about it – I would hire some decent body to seduce him.

Mama's birthday, but she is away in Scotland. Worked all day till the evening. Went to Doreen at 6 o'clock, my head full of other matters than Doreen. But she talked me into interest on the subject of remarkable women we have known, or known about. She says that in Edwardian days to be successful women had only to be beautiful. Today they have to be intelligent. That is certainly some improvement.

Patrick O'Donovan dined. He goes to Singapore on Tuesday. He has made a success on the *Observer*, but little money. He is very funny about himself, a huge joke he considers, yet ponders over life and death, and sex. Has never yet slept with a woman, he so natural and hearty. He is a strong Catholic by temperament, but not by faith, like many of us, including James. Says the Greek Communists are fanatics and die bravely; but Communism must be extirpated. How?

To Knole this morning by train. Robin and Mason [Lord Sackville's agent] and I went round the furniture, sizing up what has been done to date and what must still be done. All rather worried that so much necessary deworming has not yet been tackled and only 1/5th of the fabrics have been taken in hand whereas we have already spent £500 out of the £1,000 allotted by the Government for reparations. Looked over Quebec House, Westerham. A dull house with little visible reminders of General Wolfe.

Audrey came to stay here last night and leaves Thursday. She is very sweet and pretty and a charming guest for she is happy doing anything, or nothing. Today Baron Ash and Sibyl Colefax lunched. Audrey thought Sibyl full of charm – I would not say she had charm – and was mightily struck by her personality, which I suppose is strong. Sibyl had returned this morning from Stratford where she went yesterday for *Hamlet*. Speaking to me she said, 'You and I are happy.' I said, 'I am not happy, Sibyl. Are you really?' She went on, 'I haven't finished my sentence – I was going to say happy in having been born with no possessions. No, I am not happy. Old people are not happy. But I *was* happy. Now I am only interested in the young.' This is the one occasion when I have heard her speak of her inmost self. I believe I am rather fond of this old woman, if only because she is so invariably kind to me. She said she would write by airmail tomorrow to that horrible old Berenson

[93]

giving him my Rome address. And she will too. Now as to possessions the fewer one possesses, and of course I have a very few, the more one loves them. People like the Hartingtons who own priceless works of art are not so fond of their Inigo Jones drawings, their Rembrandts and William Kent furniture as I am of my one little watercolour by Ethel Walker.

Thursday, 2nd September

A meeting at the Treasury this morning attended by Lord Esher, the Admiral, Hubert Smith and myself: also by FitzRoy, the Princess Royal's agent, and solicitor, and accountant. To our dismay Lord Esher urged the Princess to accept the Treasury's terms to take Harewood and hand it to the Trust for five years, with the right for herself and son to live there during their lifetimes. After the five years it is to be a gamble who holds the property. Esher is so confident that it will be the National Trust that he is eager to take the risk, and for the present owners to take the risk. The rest of the staff and myself very uncertain. I was prevailed upon to tell Lord Esher so. Accordingly I drafted a letter from him to FitzRoy toning down his actual words at the meeting. I don't know how he will react to this. Perhaps he will be displeased.

Friday, 3rd September

I managed to clear up all outstanding letters and work at the office, this being my last day. Am determined in going abroad to give my work no further thought and anxiety. Went for a drink with Riette Lamington, who was alone. She is not unintelligent, but I don't want to see a lot of her. She can't relax without becoming coquettish. Very stormy day and returning on foot across the park a violent cloudburst of rain descended, so I sheltered in a temple alcove. In it were two working-class men talking disrespectfully of the Royal Family. Some women driven in by the rain joined in the conversation, and agreed that the Royal Family were an unnecessary expense. All spoke without vitriol and quite dispassionately. I was surprised, and merely said that I totally disagreed. Wished them good-day and ostentatiously walked off. Got soaked.

Saturday, 4th September

Set off with Desmond Shawe-Taylor at 9 o'clock for Victoria. We travel together as far as Rome, first class. Uneventful journey till Calais. In the corridor of the French train I see what I short-sightedly mistake to be a

[94]

pink blancmange crawling along the floor. It is Oggy Lynn's hat with Oggy beneath it somewhere below my knees. Much embracing. We have her company in the next sleeper to ours as far as Milan. In Paris D. and I leave the train for a three-hour break; drink at a café on the pavement and drive in a horse-cab to the Place de l'Université where we dine, only fairly well, at Marius restaurant. A delightful ninetyish atmosphere. It is a beautiful square and when I come back to Paris I shall stay here.

The night full of disturbances but comfortable. Our sleepers are adjacent so we throw open the door and have one compartment of adequate size entirely to ourselves.

Sunday, 5th September

We wake up in the mountains in pouring, cataclysmic rain. All day it rains which dampens our spirits. Has the weather changed, we ask in great distress and fear. We sleep on and off. One cannot read for long stretches in a train. We reach Rome at 12.45 a.m. Lucky Desmond is met by his host, John Somers Cocks at the Vatican Ministry, who drives me to the Hôtel de la Ville and takes D. onwards. Curiously enough I am given exactly the same room as I had last year, no. 88. It is not very nice, but fairly quiet.

Monday, 6th September

My first impression of Rome is that the whole city, and certainly the hotel, are slightly shabbier than last year; also the inhabitants. That bloom of expectancy has gone; and just the faintest disillusion prevails. Is it because in a foolish way the Romans expected an eldorado before the ensuing elections last year, and that now they are over and the same Government is in power, they are bored and disappointed? I pray not. On leaving the hotel my steps automatically take me past the Villa Medici to the Pincio. I then sit on the balustrade overlooking the Piazza del Popolo. It is a bright, cool day, ideal for sightseeing, with a breeze. I descend and look at both sides, Vignola's and Bernini's, of the great arch (the Porta del Popolo). Then immerse myself in the church of Santa Maria with its superb collection of Florentine sculptural tombs and screens. Then cash a cheque at the American Express for nearly 2,000 lire for each £1, and walk to lunch at a favourite trattoria close to the Piazza Navona.

Desmond calls for me at 5 o'clock and we walk to the Vatican City. I notice how much Bramante's Palazzo Giraud evolves from Alberti's Palazzo Ruccellai in Florence; the same thin pilaster strips to each floor. The approach to St Peter's very squalid at present with barricades everywhere, and the Borgo up and cranes working. I hope they do not mean to fill up the vista that Mussolini cleared. Rome is crammed with the Catholic girls from all over Italy wearing red berets, who smell very strong and acrid. 'What we now want,' said Desmond, 'is some Protestant boys.' More impressed than ever before by the unassertive splendour of the interior of the basilica, so vast and clear of all pews and seats. People complain of the arrogance and coldness of St Peter's. I do not agree. I find the interior, when empty, humbly offering shelter, asking to be filled and loved, offering faith and understanding. The predominant blue-grey is restful and effuses a misty tone through which the sharper colours of mosaic and gilding glow. Walked up to San Onofrio but could not enter the church. Enjoyed the western view in the sunset.

In the evening Guido Ferrari called at the hotel. Has improved in mind and body. Is now a very beautiful young man with raven hair and white teeth and eyes of bear-like brown, a Michelangelo ephebe. Is less discontented with his lot, which is a relief, no longer wishing to adopt British nationality. I expect he has a girl, but do not inquire. Italians don't like familiarity. He says my Italian is worse than ever and it is a waste of his time giving me lessons.

Tuesday, 7th September

Walk straight to San Onofrio, via the Borghese Palace, and enter the cloister, timeless and tranquil and composed of ancient and modern (which is to say fifteenth-century) columns. Wall fountains with Persians carrying baskets on their heads, the alcoves with elaborate plasterwork of trees, etc., extremely pretty. Sat here meditating for an hour. Walked past the Villa Farnesina, the Porticus Octavianus, dull, and the Theatre of Marcellus. The two restored bays give a helpful understanding of the purity of Roman architecture from which Palladio profited. Climbed to Ara Coeli and took note of the Cosmati pulpits. I love this period and its oriental display of coloured mosaic and un-Gothic architecture – Proto-Renaissance the art historians call it. Trevi fountain is again dry, which is maddening. Why do the fountains not play?

Desmond called for me and we lunched with the Somers Cockses. He is an intelligent man; she very English and nice. He says that, deputizing for the Minister, he will ask for an audience for me at Castel Gandolfo, but that I must hold myself ready to go there – twenty miles off – at the very last minute.

This evening walked to the Gesù church with its Baroque ceiling, the clouds painted over the compartments just like the spreading waves of dry-rot fungus. The *giallo antico* pilasters of Vignola are shiny green as though erected yesterday. Then to Sant' Andrea della Valle and with Letarouilly in hand to the Massimo and Linotte palaces. Peruzzi is my architect for he has a strong sense of the Picturesque without licence.

Dined with Roger Hinks, or rather we went Dutch, I paying the larger share. He is not a modest man and boasts of his conquests in Venice where – so he says – young men rush at him like flies to fly-paper.

Wednesday, 8th September

Met Desmond sitting outside the Villa Giulia which we looked at together. He admired it much. Letarouilly revealed to me that many of the stucco panels by Udine on the outside of the hemicycle are now gone. This is sad and accounts for the present over-austere surface of that side. Such a pity the water not playing and the garden ornaments in such a mess. San Prassede: the mosaics in the Orto del Paradiso glow with red and gold. I am confused by the dates of the mosaics here. Those upon the spandrels of the arch in front of the apse have faded to a heather colour. The floor is of Cosmati mosaic. Desmond has no reverence in a church and talks loudly as though he were in the drawing-room at Long Crichel while devout pilgrims are bowed and prostrate in devotion before the holy column.

There are many anti-Government chalk *graffiti* on walls and pavements, such as 'Il popolo ha fame', and abuse of De Gasperi's Black Government. Guido tells me there is much Communism even in Rome and Somers Cocks says there are 2 million unemployed. Things certainly look to me worse this year than last. 'Il Christo è morto per i poveri. Che fa Gasperi?'

One should take stock of the alterations made by time when one asks why contemporaries thought more highly of such and such a monument than we do. Usually the answer is that depreciation of a sort has subsequently taken place. On the whole it is amazing how little buildings have altered in Rome. My Letarouilly drawings done in 1810 with extreme accuracy reveal how slight are the alterations since that date.

Tonight met a charming friend of Roger Hinks, called Kop, a Pole, drinking with Desmond. Then walked to the Via Giulia to a cocktail party given by the Taffy Rodds, to which Peter [Rodd] had invited us. I met Peter while lunching in a trattoria. Gavin Faringdon was with him. D. and I dined in the Piazza Navona watching the children playing with balloons around the fountains. On my return to the hotel I found Guy who had turned up without an appointment. Sent him away. A man at the Rodds' party who lives in the Palazzo Sacchetti told me that families of dwarfs occupy the mezzanine floor of the palace. They are very agreeable people.

Walked miles this morning for quite three hours. Left notes on Gavin Faringdon and D'Arcy Osborne. Then looked at Bernini's Triton fountain. Walked into the Barberini Palace courtyard and admired the corkscrew staircase of twin Doric columns, a marvel of engineering. Then Santa Chiara something and San Bernardino, a baby Pantheon; then Sta Maria degli Angeli with vast transept, in fact the transformation of the great hall of Diocletian's Baths. The San Bruno by Houdon very pensive. Then San Lorenzo fuori le Mura, through the Porta of that name. This church was bombed by us in the war and, alas, the Cosmati work of the choir destroyed although the tabernacle remains; the ambones much injured. Restoration is in progress but by no means complete, and no admission to the nave. Some columns replaced very skilfully.

I lunched with Colonel Fothergill, a fat Colonel of fifty, whom Cuthbert Acland wants as assistant in the Lake District. No intellectual but extremely jolly. He has offered to take Desmond and me to Hadrian's villa on Saturday. D. and I looked at more churches in the evening.

I went to Sir D'Arcy Osborne's apartment in the Via Giulia at 7.30 and we dined out. He is a charming but shy man who suffers from periods of acute depression. He talked of the Pope (Pius XII) whom he sees at least twice a year and to whom he is devoted. The Pope told him the other day that he listens to the BBC course of English lessons. He loves England, speaks the language fairly well but does not understand a great deal. He seldom relaxes but works all day long, living extremely ascetically. His recreations are occasional music and talking to his half dozen friends among the Cardinals while strolling in the Vatican garden. Sir D. thinks the inner cabinet of the Cardinals should always be Italians for otherwise agreement would be impossible, and furthermore Italians are more level-headed than most nations in politics. This surprises me. He says that notwithstanding the Pope's sanctity things happen in Vatican backstairs departments that are far from edifying, such as black-marketing. The Vatican lately bought a great deal of wheat from Canada on this basis. Sir D. has invited me to attend the St Peter's ceremony on Sunday when the Pope addresses the Catholic youth gathered in Rome this week.

[98]

Walked this morning to St John Lateran. Appraised Galilei's facade. It has a severe tightness like Gibbs's church in the Strand, and Easton Neston, which make me want to pick them up and shake them looser. Again failed to find a way into the cloisters. Then sat inside San Clemente; strolled through the Colosseum and noticed some fragmentary remains of Roman stucco on two archways.

Lunched at the Taffy Rodds in Via Julia 167. She is his second wife and very pretty, fair Angle-angel type. Sat at a large circular table, five children and Peter. Agreeable talk about Communism which Peter thinks will destroy itself if only war can be avoided long enough; that the Tito break is more significant than people in England realize.

It seems that one can drink local wine in Italy with impunity. In the church of S.M. sopra Minerva it was revealed to me that the Tudor masons in England were only influenced by the earlier Florentine monuments of about 1480, and by nothing Roman. I suppose Rome was politically a dangerous city for Englishmen to frequent in Elizabeth's reign. Dined with Desmond and Roger Hinks in Piazza del Popolo. Desmond departed for the Piazza Colonna and I retired early to bed.

Went this morning to Palazzo Venezia, an exceedingly interesting building in its transition from Gothic to Renaissance. Thought that Sharington may have been influenced by it in building up Lacock Abbey. Possible? The collection of furniture, pictures and porcelain upstairs is admirably displayed. Quite exemplary. The pretty paving of old brown and green tiles makes lack of carpets not felt at all. In fact Roman palaces seldom have carpets.

At 12.30 Colonel Fothergill called for me and drove me to Tivoli, but we had a puncture and got no further than Hadrian's Villa. Here we lunched and spent the whole afternoon in exceeding heat, slowly walking over this remarkable acreage. Much is left. I was particularly interested in the remains of a plaster ceiling in the vaulted Baths. This ceiling was exactly copied by Robert Adam. The Colonel asked me if I had read a Batsford book – quite good, he thought – on Adam. The Colonel's spare tyres are made of synthetic rubber so we drove home at 15 mph, and burst a second. Never got to Tivoli.

At night the huge cemetery outside Rome is lit up, a light in each niche wherein the coffins are kept for seven years. Then the body, having disintegrated, is taken out and buried in a smaller space.

[99]

To Mass at the Trinità church at the top of the Spanish Steps. Hearing female voices issuing from persons unseen I recalled Mendelssohn's passage about his attending Mass in this church and noticing the same phenomenon. Sweet sisters of the Sacré Coeur they are. Then walked to the Farnese Palace, open Sunday mornings only. The Caracci room is a poem of beauty, an elegy rather than a lyric. Rich Renaissance, the flat of the ceiling contains the painted panels within ornate ribs. Paintings by Caracci against grey and gold. I can think of few rooms more beautiful. Every architectural detail of this palace is massive, strong and superlatively self-confident.

Somers Cocks in his car, with Desmond, met me at the Pal. Farnese, and we drove down the Via Appia. No words can describe how for miles around the Campagna has been utterly ruined. The mess and untidiness, aerodromes and, above all, pylons and wires, and revolting buildings have made a wilderness out of this historic pastoral landscape renowned throughout the ages, and painted by every artist visiting Rome. After this little tour we looked at San Stefano Rotondo. A circular aisle with central choir, enclosed by a ring of inner columns. On the walls indifferent frescoes of unspeakable martyrdoms and tortures. Against the church in the colonnade outside, at a long table, Catholic neophytes were eating their simple midday meal. With the columns as a background the scene resembled a Last Supper.

At 5.15 D'Arcy Osborne in the Chancery car motored me to the Vatican to watch Pope Pius address the Catholic Youths. We had a stance on top of the Bernini colonnade. From here I enjoyed the extraordinary medieval spectacle of nuns in a row sitting, apparently comfortably, on the sloping brown corrugate roof of a very high house with deep drop below, to watch the St Peter's ceremony. The nuns were quite unconcerned by their vertiginous perch. I liked the Pope's quiet, determined, un-pulpity voice. Saw him carried in his Chair through a central gangway to a throne and *baldacchino* placed on the steps. The cries of 'Viva, viva!' the waving of dark green caps in the air like the heads of daisies without the petals, the blues and greens of the shirts, and orange of the banners, wonderfully pictorial. The crowd stretched from the piazza further than the eye could see. That these hundreds of thousands of youths should look to the Pope as their leader is in these irreligious days astounding. A slightly disturbing element was the Fascist tinge of the meeting. The *vivas* were rather too well drilled, the demagogic voice of the Master of Ceremonies relayed from a dozen loudspeakers was reminiscent of a Nurnberg rally. Does this mean that in the Pope these youths are clinging to the next best substitute for a totalitarian dictator? For they are disillusioned with democracy. Desmond said cynically that he felt the crowd would have cheered Stalin just as enthusiastically.

I dined in a restaurant with D'Arcy Osborne. From the top of the Spanish Steps we watched the fireworks and a gathering thunder storm. The lightning lit up the dome of St Peter's. After each flash had subsided the dome remained a perceptible second as a grey ghost of itself against the deep purple sky. This seems a curious phenomenon. D. Osborne more sympathetic than ever. He confided that the Queen was the past love of his life, and he speaks of her with emotion.

Monday, 13th September

I have a bad cold in my head and chest and do not feel well. Moreover it is horrid weather, raining heavily at intervals. In the morning I looked at more palaces by myself, lunched alone and slept. Desmond joined me at 5 o'clock. We went to Trastevere where we agreed that the people, though grubbier, were better looking. Both immensely impressed by Bramante's Tempietto, but no view from the Janiculum on account of the rain. We sat in the square of S.M. in Trastevere which is like the scene in an opera, the noisiest square I have ever been in. Then we went to hear Alfredo play his guitar and sing Neapolitan songs to us in George's Café off the Via Veneto. D. considers him a remarkable artist, his art being of an intimate kind for it is difficult to hear him unless he plays close to one. It was sad for him having to perform in such noisy, unsympathetic surroundings, like expecting the late Mrs Gordon Woodhouse to play her clavichord in the middle of Paddington station. On returning to the hotel I was handed a letter from the Holy See through the Legation, announcing that I am granted a 'special' audience at Castel Gandolfo tomorrow morning at 10.45.

Tuesday, 14th September

My cold very much worse. Am feverish and my nose pours. All day without any intermission the rain also pours and pours. After a bad night I get up early and catch a tram – over one hour – to Castel Gandolfo. Am feeling very nervous because I can think of nothing special to say to the Pontiff. Arrive at the village at 10 and first look at the lake in a crater below and, over its bank, more extraordinary, at the Roman Campagna at a still lower level. A very classical situation. There are no buildings on the shores of the lake except on the Castel Gandolfo side. I go to Bernini's round church in the village to shelter from the rain, and to compose and prepare myself. A Mass is in progress. Then at 10.30 I walk to the Palace, a shapeless building of yellow wash towering above the village. At the gate are a crowd of boy scouts and the Catholic Youth. I edge my way through and wave my official invitation to the handsome Swiss guard in his fantastic Michelangelo uniform of yellow and blue stripes. I am passed from one guard to another, from one officer with a red plume to another, from one gentleman usher to a cosy butler, or majordomo, and left in the fourth chamber hung with crimson brocade and, over a table, one large crucifix. The green marble doorheads have 'Pius XI. Pont. Max. A.V.' carved on them. So this suite is fairly contemporary. It is all right but not outstandingly opulent. I sit on one of the gold chairs with crimson brocade upholstery, and wait. Presently a very distinguished old lady in black, with black veil, and wearing pearls and a few good jewels, comes in. She has what was once a beautiful face with deep black shadows under her eyes. I rise from my seat and make a gesture of politeness. She does not recognize my presence but, grasping her rosary and muttering prayers, prostrates herself with utmost reverence before the crucifix. When I next look up I hear her say, 'Giovan signore, ho grand fame', which surprises me. She dives into a capacious bag, extracts a biscuit and nibbles it. She tells me that the Pope has suddenly had to see several cardinals just arrived from South America, and our audience will be postponed indefinitely. She draws me to the window and looks out upon the lake which she supposes is the sea. She is Brazilian and says, 'An English Catholic, what a contradictory thing to be.' She speaks with great volubility about the splendid qualities and strength of the English. Then she discourses very knowledgeably on religion. All our troubles today are due to our divorcing religion from everyday life, and even the pious only give lip-service to God. She directs me never to neglect the Holy Ghost in my prayers and thoughts, admitting that it is difficult to distinguish Him from the other Two. She assures me that through years of unhappiness she has reached absolute contentment through her religion. I admire and like her, but wish she would offer me a biscuit. We are then joined by a superior young Italian Monsignore carrying a precious parcel wrapped in tissue paper and an uncouth young American from Texas. For one hour we four are together, shunted by the majordomo from room to room in a sort of silent musical chairs. It is what I suppose the immediate after-life may be, namely thrown among the same people who have died the very moment as oneself, and moving through the mansions of Purgatory towards Heaven. We pass other people without making any contact. However a young priest in a wheelchair, in a deathlike apathy and presumably the last stages of consumption, is pushed past us. I saw his face on returning

[102]

from his audience wreathed in ghastly smiles. It was an expression of resigned beatitude.

The Texan, much to my surprise, produced from a trouser pocket a gold wristwatch, a gold pocket-watch, a gold pencil and chain, and a gold cigarette case. He asked me if I supposed the Holy Father would accept them as a souvenir. I said I was sure he would not, but advised him to consult the Brazilian lady whose fourth audience with a different Pope this was to be. The American said, 'I don't think a cheque would be quite the same thing. I could not afford 100,000 dollars and I daresay he has enough money to go on with.' After a pause he said, 'I am going to be quite homely with the Pope. What are you?' And finally when we had reached the last state room and the Brazilian had complained of hunger pains and asked him for a biscuit, the Texan produced a Chesterfield cigarette and invited her to smoke.

By this time purple Monsignores were running in all directions. Whenever His Holiness was ready for the audience a vicious little bell rang and cassocked liverymen fairly scampered to open and shut doors. We were constantly moved along, now from chair to chair, the pace gradually slackening. The drill was very effective. First the Brazilian lady disappeared, and returned radiant, her hands full of parcels, saying, 'He is wonderful. He is so good and kind. May you all have every happiness and blessing from this visit. Arrivederci.' Suddenly, instead of the three of us who remained being called singly into the next room the door opened and in stepped swiftly a tall, erect, brisk figure, all in white, wearing a white biretta. Until I saw an attendant Cardinal genuflect I did not realize it was the Pope. He went straight to the Texan ahead of me – this was prearranged for the three of us were spaced on our chairs at intervals. The Pope without wasting a second talked to him with much affability. With one nervous movement the Texan fumbled in his trouser pocket, but mercifully thought better of it. The Pope turned, the Texan left, and the Holy Father approached me. I walked towards him and fell on both knees. The next one and a half minutes remain but vaguely registered. He held out his hand for me to take and I just noticed the ring, as I kissed it, to have a large dark stone encircled with lesser gems, not diamonds. His presence radiated a benignity, calm and sanctity that I have certainly never before sensed in any human being. All the while he smiled in the sweetest, kindliest way so that I immediately fell head over heels in love with him. I was so affected I could scarcely speak without tears and was conscious that my legs were trembling. His face was strong and healthy, not handsome, but made beautiful by his extraordinary charm. I noticed his nice strong teeth like old ivory. He spoke a gentle, hesitating English. Asked me where I lived and when I said London, said something of it being a 'dear place'. I told him I had witnessed the ceremony at St Peter's with Sir D'Arcy Osborne and had been immensely impressed by the crowd of Catholic Youth. He said, 'Did you see how beautiful it was. I am so glad. I want to bless you and all those dear to you,' and beyond a few other polite, but trite, remarks I can recollect nothing. He then handed me a little blue envelope embossed with the papal arms. It contained a not very expensive medal with his head on one side and his arms (heraldic) on the other. I knelt for his blessing and passed on. In turning to leave I noticed a Cardinal slip into his hand, held out behind with desperately waggling fingers, another little envelope for the next guest. I walked back through the state rooms now filled with groups of young men carrying some large images and awaiting their turn for the papal audience.

Got back to Rome in time to lunch with the Colonel and Desmond. The heavy rain made us postpone our Caprarola visit till tomorrow. Instead D. and I were lent the Colonel's car for the afternoon. So we drove to St Peter's, then to San Andrea al Quirinale, a splendid Baroque oval church by Bernini with beautiful inlaid marble floors, notably *giallo antico*, of the arms and legs of two supporters. Then to S. Agnese fuori le Mura where a friendly old priest took us and a small group of children into the catacombs. We were given thin tapers to hold. The children's faces of wonder and fear in the candlelight were very picturesque. There were ledges in the rock cut out for bodies of the earliest Christians, and remains of tombstones in alabaster giving the names of husbands and wives and their approximate ages in Latin.

Wednesday, 15th September

Raining still. Visited Keats's House and introduced myself to the lady custodian. Looked around and read that most moving letter, unfinished, from Severn to Brown the morning Keats died. Met Desmond at 12.30 and had a hectic time procuring supplementary tickets to Ischia and booking train seats. Colonel Fothergill called and motored us to Caprarola. The way out of Rome by the Porta del Popolo is the least congested of any. The surrounding country is comparatively unspoilt and the Campagna undulating. The situation of Caprarola is very fine indeed, on a hill with a panoramic view in three compasses. But ingenious though its pentagonal planning may be the building is grim and heavy. I was frankly disappointed. The palace is also very dilapidated and empty of all furniture. German troops were billeted here during the war. I admit that the circular colonnade inside with treillage work painted on the barrel vaulting is good – so, too, is the splendid twisted staircase of stone, all painted, a vastly improved version of the Barberini one which has a lift shaft in the middle of it. The dome of this staircase is painted. The rooms of the palace on the *piano nobile* are vast and likewise painted. The predominating yellow, blue and green of these frescoes produce a soft and rich tone that we associate with faded tapestries. Yet the individual scenes in large central panels of Francis I and the Farnese family are very poor when you look into them.

Unfortunately the visit was cut short and spoilt by a disagreeable incident. We wanted to walk through the garden up to the Casino but were forbidden by the custodian. Desmond and the Colonel disregarded him and persisted, pursued by the expostulating guardian and hesitant me. I was made cross both by the officious custodian and by the other two who were making his position difficult. I was so put out that I turned and walked straight back to the car.

John Bayley telephoned and dined with me. He is a tall, thin, bespectacled American of thirty-six, very bald, ascetic, yet puffy about the face. He talks non-stop about architecture. He has taken 3,000 photographs of Roman palaces which are his speciality. He thrusts a way into private palaces which no foreigner has ever penetrated before. He intends ultimately to publish the photographs with a text, in the manner of Letarouilly or Piranesi.

Thursday, 16th September

Set off from Rome at 8 o'clock. Met Desmond on the train. Both gloomy because at Naples the weather still overcast and even drizzling. We hated Naples. Began with a terrible scene in the taxi with a porter over exorbitant tip demanded. We almost came to blows, but gave way. The same trouble was repeated on the boat where another porter dumped our luggage and started raving. Instead of giving the money demanded so bloodily, we threw the coins *at* him.

The sea passage to Ischia became increasingly beautiful. We passed Prócida island on the way. A long row of small houses of oriental appearance painted lemon, yellow, pink or blue. Each house has a curious half arch in the front. Within it hang tomatoes to dry, making a splash of red. The effect one of the prettiest things I have ever seen. The little round church is staring white. The sea almost a mill pond. Occasionally the boat gave a gentle heave. Whereupon a travelling priest clutching his beads, frantically crossed himself, exclaiming, 'Mama mia!' Desmond much amused and referred to him as Padre Muff Pozzi, having heard me frequently refer to the ceiling painter of S. Ignazio as Padre Andrea Pozzi.

Ischia. Until today I have been alone with Desmond. The interlude after intensive Roman sightseeing has been a restorative. Rising about 9 we sit at breakfast, when the sun is not too strong, on the terrace overlooking the bay and Prócida beyond, and Vesuvius beyond Prócida. I have no shorts unfortunately, and wear my thin brown trousers and open-neck shirt with short sleeves. At 11.15 we sally to the shore and bathe in the delicious balmy sea. Lunch at 1.30. Desmond sleeps, I read in the hotel garden which overlooks Ischia Porto and town. Food not very good, but sweet servants. One evening we walked to the Castle, which is situated as romantically as St Michael's Mount. It is ruinous and has a Baroque and Renaissance chapel. Another day we took the steamer to Feria and back for dinner. Sitting in the street drinking innocuous aperitifs at sunset we watch the parade of youth and beauty. The boys and girls wear brilliant colours and are burnt nutmeg brown. Diminutive *carrozze* ply up and down. They are painted yellow with Edwardian pram sunshade hoods over them. There is a public garden with cut water melons for sale. The houses, clothes, human skin and fruit make a kaleidoscope, forever changing and forever new.

I left at 6 o'clock this morning and reached Rome at midday. Lunched with John Bayley and a tiresome party of American friends. After luncheon Bayley took me to the Villa Medici where we walked in the famous garden that Velasquez painted and, they say, Michelangelo designed. The back of the Villa is encrusted with panels and reliefs of ancient Rome. Bayley has some blind spots notwithstanding his long sojourn in Italy. For instance, knows nothing of Brunelleschi. Speaks disparagingly of his own countrymen. He is designing a palace for the Emperor of Ethiopia.

Dined with D'Arcy Osborne who has asked me to stay with him next year, if there will be one, and suggested we might motor to the south together. When amused he laughs till he cries. Yet he has a slightly abrupt manner that disconcerts. He wrote me a note, saying, 'If you are later than 8.30 I refuse to wait.' I arrived on time. He was charming.

Wednesday, 22nd September

At 10 o'clock Barbara Rothschild and Rex Warner drove up. They packed me into their car. Regretfully I kissed goodbye to Rome, as we dashed out of the Popolo gate. A perfectly beautiful day, hot indeed. Our first stop was a mountain town called Narni high above the valley of the Nar. We strolled into the Duomo. It was quite empty. There were no

[106]

guides and no other sightseers. A most beautiful old church with columns of travertine, an ornamented font (early Renaissance) and curious white marble screen against the south wall. Barbara remarked how unlike a museum and like a church this Duomo was, compared to the Roman ones, a very Protestant observation.

Drove on to Spoleto and lunched. The Duomo here is Romanesque. Although altered by Bernini the interior is surprisingly dull. The outside portico below the rose window is early Renaissance. It incorporates two outdoor pulpits by Milano and thirteenth-century mosaics overhead. A simply splendid Renaissance tomb to an Orsini by Milano and another opposite to Fra Lippo Lippi. In the apse are Lippi's frescoes, very sweet, gentle and appealing. The soffit of the apse has been restored and is too gaudy. The stalls of a side chapel, dated 1550, are of intarsia, a form of art which is I think underrated. This seems to be the region of choir stalls and inlaid woods.

Drove to Spello through the loveliest Italian country. Trevi, literally tumbling down a steep hill in a stream of grey walls, is from the distance the most romantic village imaginable. Spello is a small town where we stopped to look at the Pintoricchio chapel, dated 1501. After the Lippi frescoes there is no insipidity here. How moving and divine Pintoricchio is.

Then Assisi. I had never been here before. It must surely be the loveliest town in all Italy. I had no idea how beautiful. By now tired (and I have not felt well all day) we saw only San Francesco and examined the Giottos. These childlike pictures must have been repainted for there is much crudity of outline. Yet the silence and motionlessness of the seated nuns, their backs turned to the spectator, is very solemn. Rex Warner and I walked along the outside cloister, high above the valley. Women are not allowed there. It is reserved for contemplation from which they are held to distract. No allowance is made for women's contemplation from which men distract. What a view from this city! We watched two women, who had slipped in, being turned out by a young Franciscan very politely. They evidently supposed we were enjoying pornographic pictures. Another Franciscan was playing the organ in the church with an air of tranquil distinction. All the while Barbara waited for us outside, seated with a book on the floor in a tumble of flounced skirt, totally unaware of the beautiful picture she made.

On our way to Perugia we stopped in the dusk outside Sta Maria degli Angeli and looked at the Golden Madonna over the portico. I fancied she was bowing, but the others said not. Drove on to Perugia where I stayed at the Hotel Brufani and they left me.

This afternoon, all three of us feeling languid, we decided to have a *piccola siesta* at the source of the Clitumnus, a romantic spot where the water bubbles up from the earth. It is crystal clear and pure to the taste. In the pool to which it runs it lies green as emerald. The grass is lush beside it. Barbara was amused as I hung my blue coat solemnly on a tree, propping myself uncomfortably against it, my body stretched upon my topcoat for the damp. In a Hilliard-like attitude, head on elbow, I remained for ten minutes in great discomfort, wondering how the Elizabethans managed to look so happy and natural in such awkward circumstances. The truth is that anything done comfortably indoors is always uncomfortable out of doors.

Barbara is enchanting. She refers to the Sibyls on the ceiling of the Spello chapel as 'those Colefaxes on the roof'.

Thursday, 23rd September

A very full morning sightseeing for I was out at 9.30. Determined first of all to visit the thing I had come to see, the choir stalls in San Pietro. So trotted down the hill, but on the way went into San Domenico. A large open church, a funereal Mass in progress, one small draped coffin in the middle of the nave, much incense, a priest before it and only two veiled women mourners. So I knelt and prayed for the poor lonely corpse at a discreet distance. Prayer can never do any harm. It may not do good. The fact that for more than two millennia human beings have prayed without thereby doing the slightest harm to anyone speaks well for it. Indeed to my way of reckoning it proves that it must be a positively beneficial thing. We can't have enough of it, and we can all do it when we are too infirm to do anything else. Then I wandered into the choir where the intarsia stalls are of great beauty: inlaid arabesques between little pilasters. I soon came to San Pietro where I was rewarded by a golden hour, and was uplifted. There was a rehearsal of Mozart's Grand Mass in D Minor, with full orchestra and choir. No one stopped me walking into the presbytery. I spent a long time among the incomparable stalls by Zambelli, carved about 1535, the most exquisite of their kind I have anywhere seen. They surpass in delicacy those in King's College Chapel. I was lost in amazement and delight. All the while the rehearsal was in progress. I then heard the loveliest voice in the world singing solo. It was Elizabeth Schwarzkopf's. I was much taken by her appearance, short, almost stocky, fair hair and complexion, unaffected, earnest little face. Could hardly tear myself away. Have been haunted by her all the day. A blue patch of heaven through white clouds.

Met Barbara and Rex coming out of the Perugino place – name forgotten – where are more stalls, again very fine but later work I take it, who persuaded me to go inside. After luncheon I took a bus for 800 lire across Umbria into Tuscany. Like all Italian drivers the bus driver galloped, his finger permanently on the horn. Reached Florence worn out, with emotion and fear.

I drove in a *carrozza*, which made me feel self-conscious – idiotic – from the bus station to the Grand Hotel. All I did this evening was to look at Ghiberti's door, now back at the Baptistery where it belongs. Far from being gold it is bronze covered with a veneer of gold leaf that in parts has quite worn away. I cannot see how it will endure the rain and dust, not to mention the exhaust fumes from motors and buses.

Saturday, 25th September

Siena – I lunched in the Campo overlooking the grotesque palace and its toy tower of vertiginous height. In the Duomo baptistery two babies were being christened, the priest holding a candle and the parents and friends all very jovial and good-tempered. More like a family party than religious ceremony, the sort of conduct that shocks Protestants.

A funeral procession passed outside. One of those black and gold motor hearses preceded by figures – paid mourners I presume – wearing black masks completely covering the face, allowing slits for eyes, and falling in a peak over the chest.

I returned to Florence by bus and stood for half an hour, which was agonizing. We passed over the grey hills, the brown earth bearing grey olive trees with incredible green berries, and vines bent down with purple grapes. The cypress trees on these hills like snuffed candles. This terraced Tuscan landscape unchanged since the days of Pintoricchio.

Sunday, 26th September

An unsuccessful day. Went to the bus station preparatory to going to Pisa, but the crowd was so overwhelming that I funked another long journey, possibly standing and certainly fighting for a place. It seems that one can book seats only for long journeys. So I came away. A pity. Instead I idled around Florence. A most beautiful autumnal day and rather hot. Walked to San Lorenzo and studied Brunelleschi's sacristy which is most moving. Geoffrey Scott has taught me not to suppose that Bramante's generation was necessarily an 'improvement' upon Brunelleschi's, an absurd assumption which the Victorians maintained. This conventional argument is a complete fallacy. Once again I found myself by chance with Barbara Rothschild and Rex Warner, meeting in a café at midday. What joy! So together we visited the Bargello. Barbara lost in admiration of Michelangelo's Brutus, which is indeed the quintessence of masculinity, and may be the greatest bust in the world. I can think of none greater. Then we lunched in the Piazza della Signoria. I had a siesta in the afternoon and then returned to San Lorenzo.

Monday, 27th September

Cashed my last cheque at the Grand Hotel and paid the bill. I much like this hotel and cannot speak too highly of it. Everything done for one's comfort, and the bill not exorbitant. This morning said farewell to Botticelli's St Augustine in SS Ognissanti next door, and went shopping. Bought pants, ties, socks, a belt, handkerchiefs and more photographs. Now wonder if I have enough money left. Arrived at Milan at 4 o'clock and went straight to no. 41 via Manzoni which is the Palazzo Borromeo. Orietta Borromeo, the mother, met me and showed me the palace which Carlo [Borromeo] has had repaired. It received a bomb during the war, one of ours I daresay. Orietta is a very seductive woman – her flashing eyes, her floating hair, dark, romantic, ruthless I guess. She is half-Italian (*née* Doria) and half-English (her mother a Pelham-Clinton). We went shopping together and wandered through the Cathedral. Much of the glass has been put back since last year, so there is more light. If ever Gothic embellishment needed justification it has it here. The splashes of colour upon pavement and monument are stupendous. Interior impressive, but I do not like the monstrous capitals. Carlo joined us at 6 o'clock and motored us out to Senago, the Borromeo villa which was bought by the Saint's nephew at the end of the sixteenth century. It is a very large country house. Appears to have been modernized about forty years ago. Carlo is quite unlike his mother in appearance and temperament. More the phlegmatic Englishman than the mercurial Italian. Resembles his cousin, Michael Rosse, good, dutiful and chaste. More than can be said for his Fascist brother who, I am told, takes after his mother in looks and character.

Tuesday, 28th September

This morning out at 10.30. No one else about. It is a fine autumn morning with just a little dew, but no yellow leaf on the trees. Carlo appears and conducts me round the garden which consists of a long, wide vista made by himself, not very successful because too wide for its length, and ends in nothing but some scrubby little trees. It is lined with

[110]

small statues between each of which is a terracotta oil pot. Ignoble and too small in scale. There should be cypress trees. Nothing inside the house is visibly old except some cinquecento ceilings, the soffits and rough beams painted in monochrome. But in two rooms on the first floor are a suite of gold console tables, shaped like tree branches, and mirrors and wall sconces of elaborate gold ribbons in knots, made of wood. Very Baroque and ornamental. There are few pictures of any consequence.

After luncheon we motored into Milan. The old lady, Maddalène Cotta, a notable gossip, and I looked at San Satiro church. The perspective eastern apse is a successful piece of make-believe. Deplorable additions in the last century, notably the pulpit, and ceiling of nave.

Wednesday, 29th September

Today the four of us – Carlo's wife Baby always stays behind with the children – motored to Pavia. Spent two hours at the Certosa di Pavia. Delightful setting, away in the country, remote and splendid. There are no monks here at present. It is deserted. I like the panels of Luini in the gatehouse. The façade of the church is horrible, bedecked with minute carvings. As a museum screen of late-Gothic-early-Renaissance sculpture it is unrivalled. The inside is mostly Baroque but of a boring, restless, dreary kind. Did Geoffrey Scott really like this stuff?

We lunched in Pavia town excellently. Soup with a raw egg in it – *stracciatelli*, a speciality of Pavia – and marrow meat with saffroned rice. After luncheon looked at three early Lombardy churches, one containing relics of St Augustine.

Thursday, 30th September

The loveliest day imaginable. We motored down the *autostrada* to Lakes Varese and Maggiore. Took the ferry to – not Pallanza – but the town next to it where we lunched very well on the pavement. What I have greatly missed during my visit is wine, for my kind host is very abstemious in this respect. Motored to Stresa and took a rowing-boat across to Isola Bella. This is a little paradise. I could find nothing wrong with it – rare for me. The mist dispersed and the sun came through, serene in a cloudless sky. The island still belongs to the Borromeos and the palace is inhabited by them. The present owner is the father of Carlo's wife, Carlo having married his cousin. The father of Baby Borromeo is the son of a husband and niece who married each other, with papal dispensation, in order to keep the island in the family. So

[111]

sensible. The situation is of course ideal and well-known. The palace built about 1650 by Fontana and other architects in living Baroque. The central portion was never completed and is a vast shell. The state rooms are remarkable for their white stucco in deep relief against blue, buff and pink walls and ceilings. The staircase has panels in stucco of the arms of the noble families who have married Borromeos. Most of the rooms are pretty. A few are over-ornate. I like the big Persians upholding the ceiling of the Throne Room painted to resemble terracotta, but actually made of wood. The bedrooms for Queen Caroline of Brunswick and Napoleon are shown; also the chamber in which the Stresa Conference was held by Mussolini. At the end of every passage or vista is the blue lake, with yellow villas dotted against the hills, and Isola Madre. Through a long gallery ranged with Flemish tapestries of wild animals fighting each other you walk into the garden. This to my mind is perfection. It is set upon six tiers of terraces, of which the last is built on piles over the water. You approach a theatre, formed of grotto work, the terraces adorned with obelisks bearing copper tufts of fruit, statues crowned with copper wreaths and the great central unicorn, which every Good Friday leaves his pedestal and descends into the lake. The view from these terraces is unsurpassed. The flower borders and urns filled with plants beautifully kept by the Borromeos. We did not see the owners who were away in Milan. Two little garden houses are set at the end of the lowest terrace over the water. An enormous camphor tree dominates the entrance to the garden, exhaling a strong and sweet smell.

We motored into the mountain above Stresa to tea with some friends of Orietta in a small house like a chalet overlooking the lake. Christopher and Betty Hussey were staying next door with a sister of Joan Haslip, married to an Italian. Christopher surprised me by saying he did not care for the garden at Isola Bella because there was not enough green. But there is enough of everything else, it seems to me.

Friday, 1st October

This morning I had a poke around Senago by myself. There are several relics of San Carlo, including bits of bones and his biretta. But what an ugly man with his great nose and huge mouth like a slice of water melon. Carlo motored me to Milan. At the station I was only allowed to buy a supplement to my second-class ticket as far as the Swiss frontier. Consequently was unsure whether I had enough money for the rest of the journey. Nevertheless rashly bought more ties and handkerchiefs in the town. Left at 3.30 and had a hideous journey, fraught with *angst*, all the way to Paris. Desperately uncomfortable and dirty. Unable to wash for over twenty-four hours until my return to blessed Thurloe Square, on

Saturday, 2nd October

at tea time. It is pleasant to be home amongst one's own things. How I love them and the cosiness of my flat, small and insignificant though it be. I look back upon the Italian tour with satisfaction and much happiness.

Monday, 4th October

Saw with joy that Elizabeth Schwarzkopf was singing in *Traviata* tonight at Covent Garden, so bought an expensive ticket for myself and went full of expectation. To my dismay it was announced from the footlights that she was ill and not performing. Her understudy, Blanche Turner, had a little reedlike voice. The words were in English and the whole performance disappointing.

Friday, 8th October

Left at 9 o'clock with Robin and his wife, Renée, in their car to Hughenden where we spent a busy morning putting finishing touches to the house which is to be opened next week. Robin extremely good at this sort of arrangement and under his hands the house resumes its Victorian flavour, helped by the Disraeli relics and association. The portraits of statesmen who were Dizzy's contemporaries are fascinating. Then back to London and caught a train to Bradford-on-Avon to stay the weekend with Ted Lister. He has had an operation for prostate but is little the worse, only rather bent which worries him. But he is seventy-four now, rising seventy-five. He is rather deaf and dense. Secretly I find the house *incommode* these days with its upright chairs, oil lamps and no alcohol at all, though it is heresy to say so. Ted allows no relief for reading, but talks ceaselessly without hearing what one says in reply. Christo is a perfect servant, attentive to all Ted's needs yet under no illusion as to his selfishness. His politics are amazingly sensible. He regards Churchill with the utmost disfavour for landing us in the present mess with Russia. When I asked him how Churchill could have avoided the alliance with Russia in 1941 he said he should never have supplied her with arms but should have let the Germans exhaust themselves in defeating Russia, as the Kaiser did in 1917. Then we should have had the two Powers at our feet. He is not a Balkan for nothing. There is a good deal of the

[113]

intelligence and cunning of his compatriot and former sovereign Foxy Ferdinand in Christo.

Ted insisted on driving me, instead of me him, in his dreadful old car to Norrington Manor, the other side of Shaftesbury. The car broke down en route but we reached the house. Its merit is that it is perhaps the last Gothic house in Wiltshire still to be unrestored. It might of course be made into another Westwood, but never as good, for it has no plaster ceilings or panelling of the date. It is at present in the most awful state. Is inhabited by an old man called Parham, aged eighty, and his horsey daughter. The Parhams have rented it for 120 years from the Wyndhams, to whom it still belongs. It has an interesting porch, late fourteenth-century, with central vault boss of a monster's head baring its teeth, and protruding a great tongue. The hall has been ceiled over but could probably be put back for it has, Ted tells me, a good open roof now hidden. Beneath the hall is a vaulted undercroft. There are two wings of Elizabethan date and in the ruinous 'banqueting hall' on the first floor can be seen a late Elizabethan stone fireplace. The Parhams gave us tea. Seldom have I witnessed gentry living in such squalor even in these post-war days.

Luncheon at Sibyl Colefax's – Vita Sackville-West, James P.-H. and myself only. Sibyl so monopolized the conversation, shouting us all down, that discussion was out of the question. James tried once or twice to speak to Vita, gave up and merely giggled. Vita smiled when Sibyl aimed a sharp reproof at her because she made one spirited attempt to open her mouth. 'Just let me finish what I was saying.' Sibyl is not at all well, and the whole charade was piteous. It is inconceivable that the poor old thing can live long.

Anthony Blunt lunched. He now asks to be appointed to the Historic Buildings Committee and says that where he is deficient, i.e. in English portraiture, he will get young Oliver Millar to deputize for him. My fear is that he will be too busy and not answer letters. But he has an agreeable manner, though distant. He told me in confidence that Ben [Nicolson] is 'no good at pictures'. One must discount this a little. All art experts are notoriously uncharitable about each other, especially if they are friends. He says someone must warn Ben who has made himself the laughing-stock of Europe over Carritt with whom he is madly in love. After luncheon I tubed to Blackheath, walked across the heath and inspected no. 32 Dartmouth Row, a pleasant little late eighteenth-century house in a terrace over which we are offered covenants.

Went through a gruelling drilling of a wisdom tooth by McKechnie who warned that next time I must lose that tooth. Barbara Moray, Midi and Colin Agnew dined. Midi arrived, wearing a black hat tee'd on her head like an eighteenth-century headdress which made her look like the Eiffel Tower. She's evidently lost a sense of scale. She has novel theories such as this one: children must not be thwarted by learning good manners, but must be rude if they are to become witty. Colin complained that he suffered violent diarrhoea again this year from the first day he arrived at Calais until he returned to Dover six weeks later. He seems to think diarrhoea is a germ in the foreign atmosphere. He is certainly thin as a wafer. He was a little put out that I had not suffered the same complaint in Italy. I regretted later that I had not pretended I had.

Wednesday, 13th October

Historic Buildings Committee this morning of inordinate length, but satisfactory. Lunched at the Ritz with Michael, Bridget and young Princess Doria. She is a giant of a girl, but gentle and genial. Is heiress to immense riches, possessions and position. Yet she cares only for horses and cats, hates society and intellectuals, and her spiritual home in Birchington-on-Sea.

Eardley greeted me sheepishly in disclosing that he is going to Rome on Saturday with Raymond Mortimer and Paul Hyslop. I told him straight out what a cad he was. There was laughter and forgiveness. He took me to tea at The Brook, Stamford, with Madame Lucien Pissarro, aged seventy-eight, an old bent Jewess, and her hideous daughter Miss P. who likewise paints, but E. says is no good. The mother wants to leave the place, overgrown, ramshackle, cottagey house and weed-infested garden, with what remain to her of Lucien's and Camille's pictures. She makes a condition that the daughter must retain the rents during her lifetime. It is remarkable that such a rural property remains in what is now London. Mother and daughter kept sparring in French *argot*. The daughter is a sort of monster with black, greasy face, and rather bald; fat elbows like rolling-pins. I am so envious of E. going to Rome that I can hardly bear it.

This evening dined with the John Wyndhams. A young marrieds' party. I sat next to Mrs Alaric Russell and Miss Elizabeth Winn, a niece of Nostell. Venetia Montagu's daughter there – a tall, rather plain but commanding girl, with her mother's sharp Stanley intellect. Jock Colville greeted me by my Christian name as an old friend, but I scarcely know him. He is Princess Elizabeth's secretary and is marrying her lady-in-waiting next week. He worked under Churchill during the war. Very intelligent. Much charm. I liked him. Royal servants are trained to be come-hitherish. It must be a ghastly effort at times. After dinner, when the women left, talk was about how little we knew of the everyday life of our ancestors in spite of George Trevelyan's history. Jock Colville suggested we ought to go home tonight and write down in minutest detail how we drove to the Wyndhams' door, left our car at the kerb, its doors firmly locked, rang the bell, were kept waiting on the doorstep; how we were received by a butler wearing a black bow tie instead of a white one, what the hall smelt like, how the man took our coats and hats, putting them on the chest downstairs, and how he preceded us upstairs, one step at a time, etc., etc. He said that Princess Elizabeth's child would be the first heir to the throne born without the Home Secretary being in the room; that Chuter Ede was to stand in the passage. Said there is no record left of how Asquith treated George V when threatening him with the creation of 500 peers in 1911; but that the King told his mother, Lady Cynthia Colville, at 9 o'clock one morning, when she had a splitting headache, the whole story which she felt too ill to record and has now forgotten. Thus does history pass into the shadows. He spoke of Churchill with great affection. I left at a quarter to 1 o'clock, having drunk too much champagne and port. A fatal mistake.

Thursday, 14th October

Eardley and I visited the Victoria & Albert cellars, looking for surplus pictures for Montacute. Graham Reynolds showed us such awful Victorian trash that I signalled E. a suggestion not to accept more than three small pictures. We don't want the N. Trust's houses to be dumps for rubbish not good enough for a roadside pub. Talk of looking a gift horse in the mouth. Polite Mr Reynolds did not know what was going through our minds or behind his back.

Friday, 15th October

Committee meetings today and the Trust's Annual Meeting at Goldsmiths' Hall at 4.30. The Bishop of London the chief speaker. He said that the social revolution we were going through would prove disastrous if this country did not preserve for the masses the culture which had been lost to France during the French Revolution. Mrs Hugh Dalton was present, smiling blandly like a crocodile, and I hope took it all in. The Goldsmiths exhibited for our benefit some of their choice plate. There was one salt dated 1522 that was absolutely classical. I took the 6.30 train to Taunton, but could not get a seat till after Reading. Then had to buy a first-class single supplementary ticket for which I was charged 52 shillings! On arrival at the Castle Hotel could not get a pot of tea or a biscuit, far less dinner which I missed on the train owing to all the restaurant car seats being taken.

Saturday, 16th October

Stinking day – pouring without intermission. Collected my car from the garage. It has been rebored, whatever that means. Pray God it behaves itself in future. Had a filthy luncheon at the George, Frome where I am staying tonight with Alex, and drove to Longleat. Kind Miss Coates received me and gave me tea. I looked through one of three volumes of the letters of Sir John Thynne on the building of Longleat. Fortunately nearly all had been transcribed fairly accurately by Canon Jackson in 1888, or I should have made little headway. Miss Coates lives with her sister in the Stables, not in a loose box, but a charming flat. They are nice, cosy, sweet-tempered women. They keep a dog, and a pleasant life theirs must be. Returned to Frome at 7. These country inns are hellishly uncomfortable, but we had a fairly good mixed grill and half a bottle of red wine for 9/-, which in Italy would have cost 9d.

Sunday, 17th October

Alex and I motored to Longleat in the morning. Miss Coates took us on to the roof which is fascinating. Here you see Chapman's pointed gables and carved beasts just like the Lacock Abbey ones, and the scale-capp'd towers with little lanterns like Bramante's on San Satiro, Milan, and the balustrade brattishing of great acanthus leaves. Today I finished the other two volumes of Sir J. Thynne's letters. Alex left in the morning. I motored to Wickhamford without my headlights which have fused. Mercifully the sidelights worked and in spite of tempestuous rain I managed to see by keeping close behind the cars ahead.

[117]

Monday, 18th October

Spent the whole day at Charlecote endeavouring once and for all to compile a list and description of every portrait for inclusion in a new edition of the guidebook. There is always a lot to do at Charlecote. I had tea with Alianore [Fairfax-Lucy] at The Malt House. She is an eccentric. Hollyoak the agent, who is very loyal to the Lucys, told me that yesterday she fell off her bicycle, grazing her ankle. To relieve her feelings, she silently walked to the newly painted stable door and kicked it out of all recognition.

Tuesday, 19th October

To Charlecote again all morning, trying to finish off. The portrait of Queen Elizabeth is too big to get into my car even without her frame. Drat the lady. Walked into Wellesbourne church, saw nothing but several tablets to the Granville family who, I now remember, lived here, but I think have gone. Anyway an aerodrome is right in front of the Hall, rather a nice red brick William and Mary building. I suppose the old Fairfax-Lucys would have looked down on the Granvilles, themselves an ancient family whose house, a mere mile away from Charlecote, was small by comparison with their large seat. How funny it all is or, rather, was. In Alcester church I saw a recumbent effigy of a Lord Hertford by Chantrey – what a prolific man! – and, under the tower, a seated effigy of a later Seymour in the Chantrey manner, signed Gleichen, that semi-royal person, and half-niece of Queen Victoria. It is good in a realistic fashion.

On leaving Alcester I drove to Ragley up the Worcester drive, not the Arrow drive. Arrived 3 o'clock. The house stands on an eminence and the ground slopes from all four sides. This is unusual. Consequently there are distant views from each front. Moreover there are no modern annexes to mar the house which was built in 1683 by a Seymour. My hostess told me the architect is thought to be Robert Hooke. I should have guessed Talman or Francis Smith for it has affinities with Dyrham and Sutton Scarsdale. The material is blue lias stone, of the off-Cotswold, Bidford-on-Avon variety, and some sandstone, which has perished, notably the dentils of the cornice. The great columned portico may be of later date than the house. You enter by an opening below the perron, (added by Wyatt) and, as at Kedleston, pass into an undercroft.

Lady Helen Seymour was awaiting me in the library. She is tall, about fifty-eight, with lovely blue eyes, and must have been a beauty. *Très*

[118]

grande dame. Was the youngest daughter of the 1st Duke of Westminster. Her son, Lord Hertford, the owner of Ragley, is only eighteen, and has just left Eton. She showed me over house and grounds. The great hall magnificent, now quite empty. The stucco-work might be by Gibbs's Italians, or even the Italian who worked at Ragley, called Vassali. The other rooms on this floor have rococo plaster ceilings of 1740 or thereabouts, which Lady H. believes to be original, and later ceilings in a thin Adamish style with small round grisaille cameos, perhaps by Holland, but this is all guesswork. I have as yet read nothing about the house. In the library is a large Reynolds of Horace Walpole as a young man. He was cousin of Marshal Conway, a Seymour, to whom he was devoted. There is a Reynolds of him too. Altogether some eight Reynoldses. There are magnificent Chippendale hall benches, the finest I have seen; two panels of carved fruit in the library that might be by Gibbons; some Louis XV marquetry commodes; a huge bed under a dust-sheet or, rather, very pretty chintz curtain, so that I could not see it, in the Royal Bedroom that once had lacquer wallpaper. The woodwork is still painted black and gold. Doorcases and dados are nearly all 1683. There are excellent Moorlands and a huge Wootton of three packs of hounds meeting at Ragley. I think it is one of the most interesting great houses I have seen. The stables are enchanting, built round two courtyards. The laundry yard has a colonnade. The lower courtyard is elliptical. Lady Helen fears they will have to leave the house and move to a smaller one on the estate. Heating is a great problem and they have only two servants, one Swiss. I liked her much.

I dined at Bretforton Manor with Harry Ashwin who showed me photographs of the Ashwin family and us as children when we played Red Indians, which we did in the shrubbery there for days on end.

Wednesday, 20th October

Got to Attingham at 3 o'clock but Charlie Brocklehurst not arrived and Lady Berwick still out. So I walked in the deer park. They came in to tea and so did Lady de Vesci to say goodbye for she leaves Monk Hopton next week. She grumbled a good deal about leaving and having to live in Ireland. Lady B. very tired and worried about everything. Two most melancholy ladies. Charlie and I stayed the night at the Mytton and Mermaid at Atcham. We agreed that Lady Berwick's moans and tragedy queen acts are a trifle overdone, and she needs just a little shaking.

[119]

God, these English hotels! The food, too little of it and that barely eatable. This morning Charlie and I looked over all the Attingham pictures. Interesting, chiefly on account of the Neapolitan connection. The Picture Gallery and Blue Drawing-room, now cleaned, are very splendid rooms. George Trevelyan, who runs the Adult Education College, tackled me about the hall walls which he finds gloomy. I said perhaps they were but no consideration would persuade me to have them touched. Charlie and I planned how to hang the pictures. When this is done and the furniture and the bibelots are put out then I shall go there again with Charlie.

After luncheon motored to Dudmaston, 4 miles south of Bridgnorth on my road home. Very pretty, lush, green Shropshire country with blue hills in the distance. The house is typical English squirearchical – not grand like Ragley, but of the same date. The main block William and Mary, or Queen Anne, red brick with stone dressings, a provincial rendering of Wren with parapet added about 1830. The windows, alas, on two of three sides have plate glass. To the fourth side is attached an older Jacobean wing, overlaid with a harder brick. The house has been inherited since the twelfth century. Mr and Mrs Wolryche-Whitmore are my parents' age and delightful. Both very deaf, with instruments. She is a little slower than he and, like all couples who live together and see few outsiders, they think the same thoughts at the same time. Consequence is she repeats word for word what he has just said and she has not heard.

The best room is a long central hall with contemporary oak wainscot and a plain ceiling but for one oval band of acanthus or oak leaves and fruit. Many family portraits here and throughout the house, all in pretty carved wood frames. In this room two unusual portraits, one of a seventeenth-century gamekeeper with a rugged, square, unforgettable face, another of a gentleman in a large crimson hat, smoking a long churchwarden pipe and holding up his foot in a crimson shoe. Behind this room is another long room (double pile) of less interest, facing west, and the garden with 17-acre pool at the foot of a slope. Views of a church, village and the Wrekin in the distance. Heart of England. A spacious staircase of *c*. 1800 of white painted, thin, iron balusters and wooden handrail. Doorways of the simplest description with stalwart surrounds and big brass locks and handles. I saw little furniture of great account, though most of it decent old country house stuff. The Wolryche-Whitmores say their niece and heir Mrs Labouchère has some very good Coalport china and Chippendale chairs which she will bring to the house when she lives here. The estate is 3,000 acres. He talks of handing over in his lifetime so as to avoid death duties on his demise.

Dudmaston is not grade 1, but a charming old family home. Mrs W.-W. wearing a neat tweed made from the wool of the black breed of sheep which were kept here until quite lately when they had to be slaughtered for lack of foodstuffs. They have made two flats in the house which is big and rambling. They have only two servants. Yet these elderly people are cheerful and content; a typical squire and his lady of whom no man high or low could speak ill.

This morning Papa and I motored to Ombersley, the first time I have ever been inside the house. We were asked to go by the new Lord Sandys who has just succeeded his cousin, dead at the age of ninety. The present lord is seventy-two and as Colonel Hill was a friend of my father. He and his wife charming and hospitable. In return for asking me to wander round the house and assess the contents (a curious request) he gave me a present of four pots of honey, some pears and a box of cigars. The front of the house facing the road is dull Grecian, *c.* 1810, with plain portico, added in stone by the Marchioness of Downshire, the last Sandys in her own right, to a William and Mary house behind. The old house consists of a central hall comprising two storeys, a gallery connecting the upstairs bedrooms, and a ponderous ceiling of the *c.* 1810 period. The bedrooms all wainscoted in oak of William and Mary time with nice panelled doors and brass locks and handles. Handsome staircase of three balusters to each tread. One corner room contains elaborately raised door cases with small pediments. It is a treasure house, full of good, but not exceptional, and some junky, things. Many portraits of Sandyses, one mid-sixteenth-century portrait of Sir John Cheek, a good Jansens of George Sandys, poet and traveller, a charming Dobson of a Sandys and Prince Rupert at a junketing, Sandys dipping the ribbon of a third disaffected friend's hat in the Prince's glass of claret. A delightful portrait of Lady Downshire, her little foot peeping out of her skirts and resting on a footstool. There is some nice Regency furniture in the bedrooms, the remains of a George II state bed, of splendid red Genoa velvet, but mutilated. Several gilt gesso mirrors and gilt gesso tables of Queen Anne date, very good indeed.

We were given a picnic luncheon with sherry and white wine. Lord and Lady S. have not moved in yet.

Indoors all weekend. Made some further discoveries about Smythson having worked at Wardour Old Castle. This evening went with

Geoffrey [Houghton Brown] to Curzon Cinema to see *Monsieur Vincent*, one of the best films, and one of the best actors in Pierre Fresnay as the saint. The society ladies were bad indeed. They always are bad on stage and screen for, with all their tiresomeness, real society ladies are not common. The poor folk admirable; but what a depressing affair.

Monday, 25th October

To an exhibition at the Arcade Gallery of Italian late Renaissance pictures, over-restored I thought, and very chalky faces. One excellent portrait by Gentileschi of a young woman.

Tuesday, 26th October

Rather ghastly meeting of the Keats-Shelley committee at Lady Crewe's house. She makes acid remarks which she instantly corrects with something worse in a low voice which mercifully can seldom be heard by the victim. Has a great sense of malice, which is entertaining.

To *La Traviata* with John Fowler. It was excellent. Schwarzkopf has a beautiful face as well as incomparable voice, sure and impeccable. A bell-like tone that is uniquely hers. Also she acts well. Silveri, the father, a sound base, and Neate the tenor singing better than the last time I heard him.

Wednesday, 27th October

Sir Francis Rose with his pretty wife at Lady Mander's this evening. He is a patient of Pierre Lansel who told him only yesterday that he had one other patient (me) suffering from the same complaint as his – what Lansel calls counter-diabetes. I think Lansel invents complaints as he goes along. Sir F. Rose lisps and is rather unctuous; and clasps his hands before his stomach like a curate.

Thursday, 28th October

At Osterley this morning I walked round the gardens for the first time for ages, never having done so with Grandy. Accompanied by Carew Wallace and old Mr Little, Grandy's agent. Behind the cedars to the west of the house is a circuit of trees. It is sad to think what the place is bound to become when made over to the public. The temples are all dilapidated, beds over-grown. Before the war they were immaculate, possibly too immaculate. This afternoon I went to a meeting with Sir Walter Jenner's lawyer and trustees. Eardley and I will have much work to do at Lytes Cary [Somerset] sorting contents, for the Trust may choose anything it wants.

Friday, 29th October

Riette Lamington took me to hear Rubinstein at the Albert Hall. The old man's hair is grizzled grey now. He played the piano with utmost vigour for two hours with only ten minutes' interval. He never gives one a moment's anxiety. Extremely impressive. We dined at the Ritz with the Denis Ricketts. This was the first time I ever talked to them properly. Liked them. She is very shy and very clever.

Saturday, 30th October

Walked this morning from Thurloe Square to Portland Place. In the RIBA library looked through three box files of Smythson drawings. They are more exact than Thorpe's, which are scratches in comparison.

A lovely weekend. A slight yellow fog, the sun occasionally filtering through; no wind or rain. Nothing. Utmost cosiness of approaching winter, and no desire to be out of London or anywhere else on wings.

Monday, 1st November

Patrick Kinross had a few people to drinks, amongst them Fitzroy Maclean, the MP and abrasive hero. A very tall man. Patrick's house is upside-down, he living in one rather bare room. Old pullovers and shirts scarcely hidden having been thrust under the window seat. He gave me dinner at a bistro kept by a tiresome, rather drunken old Norwegian woman who spoke affectionately of Nancy.

Tuesday, 2nd November

George Wingfield-Digby lunched to talk about how to clean tapestries. The information imparted was too technical to be helpful to me. A matter for the experts. I said I would consult him before having valuable Trust tapestries cleaned. A rather interesting lecture at the Courtauld Institute on Medicean patronage of sculptors.

Wednesday, 3rd November

The Devonshire collection of pictures at Agnew's is noteworthy. There are three Rembrandts. Lunched Alec and Frances Penrose to discuss

Blickling problems. Then went to talk to Mr Harry [Batsford] about my books generally. Had tea with Lady Binning at Fenton House. She asked me to get Cliffy [Clifford Smith] to do an inventory of her collections. I promised her I would make him settle question of fee with me; I would act as intermediary because he is very tiresome over money matters.

John Summerson gave a brilliant lecture this evening in Chelsea on Victorian church architecture in London.

Thursday, 4th November

Margaret Jourdain lunched in order to talk about her prospective book on National Trust works of art. We agreed it was a bad idea, and a better would be for her to write a booklet on each collection which could be sold at its particular house. Drinks with Dig Yorke and dined with Malcolm Bullock at the Turf. Excellent dinner as usual, grouse and Burgundy. Have finished my review for the *Spectator* on George Lloyd's Life.

Friday, 5th November

Sibyl Colefax lunched with me alone. She has a slight grievance against the Nicolsons. She says Vita is selfish and that neither she nor Harold does anything to get the boys married. It was bad for them to live with their father all the week and both parents every weekend. Then she discussed Ben's new love, Carritt, so I thought it best to change the subject. She also wants to join the Keats–Shelley Committee, but James says Lady Crewe will not hear of this.

Philippe Jullian dined with me at Brooks's, a little, dark, bespectacled Frenchman, very serious and very mischievous. Tells me he designs modern tapestries and book jackets.

Saturday, 6th November

At the Soane Museum all day. John Summerson told me of his new discoveries concerning John Thorpe. He knows the dates of his birth and death and details of his whole professional life which was that of a Crown Surveyor. All the old theories about Thorpe the architect are thus exploded. I find my interest in Thorpe and his drawings dissolved immediately now there is no longer mystery about him. What a clever man is Summerson. He is generous too in imparting his immense knowledge. He is sure that the classical influence upon design in sixteenth-century England came from France before any other country.

[124]

James dined and gossiped. He told me he had slept with a woman 'of our acquaintance'. He has got the subject on the brain.

Motored the Eshers to Knole to see the state rooms and the furniture. They were delighted. He says he always has good weather on NT expeditions. I tell him he brings it. In the afternoon we went to Wierton and Boughton, two adjoining estates bought by Mr Cook. The Eshers do not consider them beautiful enough to be held by the Trust.

Lord Esher told me at luncheon that he had seen Jack Rathbone and liked him immensely – he was so cheerful – and would have appointed him (to the Secretaryship) straight away if it had been in his power to do so. But he says the Admiral who saw him did not think him suitable. As it happens Hubert Smith, Christopher Gibbs and I had already written a memorandum on the qualifications we thought the new secretary ought to have. After a good deal of altering Smith's draft I agreed with his points, it being essential that we three should be in unity. We did this lest the Admiral might interview and select a candidate of his own choice without consulting us. We have this evening presented our memorandum to Lord Esher, who told me we might do so.

Christopher Gibbs and I then took a train to Leeds, staying the night at Bramham Park. I was last here in 1937 on the same errand. Now our hostess is the late Lord Bingley's daughter. Her husband has taken the name, Lane-Fox. Old Lady Bingley still lives in a wing, a dear old lady, very bent but active; a sister of Lord Halifax. Charming family they all are.

Foggy, calm and not cold. It is too late in the year properly to appreciate this place. Even in this season it is very beautiful. I find the pre-Palladian house lovely. The gardens have deteriorated since my last visit. We walked round them carefully. I made notes on the conditions of the temples, garden statuary and ornaments, and the ponds. We think about £3,000 p.a. is needed to keep them in order.

Anthony Martineau with whom I lunched told me that the Admiral had warned him he ought to look for another job. I told Anthony I thought it an outrage and would speak to Lord Esher, which I did before the Executive Committee meeting. Esher said, 'Tell Martineau to do nothing whatever for the Admiral will soon go and I will support him through thick and thin.'

This morning paid my first visit to the Public Records Office reading room. After a long wait I was brought several long parchment rolls of accounts of royal building works, dated 1585. When I had unrolled them I endeavoured to anchor them with a heavy book. But they have a habit of releasing themselves, rolling themselves smartly up again and covering one with a shower of Tudor dust. The separate sheets also get entangled. Both sides are written upon. They are devilish things. Noel Blakiston came and read through some of them for me. With his help I became almost expert. With practice one's eye becomes accustomed to the script. The Elizabethan scribe abbreviated his script far more than we do ours. Hence *Ye* for *the*, and a squirl (˜) for *ion*.

Looked at da Rovezzano's sarcophagus made for Wolsey's tomb, which now adorns Nelson's in the crypt of St Paul's.

Newman, the hall porter at Brooks's, told me I would be surprised if I knew which members, to his knowledge, stole newspapers out of the Club. I said, 'You must not tell me,' so he promptly did. Queen Mary's equerry, Coke, he says, an old member, steals the *Sporting and Dramatic* the very morning it comes out. He does it every week and Newman has often watched him.

Soaking in my bath this morning I decided I should not have such hot baths for my body is becoming horribly soft. Of course if one has no features or bone structure one cannot remain handsome after forty. So is it worth bothering about?

Noel and Giana Blakiston dined. An enlightened, humorous couple with whom one can talk of absolutely anything. Both highly civilized and fun to be with.

Went to the Leicester Galleries to see Oliver Messel's exhibition of designs for the *Queen of Spades*. Extremely pretty. I suppose connoisseurs would call them meretricious because they are pastiche, but I don't know, I'm sure. At the gallery some pleasing pictures by Paul Maitland (who died in 1909) in Sickert manner, but calm and well bred, of Hyde Park and London square scenes. Also some gay, sparkling pictures by Barbara Gillighan of domestic, nursery, nanny scenes, very colourful.

Dined with the Eric Dugdales to talk to Carol's old mother and Philip Frere, her solicitor, about Matson House. Delicious meal with champagne. Mrs Frere was the former wife of Toby Glanusk, pretty and sweet. When I reminded her that we met when the Glanusks rented Benmore Forest from my uncle in 1930 she tried to change the subject, which I thought foolish. She must have to make a blank in her memory of some thirty years, a difficult task. Eric D., heated with wine, became very funny. Is he a *faux sage homme*?

Tuesday, 16th November

A terrible meeting at the SPAB when it was revealed that poor old Mr Horne had spent £10,000 on restoring one of their lesser houses at Goudhurst and still wanted to spend a further £1,000. No one on the committee had an inkling of this. I suggested a subcommittee of inquiry should be set up; and so they put Rick and me on to this committee. Horne was sent out of the room like a disgraced schoolboy and much embarrassment ensued. I notice that although decent people profess to be saddened by another's discomfiture on such occasions they derive a nasty kick out of it (*Schadenfreude*, in other words).

Wednesday, 17th November

Lunched with the Eshers to meet Mrs Wyndham, John's mother, who cannot raise her head since she broke her neck hunting. Then to the Tate Gallery with Sir Geoffrey Mander to choose Pre-Raphaelite paintings for Wightwick from Mrs Angeli's collection. Tea with a Mr Bryant in a large block of flats in Putney. He has a card index of some 50,000 country houses of England, Scotland, Wales and Ireland, with detailed particulars of the architecture and previous owner. It knocks my list into a cocked hat. I have never seen such an achievement.

Thursday, 18th November

Motored today to Attingham, making first of all for Astley, Warwickshire. This adjoins Arbury and belongs to the Newdigate family. Called on the Vicar who took me to the Castle, now deserted and empty since the war. It is where Lady Jane Grey's father lived and is not of much architectural merit. Is partially moated and surrounded by a curtain wall of Severn sandstone. The exterior is embattled. It has one early front of 1554 with cusped windows. Nothing much inside but a wide oak staircase with very ordinary balusters. The house has dry rot and is quite empty. I fear doomed. The fine, tall church has painted stalls of the fifteenth century which the Vicar tells me are unique in this part of England. He is a dear, unworldly old creature, wearing a wide-awake, his talk full of genealogy. The church is threatened with subsidence if the Bishop of Coventry sells to the Coal Board the remaining pillar of coal on which it stands. I stop at Wall where the Museum had been freshly painted. Arrive Attingham after tea and find Charlie there. The drawing-room has been beautifully arranged by Lady Berwick.

Friday, 19th November

This morning walk with Lady B. into the park and she shows me the site for her husband's cenotaph where his ashes are to be buried. The spot is disappointing at present because it is close to a wire fence, but the plan is to remove this when the army camp leaves the park. Then the site will be more romantic. Her idea is that the deer should roam up to it as they do in Constable's painting. I left after luncheon and stopped at Coughton Court to look at two bedrooms which Lady Throckmorton means to make into one sitting-room for her new tenants. Terrible drive in dark and rain.

Monday, 22nd November

This evening called on Doreen Baynes, looking very delicate and frail. She thinks all laws against sexual offences should be abolished. I said, 'Even if cruelty against children is involved?' Her head shook and she said after a pause, 'Yes.' She wanted a detailed account of my Saturday in London from dawn till bedtime, in detail, nothing omitted. I said, 'Nothing, Doreen darling?' 'Oh well, you know what I don't need to hear.' She has the novelist's curiosity. She writes in bed every day till 1 o'clock, lunches alone, then walks at breakneck speed, she says often running; returns for tea to receive some friend or other; reads at dinner alone and retires to bed immediately. She says happiness consists in finding the right rut and never leaving it.

Tuesday, 23rd November

Lunched with Sibyl Colefax. Oriental incense from joss-sticks in the hall. Rather highbrow party consisting of the Ronald Trees (perhaps not very highbrow), Vita Sackville-West, Willie Maugham, Desmond MacCarthy, Ruth Draper and me. I sat between pretty Mrs Tree and Ruth Draper. Latter is an enchanting woman, with great perception. She misses no nuances, has a low, modulated, seductive voice, like her sister, Mrs James. They belong to the aristocracy of American women who are exceedingly gentle in manner. She told me that her performances tire her, but she *loves* them. Only once in her life has she missed one through illness. At present she has a cold and this makes work a great strain. She thinks she ought to stop acting soon or she will make the same mistake of most actors and actresses who do not know when to retire from the stage. She senses the kind of audience she has in front of her at once and always knows whether they have seen her before or not. She loves England. Towards the end of luncheon conversation turned to the Russian temperament. Macarthy said all Russians were children, with children's sense of fun and cruelty. He is very entertaining and laughs a lot himself like a child for the sheer fun of being alive.

Wednesday, 24th November

The new Lord Bearsted came to see me. He said that several of the pictures his father gave us at Upton were not his to give. Would we please strike them off our list. I am always willing to oblige donors but I can't very well do this without my committee's consent. I have had a victory in getting authority for Lady Berwick to be paid £5.10s per week for her servant's wages as from the date of her husband's death. I was asked by the Henry Yorkes to a party to celebrate publication of Henry's new novel *Concluding*, but couldn't manage it.

Thursday, 25th November

Lunched at Mrs Wyndham's in Portman Square. Then met Rick at Trinity College of Music where the interview I had been dreading took place. It went well. The NT got what it wanted, namely control of the instruments. Having met Ruth Draper I thought I should see her on the stage. So went this evening by myself. Her monologues may not be, are not, I think, great art, but they amount to great virtuosity. It is a remarkable physical and mental feat for one woman to hold crowded audiences night after night, with matinées too. She is amusing as well as moving in the role of the Irish mother of a son killed in the 1914 War, and that of the village postmistress in *The Return of the Soldier* in 1945. This role was astonishingly evocative of a poignant subject.

Called on Eddie Marsh this evening. He lives in a rather down-at-heel house in Walton Street. Old food from previous meals still lying upon the table at which he sits. A sweet black and white cat, which he adores, curled on his knees. This cat follows him everywhere. His picture collection a delight. There is scarcely one among the lot that I do not covet. Ninety per cent are moderns. He repeated many current witticisms about the Belcher Case★. People say, 'After all this Government is not so bad. It is the best money can buy.' And 'There is to be a new pantomime called Ali Baba and the Board of Trade.'

Dined with Sheila Plunkett, her husband and Lady Forres (white hair) in the little house Sheila has taken in Montpelier Walk. Lady Forres left and I stayed till 12.15 drinking brandy, which kept me awake during the ensuing night and gave me such palpitations that I thought I was going to have a heart attack. This was at 4 o'clock. We talked of her brother Johnnie Philipps. Sheila, who was in excellent form, said he was settling down and becoming more serious, working at his film and drinking less. Laughed over a story of him play-acting with their father, who was mad and when dying imagined he was in a railway carriage. Johnnie had to coax his father back to bed in the middle of the night on the pretence that the train was about to leave the station. Now while we were sitting and laughing about Johnnie he was dying in his bath in Albany a mile away. He was found drowned early next morning by the night watchman who had heard the overflow of his bath water. The papers say he had a heart attack. He was thirty-three. An erratic, whizzy creature, he had charm. He led a pre-war sort of life of dotty irresponsibility which was rare and only fairly acceptable. This death has upset me without moving me to tears. I am terribly sorry for poor Sheila who loved him very dearly.

Saturday, 27th November

At the British Museum all day looking at photostats of architectural drawings from Hatfield and old tomes in the reading room. A dense fog has lasted several days. I like it.

★J. M. Belcher (1905–1964) was Parliamentary Secretary to the Board of Trade (1946–8). A judicial inquiry was instituted by the Prime Minister, Mr Attlee, to examine charges of bribery against Mr Belcher, who resigned on 15 December. The tribunal reported adversely on Mr Belcher on 25 January 1949 but no criminal proceedings were taken against him owing to the comparative triviality of his misdemeanours.

I dined with Malcolm Bullock after he had taken me to the *Prodigal Returned*, a play of little substance, but décor and dresses by Cecil Beaton extremely pretty. Also acting thoroughly good. John Gielgud as the young man of twenty-nine looked the part in spite of his forty-five years. Sybil Thorndike excellent too. At dinner at the Savoy I felt my heart racing and talked to Malcolm about it. He advised me to see Pierre Lansel at once. So I walked there this afternoon, in black fog and cold. However the walk heated me and Pierre was rather shocked that I was hot. He gave me three different sorts of pill to take three times a day. I decided that this sort of treatment was out of the question and threw the prescription into the wastepaper basket when I got home.

Wednesday, 1st December

Lunched with Tony Pawson at a restaurant in Duke Street; Loelia Westminster and Margaret Sweeny. The last was the great beauty of my generation, and is still so. Loelia took me to a picture-framer in Blue Boar Yard. Wearing extremely chic clothes and wrapped in furs. Not once or twice, but three times she asked for my picture to be framed in the *very cheapest* possible manner. Kind of her, but I caught the old aproned craftsman casting a glance of amazement at her expensive presence.

Thursday, 2nd December

At 9.30 to the Aberconways' house, no. 12 North Audley Street, into which they have just moved. It was the Courtaulds' and has a gallery at the back with central coffered dome of Lord Burlington's time. Indeed might be a gallery at Chiswick House. The Aberconways' furniture is of the Knole settee type and they will decorate the house in, I suspect, a conventional cream.

Harold [Nicolson] having dined with me at Brooks's took me across the way to Pratt's. Talk was of the appointment of the new National Trust secretary and the pains the small committee were taking to choose a man who would not interfere with Hubert Smith's and my work. Harold observed that all scandals derived from written indiscretions. He told me that the Philip Trotters, the toads, brought a libel action against him when he was Parliamentary secretary at the Ministry of Information during the war, and how Duff Cooper and Monckton made them drop it. Harold spoke too openly at Pratt's of his being ignored by the Socialist party who persistently overlook his very existence except when they make him stand for Croydon, and then do not thank him afterwards.

Last night I motored to Upton. Stayed with Richard and Heather Bearsted at Sun Rising. All day we spent sorting out pictures, there being no little embarrassment over the father's having given away some that he also left by will to his widow. Unlike the father the son cares little for art. Fortunately all the pictures he wants reserved for himself amount to a handful of horse paintings by Sartorius.

Yesterday before leaving I lunched with Loelia W. at her flat in Grosvenor Square. Hamish [St Clair-Erskine], back from Italy, was there. He made us rock with laughter over his war stories, some exaggerated no doubt but all extremely funny. Loelia laughed till the tears coursed down her cheeks.

Trained to Lancashire to spend two nights with Roger Hesketh. Meols Hall is a little red brick house in a tiny park on the fringe of Southport which practically surrounds it. The garden front faces a flat, mossy, soggy landscape, dotted with blackened and stunted copses. The house has been so altered that it belongs to no period. Some good taste early Georgian pastiche has been applied by the Heskeths. But the house contains beautiful things – Breughels, Sandbys, besides family portraits, and nice Georgian furniture inherited. I do not see how the place could be accepted by the Trust. However Roger sees it through argent- and gules-tinted spectacles because it is what remains of an ancient family estate round Southport. His father sold practically all the land. Roger bought back what he could, namely about 400 acres. He lives a secluded life as King of Southport, devoted to chairing local committees and doing his duty very conscientiously.

Came back in time for the Handel *Messiah* in St Paul's Cathedral. Had a glass of sherry with the Dean – Matthews – then sat in the Dean's Gallery under the dome. Mounted a beautiful stone twisting staircase. Very high up, we had a fine view, but it was cold and draughty. The *Messiah* is a bit too long for sitting on a hard chair at such a vertiginous height. But it was glorious to gaze at close range at the illuminated

Thornhill ceiling. I admire the Alfred Stevens mosaics. The later ones by Sir William Richmond are horrid.

Historic Buildings Committee today. Peter Hesketh who attended for the first time said he was immensely impressed. Eardley and I later lunched with Ronnie Brocket at the Marlborough Club. His geniality is perplexing and a little unconvincing like an ingratiating spaniel's. Then I left for Belgrave Square at Lady Crewe's invitation to attend a concert given for the Keats-Shelley Committee, of which the Queen is patron. Those of us on the committee were aligned in a small room. Lady Crewe said to Jamesey in her sepulchral voice, 'I shall pass the Queen round from left to right like the port.' The Queen arrived dressed in red velvet. When my turn came to be presented Lady Crewe said, 'And you won't know Mr L.-M. of course,' which was not calculated to put either of us at ease. But the Queen replied, 'Yes indeed,' with marked emphasis on the last syllable. For this I gave her the highest marks for she did not know me from Adam. She speaks in a clear, soft voice, is sweet and abounds in charm. Her voice is her secret weapon. It could disarm the most hostile adversary. She looked pale and would, I thought, have been improved by a little colour or rouge. We followed her upstairs to our seats. I was close to Quentin Crewe and just behind Midi. Vita recited two odes of Keats but was nervous and a little halting. Silveri sang Neapolitan songs in a huge, resonant voice far too big for the room, but I liked his singing. Finally Cecil Day-Lewis recited the last seventeen stanzas from *Adonais* in a measured, rhythmical voice, emotional enough and yet so firm that I don't remember being more moved by a poetry reading in my life.

This evening Sarah Churchill invited me to a party given by her sister Diana Sandys, that sweet, chirpy little creature. Two men, one called Bunny Austin (not the tennis player), and Anthony Beauchamp, a dark gigolo with a scar (I take it that he is going to marry Sarah), and Mrs Winston Churchill. I sat next to Mrs Winston at the theatre, a new review called *Oranges and Lemons*. I don't really like her, and never did in the old days. She is jerky and precise in manner, and yet miauly; laughs and speaks as though she feared to touch or swallow dirt. She is, I suspect, *au fond* snobbish, exclusive and disapproving. With her white hair she is still a beautiful woman. We had nothing to say to each other and at dinner at Sarah's flat later, all perching on chairs and sofas, I avoided her. I was very tired this evening and did not like the company at all. Don't suppose they cared for me.

Clifford Smith lunched and we went to Fenton House, to Lady Binning's. Tiresome, because there was nothing for me to do and I am overwhelmed with work. Dear Lady B. said she would feel safer if I were present – safe from old Cliffy! I am feeling very unwell, doped with the Luminal Pierre Lansel is giving me, over and above the pills which I have not admitted to him I threw away. Went with Michael Rosse to Anthony Wagner's party at the College of Heralds, a curiously academic, dry assembly of desiccated, hirsute pedants, but lots of drink and quite enjoyable. Am terribly put out that the bill for work on my motor this autumn has come to £150.

Had a talk with Lord Crawford after today's meetings about various things. I asked if he would raise at the Fine Arts Commission the projected removal of Onslow Ford's Shelley monument by the dons of University College – a monstrous proposal; also discussed the Bearsted pictures. He was disturbed to learn that so many were to be withdrawn, and felt sure old Lord B. never intended such a thing.

Burnet Pavitt took me to Sadler's Wells to see and hear Verdi's *Simone Boccanegra*. Quite well done and some pretty arias but the audience ugly and unwashed. Smelly.

Worked over whole weekend: Saturday morning in the Public Records Office on Henry VIII's accounts of the building of Hanworth Manor, the script of this reign being Gothic and difficult to decipher. Last night Henry Henry dined. He is like some big, floppy sunflower with a radiant face which one watches slowly unfold when recognition of what one is endeavouring to impart slowly dawns upon him. He is not clever and rather backward. Is a gentle child. Tells me he is extremely in love with someone who inadequately requites his sad passion; that he is very undersexed, is seldom aroused and when he has had his pleasure takes two whole days to recover his senses. A poor look-out.

Had a dinner party tonight of Riette Lamington and Johnnie and Mary Churchill. Johnnie unchanged, also (like H.H.) a child in his approach to life, sweet and funny. Every person and thing is a rollicking joke to him. He loves giggling with me as we used to do at our crammers at Stanway. Mary seems a perfect wife whom I hope the volatile Johnnie will retain.

Charlotte Bonham-Carter gave what she calls a fork dinner at 7 o'clock and then took me to the Albert Hall. She is an extraordinary character, flitting to and fro, from one idea and one place to another. Clever, charitable and engaging. I mean she can boast of possessing faith, hope and charity. The Vere Pilkingtons, Patrick Kinross and the Lennox Berkeleys there. Lennox had his new concerto for two pianos and orchestra played for the first time, Malcolm Sargent conducting. It was enjoyable, full of melodies and vigour. I watched Lennox sitting in profile with his long nose turned to the orchestra like a serious salmon, in his tense, shy, modest manner. At the end there was much applause. He appeared on the platform three times and bowed sweetly as though wondering why he was there. He is another childlike person. Charlotte insisted on dragging reluctant Patrick and me behind the stage to shake hands with Malcolm Sargent. Such visits to green rooms always embarrass me. I dislike seeming to be on the lion prowl.

Lady Anderson asked me to lunch with her alone today. She has been appointed by Stafford Cripps to the Royal Commission which is investigating the future of historic country houses, and wants to learn about the Nat. Trust of which she is abysmally ignorant. She does not even know the terms of reference of her Commission. She fancies it is to take away from the Trust the houses it already possesses. She made herself out to be very uninformed and foolish. Yet she is well disposed to the Trust.

This afternoon in pouring rain I motor Sisson to Godmanchester. I stay the night at Farm Hall.

I motored Sisson from his house – it is awfully dirty and too big for him – via Houghton to Wisbech where we looked at a farmhouse offered to the Trust. Sisson, of whom and his wife I am dearly fond, was intolerable. He practically told Penrose and Mrs Munday, the gentle and enthusiastic Wisbech Society lady, that he was not going to cooperate in getting the house repaired. I think he is overworked and on the verge of a breakdown. At the Penroses after dinner he became drunk and his bitterness and morbidity were frightening and distasteful. He gave a graphic description of a blow-fly alighting upon his father's corpse. He gloated over the prospect of worms devouring not merely his body, but mine, and was behaving like a cannibal. 'Nature *will* get you in the end,' he kept repeating. 'The worms *will* have you,' all the while looking like a death's-head himself. 'No, they certainly won't,' I replied. Poor Sisson went black with rage at this contradiction. 'I said, "They will",' he repeated. 'They won't,' I said again, 'because I am going to be cremated.'

Thursday, 16th December

To Blickling where I suppose I did some good going round the house suggesting improvements with Alec Penrose who was most helpful and quite charming. It was a clear, sunny day. The house and grounds in their sleeping beauty I know and love so well. I am sure many of the Hatfield artificers went to Blickling, for more and more affinities in the architecture strike my eye, viz. the *putti* on the gable apexes on the south front resemble those wooden ones on the stair newels at Hatfield. We motored back to Godmanchester where Sisson retired to bed and was seen no more.

Friday, 17th December

Motored back to London after much trouble getting the car to start. The battery had not been charged by that blighter, Druce, and I had to be towed. Dined with Patrick Kinross and sat next to Dig Yorke and Peter Derwent. Peter D. who is newly engaged to marry Carmen Gandarillas is not easy at all and casts a supercilious gloom. Dig told me that Henry [Green] her husband, writes his novels in the drawing-room with people about and never retires into seclusion. Prefers writing with distractions around him.

Sunday, 19th December

Work over weekend. Have now finished note-taking and by the New Year shall begin writing book. I want to call it *Classical Tudor*. My notes are so full I fear the book will be far too long and too crammed with facts. Weeding will be a serious difficulty and a hard task.

Leigh Ashton, Olga Lynn and Loelia Westminster dined with me tonight. Very successful party. I love Oggie and Loelia. Leigh, consumed by jealousies and touchiness, is of course a common man.

Monday, 20th December

Lunched with Captain Hill who told me that Mr [Ernest] Cook was very worried about the Commission. He feared the Government would seize his houses on his death and they would never come to the Trust after all.

Motored Lord Esher to Ham House to approve plans for a curator's flat, which we did after examining every detail in our fussiest manner. Ralph Edwards was there and showed us the rooms he is arranging. I told him I disapproved of his wish to delete the perspective views under the front colonnades, and also to remove the Edwardian radiator protectors. Lunched with Margaret Jourdain and Ivy Compton-Burnett. Rose Macaulay there. She becomes more and more like a wizened damson and her voice sets my teeth on edge. But I like her. Then a friendly meeting over Matson House with the Ministry of Planning, Philip Frere representing Carol Dugdale. Cocktail party at *Architectural Review* office. Malcolm Bullock and Mark Ogilvie-Grant dined.

Thursday, 23rd December

Today worked slackly for there is a distinct Christmas feeling in the air. All the girls and women in the office are agog. Women revel in Christmas. My Mama is a genuine exception. I gave the girls some chocolates but, generally speaking, am cutting down presents this year because I am so very poor. Went to the exhibition of David portraits at the Tate. The famous Madame Recamier a poor thing; the self-portrait is fine. Also went to Danish exhibition which bored me very much; early stuff dull, the late stuff jejune.

Friday, 24th December

Motored home and stopped at Oxford to look at the Merton, Wadham and Bodleian frontispieces. At home this evening wondered how I could possibly survive Christmas: Deenie, Mama and Papa. My father's thin jokes, my mother's fuss about the cooking, Deenie's fuss lest the robin might not return to its bird-bath and her radiators freeze during her absence from home, made me irritable and snappy. Of course I am an absolute beast.

Christmas Day 1948

At least I was devout at Mass in Broadway. It was a bright sunny day and after church I motored up Willersey Hill and walked to Dover's Hill along the edge of the Cotswolds overlooking the Vale. It is a fine sweep of a hemi-cycle, like a Greek amphitheatre in terraces, a curious, primitive, isolated formation with distant views towards the Malvern, Bredon and Dumbleton hills. This Christmas I have visited Campden Market Hall, Hidcote, Charlecote, Packwood and the Dial House at Knowle, which a solicitor named Parr wants to leave to the Trust.

Thursday, 30th December

To an exhibition at the Arts Council of Constable drawings and sketches belonging to a Mr Gregory who, Philip James tells me, is a Ukrainian refugee. Two practically thumbnail sketches, coloured, of ships in full sail on a rough sea, tiny specks on the horizon, drew the soul out of my body. Constable is *very* great.

Friday, 31st December

So soon after my return from several days' rest I find my nerves ajangle in the office, with nothing to account for it. It is in the mornings that I feel so ill. This evening Alvilde took me to *Scott of the Antarctic*. John Mills as Scott looked very like Peter [Scott]. Diana Churchill played the young wife, Kathleen. How strange to see featured in a film a woman whom I had known so intimately as K. How strange. She played the part quite well and K. would not have objected, I fancy. No sentiment she would have been ashamed of. It is a good film and the frostbitten heroes in their tent just as I imagined. The horror of it. How foolish I was not to have learned more about this epic story from Kathleen when she was alive. Returned and changed, and went to Savoy with Alvilde and her child Clarissa to join the Kenneth Clarks' party for New Year's Eve. It was horrid. Such a noise, with people whistling, pulling crackers and blowing streamers, that I could not hear a word anyone spoke. How can people enjoy this form of entertainment? I hate the New Year anyway.

1949

Sunday, 2nd January

Helen and Johnnie Dashwood and Alvilde Chaplin dined. Johnnie embarrassed Helen by *risqué*, schoolboy stories, and Alvilde looked unamused. Yet next day I received from Alvilde a note of warm thanks and invitation to dine Monday week. I began, with the New Year, writing my Renaissance book this weekend, but was disconsolate.

Monday, 3rd January

Lunched with Loelia and the editor of her paper, *House and Gardens*, to discuss my doing an article on the Nat. Trust. Loelia says that if they publish the article in the States I may receive £40. Since I am overdrawn more than £600 a £40 reduction will be one drop less in my ocean of debt.

Called on Sibyl Colefax who was lying in her bed, coughing. Yet she talked and made plans for the future and was interested in everything. She is a courageous woman. She looked like a tiny dried leaf that is crumpling at both ends. I asked her about Kathleen Kennet who always told me that she disliked Sibyl for her lion-hunting. Just a slight case of pot and kettle. Sibyl told me she knew K. very well when she was engaged to Scott who was always unhappy with K. on account of her 'cheapness'. Said Sibyl, 'She was a self-advertiser. She dramatized her widowhood, seeking publicity at all turns.' Sibyl told a mutual friend that Peter, then aged three, would die of pneumonia if K. allowed him to walk about London in winter stark naked. When this unwelcome piece of advice was conveyed by the mutual friend to Hilton Young he repeated it to his wife and charged Sibyl with malicious intent. Sibyl also told me that K. was a snob who tried to vamp all distinguished men. I told Sibyl that it saddened me to hear this. How odd it is to hear conflicting explanations of mutual dislike from two women at different times, both women of more than normal intelligence and integrity.

Tuesday, 4th January

Lord Esher at luncheon at Brooks's said that the present Lord Methuen had refused to allow his neighbours, the Hobhouses, to publish love letters between John Cam Hobhouse and a Lady Methuen written in Hobhouse's extreme youth, presumably 130 years ago now. Esher gave this as an example of an intelligent man's silliness.

I trained down to Salisbury and was met by Eardley. I stayed two nights at Long Crichel. Only E. and Desmond Shawe-Taylor there, Eddy and Raymond being away, for which in all the circumstances I was glad.

Wednesday, 5th January

E. and I motor to Lytes Cary, look round house and garden, and discuss questions of liability for death duties on the furniture with Sir Walter Jenner's agent, old Major Hodgson, whom we think a silly old pet. He told us he was tearing up letters and papers of the deceased Sir Walter as fast as he could go. He added, 'Thank goodness I have already thrown all the music away. You of course will get rid of that piano; good for nothing. People no longer play the piano these days.' Presumably when he hears music on the wireless he imagines it is never *live* but was recorded once and for all years ago.

Thursday, 6th January

I have a bad tooth. I knew this would happen. My face is swollen on one side. I telephoned Mary Kearney [my secretary] to fix an appointment for me tomorrow with McKechnie [my dentist]. I am terrified at the prospect of it being pulled out. E. and I motored to Montacute and discussed the proposed new flat for the Yateses [custodians]; then to Stourhead and looked around.

The day I left I received another communication from the Bank which threw me into such a panic that I wrote at once to Papa imploring him to sell for me the few shares that are in trust.

Friday, 7th January

This morning went to the dentist who gave my swollen face one look and in his heartiest manner said he knew the old tooth was on its last legs and must now come out. *His* face was wreathed with sadistic jubilation. I who am a perfect funk begged for a reprieve. He said it could not remain a minute longer and must be extracted at once and, what was more, with an anaesthetic. When I begged for it not to be gas which I hate because of the mask he said I could have an injection. He accordingly telephoned the anaesthetist who came into the room as though he had been waiting next door at the key-hole. What a strange experience to be awake and alive, and within sixty seconds as it were dead, in a different world. Scarcely had the needle come out of my arm when I was off, but not before they put a sponge of gas before my mouth, which was cruel and deceitful of them. Accordingly I had a moment's agony, only a moment's, but to me eternity's. I was under for thirty minutes and the first thing I remember on coming round was a sensation of acute regret at leaving an elysium and returning to a real and less agreeable world. My eyes were literally pouring tears, although I was not sobbing. How dull an experience for the dentist and his assistant, yet what a thrilling one for me. It was proof beyond all measure that time does not exist and is a figment of the imagination.

I talked this over with Doreen Baynes this evening. She was convinced that my experience had been of the other world and the fact that I recall it as elysium proved her point. Of course I was not actually dead this morning, but was still alive, because my heart was beating. So in what world was I? On the threshold of another? Doreen was perplexed and could not give a satisfactory answer. No one ever can. We talked a lot about death of which she has no fears. She looks forward to it. As for gas, she loves it, and says she and Noël Coward are the only two people who do.

Sunday, 9th January

I made a little more progress with my book this weekend, but no 'through leaves' as I should like. Laboured, factual and stodgy stuff churned itself out. Essentially dull it is because my skeleton is too big. The word skeleton in this context does not relate to yesterday's preoccupation with death. There is a young man called Giles Eyre staying in this house who is bright and jolly and has probably never heard of death.

Tonight Paz Subercaseaux, Rose Macaulay and Roger Senhouse dined. Paz, whom I like, is a well-educated, cultivated, rather earnest Chilean. Miss Macaulay is very spirited in spite of her desiccated appearance to which Stuart [Preston] took such exception. She can and will talk of anything. She is wizened in feature and her lower jaw – false teeth, ill-fitting – juts out at you in speaking. But do not be alarmed. She has no airs of any kind and fills her intellectual inferiors with enthusiasms that flatter their mean understanding.

Called on Sibyl still in bed. There were present when I arrived Bogey Harris and Lady Anderson, who was the first to leave. After her withdrawal the other two started gossiping about her, supposing that she had only called in order to verify that the orchids she had sent Sibyl, and for which Sibyl had already written to thank her, were still there and had not been given away. Sibyl talked fairly sensibly about the Chancellor's Committee on Historic Houses and suggested that we sent it a list of those houses that have disappeared within the last year.

Then dined with the Chaplins who have rented Cecil Beaton's house in Pelham Place. Amongst others were Paz again, Eddie Marsh and a new young man, called Christopher Warner who has taken John Philipps's flat in Albany. He is tall, dark and handsome, a tea-leaf fortune-teller's delight. Eddie Marsh tells countless stories of people he has known in the dim past and recites reams of poetry whenever conversation touches one hair's breadth upon a quotation. He must have been the perfect Edwardian house party guest. He told us how he saw Sarah Bernhardt act in 1887. No actress in his opinion has ever eclipsed her. It was an experience he can never forget. He saw her frequently but the first impression was the indelible one. Anthony C. teased a lot in pretending to be pro-Russian. He asked who would not prefer to live under Bolshevism than not live at all. I said I would.

Somerset de Chair who lunched with me said he had found at Blickling all the original building accounts and the names of Thomas Thorpe and Lyminge referred to. He read that the gallery plaster ceiling cost £60 to erect. He said that his boy aged eleven went before a medical board for the Navy entrance examination. They ploughed him because he has incipient varicose veins of the testicles.

Went to Bourlet's to check which of the Pre-Raphaelites belonging to Mrs Angeli were to go to Wightwick [Manor]. Then to Batsford's where Mr Harry had some rare books to show me; then to Holder's and Drown's, the picture restorers, and then the dentist. My extracted tooth, or rather the cavity, still aches furiously. The dentist said he had to tear the jawbone a bit in taking the tooth out. Hence the pain.

Malcolm Bullock telephoned that Peter Derwent died today in Paris. He had just returned with Carmen and Tony [Gandarillas] from Switzerland and was very fit. He had been shopping in the afternoon with Carmen, buying her wedding dress and presents, went to lie down because he was a little tired, fell into a coma and never regained consciousness. An abscess on his lung suddenly burst. He had been very ill towards the end of last year, I knew, and presumably caught tuberculosis from Sabine, his first wife. Poor Peter, I sat next to him at dinner with Patrick a month ago and thought him rather morose. I congratulated him on his engagement and he said, 'Yes, Carmen is a splendid person,' which I thought lacked enthusiasm. I noticed how white his hair had suddenly become. He was a pernickety, touchy, sensitive man, often taking and causing umbrage. He was more French than English in culture and tastes. He looked more like Byron than any man I have seen. I liked him without ever knowing him well. I first met him in 1937 when he and Robert [Byron] first conceived the Georgian Group, and I well remember going with Robert to stay with him and Sabine at Hackness [Hall]. What with the Louis XVI decoration, the French furniture, French conversation and overheated rooms, Hackness was like the Ritz Hotel dumped in the Yorkshire dales.

Dined with Cyril Connolly and Lys [Lubbock]. Alan Pryce-Jones and Alan Ross there. Alan P.-J. likes to pretend that he is sodden with middle-age defeatism and gloom whereas he is the soul of youthful gaiety and charm. Cyril is the most brilliant talker I have listened to. He surprised me by saying he had read no Trollope, no Dickens and only one Jane Austen novel. After dinner a lot of people dribbled in for champagne. I believe Cyril and Lys frequently entertain like this. I left at 12.30 without saying goodbye. Must write.

Sunday, 16th January

Eardley, Alvilde Chaplin and Loelia Westminster dined. Eardley pronounced Loelia 'brave' in the French sense, and Alvilde beautiful.

Wednesday, 19th January

Dined with Alvilde and Anthony Chaplin; the Sachie Sitwells there. Anthony, who is sensitive about such things, was furious with Georgia for scolding him for not wearing a dinner jacket. Anthony claimed that he had worthier things to spend his money on, and I agreed with him, having no money of my own to spend on anything. Accordingly I got back into Anthony's good graces, so I was told later, without realizing that I had been out of them.

To the theatre with Alvilde – Ibsen's *Wild Duck* – most lugubrious but excellent, particularly the girl and Fay Compton. The latter had no words to speak but acted in most telling silence. Saw the Bearsteds at the theatre, he and his wife having been robbed of £23,000 worth of jewels the previous evening by a cat burglar.

Lunched with Christopher Hussey at the Garrick Club in order to talk about my discoveries amongst the Longleat papers. It transpired that I was unable to impart much that he did not know already.

Dined Sibyl Colefax at her house. She was dressed and up, and though bent more than ever, was quite bright. A most excellent meal, the best I have had in England for years. I knew everyone there but the Angleseys, and sat next to her. Nigel [Nicolson], who is devoted and wished to marry her, and Diane Abdy present. Also John Sparrow, Paz Subercaseaux and Alvilde, with whom I went. Sitting with Sibyl after dinner we discussed sanctity and S. said quite seriously that I was probably a saint. Felt obliged to disabuse her.

At 11 went to Peter Derwent's memorial service at St Mark's, North Audley Street. The choir sang well and the music was beautifully chosen. I was moved by the hymn, 'Lord of our Life, and God of our Salvation'. Alvilde was present, wearing a snood over her hair, looking very romantic like a nun. We walked away from the service together and there, ahead of us was Nancy, not walking but running along the pavement to Heywood Hill's shop. We took a taxi to Cook's to inquire about fares to Portofino where she has asked me to stay in mid-February. I fear I cannot afford to go. The editor of *House and Gardens* lunched and asked me to write an article for him on country houses.

Today I finished Chapter 1 of the book and sent it to Mary Kearney to type out. Sheila Plunkett dined. She told me Lord Milford had offered to purchase Picton Castle from her and she wanted my advice. I advised selling to him since he was a Philipps, descendant of those who had owned it since the twelfth century and her brother was anyway about to sell it to him before he died. Moreover Lord M. undertakes to leave it to the National Trust if his grandson on coming of age declines to live there himself. Sheila is determined to do the best thing for Picton as she thinks Johnnie would have done. I regard her piety greater than was his. S. is carrying on with his film companies in the hope that she will not lose money and may improve the quality of British films.

Monday, 24th January

Eardley and I set off in my car at 9.30 in pouring rain to Upton where we arrived at 11.30. We watched Kiddell and his assistant, Clark, from Sotheby's listing and valuing the porcelain that belongs to the NT. It was fascinating. He valued some pieces at £500 each, i.e. Chelsea figures, Sèvres *jardinières*, and the Gold Anchor set of the Muses, eight figures, at £4,000. Kiddell, modest and kind, very ready to teach. We were favourably impressed. We lunched in the house with Dorothea Lady B. and the young Bs. Easy to see they think the mother bossy; she thinks them feckless. Who is right?

We motored to Warwick and Hollyoak took us to the Castle where we found Happ, the middle-European, in process of restoring the Batoni portrait of George Lucy from Charlecote. He has stripped off all the overpainting, leaving a lot of injuries which had been badly restored and overpainted a hundred years ago. These he will himself paint over. He was very self-confident and E. gave him bad marks for boasting how *he* knew how to remove overpaint without touching the original under-paint. We stayed at the Shakespeare Hotel, Stratford and went to a British film, *The House of Darkness*, about a family *c.* 1902 who were either killed or driven away from their home by the evil machinations of a young, handsome brother. Finally this brother, left in possession, died of fear brought about by one of his dead brothers' ghosts accompanying on a ghostly violin his piano playing. An involved story. We liked the film very much.

Tuesday, 25th January

To Charlecote. Brian and Alice Lucy there. We all succeeded in choosing the final position of each picture. A great feat. E. far and away the expert at this task. It means that when the walls of the great hall have been cleaned down and the picture-hangers have done their work, I can attach

[147]

my labels to the pictures and all will be finished. The Lucys having motored over gave us sandwiches in the little dining-room and were, as usual, generous and charming. Brian confided that until today Alice had not left home for eight months. Even so he feared she might not start until the last minute. She gave birth to two babies within one year late in life. E. stayed with a cousin in Broadway; I went home. Both parents very good to me.

Wednesday, 26th January

Picked up Mr Clouting (of the Ministry of Works) who stayed last night at the Crown, Evesham, and Eardley at Broadway. The three of us motored to Chedworth Roman Villa. Clouting reassured us about the condition of the stone capping he has put on the Roman walls. Their restoration and the rearrangement of the museum and redressing of the lawns show that progress is being made at this property. We lunched at the King's Head, Cirencester, leaving Clouting there after a visit to the Abbey church. E. and I drove to Horton Court and were horrified by the damp. Then to tea with Mr Cook at Bath whom we found an affable old man instead of the foxy old thing we imagined. E. even admired many of his pictures which he considers quite good – English school mostly – and I gave him a copy of my NT guidebook. We stayed with Mrs Knollys at Richmond Lodge.

Thursday, 27th January

Left for Lytes Cary, spending whole day there. We practically completed our selection of furniture, but have yet to arrange the rooms and sort the books. A successful day. Old Major Hodgson, who is one of Sir W. Jenner's executors, is a character. He shouts and yells at the servants and is loved by them all as a bluff, warm-hearted creature. He makes E. and me shake with laughter, for he is Colonel Blimp incarnate. At 5 o'clock we left for Exeter, staying two nights at the Clarence Hotel.

Friday, 28th January

Senior [Area Agent] called for Eardley at The Clarence early and took him to Plymouth. I motored to Lindridge to look at the house offered by Sir Edward Benthall. Was greeted by a Miss Reynolds, acting as lady housekeeper. I think her father was Rector of Stanton near Broadway. She remembers playing tennis with me. I pretended I remembered playing tennis with her. My committee accepted this property last month on E's recommendation, but I don't think it is good enough. The outside has been refaced with red brick. It has a modern projecting porch and dining-room window. I question the cornice's claim to being seventeenth-century. The staircase is early eighteenth-century. Great Chamber ceiling of copper wreathes painted a uniform cream. One other plaster ceiling of *c.* 1720. Unsightly additions.

I motored over Dartmoor, lunching at Two Bridges. Reached Cotehele. An exquisite day, strong winter sun slanting so as to penetrate the hearts of things and so warm that I drove without a coat. There were tortoiseshell butterflies on the wing which for January is unprecedented. Met Eardley there. We went round the house with the Ministry of Works letter of objections to our proposed alterations in hand. Back to Exeter for the night. Had a tyre puncture in Exeter last night; and on return from Cotehele this evening just missed by a bee's knee a head-on collision with a lorry. E. said it was the most miraculous escape from sudden death he has ever had. I kept my head but nearly died of shock when it was over.

Saturday, 29th January

Left in thick fog which cleared when we reached the heights. So we turned north to the Wellington Monument and examined [John] MacGregor's work there. We thought the spilling of cement down the obelisk and the substitution of cement blocks for stone a mistake. Called at Montacute and were pleased to find the garden beds had been dug. I dropped E. at Salisbury. Hesitated whether to give a lift to a sailor bound for London. Luckily I did so for at Staines we were plunged into dense fog as far as Osterley and by leaning out of the window he guided me until it cleared again. I could not see the kerb on the sailor's side and only the white central line of the road from mine.

Sunday, 30th January

Finished chapter on the French Renaissance. This evening dined at Alex Beattie's studio in Fulham Road very late, with Alan Lennox-Boyd and Gerald du Gouray. The latter told me he is writing the history of Meccan pilgrimages. He returns to Iraq in two days time. He does not want to live in England. Says he can only be happy in the East. I can't make out whether he is a second Lawrence of Arabia or a complete fraud. Wish somebody would tell me. Beattie is a good-looking and amiable ass. He asked me if I had ever been in love, and when I said 'Yes, of course', seemed surprised. He vouchsafed that he liked sleeping in one bed with

[149]

people he was fond of, but did not care much for sex. It left him cold. Is, I suspect, a Narcissus. 'As for women,' he said, 'they are so damned soft. Their bodies have no firmness. That is what I dislike.' He is confident that the Conservatives will be returned at the next election. How can he possibly know beyond what he has gleaned from high quarters?

Tuesday, 1st February

Dined alone with Barbara Moray who spoke of her deep friendship with Tom Mitford, of how devoted she was to him, and how she deplored his attitude to women, whom at bottom he despised. I feel sure that after the war, if he had survived, he would have married her, for she was one of the few women whom he didn't despise. We became extremely confidential as we drank whisky. I left at 1 a.m.

Wednesday, 2nd February

X. dined with me here and we drank Beaujolais over the fire. Became very tipsy. I had the greatest difficulty in getting her away for she wished to stay the night – a thing absolutely out of the question. This sounds as though I were as virtuous as St Anthony and like him desired by every female I encounter. Both assumptions are very, very far from being the case. When one is a foot away from X. her cat-grey eyes dilate like those of a film star in a close-up. She is very bewitching and seductive, is always gay, loves the ludicrous and makes me laugh. Above all she is genuinely affectionate.

Friday, 4th February

Stayed last night at Long Crichel alone with my dear Eardley. Thank God, with him my relations are absolutely straightforward. The relief of it. We motored early to Lytes Cary on a still, clear, frosty and beautiful morning. We got through a lot of work and made our final selection of furniture, even arranging the rooms except for pictures and ornamental china. We were pleased with ourselves, no doubt too pleased. We feel sure that a great deal of Sir Walter's furniture supplied by Angel of Bath is made up. We kept what we thought best and most suitable, rejecting the rest. We like to believe we make a perfect combination for we criticize each other mercilessly, usually laughing like mad, for alone we are very funny. A third person overhearing us might not think so.

[150]

Corrected my chapter on the French Renaissance, now ready for typing, and dined with Riette Lamington. She was rather *distraite*. I really don't like her very much. She is too self-conscious, prim and disapproving. Nature's governess, yet amorous. I always remember Jamesey deliberately setting fire to her sofa with his cigarette in order to effect an escape. The Ivor Churchills were the other guests. She is a new wife, young and pretty. Lord Ivor says he has given up collecting pictures and is selling what he can in order to live – good enough reason – in the Ritz Hotel – which seems a bad one. He is an affable man, not stupid and not arrogant like many Churchills. He said Lady Anderson has cultivated an unerring gift of flattering men who like her. This explains why women hate her. She has a caressing, insinuating voice like the serpent of old Nile.

Took Bridget to see Doreen Baynes at 6 o'clock. Doreen liked her very much. Conversation flowed along as it always does with this darling woman who told us that she often reads her own books, putting herself in the place of an admirer, in order to discover what in her writing it can possibly be that they enjoy. I said I never re-read my own writings, a thing I likened to a dog returning to its vomit. Bridget dined with me afterwards. We always have much to pick over.

A long special meeting of the Finance Committee to discuss the Memorandum to be submitted to the Gowers Committee. It is agreed that our points are of the utmost importance. We have reached a crisis in the Trust's affairs. [Sir Ernest] Gowers is taking the matter most seriously. I strongly deprecated a proposal that we should surrender to the Government all 'museum' houses, i.e. those which the families have left and which may not be inhabited again, because I foresee all families leaving these anachronistic white elephants in time. And then what will be left to us?

At SPAB meetings I find myself listened to now for Esher (the Chairman) always appeals to me for help. This sounds to me conceited. I hope it doesn't to anyone who may read these words. They have put me on to a subcommittee to work out the Society's evidence to be submitted to the Gower's Committee.

[151]

Dinner party given by Y. When the other guests left I stayed behind, thinking no evil, fearing no evil. Silly fool. I had put my head into a noose, and soon scented danger, too late. My hostess expected me to make love to her. How insatiable these women are. Any youngish man in a calm, it seems. Inventing an urgent excuse – one cannot have a committee meeting at midnight – I bolted, and heard the clang of the front door behind me. It made a terrible sound which echoed down the street. 'Heaven has no rage like love to hatred turned. Nor hell a fury like a woman scorned,' it seemed to shout at me. With my tail between my legs I shouted back, 'Damn, damn!' for neither heaven nor hell was of my seeking. Passionless friendship is all I need these days.

Wednesday, 9th February

Historic Buildings Committee this morning. Nearly all the area representatives present. Had my time full talking to them before and after the meeting about various problems. The Feddens gave me luncheon at Prunier's. I had oysters and *moules* and chocolate cream, and felt rather sick.

Thursday, 10th February

At 4.30 to the Society of Antiquaries as a guest of Clifford Smith. Cliffy's wife, that sweet, simpering old dear, and Lady Catherine Ashburnham of Ashburnham Place, also invited. The last, a simple, shy lady to whom Cliffy deferred in the most subservient fashion. His snobbishness and sense of class is Austenian. [Tom] Kendrick lectured with verve on English Renaissance antiquaries, a dull subject enough. The lecture room filled with the dreariest old crones imaginable, just what the ordinary person supposes archaeologists to look like – dry as dust. Rather splendid formality here, the Chairman with mace welcoming John Harvey as a new Fellow.

Friday, 11th February

Long discussion again today at both Committee meetings about the draft Memorandum for the Chancellor's Committee. Our people are now seriously concerned. Esher, to my surprise, read to the Committee my letter to him suggesting that a third body be set up to hold historic houses. Committee did not much like it but the result was, as is so often the case, that they modified their previous decision to surrender quite so many houses to the Ministry of Works. Lord Crawford and George

Howard lunched with me at Brooks's. Crawford said that at the party given by the National Art Collections Fund one old woman came up and thanked him personally for having bought for the nation all the beautiful pictures at the exhibition – the Chantry Bequest!

This morning motored the Eshers to Steventon in pouring rain. Later it cleared. We were given coffee by Walter Godfrey who conducted us to the Priory Buildings. Esher modified some of MacGregor's proposals for restoration. Then on to Faringdon to lunch with Gerald Berners who looked very ill, shaky, twitchy. He shuffles rather than walks, a bad sign. He told me he suffered from acute, unrelieved melancholia and can neither write nor compose; an awful predicament for a creative man. Robert Heber-Percy came straight from the farm to the table in corduroys, covered with chaff and straw in his hair.

Worked all day finishing chapter on English humanists, now fit for typing. Rick [Stewart-Jones] called at 7.30 and drank with me. I had to drive him away, or he would have stayed till dawn talking. Anyway I was dining with Rory Cameron at Claridge's at 9.30. The Sachie Sitwells there. Sachie never sticks to the same subject for any length of time. Flits like a swallow and like a swallow never perches. Georgia said he lectured to a school the other day for one hour, having prepared no speech in advance. Instead, after his introduction by the headmaster he asked his audience what they wanted him to speak about, and then spoke. I was dog-tired before dinner began.

To see Sibyl this evening; she up and much better. Victor Pritchett, Alan Pryce-Jones and Eddie Marsh present. Talk about there being far too many writers. You can't of course prevent people writing any more than copulating, but there ought to be some sort of contraception to prevent publication. When I was left alone with Sibyl she said how important it was that friends should be possessed of human feelings for intellect was not enough. This woman, regarded by strangers as worldly, has great warmth underneath. When I got home I wrote a brochure for the National Trust, thus at once contravening my view expressed above.

[153]

Stayed at home this morning and wrote an introduction to the catalogue of the Attingham Park collection. Then lunched with Hubert Smith and Christopher Gibbs, discussing agenda for Lord Esher's subcommittee on the new Secretary's duties. A sticky meeting with Barker of the Ministry of Works about the lease of Osterley, the Ministry strongly objecting to our imposing onerous terms. I began by adopting a stiff front on the general principle, then giving way over details. These were my tactics.

On Sunday Alvilde telephoned me from Amalfi urging me to join them in Rome. This evening I consulted Rick who instantly offered to pay for my ticket there and back, which is angelic and typical of him. He said he preferred it to be a gift to a loan. So now I shall fly to Rome on Saturday. I dined with Paz Subercaseaux who gave me 7,000 lire for my journey which was equally angelic. Jamesey, who was present, talked in raptures about Norway. Of course he is in love with a Norwegian, as he confessed to me after dinner. Tony Gandarillas's wife, hitherto kept in purdah, and married daughter there, and a Chilean composer just arrived from Chile. Several different wines to drink which always disagrees with me.

Dined with the Aberconways in their new house left to Christabel by Samuel Courtauld, in North Audley Street. A splendid house of Burlington date and style, with gallery on the grand-miniature scale; a central coffered dome. Many well-known French Impressionist pictures (Courtauld). Opposite my place at dinner a ravishing Renoir of women with parasols in a punt on blue, sunlit water. I sat next to Betty Hussey to whom I am devoted for she is gay and buxom, natural and forthright, and Lady Elizabeth Hofmannsthal who is a great beauty with the soft, peony skin of all Pagets. The David Bowes-Lyons, he insinuating all sorts of forbidden things in veiled terms and proposing a trip with me in the spring. He is an extraordinary, complicated, buttoned, perhaps not so buttoned-up man who cannot call a spade a spade and is a walking riddle. Anthony Blunt and Christopher Hussey with whom I had Tudor talk. Hussey is sure that Longleat is of French inspiration. His articles on this great house appear in April. Lady Aberconway, with her milk complexion, wants to appear a pretty goose, but is as clever and calculating as a monkey. He affability and big business. He holds up a hand as a dog holds out a paw to be taken. But one is not disposed to stroke him.

To the theatre with Lady de Vesci (Bridget being ill in bed), Rory [Cameron] and Helen Dashwood. Rattigan's play *The Browning Version*. Did not care for the first set but liked the second, called *Harliquinade*. They dined here after. Sticky.

Lunched at the White Tower with Rose Macaulay, Roger Senhouse and Jamesey. Rose M. is writing a book on ruins and wants to be told where to go. James gave me another book to review for the *Spectator*, on the architect Godwin, a tormented aesthete.

Called very early and breakfasted. Druce motored me at 7 o'clock to the air station at Kensington where I straightway put my bag on what I mistook for a ledge and was in fact air. It tumbled down a staircase and emptied itself of all my precious luggage at the bottom. Found John Lehmann on my bus going to Rome likewise. This very agreeable although I know him but slightly. He is about my age, was at Eton with me although we never overlapped and is, like me, suffering from sciatica, seeking relief from the Mediterranean. Journey very easy. Within half an hour we were over the Isle of Wight, then across the Channel, Le Havre and all the way down France under-populated. Weather very fine in England, in mid-France cloudy, at Marseilles where we halted for half an hour extremely warm. I was told it might be cold so took my fur-lined coat. Over Riviera, Corsica, Elba, and Rome itself. Landed at 3.30. I am less scared of flying than I used to be, yet I do not think it any less unsafe. Even a little flying experience inculcates humility and a capacity to view the earth and life thereon as insignificant and transitory.

It is heaven being in Rome again after so short an interval. I drove in an old *carozza* round the Pincio to the Hotel de Ville where I supposed the Chaplins would be staying. But no, they were at the Inghilterra. Having engaged a room and unpacked I shall stay here until we move on Tuesday.

Went at 7 o'clock to the Chaplins' room at the Inghilterra which is Henry Jamesean, not unlike Brown's Hotel, Dover Street, with prints of Chantrey Bequest pictures in maplewood frames. In a pretty big double bedroom Alvilde has a white pekinese called Foo. Anthony asked if I wished to see his toad found at Paestum. I said yes. Whereupon he fetched a chamber pot covered with a face towel. In it lives the toad which he says is over sixty years old, possibly eighty, and has all its life been in the same garden avoiding the peasants and death, since all primitive people kill toads for being evil, which they are not. Anthony also has several lizards and frogs in cardboard boxes. They seem to be given nothing to eat yet thrive. Toads can live three months without food. We dined sumptuously at Alberotti's restaurant where D'Arcy Osborne once took me. I am so happy to be here – lovely Frascati wine, scampi and chocolate cake. It is warm tonight. No topcoat needed.

Sunday, 20th February

Sun shining. I dress with the double window wide open. Walk up the steps of Charles VIII's and Mendelssohn's church to hear the very end of a Mass, the nuns behind the grill. Then via the Corso to San Lorenzo in Lucina, and hear a complete Mass. An old monk takes the alms-basket round. He wears an expression of contemptuous boredom. Called at the Inghilterra where Anthony and Alvilde are furious because their car, left outside the hotel, had the lock broken during the night and many things stolen. However this morning they left it where it was and it was broken into again, and more things were stolen. They are both very anti-Rome on this account and on that of the noise and dirt round their hotel, which are appalling. The dustmen are on strike and the streets ankle-deep in garbage. A. and I walked towards St Peter's where Il Papa was speaking at 11 o'clock. There were great crowds so we diverged into the Castle of St Angelo. I was glad to go over Hadrian's great cylinder, never done before. The rooms painted by del Vaga in Raphaelesque arabesques are enchanting.

Geoffrey Gilmour met us at luncheon and motored us in his large Lincoln to Tivoli and the Villa d'Este. None of us had seen it for years. I was not disappointed though the others were. The rooms painted *c.* 1550 by Zucchero are beautiful just as a jumble of medieval glass may be beautiful, not for their composition (which is poor) but their kaleidoscopic quality. It is atrocious how Italians carve their names and write them with indelible ink on the wall paintings. In the Ara Coeli church I noticed a name and date '1907' in pencil upon a monument at chest height. One wipe of a sponge by a verger would have eliminated it in a second. But no. Italians have little aesthetic sense and are unobservant. They find sculpture irresistible to their biros. David Crawford wrote a respectful protest to the Pope but received no acknowledgement. Pirro Ligorio's frontispiece of the Villa d'Este is noble. The pencil-thin jets and fan-like gushes of musical water are a delight. The noble arch on the terrace

[156]

framing a vast pink sky and expanse of mountain horizon is like a Panini painting. Architecture in Italy is painting, not the other way about. The Chaplins found the Villa d'Este melancholy.

At the Scotch Tea House at teatime Simon Harcourt-Smith approached and spoke. The others hid their faces in the table cloth and groaned which embarrassed me. Later John Lehmann called for me and we drank in the hotel. Graham Greene, like a raddled Noël Coward with a bad colour, talked to John. I made myself scarce. With the Chaplins dined at Nino's not too well. The sour red wine upset me in the night. Talk was of animals not having souls, and of humans being morally superior to animals. Anthony maintains this a nonsense, for even the most ferocious wild beasts are not actuated by intentional cruelty. He says that birds are just as capable of art and architecture as men.

Monday, 21st February

A wonderful day. Full sun and able to sit and drink on the pavement before luncheon. John Bayley called at 10.15 with his camera and tripod in a satchel. He is a strange man of few affections I would guess, devoted to his studies and consumed by anxiety because he has no formulated purpose in them, and absolutely no money. We walked for miles past the Colonna church, up the Campidoglio, into the Ara Coeli church, he taking photographs unconcernedly in the middle of the Corso and in churches. Then down into the Gesù which is too lavish and in the decorating of which too many pains were taken. Into the Piazza Navona, past the Farnese and Sacchetti palaces, over the Tiber, up to the American Academy on the Janiculum. John Bayley is an indefatigable talker and sightseer. He knows every building in Rome, yet he does not bother about historic facts, or names of architects, or dates. He has a studio filled with thousands and thousands of photographs that he does not know what to do with. We lunched at a long table in a vast, whitewashed room. The American Academy was built in the Renaissance palace style in 1913, and is very *bien*. Full of earnest, friendly students, with a magnificent library packed with tomes on Roman subjects and all the arts. John Bayley says I could arrange to stay here as a guest in the summer. I was attracted by the claustral atmosphere.

I took John Bayley to Keats's house and we talked to Signora Cacciatore. We concluded that between the window and back wall facing the fireplace Keats's bed must have stood. A poignant room. There is a tin – the original one – from which remains of the aromatic gums were thrown by Leigh Hunt upon Shelley's pyre and which, Signora Cacciatore affirms, preserves quite a strong smell. In a tiny porphyry urn repose some of Shelley's ashes snatched from the pyre by Trelawny.

This morning Alvilde and I motored to the Vatican Museum and walked down the long galleries to the Sistine Chapel, straining our necks and eyes towards the ceiling which she assured me had faded since she last saw it twenty years ago. Again I thought the marble screen as fine as anything there. We were horrified by the damage done to the Loggie walls by pencilled and incised names within recent years. The lower part of these famous arabesques is totally obliterated, both paint and plaster work. Even the Raphael walls of the Stanze have been mutilated. They could so easily be protected by glass panels. These Stanze always leave something to be desired. True, they are much faded and cracked. But the scale of the murals is too big for the low rooms. We went into St Peter's. The overall grey marble makes a peculiarly fitting background to the opulent golds and reds and greens. I made Alvilde kiss St Peter's toe which she did with a reluctant grace, not to mention a positive grimace.

After a vast luncheon at Alberotti's I sat in the sun in the Pincio gardens and corrected typescript. The noise of motor scooters a distraction. But what noise does not distract in Rome now the fountains are silent, or inaudible? John Leslie dined with us. A dear man, and a fount of Roman gossip. He will never dry up.

I am constipated, as usual here. At 9.30 we left for Florence. I got awful sciatica in the tiny motor. Alvilde is a perfect travelling companion. Anthony is fun but one has to play up to him continuously. Sun dazzling, slightly cold, with wind on the hills. An exhausting drive for the road winds and winds and the hills are very steep. We passed Caprarola without stopping. Memories of Desmond [Shawe-Taylor] and the Colonel ranting against the custodian. We bought sandwiches and wine and grapes, and ate and drank on the roadside, our feet on the dusty surface. Stopped in Siena for coffee. A. and I visited the cathedral and admired the floor paving, or what we could see of it. Anthony refuses to look at any buildings or pictures. He will stop only to look for frogs in ponds. This affectation is silly especially since he claims to be a cultivated man; and it is maddening for A. The road between Siena and Florence covers beautiful country. In other words – not to underline the word 'beautiful' too faintly – Tuscany with its gentle hills and little towns, large villas, vine terraces and cypresses, *is* Paradise, Classical not Picturesque like the country round Assisi and Perugia. We stay at the Grand Hotel, Florence, in great comfort, overlooking the Arno. The view from our bedrooms, each with a terrace, on the top floor is exquisite, a rushing fall of Arno water below, the campanile and cupola of Santo Spirito and the bulk of the Carmine opposite us; and the cypress- and umbrella-clad rise of Bellosguardo beyond.

Thursday, 24th February

What a day! The sun so hot that I sat on my terrace without a coat, yet inside the churches icy cold. Alvilde and I sightsaw in the morning, first the Botticelli of St Augustine in the Ognissanti church next door, then to the Uffizi to feast on Lorenzo Credi and Bronzino. In the entrance there is an Etruscan torso of a man two centuries BC, massive and powerful just like one of the rowers of a skiff on the Arno this afternoon. Yet who were the Etruscans? And were they the ancestors of the Florentines? Then we ate *zabaione* in the piazza before plunging into the sombre Duomo.

Harold Acton lunched with us at the hotel. Was wickedly funny reviling the English *litterati* whom he dislikes, including poor Raymond Mortimer who gave his book [*Memoirs of an Aesthete, 1948*] a filthy review. He said he was a Jew, which R. hotly denies, being connected with Meyer & Mortimer, the military outfitters; that as a young Bohemian in Paris he sported a cloak and broad brimmed floppy hat. One day a passerby shouted at him, 'Va-t-en, folle bergère!'

I admire Anthony for the independence of his views, if I do not admire all his views. He dresses well and is always spruce. When at luncheon the waiters made A. take her pekinese out of the dining-room Anthony said to me, 'I wonder what they would say if they knew I had two toads in my pockets.' This afternoon instead of going out he sat on his terrace reading the Shakespeare sonnets.

We dined at Buca Lapi restaurant in the basement of an ancient palace, drinking delicious Orvieto white wine. A guitarist and violinist were playing Cimarosa, who was Napoleon's favourite composer, Anthony says.

Friday, 25th February

We left Florence after I had said farewell to St Augustine, for Pisa, a dull route, houses all the way. Looked at Pisano's ugly Gothic pulpit with classical cornice in the Baptistery. The Campo Santo completely destroyed in the War. What with Dresden we have much to answer for. The Tower would be very beautiful if only it would not lean. This it must have done since 1500 at latest for it is depicted leaning on an intarsia panel in the choir of the Duomo. We lunched in Pisa. How sad the gaps from bombing along the Arno. Then to Portofino across the mountains, a beautiful route. We arrived at 5.30 to find the Cliffords had come and moved into their Castello which they had in fact lent to the Chaplins. This quite naturally made the Chaplins rather cross. We had to stay at the Hotel Nazionale, primitive, but food excellent. Cliffords dined with us. Him we did not much like, a dark, smooth, saturnine newspaper correspondent, like a schoolmaster who does not look his pupils in the eye. She the daughter of Robert Graves, very talkative and bright.

Saturday, 26th February

Still fine and sunny but fearfully cold. None of us like Portofino. It is too *mignon* and shut in. We crave open space. All morning I wrote on my window terrace while the Chaplins took their pekinese who is ill with enteritis to the vet. This afternoon we again packed up and moved to Santa Margherita to stay at the Miramare, a more luxurious hotel.

Sunday, 27th February

Wrote most of the morning in the sun but behind glass doors because of piercing winds. In the afternoon we visited the Cliffords in the Castello, the site of which is extremely romantic. There are views from the terrace in every direction, a rare thing, over the fishing village of Portofino behind, over the outward sea towards Genoa and Sestri in front. Furthermore the place is on a promontory as well as a hill.

Monday, 28th February

I had sudden but acute toothache in the night and was only saved from madness by the kind night watchman finding me some aspirin. In the morning A. took me to a dentist in Rapallo who painted the tooth with medicament and refused to accept a fee. This is typical of one of the extremes, rapacity and generosity, to be met with in the Italian character. In the afternoon A. and I left Santa Margherita for the Castelletto, Portofino, the Cliffords having left it this morning. An old gardener, Pipo, carried our heavy bags up the hill. Paola the cook walks from the village every day, carrying provisions bought in the shops. It is divine up here. Much wind but burning sun. I sat in an arbour overlooking the sea and wrote at a table Pipo improvised for me. A. and I dined at the Nazionale, the best food we have had in Italy.

I worked in the tower room till 4.30. Anthony arrived at luncheon time. His love of Shakespeare is deep and passionate. He quotes at great length and is moved to ecstasies of veneration. Music and ornithology are his prime interests, yet he says Shakespeare transcends everything, even Mozart. A. and I drove to Rapallo in the evening to deliver a letter of introduction from Eddie Marsh to Max Beerbohm. We three dined at the Nazionale. Such laughter we have. They say I must come and live with them in Paris. Alvilde is incredibly generous and I notice that she pays for everything. It is Mardi Gras today and all the young in Rapallo are dressed up and making much din.

Terrible gale during the night and all day blowing relentlessly and noisily. From my window I see snow on the mountain tops beyond Genoa. Paola brings up a tiny pot of flowers on my coffee tray. Worked all day. Anthony says all great men have been preoccupied with death. Shakespeare never overcame his awe and fear of death, so how should we endeavour to do so? The smell of the fires that burn olive tree wood and roots is sweet and not a little intoxicating. I burn it in the stove of my bedroom, which is in a detached tower.

We leave Portofino this morning, the Chaplins glad to go for they have not liked it and truthfully I would not care to have the Castelletto as my only home because of exposure to the fearsome *tramontana* we have been having. Apart from the bitter cold it brings, it is extremely tiring to listen to. Besides, on this eyrie there is nowhere to walk, except down to the village and up again.

We motor to Genoa where the climate completely changes to midwinter. It is snowing hard. The Chaplins drop me at the station. We are all sad at parting. Left alone I wander down the Via Balbi, looking at the massive palaces one after another, and the University with the marble lions descending the stairs into the courtyard.

Shared a sleeper with a decent, inarticulate South American.

How rude and surly the French are after the outgiving Italians. I found myself sitting next to the Duke of St Albans in the train from Paris. He is a non-stop talker about nothing, but very funny. Hitherto I had only met him casually in Brooks's. I was furious that at Dover he paid no duty on two bottles of brandy and six of champagne whereas I had to pay 32/- duty on one bottle of liqueur. He was delighted and said it was because he was wearing a hat and I was not, but I believe it was because he is a Duke and I am not. In the carriage to London he spoke about King Edward VII's petty nature and his awful behaviour with women, as though his own was impeccable. He said that whenever the King saw a pretty woman he sent his equerries to fetch and present her to him; then would invite her to tea while commanding her not to come wearing a hat, or veiled. He said, quite irrelevantly, 'Oliver Messel is a pervert, isn't he?' I said, 'I don't think so.' I will not subscribe to the notion of old brutes that homosexuality is wicked or disgraceful.

Monday, 14th March

I have been back a week. My mind in turmoil. A fire has been lit. How absurdly coy and genteel one is, even to oneself, about one's emotions, when they are serious. Here the weather has been bitterly cold, un-relieved by sun. A sore throat turned to a cold, so I retired to bed on Saturday until today.

Jack Rathbone, our new Secretary, has started work. We were friends at Oxford. He is going to be a success with my colleagues. Have received several post cards from Alvilde who arrives in London tomorrow.

Tuesday, 15th March

I lunched with Harold at the Travellers'. He ordered a bottle of white wine of which I foolishly partook, for I had vowed on my return from Italy, never to drink in the middle of the day. The old men at the Travellers' look askance at Harold, the Socialist, surrounded by young men whom he corrupts with wine and seditious talk, the fools. But Harold is as dear as ever and enhances the lives of his friends, young and old. I drove him to Knole and we looked at the garden wall. He was deeply shocked. He thought it had been repaired in a way an urban corporation would have done it and is going to complain to the Committee. I hope, since he thinks we cannot undo the work, there will be no need for me to see Lord Sackville on the matter. I would hate this, for I am very fond of Lord Sackville who, I believe, trusts me. He might be. hurt and angry.

Back in London I told Harold I was going to meet Alvilde on the Golden Arrow and wanted to buy flowers for her. He dissuaded me, saying it was a continental and *bedint* thing to do. I met her and she dined here, bringing me some ham and liqueur as a present – not *bedint*.

Wednesday, 16th March

Sam Carr [of Batsford's] lunched and warned me that my book must be popular, short, and not too factual. As it happens everything he said it should be it isn't, and everything it should not be, it is.

Went to tea with Lady Binning at Fenton House, Hampstead to approve the colours she has chosen for her two front rooms. The kind woman, who really likes me very much, insisted upon my accepting the present of a sixteenth-century book of Roman palaces, which I am delighted to have. I could not refuse (didn't want to of course). She promised she would never give me another present. I wanted to embrace her, but refrained.

I took Bridget to the Hills' cocktail party. We could hardly move for the crowd.

Thursday, 17th March

Lunched with Sibyl Colefax at the Dorchester in a fearfully overheated room. I thought I should die and sweated like those spongy water ferns met with in Italian grottoes. My cold is now feverish. Sat next to Juliet Duff and Lys Connolly. Alvilde there but we could not speak. Walked away with James who told me his mother is to have a serious abdominal operation. Tonight Alvilde took me to the French ballet – *Carmen* vigorous and sexy – and we dined at the Dorchester. Her beauty is proud, guarded, even shrouded. Rather Pre-Raphaelite in manner, not in substance. She has had a sad married life, if it can be called married. Cecil Beaton invited us both to meet Nancy for dinner, but we decided we would be happier alone.

Friday, 18th March

Drove the Eshers to Upton [House, Warwickshire] for the day. It was too long an outing, and with my cold I felt rotten. Bridget took me to a film première of Oliver Messel's *Queen of Spades*; beautiful décor by him; Louis Quinze dresses superb. Edith Evans as the raddled old

[163]

countess in her element. I sat next to Rose Macaulay who talked throughout the performance.

Stayed in all day on account of my cold. Alvilde called with a bottle of champagne for our dinner here tonight. Sent a car for me and we went to *The Heiress*, an absolutely splendid production with Ralph Richardson and Peggy Ashcroft. He is invariably natural which few English actors seem to be. Her performance is unforgettable. A great actress when she sheds the affected, suburban delivery. Alvilde and I dined at home over her champagne. I took her back to the Dorchester and left her there. My cold is still very bad. I am in a daze. I do not quite realize what has happened to me. This is the first time that a woman I have loved has loved me. I say 'loved' which is totally different to 'lusted after'. I have had plenty of reciprocal lust of one kind and another. I want to be with her all the time. My cold makes the situation even more unreal, and me surely unappetizing. Which goes to show . . . What? Her nobility and sincerity.

Stay indoors all day except to go to Mass. Still feel ill. Try to write fitfully. The reality of this love dawns on me slowly like creeping paralysis. One becomes a victim to a great power that is irresistible. How selfish I have been hitherto, all the stony way to middle age, in full control of my emotions, and probably cruel at times. I meet A. this evening. We tried Soho and could get in nowhere, so ended at the Mirabelle where we had a very expensive and perfectly filthy meal. Then returned home and talked and made plans for the summer. We are very happy.

A. and I lunched at the oyster bar, Wilton's. This evening she came round here and we ate honey sandwiches and drank tea, sitting on the floor in front of the fire. She left to dine with Anthony who came over from Paris this evening.

Motored Alvilde from the Dorchester to Victoria. Put her into the Golden Arrow, and left. I sent her a telegram and posted her a long letter. Then went to the ballet – Danilova in *Coppélia* – with Sheila Plunkett. Very enjoyable. Although S. said Danilova's neck and back showed age I did not notice it. Danilova's precision is wonderful. It is the steadiness and sureness of the older dancers that convey necessary confidence to the spectator. A lifetime's arrival at perfection. The young ones will dance as well in time. Dined at the Lyric. S. is a dear, so gay and laughing, and very pretty and distinguished.

Wednesday, 23rd March

This morning we had a Reorganization Committee in the office. Satisfactory for it laid down general principles. We, the staff, now know where we stand. Esher of course always says that general principles are arrived at only to be disregarded. Jack Rathbone is very sensible and understanding, and grasps the situation of our peculiar, sensitive, dedicated staff, which must be totally unlike the staff of most organizations, and maddening to an outsider. In the luncheon interval went to the Abbey to look at Ben Jonson's stone with the four words, 'O Rare Ben Jonson', which moved A. so much. In the afternoon to Dr Johnson's House in Gough Square. It has a handful of important relics compared with the quantity of Carlyliana in our Carlyle's House. It is however more attractively furnished than the other because it has carpets and curtains. Rick means to enliven Carlyle's.

Thursday, 24th March

Depressed because no letter from A. today and as yet – 9 p.m. – no telephone call.

This morning I went on a small deputation with Crawford, Esher, [Ruby] Holland-Martin and the Admiral [Bevir] to give evidence before the Gowers Committee set up by the Chancellor of the Exchequer, at the Treasury, a fine early Georgian room. It was an interesting and enjoyble experience, conducted informally. I sat between Esher and Anthony Blunt. All very nice people and I was greeted by Ansell and Sir Cyril Fox. Crawford launched the discussion. He was very nervous and repetitive and was sweating. This surprised me. But dear Lord Esher, who never lets one down, contributed wise and weighty interpolations. How excellent he is in dealing with civil service minds. The chairman and others raised a number of questions which we answered adequately. I found myself speaking up rather a lot. After all I do know a good deal about this subject. The issue lies between us and the Ministry of Works. I felt that general sympathy was with us, and believed that we made a good case. Lady Anderson asked one or two pertinent questions – and me to the ballet next week.

Jamesey came at 6 o'clock. I told him about Alvilde. At first he made wild and preposterous guesses. When I disclosed, he was amazed and delighted, and encouraged unreservedly. When he left I got worried, but at 11 o'clock she rang up. Line as clear as though she were in the room. Her usual firm, take-it-or-leave-it, fierce little voice. I knew she was pleased really, and I went to bed happy.

Friday, 25th March

That beloved man Lord Esher accompanied Rick and me to Carlyle's House, and endorsed all our ideas for improving the place, and the conditions of poor, wretched Mrs Strong, the caretaker, and her husband.

Saturday, 26th March

A fine, bright, sunshiny day, everything singing. I motored in a clean car to Stratfield Saye, arriving luncheon time. The Willy Kings and a Commander Thwaite staying. Gerry [Wellington] at his most entertaining and charming, although fussy. For example, he came into the drawing-room and saw me with my feet, in perfectly clean evening shoes, poised lightly on an ordinary footstool. He rushed up with newspapers, seized my feet, arranged the papers on the stool, and banged down the said feet, exclaiming, 'It never occurred to me that anyone would actually put a foot on a footstool.' There were similar protests from time to time. He made a considerable fuss because Viva, on going to bed, took upstairs a tumbler of water. G. confided to me in a desperate air that this would mean the tumbler never returning to its allotted place downstairs. Henceforth it would for ever belong to the housemaids' pantry where the glasses were of a different pattern. Food bad and little to drink. Thwaite a dull man, also G.'s librarian; and the party not gay. I did not on the whole much enjoy it, although I usually enjoy G.'s company and anecdotes. We motored to a distant antique shop where I bought a small oil sketch, which G. said might be by Poussin, for £2. He was rather put out, pretending that he had seen it first.

I went to Mass on Sunday morning at Heckfield House. Willy King has no manners and his appearance is grotesque – face blue all over like a parakeet. At first he is taciturn but after a bit warms up and is funny but caustic.

Monday, 28th March

At 10.30 picked up Jack Rathbone at Reading station and drove to Banbury where we lunched. On to Upton and showed him the house and garden. He was very impressed by the condition of both. Then to Charlecote which was looking perfectly beastly. He remarked on the deplorable state of the garden. We stayed at Stratford-on-Avon and went to an excellent English film with Zimmerlin, the divine Austrian girl I saw in *The Wild Duck*, as heroine of a displaced persons' camp. Went to Evensong in Shakespeare's church and were accosted by the vicar, an old queen and friend of Noël Coward.

Tuesday, 29th March

This morning to Hidcote in impenetrable mist. Nothing out for it is not exactly a spring garden; even so, tidy, and Jack admired the layout; also appreciated Albert the head gardener. Then to Packwood looking magnificently polished and shining. Then Coughton and dear Lady Throckmorton. Had tea with her. I had written explaining that I was bringing the new Secretary to make her acquaintance. She drew me aside afterwards and said, 'Jim, who is this nice little man?' Then to Malvern, and stayed at the Abbey Hotel.

Wednesday, 30th March

With Colin Jones [the Area Agent] we motored over the Malvern properties, ending with Colwall and Rayner Wood. J. has a habit of taking a person's arm, Lady T.'s, Rayner Wood's and in a confidential whisper begging them when in difficulties to communicate with him at once. Too affable, this. He is a good companion, gay and understanding, with acute sense of humour. But lacking *gravitas*.

Got home before 6 o'clock to find a note from my father. He has seen a specialist who reports a growth on his bladder. He is to go to a home in Queen's Gate next Monday to have bladder opened up and diagnosed lest it be malignant. This worries me a good deal. Mama is to stay here for a week at least. A. telephoned as arranged at 6 o'clock. She writes every day, as do I.

Went to *Coppélia* again, with Lady Anderson in the Royal Box. Danilova ill and Swanelia taken by Moyra Shearer who is far better, with beautiful legs and arms and hands. It is a pretty ballet indeed. We ate, in the little room behind the box, a course during each interval, a most civilized manner of dining. The box and room so elegant and Edwardian. I sat next to a very young Princess Murat who is in London to learn typewriting, and Susan Lowndes that was, now married to a Portuguese and living in Lisbon, charming. Was driven back to Belgrave Square in Chips Channon's Rolls. Had a drink with him and Peter Coats in Peter's bedroom, he being ill in bed. Chips imparted some astounding information not to be recorded alas, but which will be remembered.

Helen Dashwood lunched at the Allies Club to meet Robin Fedden. She was in a gay mood and liked Robin who is to go to West Wycombe [Park] and try to unravel those ghastly knots. This evening went to a cocktail party given by Mrs Carr and the Lothians. It was the usual hellish squash and agony. I literally fought my way in and out. I don't believe either the hosts or guests enjoy these entertainments. Then why are they given and attended? I then called for Garrett Moore and drove him to Hampstead to dine with the Kenneth Clarks. Admirable hosts. One other guest only, an Australian woman, artist and swimmer, pretty and rather bitchy. Talked a lot with Jane Clark who is very easy. Her husband's gracious manner – I don't think he cares for men one bit – frightens me. Yet he arouses my fervent admiration. He is a sort of Jupiter in intellect.

No letter from A. either yesterday or this morning. Drove to luncheon at St Clere, a house belonging to Mr [Ronnie] Norman's eldest son Hugh. Mr Norman called in my office this morning to consult about painting the pine panelling of the hall and asked who might advise. I said I was going to Penshurst this afternoon and offered my services, if he wanted them. So he telephoned the son and I went. Nice, large red brick early Georgian house somewhat spoilt by a rich grandfather in Victorian times.

Penshurst had a reopening of state rooms ceremony. Bill de Lisle invited me which was kind. He has greatly improved the place since I was there ten years ago. Some of the furniture is superb. Crowds of people from the museum world, Leigh Ashton, Summerson, Gerry Wellington, etc.

In the hall at Penshurst Gerry W. drew me aside and pointing at the screen said, 'Look at that classical entablature. The whole thing is pure Batty Langley and not medieval at all.' I am always ready to be convinced, and was. Then I told John Summerson who said, 'Nonsense. It is not eighteenth-century, but pure Jacobean.' I was convinced again. Now I am not sure and think it is made up.

On return to London no letter from A. today. Was worried and unhappy, so telephoned her at Jouy. She said she had written every day.

Felt quite calm and content this morning having spoken to A. last night. By the first post received two letters from her. While reading them Emily handed me a telegram asking me to ring again tonight because she was anxious. So I again fell into a state of *angst*. Goodness, the absurdities of love. Just before luncheon came a letter from Dr Astley, my father's doctor at Wickhamford, announcing that he had received a report from the London specialist of 'exceedingly grave' news. The tumour on the bladder was almost certainly malignant. I telephoned the nursing clinic where Papa is to go on Monday and spoke to the matron. She confirmed that the specialist was right in his diagnosis. She advised that we should await the chemical examination of the piece of tumour to be extracted on Monday before telling Mama, who as yet knows nothing; not till then will they be sure they can operate properly and remove the whole tumour. Everything will depend upon how bad it is. If bad, I gather nothing can be done. I telephoned Dick [my brother] at Shaw. He is a great comfort and help and strongly advised against telling any member of the family until the diagnosis is known.

I telephoned Wickhamford this evening and both parents spoke to me from their beds, sounding quite cheerful and cosy, which made me feel how pathetic they were in their ignorance. I telephoned Paris and spoke to A. who was unhappy because she had received no letter today and would not now have one until Monday. Heavens, what mixed emotions!

Worked at my book, correcting rather than composing, my mind concentrated upon Papa's illness. Dined with Alick Beattie and Ivor Newton, the pianist, an old pussy cat not attractive and rather common. He played a little Chopin after dinner.

Met Mama and Papa at Paddington at 11.30 and motored him to the Queen's Gate Clinic. Took her to lunch at the Allies Club. At 4.30 she and I went back to the Clinic and found him coming round after his operation. The specialist removed two small growths in the bladder through the penis, which is almost unbelievable. Mama is staying with me in the flat, she having my room, I sleeping in the back of Geoffrey's [Houghton-Brown] drawing-room. She insisted on meeting, with me, the specialist's assistant, who told her Papa would have to return every three to six months for observation, which alarmed her, but nothing further. I made an appointment to see Millin, the specialist who did the operation.

I lunched with Sibyl, sat next to Leigh Ashton and Lady Salter. Lady Hudson, widow of Lord Northcliffe, a rather jolly old lady, slightly deaf, was there.

At 6 o'clock I saw the specialist who told me that he had indeed removed two malignant growths. He assured me my father could only live two years at most, that the growths were bound to return. He advised against telling either him or my mother the truth unless the analysis next week reveals something even more serious than what he has already discovered.

Historic Buildings Committee this morning very long and dull. Nothing of interest beyond designs of memorial plaques. One controversial question arose over the restoration of the Roman remains at Housesteads Camp. I consider that there is no conflict between aestheticism and Ministry of Works restoration of these archaeological remains whose interest is exclusively historical. I except of course the Roman wall itself which is undeniably beautiful and romantic, serpentining across the Northumbrian hills.

Went to see Lady Berwick at 5.30. She begged there should be no opening ceremony at Attingham until the end of the summer. My father looks so well and has such a good colour that it is difficult to believe he can be seriously ill. He eats well. Mama has, thank God, accepted my equivocations. Alvilde telephoned from Paris this evening while she was in the room. A. suspected she was present and asked me. I said yes, and she rang off. Then I told Mama our story, sent her to bed, and rang up A. again after 11 o'clock. Woke her up. Mama said Clara Mitchell – foolish woman – told her today that I was handsome. My dear mother told Clara she was talking rot; and as she (Mama) had given birth to me she knew I was nothing of the sort. Rather sweet of her.

Received a letter from John Betj[eman] in which he mentioned that Basil Champneys died in April 1935 and would, if alive, be 107. Did I remember taking him to dinner with the Champneys in Church Row,

Hampstead? Architecture was never mentioned, as though to be a professional architect was not quite the thing socially, although the old man did talk about 'my friend Mr [Coventry] Patmore' and less enthusiastically about 'that Father Gerard Hopkins'. What I do well recall is our having to go into the dining-room arm-in-arm. I was to take in the daughter, and J.B. Mrs Champneys, who was very grand and correct. She had greying hair brushed back and wore a gown with train. John could not remember which arm to proffer. She gave him no help and stood up motionless like a statue, waiting. John jazzed around, caught my eye, in which anxiety and embarrassment were blended, and dissolved into giggles.

Jamesey lunched at the Allies Club and was *distrait* and inattentive, but we ended by laughing like mad over some Algerian wine. I bought some shoes for him and went to the dentist who took three-quarters of an hour extracting a nerve. This operation left me in pain and very exhausted. Then Dick came to Brooks's where we had a long talk. I was relieved to see him. He approved of what I had so far done and is sure that withholding the truth is right. I am so glad.

At 6 o'clock to Miss Ethel Sands. She is charming, the most charming ugly woman I have met. She has a delightful soft, sincere laugh, a running laugh with a lilt that misleads a little, making one suspect she may not be simpler than she appears. I was perished by the cold wind. She was kind and asked me to come again. Clive Bell there, very affable and talkative. He said Desmond MacCarthy does a wonderful imitation of Henry James recounting with much earnestness the appalling treatment Ethel Sands received, when a girl, from her mother who was a noted beauty and a cruel woman. Dick dined with Ma and me at Thurloe Square.

Friday, 8th April

Lunched at 5 Belgrave Square with Peter Coats and Chips Channon. Sat next Sylvia Compton. She told me she was fifty. She is great fun with her stories. She said George Lloyd would always ask penetrating questions about matters of world importance and expect immediate answers. He liked her company so long as she gave quick retorts, no matter whether sensible or silly.

Went to see Doreen and had a gossip.

Monday, 11th April

Papa and Mama went home today. They seemed so pleased and I pray that by some miracle he may be all right. Mama very sweet and considerate yet I find her a little tiring because she cannot concentrate upon one topic at a

[171]

time. She says she will not come to London this summer to meet Hugh Macdonell because he upsets her so much and she is now determined to do nothing to distress Papa. Evidently at the age of sixty-five she is still moved to love. She advised me to love Alvilde while I could, adding that this was perhaps not the advice a mother should give a son. James called last night while I was with Papa. They got on like a house on fire.

Tuesday, 12th April

I lunched with Giles Eyre at the Travellers', a happy, mundane youth, and a little *affairé*. At 6 o'clock sat in the Travellers' with David Crawford and the Admiral talking over the Gowers' Committee evidence. Crawford is so vague I wonder how he gets any work done. Dined with the Kings. A very enjoyable, giggly dinner. Ruth Lowinsky and Robert Cecil from the Wallace Collection, whom I liked. He too was immensely amused by Willie who was rather tipsy and beetroot-coloured. Viva shouted at him, 'Willie, do keep your mouth shut when you are eating. Nobody wants to see what you have got inside it.' And after dinner, 'Willie, don't sit so close to Robert, and Robert, don't let Willie tickle your face with his beard.' Alvilde telephoned at 10.30 and I gave way and said I would fly to Paris on Thursday to stay with her. Weakness, for I ought to stay at home and work.

Wednesday, 13th April

Dined tonight with John Lehmann at his covetable house in Egerton Crescent. Guests were Sibyl Colefax, Miss Ethel Sands, Peter Quennell and an unknown woman. Much Sibyl talk of famous people she had known, such as Robbie Ross. John Lehmann and Peter Q. complained that there were in England no young authors with any style; that in their young days their elders, like Lytton Strachey, kept them up to the mark. How often have not these sorts of complaint been exchanged by the middle-aged? Peter's wit and brilliance always impress me but his malice is without any limit. I relish it because, so far, it has not been directed at my face, and what is directed at my back I cannot mind, so long as a kind friend does not repeat it.

Thursday, 14th April

The office shut at noon for the holidays. I, who had decided after all to go to Jouy-en-Josas, collected my ticket and, having worked in the afternoon, bought A. an Easter egg made of Sèvres porcelain and another

[172]

smaller one for Clarissa [Chaplin] and left by the 5 o'clock plane for Paris. A wonderful day but I felt so full of misgivings that I was nearly sick. Fortified myself in the air with brandy and water. Landed at Le Bourget and was met by A. looking beautiful and radiant at the Invalides. She took me to a restaurant for dinner, I consuming a whole bottle of white wine and a liqueur with the result that, although blissfully happy to be with her, I was reduced to a state of nervous idiocy. We drove to Jouy-en-Josas. Her house Le Mé Chaplin most picturesquely set on a hill with Turneresque view over a valley, crossed by a Louis XIV aquaduct in the background. The village of Jouy hidden by misty trees below. The moon was shining like day, the nightingales singing like sopranos, everything as romantic as could be desired while, arm-in-arm, we walked into the garden and into the house where Anthony was playing Mozart on the piano.

Friday, Good Friday, 15th April

The actual house is modern and unbeautiful but filled with A.'s pretty things. Doors of glass and huge windows open upon a garden of enchantment. It is a summer retreat. We went in the morning to the village. The church all shut and dark and dead, the tabernacle door wide open, the dove flown as though God were deliberately withholding himself from me. This evening the four of us (Clarissa is here) motored to Dampière and looked at the outside of the Luynes château, most impressive, Mansard's work, with detached wings and forecourt and, on the far side of the road, a stone balustraded 'lay-by' as it is called today in Great North Road jargon. We dined and drank Suze which tastes of gentian. Anthony behaves wonderfully to me. We are a sort of blood brothers. His conversation with Clarissa, aged fifteen, about his love affairs and sex life makes my hair stand on end, but not hers evidently. How much, I wonder, should one believe?

Tuesday, 19th April

I return today, A. having motored me to Paris. This visit has been unsurpassed. It exceeded my dreams. Perfect weather, sun shining every day and moon at night. The eyes of God did not blink for one single second. Perhaps it would have been better if they had. The country at its zenith, the hyacinths and tulips out by day, the nightingales and tree frogs by night. Like little green toys or jade jewels they look so pretty, until they croak when their chests expand hideously like a monstrous goitre or a balloon one wants to prick. Anthony took us to a marsh

[173]

where these creatures on warm nights congregate and sing in thousands, so that the chorus is like a canonade. He says their voices were the first animal voices heard on earth – a very impressive thought. I sat on the terrace of my room writing, or in the garden reading, talking and laughing. Anthony is delighted because A. is made happy. Was there ever a more topsy-turvy business?

One morning we walked about Versailles, round the Trianon and the Temple d'Amour. Another day we took a picnic luncheon and drove to Chartres, never seen by me before. Surely no blue glass like this exists anywhere else in the world. It has a particular cerulean, jewel-like quality. The solemn grey cathedral is untouched by time and accident.

Thursday, 21st April

Motored today to Biddlesden Park, close to Stowe, in well-wooded Buckinghamshire country. It was in 1937 I went to see this house for the National Trust and recommended acceptance. Now the same owner Colonel Badger and his wife, very nice people, entertained me again to luncheon and showed me round. I had forgotten it entirely and after this second visit read my first report made twelve years ago and was surprised at the things I had noticed. I then motored to Wickhamford and stayed the night. It was Papa's sixty-ninth birthday. He is thinner and does not eat much. Deenie and Colonel Sidney, lately widowered, dined and we drank champagne in celebration of this most melancholy little event. Colonel Sidney is seventy today and is absolutely miserable.

Friday, 22nd April

Spent all day happily at Charlecote on ladders, sticking labels on the pictures or walls, the sort of occupation I most love, with the new caretaker, a nice man, having had to say goodbye to Wickers, the late caretaker and wife who were practically in tears. I felt so sorry for them. Dear people. On my return I found two letters from A., one depressed, so I telephoned her.

Monday, 25th April

After a National Buildings Record meeting I met Alvilde at Kensington air station and motored her to the Dorchester. The Bearsteds had travelled over in the same plane. As I said to A. one can never get away with any secret, however much one tries. Therefore it is better not to try. We went to the ballet at Covent Garden, Prokofiev's *Cinderella*. A little too pantomimey, but Freddie Ashton and Bobby Helpman as the ugly sisters were extremely funny. The Queen attended but since she sat right above us we saw her not. We went for a drink of champagne in the Clarks' box in the interval and dined afterwards in the restaurant of the Dorchester.

Went to A. at the Dorchester at 4.30. Then to the Courtauld Institute to hear the first of Count Metternich's lectures – this one excellent – on German architecture of the seventeenth century. Returned to A. at the Dorchester but dined alone since she had to go to the ballet again with Clarissa and the Clarks.

To the Goldsmiths' Hall this morning to look at their Renaissance silver, the Bowes Cup being very Holbeinesque; and an exquisite little salt dated 1522 quite classical by comparison, although about fifty years earlier. Lunched at the Allies Club with A. and Anthony and Oggy Lynn.

A. and I went by air to Paris this afternoon, I having to make untruthful excuses to the office, and feeling guilty and unhappy. She gave me a little gold toothpick as a present. We dined at Albert's again and motored to Jouy. We stopped at the same corner of the road near the village to listen to the same nightingale that we heard singing on my first evening a fortnight ago exactly. Anthony remains in London and Clarissa away. Terrible black moments of despair are mercifully redeemed by moments of unadulterated bliss. I suppose this is often the case. Neither can be described.

On Friday morning we were taken round Versailles by the curator, a young man called Van der Kemp, previously arranged by A. I was so shy about my bad French that I could not converse intelligently. I feel desperately ashamed because when I left Grenoble University in 1927 I spoke like a bird. Van der Kemp took us not only into the state rooms but into the *petits appartements* of the Pompadour and du Barry, not seen by the public. *Petits* they are, and enchanting. In Marie Antoinette's boudoir her own clock played tunes for us, little airs specially composed for it by Mozart, Glück and others. The pathos of it. These rooms must

[175]

be the most exquisite in the world. In my youth I used to despise French architecture for being effeminate and effete. How I dared, contemptible fool that I was. The prejudices of adolescence make one blush in remembrance. We walked upon the lead roof of the palace and admired the formal rides and parterres.

We went to George Chavchavadze's concert of Mozart and Schumann concerti, lovely works which A. said he played badly – he had a horribly inflamed eye; then to a party the Chavchavadzes gave in Noël Coward's flat in the Place Vendôme. Awful, it was. A. says French society is less intellectual and more superficial than English. It is certainly more sophisticated and alarming.

Saturday we went to Chantilly. Had the most excellent luncheon I ever ate, and then round the castle, looking at the pictures – the Clouet drawings and Fouquet illuminations. To tea at the Duff Coopers', a delightful Louis XV villa with an English garden lolling down to a lake with weeping willows and a cascade. The Walter Elliots staying. She a red-faced, horsey-looking English woman, yet clever and non-horsey, but plain and badly dressed. He speaks with a broad Scotch accent. Lady Diana wearing trousers and cowboy jacket with large silver buttons and cowboy hat. She is very offhand. When I left she was lounging across a chair, did not get up or proffer a hand, so I mumbled goodbye and followed A. out.

We are ecstatically happy alone, and dined at home. All Sunday spent at Jouy in the sun. A. is considered one of the best-dressed women in France, which for an English woman is some compliment.

Tuesday, 3rd May

I flew back from Paris yesterday morning. Today left at 9 o'clock for Barnstaple. Was met at the station by Eardley wearing corduroys and a French beret and Raymond Mortimer, with his black, now greying, but thick curly hair, always hatless, chain-smoking, dusty, talkative and enthusiastic. Typical Bloomsbury in his disregard of clothes. Do they consider sartorial elegance synonymous with mental degeneracy? R.'s exaggerated voice is like a raven's croak. We spent the afternoon at Arlington Court, a forbidding, gloomy, neo-Grecian house, stacked with some 200 cases of old ship models and chests and chests of shells and other bric-à-brac. The trees all over-mature, intergrown and 'gone back'; the park a jungle. Miss Chichester who left us Arlington was very eccentric and during her last eighteen months spent £35,000 buying whatever junk she could get hold of. She must have been cheated by agents she employed to buy these things at sales and auctions. It was

[176]

wicked of her solicitors not to restrain the poor old lady. Surrounding country very beautiful and remote. We stay the night at Lyndale Hotel, Lynmouth.

Wednesday, 4th May

Walked up Watersmeet this morning. Then drove back to Arlington, worked there, picnicked on terrace and drove to Exeter. E. and I to the Cathedral. A young verger showed us the tomb effigies repainted by Tristram. One I approved of for it was a judicious restoration, the old colours having been lightly touched up, a Siena patina predominating. The others were too gaudy. The fifteenth-century chantry tombs are very fine. Then we motored to Long Crichel for the night, stopping at Lyme Regis where at 7.45 we failed to get a meal at any hotel and finally had beastly, greasy fish and chips at a lorry-drivers' café. Raymond very indignant. Found Eddy [Sackville-West] in his crotchety, querulous and spiky mood.

Friday, 6th May

Motored Jack Rathbone to Polesden Lacey and Hatchlands. At Hatchlands where Goodhart-Rendel took us round gardens and house I was deeply impressed by the learnedness of the man. There is nothing he cannot talk about wittily and to the point. His trouble is that he speaks too much and with such rapidity that persons like me have difficulty keeping pace with the trend of his thoughts. I like him and we have many subjects in common.

Went to a poor play (Alec Guinness, that great actor) about Dr Simpson who discovered chloroform.

Sunday, 8th May

All this weekend at home working fairly well. Had besides time for reflection. No letter from A. this morning – Saturday, I mean – and great difficulty getting through to her on the telephone. Have felt very lonely.

Monday, 9th May

To the National Gallery to see the Munich pictures. Only managed three rooms within an hour, chiefly of Flemish and German painting. Colours of the Dirk Bouts startling. A Guardi of a concert in Venice and a

[177]

Botticelli Pietà detained me. The Grünewald mocking of Christ very terrible.

To Ockwells with Carew Wallace to approve a site for a Dutch barn. Went for quarter of an hour to St George's Chapel. Wonderful though this Perpendicular fan vaulting is, it is never tenuous enough. I like the theatrical monument to Princess Charlotte, her soul flying skywards leaving her shrouded body on the ground. The Reid Dick effigy of George V is pretty awful. On my way back I stopped at Cranford. The house has been swept away as has every single one of the pleasant Georgian villas of the village, now a wreck of its former self. Only some broken-down garden walls and gate-piers to the big house remain, a shocking commentary. The church very pretty seventeenth-century, with several fine tombs and mural monuments. The Berkeley family has associations with this place.

Tuesday, 10th May

Whereas there were two letters from A. yesterday there are none today. The unpredictability of the post is disturbing. I prefer to have one letter a day to two every other day. I bought two seats for *Das Rheingold* for ourselves on Thursday and ordered a table for supper at the Savoy. I ought to have asked the Clarks but want to have A. to myself. Went to the Munich pictures again and looked at the later ones, two lovely Claudes in early morning light, Rembrandts and two Poussins. Murillo fine.

Jamie Caffery dined with me at Brooks's. I drank too much – 2 glasses of sherry, ½ bottle of Burgundy and 1 glass port – and felt ill next day. When shall I ever learn? Caffery is a handsome-ugly young tough of twenty-nine, with fine straight hair like powdered gold. Face cruel in repose and mouth of no shape. Comes from the American upper crust, whatever that means. He told me he has a great-grandmother alive. His sister has a child of ten, so the old lady is a great-great-grandmother. Unusual.

Wednesday, 11th May

Went to Munich pictures again, to look at Rubens and Vandyke. Then to Sotheby's with Robin Fedden and checked the condition of the tapestries to be lent to Little Moreton Hall. Then to tea with Lady Binning who, dear woman, is becoming another cross. She is so lonely that my heart bleeds, whereas hers melts.

[178]

Count and Countess Metternich and the Eshers lunched here. Then I met Alvilde at Kensington Air Terminal. Took her to *Das Rheingold* at Covent Garden which bored me fiercely. I only enjoyed the clever way the Rhinemaidens swam round the rock upon thin wires. We dined at the Savoy.

This evening after my committees I met A. at Thurloe Square where Jamesey came to say goodbye. She and I motored off for the weekend. We stayed the night at Harleyford Manor on the Thames. This was the best night's lodging we were to have, for the food was excellent and the beds comfortable. Otherwise a squalid, adulterous place run by peroxide blondes. Nothing dusted, tooth tumblers unwashed. Yet still a country house with Clayton family pictures on the walls, a lovely house once, a true riverside villa built by Sir Robert Taylor. We were told the proprietor was a Clayton, a curious déclassé sort of man, as much gone to seed as his house, only less handsome.

Poor A. trying to choke down a bad cold. We motored to Bibury and stayed at the Swan, she spending the day at Hatherop Castle school with Clarissa whose confirmation took place today.

We took Clarissa and Barbara Moray's daughter Arabella Stuart out from school for the day, starting with a drink before luncheon with David Stuart at his house in Coln St Aldwyns. He looks a sweet, pretty little boy of eighteen, whereas he is already a widower, aged I don't know what, for his wife, Mrs Fyfe's daughter, died giving birth to a son. David lives here with the baby and his wife's ten-year-old daughter by a former husband. After lunching at Bibury we drove to Newark Park for me to see the house offered to the Trust. It is of little importance and the most desolate and gloomy place imaginable, miles from anywhere. The house, basically a mid–sixteenth-century hunting-box, has one window of that date with pediment over Corinthian columns. Otherwise done over in the late eighteenth cent. with stucco composition and fake battlements. Interior of simple, classical decoration. The site overlooking a Cotswold coomb with overgrown view towards the

Severn estuary, unsurpassed. We left this Wagnerian haunt for Nether Lypiatt. During tea a sudden storm arose out of a blue sky. Lightning struck the water tank at the top of the house, burst a main pipe and flooded the drawing-room, ruining the ceiling. Our hosts were desperately searching for buckets and in their panic producing tea cups to stem the devastating tide. What a bore children are! The two girls giggled over the disaster like zanies. I never know how one should treat them. I adopt the jocular attitude until I, and they, grow tired.

A. and I stayed the night at Cricklade. We find country hotels and narrow beds and paper-thin walls, and unbrushed carpets, and baths with rusted enamel and soap dishes with extinguished cigarette stubs in them, unpalatable. The church here has a tower of 1550 in Perpendicular style built by John Dudley. The tower is carved with Elizabethan conceits, banners coming out of hearts and playing-cards in stone. The Tudors were given to emblems, riddles, divination and subterfuge. They liked nothing straightforward and composed in allegories and mystical terminology.

Monday, 16th May

A. and I to Chedworth Roman Villa where we met both Eshers, Eardley, Smith, Jones and Clouting the Ministry of Works expert, whom we severely chastised for his pedantic treatment of the remains. A. very bored with them, preferring ruins above to below ground, and longed to move me on. We picnicked at the Villa which was fun.

After dinner in London I took A. to Victoria and saw her off in the ferry. Both full of red wine and tears.

Friday, 20th May

By train to Llandudno yesterday, and at Bodnant met Hubert Smith who arrived by car. We stayed the night with the Aberconways. I like Lady A. with her lovely skin and blue eyes, all pearly. She purses her mouth and is very affected. Nevertheless I don't understand why people laugh at her so much. He is incredibly stiff yet genial in an old-fashioned keep-your-distance manner. I find this famous garden frankly ugly and lacking taste. I don't like conifers and rhododendrons. The layout has no symmetry, and is over-packed with trees and shrubs. There are no vistas, glades or open spaces. It is not picturesque. I am not interested in rare shrubs. The garden is merely an expensive nursery arboretum. All the urns and architectural adjuncts are likewise ugly and the house the most graceless I have ever beheld. I admire the Aberconways, however, and they are both charming to me. Yet I could never love either of them. She showed me a long passage O. Sitwell has written about her in his new book which could not be more complimentary, and is a tribute to her intellect. I am suffering from terrible sciatica from much recent motoring, and sitting in the train; the worst for years.

Sunday, 22nd May

Some fiend impels me to go on writing this diary which no one will want to read, not even my great-great-nephews and nieces. I used to keep it at the end of each day. Now I allow intervals to elapse, sometimes as long as a week when I forget the salient events to record. It is a vice, an indulgence. Now that I write every day to Alvilde and tell her my days, it is a case of duplication.

Tonight I dined with Bridget in her new house in Eaton Terrace, which was, and maybe still is, Anne's. B. has made it not pretty exactly, which it definitely was in Anne's time, but conventional. Then I went to join Anne and Harold Acton at Oliver Messel's. When I arrived they were still seated round the table lit from silver candlesticks, and drinking champagne at 10.30. Harold, rather intoxicated, saying outrageous things in front of Susan, Anne's child, whose presence nevertheless somewhat cramped the adult style. Van the Dane, tiresome in boasting how he quarrelled with all Oliver's friends whom he suspected of trying 'to get things out of' Oliver for nothing. Disingenuous, I thought. In any case what gossipy, fatuous conversation this is.

Tuesday, 24th May

Went to the Chelsea Flower Show for the first time and straightway met Bridget, Diane Abdy and Lady Sibell Rowley. Diane and I made for the Aberconways' tent and had a scrumptious tea and iced coffee. Then both looked at some of the show. I never knew flowers could be forced into such size: delphiniums 12 ft high, begonias like dishes and everything too big and unnatural. David Bowes-Lyon dragged me off to see the Hidcote stall of common geraniums which we thought *quel-conque*. He came back here for two minutes and seemed keen that we should go on a motor tour in August. A curious man he is. Then went to a sherry party given by Margaret Jourdain and Ivy C.-B., both of whom have made so much money from their respective books lately that they admit to being rich. This is rather touching. I am glad. Ivy's novel is coming out next month.

[181]

Motored to West Wycombe and looked around. The grounds far tidier. Johnnie Dashwood there wearing a blue beret and carrying a huge axe. He took me to watch six men blow up a tree trunk with gunpowder. Then [Captain John] Hill took me to Bradenham House, now a school for very young children. It is the house which Disraeli's father rented, a very homely red brick William and Mary building, with terraced garden. In spite of quantities of children the gathering was more like a large family party than an institutional half holiday, in fact what a pause in a school curriculum ought to be.

As time goes by I miss A. more and more. After a month I yearn to see her and be with her. Yet what can be done? I do not know. I am longing for next Friday with great desire. Mama has written me a long letter telling me to put A. before my religion and marry her. But would A. agree to this? It would mean altering her life completely, selling Jouy in order to live in England with me, and be tied to London which she would not like. The alternative is for me to throw up my job and live altogether in France, on her money. This I could not do. So what? I cannot help looking ahead to the time when she may not love me any longer. Then where would we both be, with me an incubus round her neck? I should not look ahead perhaps. It is strange how love unfolds itself like a gigantic scroll of which only the lettering immediately under the eyes is clearly readable, the rest being lost in misty lines. Now the last time I saw my father he said that he was sorry about the condition I had got myself into; that of course there was no predicament, for being a Papist I could not possibly contemplate marriage. He spoke nicely, but knowing his loathing of Catholicism I detected in his eye a glint of *Schadenfreude*. 'I told you so,' and 'You are reaping what you have sown,' and other reproachful expressions were hovering about his lips.

Bridget and I went to *The Snake Pit*, the film about a woman who had a breakdown and was put into an American asylum. Not very convincing although acted extremely well. It was not as harrowing as it ought to have been. I don't believe nurses behave with the callousness evinced in this film.

To the opera with the Andersons in the Royal Box – *Siegfried*, which I enjoyed, especially the last act with Flagstad whose voice rolls over one like gigantic waves on shingle. Cecil Beaton in the box for two acts. He giggled with me in the lavatory during the second interval over Sir John's bossiness, for he orders everyone about and spars with his wife, but, I think, good-humouredly really. He is a dour Scot and resembles a disapproving family butler. Lady A. remarked that Daisy Fellowes was looking ill. 'I didn't notice it,' he retorted downright, 'I thought she was looking old.' Caroline Paget there too. Such a whimsical, twisted face she has. Ineffably attractive.

Friday, 3rd June

Motored to Knole this morning in pouring rain to meet members of the Gowers Committee on their jaunt to various country houses. They all turned up except Sir Cyril Fox, and were enthusiastic. Lady Anderson much in evidence, asking fatuous questions. I don't find her rebarbative. On the contrary she is always forthcoming. Anthony Blunt made a number of discoveries among the pictures, the only things in the house he was interested in. Lord Sackville, distinguished and patrician in a tidy blue suit and yellow waistcoat, conducted them round the house very graciously.

At 6 o'clock I flew to Paris. Arrived an hour late. Poor A. waiting at Le Bourget. She motored me to the Venezia restaurant where we dined happily. On to Jouy where we were happier still.

Saturday, 4th June

We are a curious party *à quatre*, for Rosemary Lyttelton is staying. Rosemary is very pretty and very slight, too thin perhaps for some tastes, but evidently not for others'. As A. says, she is *racée*. Her little face is dead-white, her hair auburn which glitters in the sunlight. She reminds me of the young Queen Elizabeth. She is musical, talented and extremely intelligent, well read for her age, and much in love with Anthony who pretends to us to be tired of her because she is too clinging. This is nonsense, of course, and a pose. I fear Anthony is determined by a concatenation of paradoxes and contradictions not to disclose what are his intentions. He treats her very sweetly, however. Anthony has breakfast with A. in her bedroom always, plying her with outrageous questions about us. He is a very strange man. His buffooning becomes irritating after a surfeit.

A. and I motored this morning to Versailles. We walked in the gardens looking at the statuary. This afternoon we motored to Fontainebleau where we went round the apartments which display a wonderful sequence of decoration and furnishing from the time of François Premier to that of Napoleon. I find the F. Premier style slightly sickening, like the monarch himself, a bounder, who was also straitlaced and lascivious. At Fontainebleau is the best of the genre to be found anywhere in France. I am possibly mistaken in despising it, for every style that is distinctive and earnest should be respected, if it cannot be liked. An architectural historian must learn to evaluate every style and not allow his judgments to be swayed by fashionable quirks and prejudices.

Monday, 6th June

Lovely hot day of brilliant sun. Lay in the garden till 5 o'clock when A. and I flew back to London. Were met by her Clarissa and dined here in Thurloe Square.

Tuesday, 7th June

Tonight I had a dinner party – A., of course, the Kenneth Clarks and Paz Subercaseaux. I was alarmed by the prospect of the Clarks and the evening was a strain. But A. came early; so did the Clarks before I expected them. K. walked straight round the room looking hard at everything and assessing everything. He rejected everything out of hand as rubbish beneath contempt except my Renaissance bronze of San Sebastian which he started to polish with the ball of his hand, saying it had silver in it and would brighten with this treatment. He was very agreeable and gracious, but does not put one at ease. I told Jane I was terrified of him and she said, 'Don't let him know.' He is for ever instructing. I admire him more than anyone of my generation for his universal learning. Talking of modern art he said there was only one contemporary English portrait painter, Lawrence Gowing. I don't know how unbiased his judgments of modern art are. I suspect he only recommends artists who are among his circle of friends. We talked of Hampton Court. He agreed that the *grisaille* of the Pope being stoned must be Flemish, certainly northern and not Italian. When the Clarks left the three of us sank back exhausted by the tension and discussed him. We all agreed in giving him unqualified praise for mind and scholarship, and prose. Paz said he was not as great as T. S. Eliot who is creative, and K. is not creative. We agreed too that he lacked the fine human instincts that make people sociable and beloved. Clarissa, aged fifteen, who formerly was frightened of him, told us that having stayed with the Clarks over the weekend, all her fears fled. 'You need not speak to him,' she told A. confidently, 'I have breakfast with him and never address a word to him. He is very easy and mild'!

A. and I lunched at Wilton's, fearfully expensive and very little to eat. Agreed not to go there again when hungry. I motored her to Shalford (Surrey) to look at the Mill House, a National Trust property which I had never seen before and do not wish to see again. Then to Polesden Lacey. Went to *Daphne Laureola*, a very good play with Edith Evans, whose performance was brilliant. A joy to listen to diction which is always clear as a bell. She is as trained as a circus horse. Dined excellently at the Savoy Grill and back to the Dorchester at 11 o'clock. On arrival A. spied her mother-in-law on the doorstep and with utmost presence of mind told me to go on while she jumped out. I asked the cabbie to drive to Chesterfield House. Got out and walked back to Dorchester.

Thursday, 9th June

Trooping of the Colour this morning. The whole of London's traffic disorganized. I had a terrible time getting a new ticket for A. back to Paris. By a stupid mistake I tore hers up thinking it was my old, used one.

I dined with Harold [Nicolson] at the Travellers'. Over a bottle of champagne I told him I needed his advice how best I could work half-time for the National Trust in order to spend the other half with A. in France. Harold mumbled that love was a wonderful thing which must not be thrown away. That was not much help. Then he rambled off in talk about Vita who is ill with a weak heart. Consequently I did not press my point, seeing that I would get no sympathy if I did. I had told A. I would ask Harold for his advice. I failed.

Friday, 10th June

A. has gone. For five weeks I shall not see her, and already the agony has begun. After committee meetings all day I went home to change for the opera. Jamesey, returned from France, came in to talk. His advice is that I should do all in my power to marry by letting A. divorce Anthony, if she wants to. He says it is middle-class to have financial scruples because she has money and I have none, and ridiculous to have religious scruples about divorce; also needless to have moral scruples about Anthony who is a thoroughly selfish, if charming, cad. At least his advice is considered and direct, if expedient. He took his bus conductor friend to France and is taking him to Norway. The friend loves women and treats James with good-natured but rough bonhomie which J. likes. J.'s last remark to me as he jumped into a taxi cab was: 'I am having boxing lessons now.'

[185]

In the Kenneth Clarks' box at Covent Garden heard the last performance of Tristan with Flagstadt as Isolde. She surpassed all criticism. Everyone I spoke to agreed that she is the greatest singer of our age. I was extremely moved throughout. In the box were Christabel Aberconway, Leigh Ashton, the Italian Ambassador and Duchess Gallarotti-Scotti. Drove back to dine at the Clarks' beautiful house and sat next to the Duchess and Yvonne Hamilton who spoke high-speed Italian across me.

Monday, 13th June

A. writes that Oggy Lynn, Paz and the Duff Coopers know all about us. What does it matter, she asks? So now this is general knowledge and she doesn't mind I shall take no pains to conceal it. Took the train to Windermere arriving at 5.30. Stayed the night with the Bruce Thompsons. They are dears, particularly Bruce, but by no means exciting.

Tuesday, 14th June

Bruce motored me to Town End, the little yeoman's home of the Brown family of Troutbeck. He has in his meticulous way tidied it up and made it very neat. It is open daily to the public. The house is pitch-dark and crammed with black varnished oak settles, chests and lace. Then to Hill Top, Beatrix Potter's house, filled to the brim with her things. I cannot help wondering whether the public will be interested in her 100 years hence. Then to Wray Castle, a fascinating, castellated 1840 structure which the National Trust has contemplated pulling down. It has some period charm and a pictorial quality and, although not architecturally important, should be spared. From a distance it is an ornament to the shores of Windermere.

At Ambleside I was handed over to Cuthbert Acland. I now like this severe, censorious man. He took me to Sizergh Castle where we were given luncheon and tea by the Hornyold-Stricklands. Both the Hornyold (he) and the Strickland (she) come of Papist families which survived the bad times, indeed since the Reformation, without a break. Very nice, solid, worthy people too. He may be a bit of a bore with his family pride and genealogy talk. This castle is nothing like so good as nearby Levens, but it is an historic place and worth holding. There is some indifferent furniture, but there are several pictures of interest, notably the Rigaud portraits of the Stuart family. There are Jacobite relics, including diamond earrings given to a Strickland by Charles II. After a deal of talk Mr Hornyold-Strickland agreed to supply in cash the endowment for which we asked. So it was a successful visit and worth my going all this way. Returned to Cubby Acland's charming little plain white house, set at the foot of a wild moor up which we walked among the curlews and seagulls and snipe. Smells of peat bog and heather in the nostrils. Distant fringe of the Lake mountains. I was much struck by the isolated, bachelorish charm of this little establishment, so stark and pretty inside. What a curious fellow he is: very intelligent and quick, with proud craggy features, and deep-set quizzical eyes of a romantic cast. Puritanical, and exuding continence. I took a sleeper back to London.

Wednesday, 15th June

Found my father at Thurloe Square, he having come to stay yesterday. He is a bit thinner but looks extremely fit and feels it, I am glad to say. But he still passes a little blood, which is a worry to him, and to me a horrid prognostication of his fate. He goes to Ascot every day. This evening I went to Jamesey's flat. His new friend, a house painter, was there, wearing a battle-dress and rather grubby. Has a nice open face and laughs in raucous guffaws. I think this sort of association pathetic. What can J. get from it beyond the one thing which is not dispensed because the boy likes girls? Paul Wallraf who walked away with me deplores it very much. He says J. is becoming amoral about money and borrows from his mother and poor friends what they cannot afford in order to make frequent trips abroad, taking friend. Silly business.

Thursday, 16th June

Rather unhappy because I cannot communicate with A. There is a strike in France of telephonists and post offices. So no letters or telegrams, and no talks.

At Batsford's Sam Carr told me they were sacking Charles Fry who has become quite impossible. Their American branch has suffered badly from him. I am not surprised. Yet I am sorry for this clever and deplorable man losing his livelihood in his middle age.

Motored to St John's, Jerusalem to meet the Gowers Committee whom Sir Stephen Tallents showed round and entertained to tea. I can't quite fathom what is in their minds. St John's is merely a pretty little house, readily lettable, without problems. Then I went to Stoneacre which does look rather startling, like an ice cream. We have had it whitewashed over the timbers. Even the mullions and window heads have been so treated which is going a bit too far.

[187]

Friday, 17th June

Jack Rathbone and Mark Ogilvie-Grant dined. Odd little party but Midi, whom I had asked, chucked. Jack determined to subdue any exalted sense of importance as the new Secretary of the National Trust, and succeeding well. I have never met a man more eager to please and be liked. If he only knew, he has no need to try so hard.

Sunday, 19th June

Carmen Gandarillas dined. Much bereaved and pathetically talking of Peter Derwent without cease. Dressed in deep black with her jet-black hair she looked beautiful as the picture of woe. The unfulfilled wife and widow, and yet neither.

James called once yesterday, and once today. Reiterated his advice of the other day – marry A. at once, *come* what may. He says I am blessed beyond my deserts; that my weakness is indecision; that few men are vouchsafed such an opportunity; that if I drift it will peter out, for that is the nature of things. Then I shall become a dreary old failure and he will wash his hands of me. A little nettled, I said that that would save me money.

Monday, 20th June

To the Tate Gallery and an hour's revel in the Vienna collections. The jewelled boxes, the rock crystals fascinate me. Jack Rathbone dined with the Hugh Daltons and delighted me by saying that Mrs Dalton read him an extract from my preface to *Adam* as an example of my 'intransigence'. I always hoped it would reach her eyes, the bloody woman. Reflecting upon James's words I feel how skunkish I am even contemplating disregard of the Church's rules. I who have always been a noisy partisan of Papistry and whose profoundest principle has been to uphold it against the devil and all his ways, Communism, puritanism, etc., etc., while overlooking those other little ways that seem to me unharmful and even pleasurable.

Harold Acton had a dinner party of twenty at the Ritz. I knew everyone present and hated every moment. Harold is the least vulgar man I know. But this cannot be said of some of our mutual friends. Often my loyalty is severely strained.

Tuesday, 21st June

Vita has asked me to stay at Sissinghurst on Wednesday of next week. John Wilton dined and was charming and percipient. He has lost that

[188]

marmoreal cast of feature which no man preserves after reaching his quarter-century. He told me he had definitely bought Ditchley from the Trees and, when all was settled, intended to make it over to the National Trust. That would be splendid but I shall not believe it until it has happened having had other disappointments of this nature before. James says Princess Margaret is high-spirited to the verge of indiscretion. She mimics lord mayors welcoming her on platforms and crooners on the wireless, in fact anyone you care to mention. A considerable gift. She has a good singing voice. In size she is a midget but perfectly made. She inadvertently attracts all the young eligibles to her feet, which doesn't endear her to the girls.

Wednesday, 22nd June

Took a morning train to Nottingham. Looked at the classical castle built in 1674 by one of the Smythsons, and made notes. It is an interesting building outside. Then was driven by the Town Clerk's people to Rufford Abbey and conducted all round. It is deserted and depressing. I cannot call it a first-class building but it is better in the stone than the illustration. Inside deplorable apart from the twelfth-century undercroft. Nothing old left otherwise. It is suffering cruelly from dry rot to the extent that all the floors and the ground storey of the Stuart wing have had to be ripped up and the earth is showing through. The property has been bought by Harry Clifton who is now anxious to demolish it. It seems a pity to let it go, but no use can be found for it. Myles Hildyard met me and motored me to Clumber. We looked at Bodley's chapel, a veritable small cathedral, noble both in- and outside. Then to Welbeck. Then to Flintham to stay the night with his elderly parents. Flintham Hall, *c.* 1850, is a sort of Venetian classical. Myles loves it. He is the perfect squire in embryo, the cultivated countryman in the still living tradition of Gyles Isham and Wyndham Ketton-Cremer, versed in their counties' history and culture.

Thursday, 23rd June

A letter from A. saying she cannot make up her mind to divorce Anthony and that anyway she thinks we had better live apart lest I get tired of her. I? Does she mean lest she gets tired of me? This has depressed me somewhat. Dined at old Mrs Carnegie's in Lennox Gardens. I and Sir Francis Humphreys were the only men wearing black ties, all the others wearing white. Too ridiculous. Sat next Lady Humphreys, now an old lined woman, but friendly, and Diane

Maxwell. The whole performance was over by 10.30. There was no flourish to this tail-end of Edwardian Kensington entertainment, which there was the last time I dined with this splendid old lady. She is still upright but her rapid deer-like movements have degenerated into the gait of a stricken hind.

Friday, 24th June

Luncheon party at Sibyl Colefax's house. Wonderful food, but so wedged was I between Cynthia Jebb and Hamish Hamilton that I could scarcely raise the fork to my mouth. John Gielgud is very shy and retiring on these occasions, which is strange. He is very bald now. Told me he has long since given up trying to stop his hair from falling out, and is resigned.

Gerry Wellington called at Thurloe Square for tea and we motored off to Stratfield Saye. John Steegmann, author of that inimitable *Rule of Taste*, Rupert Gunnis and Esmond Burton staying, all of us enlisted as guides to the party of National Trust members visiting the house tomorrow.

Saturday, 25th June

Everything went well and fortunately no one misbehaved. Each one of us was posted in a different room. Gerry, quite ruthless, would not allow a moment's relief. We were coached what to say and he took infinite pains labelling the exhibits and providing a printed brochure. The usual ignorant, dreary lot of members came. After a high tea we were driven, the five of us, in G.'s tiny Morris (the Rolls being away having its door mended which Harold [Nicolson] smashed off its hinges the previous week, greatly to G.'s annoyance) to Bradfield School to see a performance of *Agamemnon* in Greek in the outdoor theatre. This theatre is a disused chalkpit converted. Stone seats *à la grecque*. Trees surrounding. Very picturesque. The boys performed extremely well and Clytaemnestra brilliant. I think boys prefer melodrama to less emotional form of acting. I was a bit bored at times, but the seat was too uncomfortable to allow dozing off. As the night drew on, so lights were turned on to the stage. The beauty of the setting, birds and doves cooing from the trees, the coloured togas, the chorus of boys declaiming, certainly made a picture. The Duke and Lord Montgomery were the guests of honour. They walked in with the headmaster, Hills, late of Eton. I sat immediately behind Montgomery, now a little bent man, with small, mean hatchet face like a weasel's. He has ugly hands with crooked, gnarled fingers. The knuckles nearest the fingertips stick out like twigs from oak branches. I hated his little brown bald skull a foot below me.

Went with Esmond Burton to Mass at Heckfield Park family chapel, the doors wide open, the misty heat sizzling pale blue outside, blackbirds singing crisp, dewy bars, the butler in the pantry next door clattering breakfast cups and silver spoons. This kind of Mass makes me feel devout. After luncheon Gerry took us in my car to Silchester. We scrambled about the walls for he wished to show me how well the Ministry of Works had repaired them by cementing the top courses on which the lichen and moss were happily growing. Reluctantly I had to admit the Ministry's successful treatment.

Lady Hudson and Lady Granville came to tea, and Lady G. suddenly developed St Vitus's dance and jangled her cup in her saucer, spilling scalding tea through a thin silk dress on to her knees, and smashing the saucer to smithereens. Gerry leapt up, seized the table upon which a few drops of the tea had sprinkled and rushed away with it to have the surface repolished. He made not one gesture of help or sympathy to poor Lady Granville who was in considerable pain and distress. Typical Gerry behaviour! Oh I do love him. He never lets one down. His patent anxieties about his possessions bring these catastrophes about. I enjoy teasing him in a subtle way. Oblique references to sex make him bridle with a nasty covert leer. Now that he is a duke he thinks it unbecoming to let himself go.

Motored to Wickhamford after 5. In Oxford stopped at Wadham Chapel to look at the glass which is signed and dated 1622: a wonderful chapel with Jacobean screen and this glass amazingly colourful and clear. At home found a cocktail party on the lawn – hellish. Mama talked of Alvilde. I showed her my photographs of her. She looked at them very attentively and pronounced A. beautiful, which she is.

Very hot day indeed. Motored to Castle Bromwich. Rich warm smells of hay, eglantine and elder now in full flower looking like side plates. A completely rural drive. Spent several hours making a survey of the late seventeenth–century Hall and gardens which are under a covenant with the N. Trust. The garden temples and piers, etc. in a poor way. The sphinxes on the end garden piers are noble. In the house the stucco ceilings are in very deep relief. Stopped at Kenilworth Castle; little to see beyond Leicester's building of 1570–5 which has remains of two fireplaces of a classical type, high up in moulding Severn stone.

Motored to Sissinghurst to stay the night with Vita. When I arrived she and Mrs Lindsay Drummond were drinking sherry in the long room. I told them the story of the tea disaster at Stratfield Saye which amused them very much. The garden here is almost blowzy with bloom – an incredible spectacle. Surely no other county in England but Kent can be so lush and rich. No wonder it is called the Garden of England. I asked Vita why she liked the old-fashioned roses so much. She said because they reminded her of Tudor heraldic roses and Caroline stump-work. The Sissinghurst garden enchants because it is both formal and informal. The straight paths lined with yew and the pleached lime alleys lead to orchards, their fruit trees swathed in ramblers and eglantines.

She and I sat down to dinner at 8 o'clock. A cold meal with white wine which we drank and drank until 12.20 when we left the table. Vita is adorable. I love her romantic disposition, her southern lethargy conceal-ing unfathomable passions, her slow movements of grave dignity, her fund of human kindness, understanding and desire to disentangle other people's perplexities for them. I love her deep plum voice and chortle. We talked of love and religion. She told me that she learnt only at twenty-five that her tastes were homosexual. It was sad that homosexual lovers were considered by the world to be slightly comical. She is worried about Ben's love for Carritt who doesn't reciprocate and is perpetually unfaithful. As for my predicament her advice was to marry if I had the chance. She protested that it was nonsense for the Catholic Church to discountenance a Catholic marrying a divorced Protestant whose previous marriage it has not regarded as a sacrament. Was very emphatic on this point. The memory of this evening will be ineradicable.

Motored to Smallhythe. The 'Trouts' as Vita calls them, very old. Miss Atwood wearing trousers, a tight little brimless cap, from which her white, man-cropped hair obtrudes upon her cheeks, and a white coat like a waiter's. Their little old Priest's House pretty, and untidy, reminds me of Madame de Navarro's house in minute miniature, I mean as regards ninetyish Bohemian flavour. Mrs Chaplin, the curatrix, is Ellen Terry's niece, a very beautiful woman with grey hair.

This evening Barbara Moray took me to the Hugo Pitmans' lovely house, 16 Cheyne Walk, where Rossetti lived. Inside it is like a country house, so large and quiet and filled with splendid pictures by John, Tonks and others of the early years of this century.

At 9.30 picked up A. E. L. Parnis, [Secretary of the Gowers Committee] and Mr Ansell and motored to Hughenden where we were joined by the rest of the Gowers Committee. They all liked Hughenden and thought it well kept. Then to West Wycombe, rather shabby by contrast, but Helen [Dashwood] very sweet to them after a sticky start. Then to Hatchlands. At the end of this trip I was dead tired. Called on Midi and dined with her. On arrival the place teeming with children. Midi seemingly insensitive to their clamour which would get on my nerves after half a day.

Extremely tired after my week of dashing around. Tonight I motored to Send to dine with Loelia [Westminster]. The Hofmannsthals there. Dinner talk was of the awful austerities forthcoming as the result of Cripps's speech this week – more tax on tobacco, and less petrol. Everyone says we are in for a bad economic crisis and that America is already undergoing a slump.

To Doreen Baynes for a talk. When I told Eddy West that I considered her nearly a saint he laughed me to scorn. He said she used to lock her sister up in a cupboard when her friends came to the house because she was so ashamed of her. Indeed I do recall a luncheon guest before the war going to the lavatory in her house, finding the door unlocked and the sister on the seat, a pekinese on her lap, reading a novel. But I attributed this to the sister's intense shyness and reluctance to meet Doreen's friends. Doreen talked of love, of King Edward walking into Queen Alexandra's ladies' room and asking one of them to go to bed with him, like picking out a whore in a brothel. Doreen does get hold of the most improbable tales. She is extremely credulous.

John Russell lunched. He has recovered his young Shelley looks and is handsome again; and more mature. He and his wife now live in Essex

[193]

where they have a farm. I cannot envisage John milking cows or cleaning pig stys or spreading manure. It is splendid how this young man, the son of a bicycle shop proprietor, became rich and established at the age of twenty-three.

Mama came to stay and went out with Hugh MacDonell, in spite of her pious avowal. This clever man is tremendously dull. I dined with Mark Ogilvie-Grant, and took the Rosses to Kew. It is curious how every human being believes the set he moves among is superior to every other.

Thursday, 7th July

Had a drink or two of champagne at Diane's. She is always affectionate and always sparkling like a nymph by a fountain in a landscape by Lancret. Anthony Devas, a sympathetic man, looked out of place listening to Diane and Bridget discussing what they should wear at Mrs Hulton's ball. Mama and I dined alone. She is exceedingly worried about my father, who is not well: haemorrhage and clots in his urine.

Friday, 8th July–10th July

Weekend with the Eshers at Iford [Manor, Wilts]. I motored Sibyl Colefax there. She never ceased chattering for one instant and I could barely hear a word for my car is so noisy. In bending down my ear to listen my head was well below the dashboard and windscreen, a hazardous operation. Eddy Sackville-West and Lady St Germans the other guests. Eddy says outspoken things in a way I do not always like, my reason probably being that what he says is usually true. Weather hot. The deep blue sky over Iford with its terraces and statuary allows one to imagine one is in Italy.

Wednesday, 13th July

Had a sebaceous cyst cut out of my ear. No pain at all, but this day ill with fits of unconsciousness. Stayed at home.

Thursday, 14th July

Better today, but not very well. I went to Paris this evening. A. met me. We dined at Jouy with Anthony.

[194]

A. and I left Jouy at 9.30 and motored to Chalon-sur-Saône, staying at the Royal Hotel. After dinner we walked in the moonlight. On the bridge I made a confession which greatly disconcerted A. Slept in a large bed, if sleep is the right word, for some demon kicked a tin can in the street below our window all night long. En route we had stopped at Sens Cathedral with twelfth-century façade. A renaissance tomb with stars and lime leaves sprinkled over the canopy in carved stone. A large handsome rococo tomb to Louis XV's son buried here. Auxerre Cathedral very fine. Saulieu has remarkable Romanesque capitals.

Saturday, 16th July

Weather gets very hot indeed after Lyons. With the wonderful Roman triumphal arch at Orange Provence begins. I like to think the arch was expressly built by the Romans as the entry to the exquisite, mysterious South. A. drove nearly all the time, I only occasionally for her car is new, a Hillman. It has steering wheel gear change. A. is a fussing car owner who shouts directions all the time and gets rather impatient with me. In fact she is impatient with inefficiency, hesitancy and hopelessness, which are among my many failings. We arrived at the Riviera Hotel in Aix in time for the first of the Festival's concerts, chiefly Mozart, given by Casadesus in the Bishop's Palace. The courtyard of the palace has been made into an open air theatre, the stage contrived by Cassandre. Pretty in a Rex Whistlerish way. An adjoining exhibition of his designs for the stage and dresses for the Don Giovanni opera. Casadesus, A. says, is the best Mozart player she has ever heard. Rory Cameron, George Chavchavadze and a large party all in rich, huge American limousines, with chauffeurs and valets, arrived from Paris last night. A. and I have adjoining rooms, a bathroom each. Rory guessed all and in fact everyone now knows. A. doesn't care at all. So why should I? The hotel very comfortable and food excellent.

Sunday, 17th July

Aix is a ravishing little town set like a jewel in the open country. It has rows of very old palaces in a sort of Florentine late Renaissance style, but with a character Provençal rather than provincial. The Cours Mirabeau is completely over-arched with planes which form a vault of shade. A. adores Provence and is determined to buy a house here or nearby, but I am a little depressed by this thought for I would prefer to live in Italy. Our idea is to live together, married or not, dependent upon whether she and Anthony divorce and upon money arrangements, for I could not have a job in England if we were married owing to her domicile abroad. That raises a major problem. This evening a Haydn concert in the Cathedral, we having first dined with Rory's party.

I visit George Chavchavadze and Rory in the morning, they sharing a room, *faute de mieux* I gather. George was lying in bed having his toes pared by a valet and reading to me the whole of *The Young Visiters* amid shouts of laughter. He is such a sweet fellow, unchanged by opulence since his Kensington bedsitter days. We motored to St Cannat, lunched, and continued to Arles. Squinted at the Cathedral, the Roman theatre and amphitheatre, then drove through the Camargue looking for birds. Saw a roller which flies in a rolling motion and a bevy of white aigrets. Back to Aix to find Nancy Mitford and Mogens (pronounced *Moans*) Tvede, a Dane with whom she is staying in Marseilles, a friendly man. We went to *Don Giovanni*, beautifully performed in the courtyard of the Bishop's Palace. The Don a young baritone of twenty-two who really assumed wickedness. The stage effects deliberately contrived on a small scale in the eighteenth-century fashion. A blackbird accompanied the sopranos at the top of his darling voice. The louder they sang the louder he followed suit.

Motored to the aqueduct of Roquefavour and lunched there. Then lay in the sun a little beyond. A. is determined to make me brown and fatter, for she says I am a white Gandhi-like skeleton, which must be very unbecoming.

Motored through Marseilles to 157 Avenue de Montredon to spend the day and bathe with Tvede and his wife Princess [Dolly] Radziwill, an old witch, intelligent, witty and gossipy. Nancy very well and happy; her new book just out. She told me she enjoyed life to distraction.

This morning stayed late in my room trying to burn myself for A.'s sake at my window. I don't really like it. Sunbathing is a modern craze. The

Ancients would never have done it. At midday we met Mérode de Guevara at a very bohemian café in Aix. We followed her in her jeep, containing herself, daughter, friend, cook, dog, casks of wine, bread and sundries, to her house. The road became so bad that we left our car in the shade of a bush and climbed into Mérode's jeep, I sitting over the wheel, my legs in great danger of being amputated by passing rocks and trees. We arrived at a barn-like structure up a hill. There under some scruffy trees we ate a truly bohemian luncheon, the remains of our fish being thrown to the cats and dogs hovering in droves. We left for Les Baux, stopping at the Pont du Gard on the way, and staying at the Beaumanière Hotel, the most luxurious of all the hotels so far. The bill for dinner came to over £5.

Friday, 22nd July

The drive from Les Baux to Saint-Rémy covers the most beautiful area of Provence to my mind. It is low-lying and fertile, intensively cultivated. It is partitioned into rectangular sections between high cypress hedges. As we flash past in the car we see a peasant in blue trousers driving an ox, then an old woman with wide straw hat tending a vine, then a mahogany-brown body on a ladder mending a roof. The Roman mausoleum at Saint-Rémy, standing in a clearance of olives, must be the most complete Roman monument in existence. Avignon disappointed me. It is a poor version of Florence. Unsympathetic texture of stone, and architecture mediocre. The Cathedral has little to recommend it. A. is more keen than ever to buy a house in these parts. She says she could not live in Italy because of the Italians' cruelty to their animals. It is so frequently the case that people who care so vehemently for animals do not care for humans. Both Chaplins and my mother are like this. We stayed the night at the Beau Rivage inn at Doudieu on the right bank of the rushing green Rhône – a quiet little place. But owing to relentless mosquitoes did not sleep a wink. We do not book rooms ahead. We just turn up and are never sent away.

Saturday, 23rd July

A very tiring day indeed. A. exhausted by sleepless night allowed me to drive most of the journey. The long straight roads and chequered light and shade under the plane trees have a mesmeric effect. Terribly hot driving. We covered nearly 300 miles and on arrival at Jouy for dinner I felt quite sick, to be revived by the flat champagne we drank. Then sat up late with Anthony discussing our affairs. It was settled that in September

[197]

he and A. would consult a lawyer in London as to whether it would be advantageous for them to divorce, or have a legal separation. Anthony says he wants a job in London where Rosemary will be, but doesn't wish to marry her, or she him, which I doubt being true. A. does not necessarily wish to marry me but wants me to leave the Nat. Trust if they will not give me a half-time job. If they will, I can live half the year in England and half with her in Provence. She will definitely not surrender her French domicile. With this decision I sympathize. It is difficult for me to know what to do. I am in great confusion.

Monday, 25th July

I am back in the London office. Eardley dined and I told him all. He is so patient with me and listens to all my problems. We drove to Fulham at midnight, walked along the river and drank coca cola from a night shelter, which he considered very paintable. It was on wheels beside some bollards on the embankment. E., who is incurably romantic, said that he would chuck up Long Crichel and his perfect life there for love and give all he possessed to the loved one. And he would too. The heat in London is as oppressive as lead.

Tuesday, 26th July

Lunched with Lord and Lady Ilchester at their house in Montagu Square, filled with lovely and historic possessions from Holland House: portraits of Foxes, a lovely Hogarth group including Butcher Cumberland, paintings of all sorts, a commode by Cobb. Sat between Lady Ilchester and Mrs Kendrick, plain, Viennese wife of Kendrick of the British Museum, not a distinguished man in appearance. Eddie Marsh, Freda Lady Listowel and Mrs [Muriel] Warde present.

Raymond Mortimer and Paul Hyslop gave an evening party. The heat was so great that every time I turned my head I broke into a sweat. Drank lime juice to keep cool. Hundreds of people I knew as friends or acquaintances. Eventually I sat out on the roof talking to Paz Subercaseaux. David Carritt was trying unsuccessfully to vamp Garrett Moore when Joan came up to them quizzically. Carritt asked G., 'Who is that glamorous female?' 'My wife,' said Garrett.

Thursday, 28th July

Dined at Alan Lennox-Boyd's punctually at 8.30 to meet the Regent of Iraq and his new wife. They came at 9.15. Then dinner at separate tables.

[198]

I hated the evening and talked to Gerald du Gouray and Alix Beattie and Svelode of Russia and Mamie Pavlovsky. The party did not break up till 1.30 so I was obliged to stay on, drinking more and more and getting more and more tired. Mamie resolutely refused to go on to a night club with the silly Iraquis, and I did too. They went to the Four Hundred and we stayed behind. Mrs Iraqui only interested in film stars, horses and night clubs, so I was not a great success with her. She is a pretty little thing, plastered with jewels. How people like Gerald can be bothered with them I don't understand. He dances attendance. For what reasons? He is *éminence grise*. Is he a spy, and if so, for whom?

Sunday, 31st July

I took Papa to Paddington station this morning. He had had no operation. They looked at his growth and cauterized it a little, although he declared they did not touch it for he felt no pain. The doctor told me there was nothing they could possibly do and that he might live eighteen months to two years at most. Dined with Ivy and Margaret. Ivy, talking of the uneducated English masses, said that hitherto England had come out on top because she had been pushed along by the educated few. Hence her success in the world. Now that there was open competition between nations England must go down owing to her standard of education being lower than that of every other European country. I agreed, adding that the situation seemed to me even more serious in that the educated few were being pushed around by the uneducated many.

A. keeps on writing me letters nobly offering to do anything I ask, even to live with me in England in spite of losing money. I am in a quandary. I dined with Burnet at St Paul's, Waldenbury, motoring there and back.

Friday, 5th August

Lunched with A. E. L. Parnis at La Coquille to meet the editor of *Vogue* who asks the favour of the National Trust to photograph women models in front of its country houses. Next to our table sat Herbert Morrison, napkin tucked under his chin, with two tarty elderly ladies on either side and a pot-bellied gentleman, all eating voraciously and drinking two sorts of wine.

Monday, 8th August

Lunched with Countess Borromeo who had lunched with me yesterday. The Italian Ambassador and Peter Tunnard the other guests.

[199]

At Mass yesterday in the Oratory, while kneeling before the Gospel at one of my favourite stances in the west transept, it came to me that of course God alone was worthwhile because enduring; that nothing human, animal or vegetable endures, neither love, sex, friendship, hatred, oneself, one's ideas, ideals, nor anything man-made, even by Pheidias, Michelangelo, Shakespeare or Mozart. Only God remains immutable, unchangeable. A very commonplace revelation certainly which dawned upon me extremely forcefully in a new, clear understanding. Then I qualified the satisfaction the revelation gave me by asking myself if God was not merely a fiction, made by each man in his own image. I decided perhaps not, because in thinking of, or worshipping God I do not picture him as possessing all the particular virtues which I venerate. Instead I purposely keep him rather vague and woolly, wholly beneficent, perfect certainly, and of course omnipotent. I don't investigate his ingredients. I don't inquire of myself if he is handsome, ugly, has a sense of fun (this would be a surprise), is gloomy, likes art or horse racing, is normal or queer, nice or nasty. In fact I can't believe in a personal God the Father. I do believe in the divinity of Christ, a human being wholly possessed of God. Thus I accept the Father and Son. The Holy Ghost perplexes me. Must get to grips with, and the Logos.

I have just finished Ivy's book [*Two Worlds and their Ways*]. Now this novel really is worthwhile, is literature after the tosh some of our friends write, for which they receive acclaim. Yet it will never be popular.

Tuesday, 9th August

Motored to Stratfield Saye and took Gerry Wellington to Selborne Hill. Getting into the car I fell over the bumper and badly cut and bruised my leg and hand. All Gerry said was, 'Some people make a terrible fuss over a scratch. Now the other day I fell, cut my head open to the skull, bled, was dreadfully messed about, and never turned a hair.' Neither had I turned much of a hair, nor uttered one word. I merely sucked the wound in my hand and limped. G. was very good at Selborne though ducal with the local people. He came to an instantaneous decision about the watch-tower, dismissing the design they proudly showed him with the wave of a hand. I lunched at Stratfield Saye with him. In the afternoon we went round the disused bedrooms of the house. He showed me the Great Duke's Garter robes unpacked for the first time since his death and in perfect preservation, even the long brown curl with the wig-maker's name attached to the label. Gerry held up the

Great Duke's underpants to the light, looked intently at the fork and said solemnly, 'I am glad to see no signs of sweat – or anything else,' as though this were occasion for personal congratulation.

On returning to London I called at Bramshill. Ronnie Brocket was away but his daughter aged eleven, a fat little dumpling, showed me round. A disappointing house because too much restored, too stockbrokery. No antique spirit left; no good furniture. Bad taste pile carpets and curtains. The long gallery with dappled panelling is the only good room left. The garden done in poor taste, inappropriate Italian well-heads and urns introduced, and looking forlorn and homesick for Italy. Not so long ago this great house was shabby and romantic, with its continuity unbroken since James I's reign and the breath of hereditary lunacy still heavy on the stagnant air.

Wednesday, 10th August

Dined at Colin Agnew's. Bogey Harris there, talking of Edwardian days, said that when he stayed at a great house he always took in addition to his valet, a man to shave him and do nothing else. He and Colin told me Berenson was an old pansy in spite of kissing in the garden every pretty woman who came to the place.

Thursday, 11th August

Tom Driberg, reeking of a very adhesive scent, called to tell me he must sell Bradwell, his eighteenth-century villa in Essex, which he had left by will to the National Trust. Dined alone with Jack Rathbone. Before and after dinner Raymond Mortimer, Paul Hyslop and Desmond Shawe-Taylor came in. A good deal of puppyish embracing which I take in good part, but don't really care for. Like Berenson I prefer to kiss women and even in amity or affection don't relish kissing men as a form of salutation, though it is becoming common. The embracing of women has even got out of hand. Once you give way you can never stop it. And there are times when I sense that women friends, however intimate, are not in the mood to be mauled. Nor can one always be in the mood to maul them, poor things.

Friday, 12th August

Drove away at 11 o'clock to the west. In a bad, bad mood, feeling ill and miserable. Called at Longford Castle. Lord Radnor conducted me round the grounds and principal rooms of the house. This house is interesting on account of its triangular plan, a Tudor conceit. Salvin's alterations did not improve its beauty. He added too many towers and turrets. They began in the nineteenth century to turn it into a hexagon but got nowhere beyond one extra round tower and one square tower. The three inner turrets that figure in Thorpe's drawing survive. The main elevation was rebuilt in three parts, the upper recessed. I wonder if Smythson had a hand in it after Wardour and before Wollaton.

Called on a man Tibbits in the grounds of Wilton to talk about his house at Warwick. Then motored to Iford to stay with the Eshers.

Saturday, 13th August

We drove in slow stages to Attingham. My car was simply packed with the Eshers' luggage, he squashed in the back seat, she in front with me. We stopped at Gloucester, lunching vilely at the New Inn. Visited the Cathedral and I showed them Edward II's tomb and Duke Robert of Normandy's which I think particularly impressive because of its simplicity; the crossed Crusader leg and pointed toe in a recumbent ballet dancer's pose. The marvellous cloisters too we saw, deprecating the opaque glass in the walk lights. We stopped at Tewkesbury to look at the Abbey and canopied tombs. A pretty wedding was in progress, the bride and groom coming out into the full sunlight. Then Worcester Cathedral, King John's tomb, the Cathedral so grossly over-restored. These three cities horribly crowded with people and cars. One couldn't put a pin between them. We turned off the main road, proceeding via Stourpourt and Ribbesford to show them the house, and glanced at Bewdley. Dined at Lady Berwick's. Charlie Brocklehurst there. Delicious dinner with champagne from her cellar, the Eshers drinking nothing. Lady B.'s sighs and tragedy queen gestures irritated him, and in consequence he talked to me on his other side throughout the meal, which was rather rude.

During the drive I told him that I wanted to retire from the Trust, or work part-time. This announcement caused quite extraordinary concern. He said that nobody else could do my job but me, whereas hundreds of people could write books better than me. I said yes, I was sure of that, but my health was not good and I was tired. His last comment was, 'Well, we must find you a very rich deputy,' presumably so that he needn't be paid anything. Alvilde's fortieth birthday and she away from Jouy, somewhere in mid-France, I don't know where. Oh, lack-a-day.

Sunday, 14th August

Rather a ghastly day motoring Lord Esher round the estate and showing him the house. In the afternoon the opening ceremony took place and he

[202]

delivered the speech I had drafted for him. Of course he altered and embellished it so that it turned out inimitably his. Tiring, hanging about, talking to people unknown. I left at 5.30 and arrived at Wickhamford at 7.30. Found my mother in the kitchen worn to death and my father looking, at first sight, well. But his haemorrhage worse than ever. In fact he is not at all well. he is always languid, gets up late, goes to bed at 5.30 and when up lies on his sofa. I saw his doctor who is much worried; gives him six months at most and told me he is now probably dying.

Monday, 15th August

Mama terribly worried. It is awful leaving her in this predicament. I had to tell her that everything depended upon her. Until he becomes bedridden I don't think we should tell her the truth, or go there too often, or do anything to arouse suspicion. Haines [the old chauffeur] took me aside this morning to say he was certain Papa is failing and moved me greatly by adding that he could think of little else. 'When he does not come to talk to me in the morning then I knows how ill he is.' I left exceedingly depressed for Bath, calling for Eardley who was with his mother in a nursing home. We motored to Wells, lunched there and visited the Cathedral. Early English is not my favourite style. Arrived at Arlington Court at dinner-time. A most glorious drive, the fields peopled with corn stooks. We stay till Friday at the Lodge with Woodrow, the clerk of works. Ensuing days with Eardley very happy, we working like blacks arranging Miss Chichester's collection of ships as best we can. The ship expert from Greenwich Maritime Museum, Mace; the pewter expert, Michaelis; the agent, Reeks, all came over at different times. Only one letter from A. has followed me. This house is awful outside but inside there are four very pretty 1825 rooms. These, alas, we cannot arrange as furnished but must cram with ships and show-cases, save one exquisite little boudoir. There we shall put all the china, of which some is good. The boudoir has beautiful yellow curtains and the walls are hung with rose silk.

One evening we called at East Down Manor a mile away belonging to an old family called Pyne. An enchanting Queen Anne House. Several nice rooms with coved ceilings, panelling and watercolours by W. H. Pyne, founder of the Watercolour Society in 1804. I have a tiny picture by him, of peasants round a camp fire.

Saturday, 20th August

At 6 o'clock went to Carmen Gandarillas's house to meet Jamesey who is broken-hearted, Dame Una [Pope-Hennessy] having died. James admirably brave and sensible. He says his mother had a fulfilled life, had written many good books and several first-rate ones. More important than these were her astringent mind and capacious intellect. She was one of the most important women of her day. I told him she was the best debunker of the second-rate. On Tuesday evening she was remarkably collected, and seemed filled with renewed energy. She gave him detailed instructions how he was to finish her book on Lamartine and how to put her collated notes together. Having settled these and other matters she announced that she was going to die the following afternoon. But at 7 o'clock the following morning she failed and J. said the ten minutes of her death were an experience he would never free his memory from. It was awful. He never thought such a noise could be emitted from a human frame. Her face became a skull with a veil of torment drawn across it. She was unrecognizable except for her hair. He held both her hands and tried to help her to die. Meanwhile she was kept conscious while extreme unction was administered by a clumsy, fumbling priest. Otherwise there was nothing terrifying about her death, James said. What he described sounds terrifying enough to me. He oversaw everything; dressed her head with her favourite lace veil and surrounded her with piles of all the books she had written. Then he broke down utterly. Poor James, as sensitive as a film on which every impression is registered. John returned too late, and James is glad he did not have to witness what he did.

Monday, 22nd August

Carmen took me to Dame Una's Requiem Mass in the little chapel of Saints John and Elizabeth. Not many people there, and it was extremely hot. James and John in dignified distress. I sat next to Rose Macaulay who looked terribly thin and unhappy. The old nanny sat at the back and looked broken and ill. Her poor old hunched shoulders, worn navy blue coat and skirt and frozen grief very poignant. I shall not quickly forget the spectacle. A sight to rend the heart-strings.

Tuesday, 23rd August

I motored to Bexleyheath for an interview with the town clerk and several councillors, all extremely amiable, sensible and conscientious. They wish to vest Hall Place in the Trust if we can help them to raise the money for upkeep. Ivan Hills, our nice agent, and I went to the house later. It is in far worse state than it was in 1938 when Archie Gordon took me to see it. But it is very fine, set in a beautiful old walled garden and enclosed by green fields. It might be in the depth of the country instead of the middle of suburbia. I drove to Midi's for dinner. Stopped en route to look at Nonesuch House. Well kept by the Ewell Council, and now a show place. Gardens not urbanized. There are no disfiguring notices, no wire litter-baskets. The house was shut. It is not the least like what one pictures the famous Nonesuch Palace which Henry VIII built. It is a plain neo-Gothick, cement-rendered edifice. In discussing my problems Midi declined to give advice. She has never met A. She merely said, 'You have to bear in mind that you may be sacrificing your country, your religion, your career and your independence.' That was food enough for thought.

Monday, 19th September

I got back from my three weeks' holiday in Italy today. During this time I did not keep my day-to-day diary, and I have now little doubt it is high time I stopped it altogether. Anyway, a diary of travel to the continent is of little interest unless it is a learned disquisition on the arts and manners, containing profound and stimulating thoughts. Nevertheless . . .

On the 26th August I flew to Paris (this sounds as if I am contradicting the gist of my previous paragraph), stayed that night at Jouy and next day motored alone with Alvilde in her new car, a Plymouth, which is a treat to drive and runs smoothly like the wind after my lumbering old Rolls. We stayed the night at the Grand Hotel, Nancy, that wonderful city. We wandered in the *place* and down the street leading to the elegant palace by Emanuel Héré. Indeed the architecture here is superbly elegant. Elegance may not be the foremost quality of great architecture, yet no country in the west has eclipsed the French manifestation. The ironwork by Jean Lamour is grander and more elaborate by far than Tijou's at Hampton Court. Next day we stayed in Zurich at the Belle Rive au Lac, clean and well-appointed after the French hotels we experienced. On the 29th we reached San Vigilio on Lake Garda, staying at the Locanda, picturesquely situated on a small quay projecting into the lake, and run by Walshe, an old English horror who is the best cook on the south side of the Alps. Mosquitoes, however, were appalling and the rooms so hot that we were only free from torment when bathing. So we soon moved to the Ermitagio, an annexe away from the lake. Some embarrassment caused by Sir Eric de Normann and wife staying. He is head of the Ministry of Works and knows me. Since A. and I were sharing a room we had to be on our guard and pretend we were not together.

Thereafter Verona (the thirteenth-century statue of the black Bishop San Zeno 'che ride', with face of radiant benignity), Milan (while A. shopped I visited San Satiro baptistery – life-size medallion heads in bronze). On the 7th to Venice, staying at the Danieli (two rooms with a bathroom between). Weather here cooler. Too many English people about. To my amazement Cyril Connolly meeting us in the Piazza solemnly congratulated A. on becoming a viscountess on the death of her father-in-law. He should have known better. K. Clark accompanied us one day to Padua, conducting us to his chosen monuments. A signal honour. Bergamo and Vicenza visited. At the former the intarsia choir stalls in the presbytery of S. Maria Maggiore of Old Testament scenes to the designs of Lorenzo Lotto, about the loveliest things seen this visit. In the latter city the streets are more crammed with masterpieces and less messed about than those of any other I can think of. As for the Palladian palaces words are superfluous. In Venice we visited all the architect's churches with Hiram Winterbottom, a great Palladio enthusiast.

We lunched one day with Bertie Lansberg at the Villa Malcontenta. I was disappointed. The elevations are grim and that not facing the Brenta positively ugly. The planning most ingenious, for the rooms fit skilfully one above the other, though of varying heights. The lack of a staircase is conspicuous. The same afternoon we motored to the Villa Maser which is over-restored. The church is exquisite. On our return to France we stayed a night at Vicenza to see the exhibition of Palladio drawings in the Palazzo Chiericati. We also visited the Villa Capra which eclipses all the Palladio villas I have so far seen. The lesser rooms like satellites revolving round the great sun of the central domed hall are all pretty. Even so the quality of the interior decoration is clumsy compared to that of Chiswick, when looked into closely. We were shown the kitchen by a charming, handsome son of the house, Count Valmarana, aged about twenty. It was whizzing with peasant women, with scarves over their heads, singing, and scouring pots and pans.

Our Italian tour was punctuated by some unforgettable little scenes and incidents that make me love Italy. 1. The small urchins, to one of whom, the leader, we gave a few lire for guarding the car while we visited the Villa Capra, waving and cheering us as we drove away. 2. After horrible difficulties in the garage in Venice, when we were driven to exasperation, the lift boy kept lighting Hiram's cigarette which for some reason refused to take flame, while bubbling with laughter. 3. Three extremely well-bred old ladies drifting in a superbly groomed gondola to the steps of the Danieli and being helped to land by a pair of gorgeously liveried gondoliers. 4. At a restaurant a mother and daughter licking their handkerchiefs and scrubbing with all their might the lapel of a man's coat which had been stained by food. 5. Women and men with their hands on St Anthony's tomb in Padua cathedral, wishing, as they prayed with the utmost fervour and faith, for what? A new pair of shoes?

[206]

A new carpet sweeper? Renewed faith? Or new lovers? 6. The night on Lake Garda when I left A. in the garden in anger, and walked by myself under the moon along the shore, and sat on the shingle hoping for help from the lapping waves. When I returned A. was in tears. I was all penitence. I was forgiven. The relief and bliss ineffable. Perhaps not concerned with Italy, and could have happened anywhere else. But did happen in Italy and will always be registered with it.

Now my relations with A. have entered a new phase, undergone a sea change from the first fine careless raptures into something certainly richer and possibly stranger.

Tuesday, 20th September

A. and I returned by the ferry boat on Sunday night, reaching London at 9.30 yesterday. I am glad to be out of France. I hate the beastly country and its ferocious, mean, cruel inhabitants. I lunched with A. today. This evening she left for Scotland with Anthony and her mother-in-law to attend Lord Chaplin's memorial service at Dornoch. A. did not telephone me before leaving so at 6.55 I scribbled a note, hailed a cab, rushed to Euston station and gave a porter half a crown to deliver it in the two minutes before the train left.

Wednesday, 21st September

Alec Penrose lunched to discuss how we could save Holkham now Lord Leicester had died. We concocted plans for him to put to the new peer. At 4 o'clock I trained to Manchester and stayed the night with Dick and Elaine at Park Cottage. We deliberated how best to tell Mama the truth about Papa's illness and agreed that on the next occasion when he was taken worse whichever one of us was present should tell her, with Astley the doctor present. D. and E. are devoted to each other. Their little house is bright and comfortable and they are, I believe, perfectly happy. But oh! what a district of solid rain like stair rods, black tearing clouds across the blacker moors and scarlet cottages, and tall chimneys like prison warders at every corner one tries to escape from.

Thursday, 22nd September

To Lyme Park this morning with Charlie Brocklehurst. Back to London and joined Bridget [Parsons], Lady de Vesci, the Dorias, and Orietta Borromeo at the musical comedy, *Tough at the Top*. Dined at Bridget's afterwards.

[207]

Lunched A. and Anthony and Mr Harry Batsford, to whom I introduced Anthony, and upon whom Anthony exercised all his charm. We want him to write a book on reptiles for Batsford's. On leaving I walked with Anthony who said he could not think why I hesitated to live permanently with A. A. tells me that Anthony says to her she is a fool to be cross with me. Poor A., it is as much my fault as hers. I should be stronger and capable of helping her instead of throwing up my hands in despair and running away. She dined with me at Thurloe Square and is very sad indeed that we separate tomorrow.

Lunched with A. I believe and trust I left her happy. I motor home this afternoon and send her a devoted telegram from Oxford. Call upon Deenie at Stow-on-the-Wold and talk about my father. She wants him to have a nurse in order to spare my mother, but I am against that. Twenty nurses would not spare her and it is better for her to be occupied now she is so wretched. She would be more wretched if she had nothing to do but be irritated by the nurses. However the situation at Wickhamford is very sad. Papa remarkably cheerful and getting up again after a strangulated hernia trouble of a fortnight ago. Yet he passes water every hour, some days and nights every quarter of an hour, and during the nights Mama wakes too. To pass water (terrible doctors' phrase) gives him much pain. After a talk to Astley on Sunday morning it became clear to me that she should now be told the truth. It fell to me to tell her.

I took her for a stroll along 'the donkey patch' in the sun and said that Astley took the gravest view and wished to speak to us both at a convenient moment. Thus I tried to break the news to her gradually. She said at once that she knew what it was to be and did not wish to be told by the doctor. She wanted him to tell me so that I could pass it on to her. Her courage was wonderful. She did not weep. At one moment only I thought she might break down when she said she could not imagine life without him after forty-five years. (I marvelled that she seemed to have forgotten those long wretched years when they were on the worst possible terms. God is sometimes merciful to the afflicted.) Then she pulled herself together and said he must have no suspicions of what we knew. While we were talking old Mason called to speak to her from the road. She called back to him cheerfully, answering his inquiries about Papa as though nothing were the matter. In the house Papa was up and dressed and she joined him and laughed and joked with him. When I

[208]

confirmed later in the day that Astley pronounced the bladder growth to be malignant and gave him three months to live at longest she took it calmly. How I admired her.

Monday morning I left Wickhamford for Bath, collected Eardley in my car and drove to Arlington Court, where we worked hard all the week sorting the desultory collections. We stayed at the Lyndale Hotel, Lynmouth. Weather divinely beautiful. Autumnal sun every day. E. and I made a great discovery. One morning we spent clearing away old rubbish. There were a few broken frames, fragments of glass and trashy Pears Annual illustrations in a dusty heap on top of a wardrobe in the housemaid's pantry. We debated whether to tell Newman, the custodian, to throw away the lot; then decided we might as well complete the work ourselves. So I climbed on to a chair and handed the junk down to Eardley. I held out one picture and said, 'I do believe this is the reproduction of a Blake drawing.' It proved to be better than that; a large watercolour drawing, typical Old Testament scene, signed and dated 1821. The frame was contemporary and the name of Blake's framer, Linnel, known to Eardley, written on the back in the handwriting of Miss Chichester's grandfather, Colonel Chichester, the builder of Arlington Court. Furthermore when we took the back off some newspaper stuffing was dated 1820.

In Lynmouth we went to the *Fallen Idol*, that splendid film I always wished to see but missed in London, with Ralph Richardson and the little French boy. It was excellent and the child most moving. He never cried once; that is why he was so moving.

On our return on Saturday I bought at Porlock in an antique shop for £2 a small portrait of a man on a panel by Samuel Lawrence, quite a good bargain.

Jamesey amused me by telephoning: 'You know that picture of an eighteenth-century house which I am leaving to you in my will?' 'Yes,' I answered, 'I can't wait for it.' 'Well, I am ringing you up to say that I have sold it and it is in Appleby's shop window if you want to buy it.'

Ivy and Margaret lunched with me in the Cromwell Road and later Margaret returned me the second half of my book with her corrections. Prudence [my niece] came at teatime from Paris to stay. I took her for a walk in the Park and tried to show her buildings of interest and tell her the history of Hyde Park. But she was not interested and is, I fear, an incurious girl. 'Heavy,' Alvilde calls her. She may improve, but I like children to ask questions. Then I met A. and Anthony on the Golden Arrow and brought her to dine here.

Went this evening to see Dr Spira, the Chaplins' doctor, at their urgent request. He was certain my trouble was the old complaint persisting, and the sugar content disability was nonsense. He said it was very wrong that I should be in pain part of every day and this must be stopped. He made me write to Pierre Lansel before he would consider taking me in hand. This I did, and of course Pierre will be furious. So I have certainly lost him as my doctor without definitely gaining a new one.

Went to see a Miss Sketchley in Kensington who offers to leave some decent pieces of family furniture to the Trust, not museum stuff but the sort to be found on the second bedroom floor of a grand country house. She lives on the ground floor of a beastly house in Baron's Court, her sister having just died. She is sad, old, lonely and resigned in a bitter way. What indeed is the purpose of life for someone like this? My heart bled.

A. and I went to the Cimarosa opera *Il Matrimonio Segreto*. Very pretty Mozartian music never rising to great heights, and repetitive.

Inspired by A. I have begun the study of wild flowers. Having acquired a few books from Barnstaple I picked what flowers I could from the roadside on Salisbury plain and looked them up on my return. This is a new fascination which promises to be more dangerous than architecture in so far as turning the eye from the wheel is concerned. How shocking that I, country-bred, never learned about wild flowers in childhood.

Margaret Jourdain's corrections of my book have depressed me. I agree with nearly all of them. Nonetheless they shake my unstable confidence. She has rightly suggested my cutting out certain passages that are irrelevant, but she also suggests cutting out the little light touches which I hoped would enliven the book. After all, her own books are deadly dull.

No true and enduring love affair ever runs entirely smoothly. How can two individuals, composed of different and often warring elements, who decide to coalesce, not clash fairly frequently? The triumph of love consists, not in winning, but enduring. Marriage is a very unnatural state. But then so are logic and art unnatural. All the most worthwhile and glorious things achieved by mankind are unnatural. To be natural is to be animal. Only fly–by–night lovers may expect to have no ups and downs – for six weeks at most. Jamie Caffery, a Papist, once told me that in the eyes of the Church marriage with a divorced person was a worse sin than adultery. For adultery has no permanent purpose whereas the other means permanent excommunication, a state one cannot but shudder at being put into. Bosh, I am inclined to think.

Thursday, 6th October

A. and I went to a bad performance of *The Magic Flute* at Covent Garden; but what heavenly, transporting music.

Saturday, 8th October

All my meals are with A. when I am in London. Today I motored to Ascott, Leighton Buzzard. This is another case of a rich man's collection of treasures housed in an unworthy building – half-timber of the 1870s,– and set in poor surroundings. House and gardens spick and span. The owner, Mr Anthony de Rothschild, is a very nice man indeed, and so is his pretty wife a sweet woman (Colin Agnew told me that after their marriage she ran away but after much woe was received back magnanimously and rehabilitated). I arrived at midday and stayed till 5 o'clock. French furniture particularly good. Dutch paintings, Lawrence sketches, two full-length Gainsboroughs, one head and shoulder Gainsborough of a young man, a Lorenzo Lotto of a dark young man, two Rubenses, one of mother and child and one of Hélène Fourment, very seductive. A collection not to be sniffed at. It is sad that the rich so often have indifferent houses.

I dined with A. and stayed the night at Olga Lynn's flat which she has been lent.

Sunday, 9th October

I was amused and rather flattered that Anthony Chaplin telephoned asking me to ring up Rosemary Lyttelton on his behalf.

Tuesday, 11th October

Tonight Rose Macaulay dined, for Anthony particularly wished to meet her. She is to him a goddess. I invited Jamesey, thinking he would improve the party, but James talked incessant 'shop' to her and Anthony became more and more visibly annoyed. However after dinner he found that she knew about green tree frogs and was delighted. Talking of religion, Rose said she was an Anglo-Agnostic, explaining that she had great affection for the Church of England, in which faith she had been brought up, yet was a non-believer.

Wednesday, 12th October

At the Historic Buildings Committee there was much excitement over the Blake drawing discovery. If either of us had an exclusive claim to the discovery it was Eardley. Leigh Ashton was anxious to have the drawing for the V & A. We said *no* to this; it must stay at Arlington Court. On the other hand we promised to let him have the four Beauvais tapestry panels of the Four Continents from Arlington Court for Osterley. A very good idea.

Friday, 14th October

A. and I went to Marlow, staying at the Compleat Angler. Over dinner I said I saw no prospect whatever of my being able to leave England and the National Trust for half the year. The Trust could not be expected to approve such an arrangement. I am rather tormented by this problem.

Monday, 17th October

Dick telephoned from Wickhamford that they were bringing Papa up by car to the nursing home tomorrow, Mama to stay with me, Dick and Elaine in Ronald Fleming's flat.

After dining with A. and me at the Allies Club William McKie and Nadia Boulanger played the organ in Westminster Abbey. The Abbey incredibly romantic lit only by the organ loft lamp, deserted by the thousand pairs of feet of daytime, full of deep shadows and ghosts of the great and famous, and now possessed by us two; such a rare and extraordinary privilege, as A. and I wandered, to the strains of Bach, among the royal tombs.

Tuesday, 18th October

A. left this morning. My family arrived after a terrible journey, Papa suffering agonies. I had a glimpse of him lying in bed at the nursing home looking like a corpse. To me it is inconceivable that he can survive another operation, now fixed for Friday. This prolongation of life is a cruel and unnecessary business.

I have put off my plans for going away this week. Audrey has come up from the country to join us. We all sit around doing and saying nothing but the same fatuous things. It is a great strain. It is terrible how far I feel from them all. A bad day, this. Dentist in the morning. Luckily the X-ray shows no abscesses so again I am reprieved from having several teeth out. In the afternoon an X-ray at St Thomas's Hospital of my back. Apparently nothing is wrong with the spine, but Spira, the doctor, says I must always take luminol, the very drug that Lansel spent years gradually reducing until he put me on to something more innocuous. Worst of all Margaret Jourdain returned the first part of my book with a letter that has properly put me in my place. She says that the book does not hang together, a third of it must be cut, and my style is atrocious. In short I am flattened. Can she be quite right, I ask myself?

I am not being as nice to Mama as I should be, and it is wicked to allow her to get on my nerves at a time like this when she is so worried. Her love for my father nowadays is absolutely wholehearted and unreserved.

Thursday, 20th October

I say to myself this morning that all this moaning and groaning and self-pity must cease instantly. Circumstances may be bad at the moment but the world is not wholly unendurable, and the sun is shining. Then I meet poor Keith Miller-Jones at Brooks's who tells me his engagement is not going well. *She* is very emotional and worried that she cannot reciprocate his passion for her. She also has grave misgivings about marrying a third time; and besides is subject to recurrent depressions. Oh Lord! I was very sympathetic with Keith and inwardly cheered that others have their ups and downs as well as myself. *Schadenfreude* again. We went to an exhibition of Adrian Ryan, a young painter-protégé of Eardley, his medium in the Van Gogh manner, very forceful and sharp; also to see pictures at the Redfern Gallery by Tom Carr in a soft Corot style, which pleased me more. On parting I said to Keith, 'Do you now feel better?' 'Not much,' he said. The truth is that love makes people lunatic. No man or woman ought to be appointed to any position of authority if he or she is in love. Just imagine in time of great crisis, or war, a Prime Minister being head over heels in love.*

*At the time of writing this I was unaware that during the First World War Asquith had been deeply in love with Venetia Stanley and Lloyd George with Frances Stevenson.

I asked Jack Rathbone (who is always sympathetic and patient with his maddening subordinates) over a drink if he thought it feasible for me to have a half-time job with the National Trust. He strongly counselled me to wait until the Gowers Committee Report comes out at the end of the year, for it may affect the composition of the Nat. Trust and my job in particular.

I called at the nursing home in Queen's Gate at 7.10, ten minutes later than arranged. Went to Papa's room, he sitting up eating and very cross that I was late. He said he had seen enough people and I had better go back to the others in the flat. I felt like a whipped puppy and slunk away, tail between legs.

Friday, 21st October

Papa had his operation this evening and it passed successfully. We were all sitting round the tea table at no. 20 when Astley, the doctor, arrived long before we expected him. He told us the news for he had been in the theatre. Mama saw him through the window. There was an awful silence because we all feared his arrival so soon must mean that Papa had died under the anaesthetic. Dr Astley's kindness overwhelms us.

Monday, 24th October

I had the best of luncheons at the White Tower with Rose Macaulay and John Pope-Hennessy. They talked so learnedly of Latin medieval authors they had actually read, Josephus, Aeneas Silvius, etc. that I felt very ignorant. John spoke indignantly about Bob Gathorne-Hardy's book on Logan Pearsall Smith which he considers scandalously depreciatory; and condescendingly about K. Clark's new book on landscape painting which, while admitting the excellent style, he thinks twists facts to bear out the author's preconceived theories on the progression of the subject throughout the ages. I have already read Bob's book about which I am inclined to agree with John, for it suggests that the author had a grievance against Logan. But I have assumed that K. Clark's book must be excellent for the likes of me and ordered it from Heywood Hill's shop at once. John approved the little Millais of Effie Gray which I brought with me and had just shown to Harry Leggatt. Having taken much trouble in consulting several experts I told Sir Ralph Millais it was not worth more than £200. He, very trusting, agreed to sell it to the National Trust for that sum. So I have purchased it for Wightwick Manor. Hope to God we haven't swindled the poor man.

I motored to Buscot. A most lovely autumnal day after violent storms and rain, yesterday being non-stop torrential. Along the road verges I noticed toad-flax, dandelions and vetch still in flower. Am glad to get away from no. 20 and poor Mama, whom I have told to stay on in my bedroom until the end of next week, if not longer. At close quarters she gets fearfully on my nerves. She is interested in nothing I say and her insincerity amounts to positive dishonesty and an inability to be straightforward and even truthful. Yet I am so deeply sorry for her and filled with admiration of her bravery. Why can't I be demonstrative? What a stinking beast I am.

I went round the Buscot rooms with an exclusive eye upon the pictures for the very tiresome chapter on the NT picture collections which I have been asked to write for A. Blunt's volume.* Gavin's [Faringdon] pictures, as well as his Deepdene furniture, make a very fine collection indeed. Two Rembrandts and some rather boring Sir Joshuas were bought by the grandfather.

Stayed last night with Ted Lister and talked long with him till late into the night about the future of Westwood. I think I convinced him that his best hope of preserving the place was in leaving it to the N. Trust with the expressed wish that his nephew might have the right to rent it. Ted is determined to do all he can to prevent the nephew selling a single stick of the furniture, even if he leaves the house to him outright. The old man is well, less deaf and in good form. He sits huddled in his armchair before the stove in the dining-room downstairs, with one oil lamp, knitting in hand. He has just bought a new sheepdog puppy.

Today I went to Stourhead and made some notes on the pictures. This is a difficult task for me because I am an ignoramus about painting. Motored to Longbridge Deverill church looking for and finding Sir John Thynne's (builder of Longleat) tomb slab with inscription, quoted by Hussey. But of course it was put up quite 100 years after his death, to judge by the design and lettering. So the wording, from which I deduced he was his own architect, is valueless. This shows the importance of seeing *everything* one is writing about for oneself.

The Nation's Pictures: A Guide to the Chief National Galleries of England, Scotland and Wales, edited by Anthony Blunt and Margaret Whinney, 1950.

I am terribly disheartened about my new book. Am still carefully pruning and rewriting and improving (I hope), but realize that it is definitely bad – damn M. Jourdain – and there is no other word for it. If ever I write another I must on getting to the end, put it aside for two months at least, then re-read it with a fresh and highly critical eye. I think the failure of this Tudor book is depressing me more than Papa's illness, which is a wicked thing to say and a proof of irredeemable self-centredness. How, I ask myself, can a person honestly feel more concerned for others than himself? He may say he does, and may try hard to do so; he will certainly pretend that he does, but can he? Is it humanly possible? Superhumanly possible, yes. Subhumanly no. I am still subhuman.

Tuesday, 1st November (All Saints Day)

My poor mother. All her tiresomenesses are dissipated by her abundant sweetness and charm. I said goodbye to her for she is taking Papa home to Worcestershire in an ambulance on Friday. Doctors can do no more for him. The tumour in his bladder continues to discharge pus. This is a terrible disappointment to him and to her who realizes what it means. I would definitely do anything within my power and deprive myself of what I hold most dear (which is A.) if I could thus prolong his life free from pain and distress. But this is not saying that I would want to. One must be honest with oneself.

I took the 7 o'clock evening train to York, writing in the carriage. Was met by Christian Howard at York station and driven to Castle Howard. She is a plain-spoken, frank girl who has let her appearance go in favour of diocesan work. George is not back from Scotland. He does not live in the big house but in one half of the gate-house, rather uncomfortably and untidily. His wife is away in Scotland burying an aunt.

Wednesday, 2nd November (All Souls Day)

Whereas the Saints can look after themselves, the Souls need all the help we who are still on this earth can give them. Christian Howard motored me to York. I spent three-quarters of an hour in the Minster. Inside disappointing, a jumble of Gothic periods and too few monuments. Much of the famous glass is back, rearranged by the Dean in some sort of design. I am right in having written that English medieval glass lacks design and artistry, which the French can claim. It has splendid splashes of colour – I had forgotten how much bottle green and twilight violet. Before I had made any progress back came Miss Howard and bustled me off. One must not be hounded when sightseeing.

A filthy wet November day. George Howard arrived for luncheon. He is stout and uncouth; sometimes forthright to rudeness. Perhaps his heart is kind. How can one tell? He took me over Castle Howard, now empty, the school having gone. Its aspect is exceedingly forlorn. It is not in bad condition, but very unkempt. It looks sad with the dome and the best rooms burnt out, but there is enough space left for a country house these days in all conscience. The lack of symmetry in Castle Howard has always worried me. The sculpture of the stonework, cornices, columns, etc., is crisp. George intends to move himself into the East Wing and open the rest to the public. We drove to the Temple of the Four Winds, now in a state of dereliction, but a very elegant building, more Palladian than Baroque. The monopteral, Doric Mausoleum is a splendid affair and the bastioned retaining wall forms an impressively massive base. In fact it is a composition of grandeur and genius. We went into the vaults where are many gaping niches unused. No one buried there since the eighteenth century. George intends to be buried there, he told me. And so he should be for he will be the second creator, or more correctly the re-creator of Castle Howard. The rotunda chapel above is faultless. The quality of workmanship is far superior to Palladio's chapel at Maser or elsewhere in Venetia. The English Georgians were better craftsmen than Palladio's men. George much distressed because hooligans have thrown bricks through the windows, breaking panes of original glass. The Kentian reading-desks, the marble inlaid pavement are of superb quality. What a wonderful building. Its condition is better than the Temple's because its construction is more stalwart.

Today George motored me to East Riddlesden Hall where we met Cubby Acland. For I suppose the sixth time in my life I went round this depressing building in vain endeavour to improve its neglected condition. I was handed over to C. Acland who drove me to Gawthorpe Hall through an endless hedge of hideous industrialism. We arrived at 5 o'clock in the dark for tea and were greeted by pretty Lady Shuttleworth in the drawing-room, one of the best Elizabethan rooms I have ever been inside. Nice small wall panels with deep fields, an interior porch and really pretty ceiling of vine patterns, the bunches of grapes like fir cones in the round. It is a very cold house. Young Lord S. is a rather stiff, too serious, but extremely gallant young man who lost both legs in the war, and is filled with a sense of duty to the locality. He sits on committees, dispenses patronage and does what is required of him, yet speaks of the inhabitants of Burnley and the neighbouring towns as one would of

Hottentots. I notice that this view is commonly held by England's aristocracy and I think they, the aristocracy, are right on the whole, although I must admit it is the unwise who reveal these sentiments in public. I am sure Lord S. never would.

A horrid day up here of drizzle and smog, blackness and gloom. The ring of industrialism has to be penetrated to reach this property. When Gawthorpe is reached one feels hemmed in and isolated from the wide world. A drive and belt of smoke-ridden trees separate one side of the house from Padiham and Burnley. The other side faces a noble sweep of orange-green fields with pits and cranes on the skyline. The Shuttleworths fear that open-cast mining may be realized at any moment so as to make their continued residence at Gawthorpe impossible.

Gawthorpe is a charming house, not large but tall and compact, built by the Shuttleworths in 1605. It reminds me of Wootton Lodge in Staffordshire. Barry made alterations in 1849, heightened the central tower – now riddled with dry rot – and put a parapet round the house and added a porch and terrace. Barry's exterior alterations lend character and interest. His interior staircase is not so good, but the warm patterned wallpapers, the mahogany-topped baths are cosy and *gemütlich*. There are many family portraits and some very nice furniture. The house is the typical home of a distinguished long line of squires. Lord S. was not too pleased when I pointed out that he had dry rot in the tower. I meant to be helpful. He would have had reason to be annoyed if I said he had bad breath which, I feel sure, he hasn't.

The Shuttleworths left early next morning and I not till midday. I had the opportunity of a good pry around by myself when they had gone off in their beautiful Rolls with less beautiful baby boy and nurse.

Got back to London by dinnertime to find that Mama had left with Papa in the ambulance for Wickhamford. He managed the journey all right but was desperately tired. Alvilde arrived in London the day before. Tonight she sent Clarissa to dine with her grandmother. She and I went to the Greek restaurant.

Alvilde left for Paris this morning. Every evening we met and dined and nearly every day lunched together. This visit was a great success. There were no crises or difficulties, and all was sunshine. I am happy and at ease. I left early this morning for Newport, Monmouthshire. Was met at the station by John Morgan flying his personal flag on the radiator of his motor, and driven to Tredegar. He has already become another Shuttleworth but absurdly pompous and puffed up with self-importance. Ridiculous as this may be he has a sense of duty, genuine, and his religion means everything to him. We spent the afternoon going round the house. Now *it* is important, and probably the best in Wales. Nevertheless I was a trifle disappointed by the coarse, unrefined quality of the craftsmanship. The famous wainscot is very rough indeed, notably the staircase. The red brick exterior is attractive, and so are the heraldic supporters of lion and unicorn in porous stone over the window pediments. It is a great pity that the cupola and roof balustrade of this Restoration house are missing. The iron railing put round the roof during the war to prevent fire-watchers falling off is unsightly. Some of the contents are superb, notably the French furniture and in particular the Adam bureau-cum-harpsichord all in one, with a clock in the pediment. John showed me the figures of his estimated income after he has paid death duties, which amount to 80 per cent. His gross income is £40,000. After paying tax it will be reduced to £3,700 and he cannot spend his capital because it is all in trust. Avis Gurney [his sister] came to stay in the evening, having travelled from Edinburgh. She is just as ugly to look upon as she was when a girl, but is very affected and amusing. One laughs with her a lot. Both siblings are devoted to Aunt Dorothy whom they call 'Ma'. I slept in the panelled room in the bed said to be Mary Queen of Scots', but I wonder. John is very dogmatic about his belongings and at the same time ignorant, like many owners. A sciolist no less. He told me that on clearing his cousin Evan's bedroom cupboard he came upon 'instruments of the most bloodcurdling nature'. He took them gingerly between finger and thumb and threw them in the dustbin. I said that in doing this he gave the dustmen ample opportunity of circulating scandalous gossip about his family. John forebore to tell me what the 'instruments' were.

Thursday, 10th November

This fine morning we motored to Ruperra Castle which the Welsh want to buy from John as a memorial to Welshmen killed in the war and vest in the Nat. Trust. I could not see any point in it at all. The castle was burnt out during the war by British troops. From vestiges of remains it must have had rather nice Adam decoration. It is rendered all over with grey pebble-dash. The windows are nearly all nineteenth-century. There remains one Jacobean two-storeyed porch which is all right. Some unsightly outbuildings, the walled garden gone to seed and deer park to thistles and nettles.

When I left Avis kissed me most fondly, pressing me to stay with her in Edinburgh and go with her on a visit to Aunt Dorothy. She is a kind soul. She wears a turban on her head as if trying to resemble Lady Hester Stanhope. John motored me to Newport and got out of the car at the YMCA branch office which he is to open this afternoon. On his express orders the chauffeur immediately furled the flag on the radiator covering it with a leather sheath. He then drove me 100 yards to the station, to return to pick up his master and, presumably, unfurl the flag. I thought only Field Marshals indulged in this state and ceremony.

Got back in time to dine with the Aberconways in North Audley Street. Not fun, but stuffy. I sat between Lady Anderson and Lady Berwick. Sweet compliments were bandied between us three.

Friday, 11th November

All today meetings. I very irritable. Is it champagne of the previous evening and of the one before – a drink that disagrees with me horribly? Or my quandaries? Or just nerves and that accursed office? We had our annual meeting in the great hall of Lincoln's Inn. I went with Harold [Nicolson] to the Travellers' where he gave me a drink. About to leave the club we ran into Crawford who called out, 'Jim, I have something to say to you,' and spoke to me. I could not very well ignore my chairman when he called. Harold walked on to fetch a cab. When we were in it he said, 'You are such a dear and old friend and I always find the failings of my old friends invariable and endearing. You dawdle today in the same way you have always dawdled since I first met you.' Until he said this I never had the slightest idea that I was a dawdler at all.

Saturday, 12th November

Patrick Kinross dined. He is back from Cyprus, Turkey and Greece. He says Greece and the Greeks are heaven. They are warm-hearted, human and more intelligent than other Europeans. They are all sensual without being sentimental, and every Greek man is homosexual. They go to bed with a laugh just as they would sneeze and laugh. I said I would not care to go to bed with anyone who sneezed and laughed. Patrick in his funny pontifical manner which I love says that true love can only exist between man and woman, true sex between man and man; that women know and hate this without understanding it, just as the Ancient Greek women did. Accordingly they resent all men's relationships, fearing them to be such that they can never attain. I think this notion is probably far-fetched.

[220]

David Carritt dined with me at Brooks's and came back here afterwards. He is brilliant and sophisticated and not entirely without feelings or scruples, but nearly so. To me he is not an attractive being. I do not like that little pinched face, over-confident eye and bad complexion. He tells me he has quite broken with poor Ben [Nicolson] who behaved in a very hysterical fashion. Ben, he maintained, and I could not disagree with him, is immature and has no *savoir-faire*. In other respects he spoke nicely of Ben – of his innocence – for which I gave him marks. Carritt told me that he [Carritt] was entirely unemotional in all his relationships. I can well believe it.

Monday, 14th November

Dining with the Johnnie Churchills I noticed how Mary has J. firmly under her little thumb. He showed me after dinner the frieze on black Welsh slate of the Battle of Blenheim which he has just incised for his uncle Winston's ornamental temple at Chartwell. I thought it far better than any painting he has ever done and told him he had perhaps found his true medium. It is entirely linear. I am going to see it put up next week. He has decided to paint the figures, which I deprecate.

Tuesday, 15th November

Lunched with George Wingfield-Digby and wife, a Viennese. Robin Darwin, the other guest, said he was renting Coleshill from Captain Hill for his art school. George Digby told me he was treated like an outcast by his parents because he took up art, although he was quite good at most sports. Now he is the youngest keeper of a department at the Vict. and Alb. Museum.

Wednesday, 16th November

I had arranged to motor to Henham Hall, Suffolk, for the day with Rick [Stewart-Jones] and start at 8.30. I arrived at his house punctually and he was still in bed. So I drove off without him. At Regent's Park the fog was so thick that I turned back. Fog cleared. In the afternoon I went to Osterley. Was conducted to a turret room and presented with a key on which was a large label addressed to me. A cupboard was sealed with a label and my name on it. All this was done by Grandy Jersey. Inside the cupboard was a mass of bills and accounts of the Child family in the eighteenth century concerning the building of the house and the making of the furniture. I told Ralph Edwards who was very excited and wanted to lay his hands on them; to which I said no, not until I had read them myself first, and then asked Grandy's permission. Presumably G. has some good reason for wanting me to look through them before any of the V & A officials [who ran, and still run Osterley for the National Trust].

Thursday, 17th November

Luncheon party at Sibyl Colefax's. Guests: the Italian Ambassador, Lord and Lady Camrose, Harold Macmillan, Harold Nicolson, Sir Arthur and Lady Salter, Thelma Cazalet, me. Sibyl so thin that it hurts to look at her. Her old maid told me as I left that Sibyl becomes thinner every day and that when she is not at a party she is in bed resting; that only within the past two months has she heard her confess to feeling unwell. I sat next to Lady Salter and Harold who reproached me for telling Christopher Hussey about the Blake discovery and allowing him to publish the story in *Country Life*, instead of giving it to Ben for the *Burlington Magazine*. I said to Harold, 'Ben's attitude is that of an editor of a parish magazine who is too proud to refer to news that has previously appeared in *The Times*.' The silly talk of politicians. H. Macmillan a pompous, inflated man full of self-importance. Sir A. Salter and Harold told fairly funny stories about Mr Gladstone and that tiresome Winston Churchill's constant allusions to Gladstone having become Prime Minister again at eighty-three. Lust for power is what it is. I liked the Camroses. He struck me as good and sincere and Lady Camrose as an intelligent, whimsical and cosy old lady, with no airs.

Friday, 18th November

At dinner at Jack Rathbone's Duff Dunbar said that Bob's life of Logan Pearsall Smith was brilliant, well-composed, honest and direct, and makes Logan, with all his warts, a kind of Dr Johnson, dedicated to upholding the English literary style.

Monday, 21st November

I stayed the weekend with Deenie at Stow, very comfortable. She is easier to be with than my mother. Twice I went to Wickhamford, yesterday and today and saw my father, the first day sitting in his chair, this morning in bed. He is pitiably thin, but his colour good. He gets extremely tired after twenty minutes of talk. Elaine says that he cannot live two months and that the cancer in his bladder has grown to the size of a grapefruit. In fact this terrible thing literally eats its victim who appreciably diminishes as it increases in bulk. There is something evil and damnable about this. Yet here is my poor father talking about his plans for next spring, how he intends to buy a racehorse if he can afford it, and go to Deauville or somewhere abroad in order to gamble. Is this put on in order to deceive us, or himself? Does such talk keep his poor spirits up? He surely must know. Perhaps God is good to one in such condition in allowing one not to despair, despair.

This morning I talked to Heather Muir at Kiftsgate. She will help us at Hidcote but says we must try and get rid of Nancy Lindsay. I looked at Quainton church where the mural tablets are all to Corbets of Adlington. At Charlecote I fetched a rare book of Erasmus, possibly illuminated by Holbein, to take to the British Museum, and the Isaac Oliver of Sir Thomas Lucy to show to the National Portrait Gallery.

At 6.15 had my first Italian lesson from an old Polish refugee, a pathetic old lady who teaches Anne Hill. She is a better teacher than that flibbertigibbet, Guido Ferrari in Rome.

Wednesday, 23rd November

Motored Johnnie Churchill to Chartwell this morning. Mr and Mrs Winston were in London so we were able to go wherever we wanted. It must once have been a nice Queen Anne house, but Mr C. has altered it out of all recognition, and it is now quite ugly; but of course bears W.C.'s strong impress. We saw his study and adjoining bedroom. If all the photographs and pictures and framed letters from Marlborough, and from himself to General Alexander and others remain, Chartwell will be interesting to posterity. His bedroom is rather austere in spite of windows on all sides and three telephones by the bed. The view from it is splendid – the great lake made by him and the dam, which I remember him constructing when I stayed here twenty years ago, and the chain of pools to the topmost of which water is pumped by a machine from the bottom lake! What a to-do went on during these operations, Mr C., clad in waders, standing up to his chest in mud and shouting directions like Napoleon before Austerlitz. The long downstairs room is now full of his paintings, of which the earlier ones in the style of Sickert, without the later ubiquitous blue, are not too bad. We looked at Johnnie's slate frieze being installed in the loggia. Johnnie is a dear old friend and we had a great gossip about his family. He says he doesn't care for Christopher Soames, but does like Duncan Sandys. Mr C. has cultivated a deafness which he turns on like a tap when he is bored: an excellent form of defence and one adopted by many old people to whom time is precious. Chartwell is fascinating as the shrine of a great man, just as Hughenden is. The moment I set foot in the house I said to Johnnie, 'I have not been here since Oxford days and I vividly remember the smell of the house. What is it?' 'Cigars and brandy,' he said. Of course. It is far from disagreeable, rather like cedar wood. Agreeable, I suppose, because his cigars are expensive ones.

Robin Fedden took me to Clandon this afternoon. The poor Onslows find they cannot afford to live in it any longer. They offer the house and garden, without further land, and will lend the contents of the state rooms. All these are on the *piano nobile* and are splendid, with some of the best Palladian ceilings in England. I last saw the house when the Blakistons were living here during the war and the rooms were piled with wooden crates of deeds and papers stored by the Public Records Office. Lady Onslow is a personage, slim and delicate, while something in the eyes and mouth denote strength of character. She has excellent taste in dress and decoration, to judge by her appearance and the way she has reanimated Clandon after the mess she found it in. He is a curious-looking man with a large mouth, capricious and 'an original', so Robin described him. He was wearing attractively bizarre clothes, check tweed trousers getting tubular towards the bottoms like the pilasters of Mannerist architects. At tea I, who normally don't eat, wolfed away; so did Robin, the Onslows eating nothing. Robin later remarked on the embarrassment of our behaviour, to which I was totally insensitive: the bloody bureaucrats from London come to take over their house and gorging on the victims' victuals.

I accompanied Audrey, Dale and Prudence to Woolwich to see Audrey and the child Dale off to the Bahamas. Prue and I, not allowed on board ship, left Audrey and Dale after a long wait at a barrier. I last saw Audrey's pathetic and taut little face, so thin and tired it looked, but smiling, in her extraordinarily courageous way: a sort of *The Last of England* scene. These past few days I have been with her a lot and overcome by that mingling flood of exasperation and pity. In the move she lost her pearl necklace and ruby ring – the only jewellery she has not had to sell. She left them on her dressing-table. Oh dear. And then her sorrow at leaving England which has always treated her abominably and worry about Papa. Now tearing off, in abject poverty, in pursuit of this husband she knows so little about. Will he be kind to her? And will she still love him?

This morning at 8 o'clock I was woken by Emily telling me Mrs Dick wanted me on the telephone. I guessed what it meant. She said my father was worse, was almost certainly dying. I said I would leave at once. Within one and a half hours I had packed, put off arrangements and left in the car. Arrived at Wickhamford at 12 o'clock. Found Mama walking in the garden, very quiet and composed. Papa unconscious. Deenie was there and before luncheon Dick arrived from Lancashire. The nurse was with my father all day and Mama went up at intervals but was so overcome that she couldn't bear it and went downstairs. Elaine also sat with him. By the evening I steeled myself and went upstairs and into his room. He was lying on Mama's bed, curled up on his side, his head twisted, almost unrecognizable. His head had wizened to a skull with skin stretched tightly across it, so shrunk and taut it was. His mouth seemed to have slipped to one side of his face and his tongue lolled out. The breathing was deep, wracked and intermittent. How he would have hated me seeing him in this condition. I felt a trespasser, uncomfortable, apologetic. I felt infinite compassion because of the indignity he was put to. Perhaps for the first time in my life I loved him unreservedly.

There he lay all through the night. At 4 o'clock I went to bed at the doctor's cottage across the road.

When I got back at 9 he was in precisely the same condition. At 10 o'clock the nurse ran downstairs and told us to telephone Dr Astley at his surgery. I went up with Mama. The breathing seemed to me louder and more laboured. Otherwise I noticed little change. There ensued a terrible hour, poor Mama on her knees at his bedside, talking to him who understood not a word and beseeching him to give up the struggle. This he did a little before 11 o'clock. The nurse, M. and I were present. The breathing became a little easier, stopped, his mouth moved, then his throat, and then nothing. Swiftly the nurse with great dexterity, her hand over his heart, pulled the sheet over his head, and I led Mama away, prostrate with grief. It was a terrible, harrowing experience, yet one which nearly every human being has to undergo, once if not twice in a lifetime. I hope never again to go through another like it. The very worst things about death are the disrespect, the vulgarity, the meanness. God should have arranged for dying people to disintegrate and disappear like a puff of smoke into the air. There are many other scraps of advice I could have given him.

Dick has been wonderful throughout, a tower of strength, so gentle, efficient and controlled unlike me who was constantly moved to tears. We acted at once; got the undertakers from Cavendish House, Cheltenham, visited the *Evesham Journal* for insertion of the announcement in *The Times*, and registered the death.

Friday, 2nd December

Dick and I motored to Cheltenham. Went to an employment agency looking for a servant for Mama, without success. Then to the cremation ceremony at the crematorium just outside the town. We were punctual to the minute, 3.45, for we had been warned not to be early or we would run into the congregation of the previous funeral service. I suppose these services go on every day from morning till night, one after the other, bodies like sausages passing down a factory belt. Behind the chapel was a round building with large central chimney. I pointed out to Dick that it was belching black smoke. We giggled. Dick and I sat alone in a hideous late Victorian chapel without ornamentation, strictly non-denominational. Behind us the black mutes of the undertakers' party. The coffin on a slab in front of us. Sympathetic C of E clergyman officiating, but the service short and devoid of the devotional and spiritual. We were completely unmoved even when the clergyman pressed a button and the coffin slid away and the tatty velvet curtains opened, and a cheap, cracked gramophone record struck up *Abide with Me*, and faded out. This disgusted us. There was nothing to be seen when the curtains were drawn open. I believe the coffin is taken off the conveyor belt and does not go to the crematorium until a number of others have been collected. And oh, the unctuousness of the chief undertaker, with his faultless manner, greased hair and black kid gloves! Enough to make one sick.

Saturday, 3rd December

Yet the memorial service in Wickhamford church was far worse. All morning the villagers were decorating the church with chrysanthemums and taking infinite pains. Mama remained in the house with Clara Mitchell. Deenie, Elaine, Dick and I went. The church was packed. We went to our pew, the manor pew, and I sat in Papa's place beside the pew door. Felt an interloper. I managed somehow to get through without making a fool of myself, not without effort. Dick, who sat next to me, and was far closer to my father than I was, sang throughout most lustily. The parson gave an excellent address, not embarrassing in any sense. He praised Papa's wisdom, courtesy and charm. Said he never refused to respond to a good village cause and was a typical country gentleman. It was rather strange that the first service at which the choir gallery (which my father gave and which it was his great ambition to see finished) should be used for his own memorial service. I noticed no one in the church. One is made insensate on such occasions, luckily. Was upset when all was over. Was full of remorse for not having been more understanding and kinder, for until recently my father and I did not get on. He never liked me from the start, for which I do not blame him, although I think he should have tried to be nice to me first. Ours was a case of biological incompatibility. Our hackles rose on the mere approach of the other. Yet within his limitations he was a good man, respected by strangers and loved by his friends and other people's children.

Wednesday, 7th December

Went to see Father d'Arcy to ask him if it would be appropriate to have a mass said for my father's soul. I explained it was a thing which I would never have dared mention to him were he alive, for he hated Catholicism and all it stood for. I didn't want to take an unfair advantage of him, so to speak, he being in no position to answer back. Father d'Arcy's reply was 'Certainly, yes. If your father is in heaven, it can do no harm; if in purgatory, he will now be glad of it.' I doubted that. Then I asked if I might be cremated, please. His answer unsatisfactory. He said it was a difficult concession and I must regard the Church's dislike of cremation as an etiquette, not a dogma, to be respected. I said it seemed to me good manners and socially considerate in view of the appalling increase in the population. If everyone insisted upon having a grave there would before long be little room left for any other purpose. To this remark Father d'Arcy turned a deaf ear in the way of priests who have been floored. Then I told him I wanted to marry. He said that if A. and A. could establish that their marriage had never been taken seriously, an annulment was possible, notwithstanding that a child was born of their union. I don't like Father d'Arcy very much. He is artful, as one would expect the Provincial of the Jesuits to be.

Tuesday, 13th December

Lunched with Midi at her club to meet George Chavchavadze who turned up with Malcolm Sargent. The meal was about the most hilarious I ever

[227]

sat through. Conversation was sheer nonsense from beginning to end so that I laughed till it hurt. None of the talk bears recording. In fact it was inconsecutive and quite unrecordable. Malcolm is a splendid foil to George. Each eggs the other on to inconceivable follies.

I have slight nightmares about corpses and coffins, which trouble me. Mama was so pleased with Papa after death that she wanted to show him to people. Very extraordinary, for it is just what she laughed at the village people for doing. She thought he looked young and serene. I thought he looked fearsome – emaciated, stern and a travesty of his former self, like an unsuccessful waxwork at Madame Tussaud's.

Thursday, 15th December

Alvilde has come back. I met her at Victoria.

Thursday, 22nd December

At Ethel Sands's this evening Prince Antoine Bibesco came in. He is oldish, with straight, thick grey hair. He is the man Proust loved and the widower of Elizabeth Asquith. Abounding in charm and I would guess the cause of havoc in many hearts of yore. John Lehmann was present. Talk was of publishers. John says only the old and established firms can make a profit and survive today.

Sunday, 25th December

Christmas Day spent at Stow-on-the-Wold with darling old Deenie and Mama. No one else. Dick telephoned from Lancashire and Audrey sent a cable from Nassau. Alone with D. it would have been easy and restful, but with Mama present it was not. She became vague, argumentative and cantankerous. Abused Elaine until I could hardly bear it and not too nice about Dick. I wrote to Dick and begged him not to pay too much heed to what she might repeat about me, for I should not pay any to what she says about him.

I walked in the afternoon down to Swell, looked in at the little Norman church and at the manor with its Tuscan-Jacobean porch; then across to Nether Swell and on to Lower Slaughter, and back to Stow. Very northern, dark, cloudy afternoon, the distant hills cold and watercolourful. How snug England is in the winter, with the cottage windows lit up, warm fires blazing and Christmas decorations hanging from the beams. So pretty all the rooms were, while outside grim and dusky. This is England in the distant heart of the sweeping Cotswolds,

[228]

with the sweet aromatic smell of log fires unchanged since my childhood.

During the walk I reflected upon my relations with my poor mother and the sad change that has come about. It may be due partly to having witnessed her perpetual nagging of my father ever since I can remember anything. In my boyhood I took her side. Years passed before I realized my mistake and cruelty in so doing. I should not have taken her side, or his. Now I must never forget that until I was about thirty my mother meant everything to me. We were as one. All things change and relationships turn topsy-turvy. Perhaps in the next world they right themselves, I mean the good ones become good again and the bad ones are totally forgotten, as they can be partially overlooked in this.

Thursday, 29th December

Went to see Sibyl Colefax in bed, looking bright-eyed but slighter than ever. This woman who has known thousands of people in her time is now near death and is content, or should I say compelled for lack of anyone better, to call upon me, who am younger than she and outside her intimate circle, to her bedside. We talked of the wickedness of mothers for being possessive, something I can never accuse my poor mother of. Then T. S. Eliot came. He is remarkably youthful in appearance, with smooth, unlined, tight skin behind the ears and on the neck. He has a mischievous manner of speaking which is attractive. He talked of his play's success at Brighton and said he feared for its reception among the wolves and tigers of America. Said the Americans owe their figures to the starch and sweets they eat. We talked of Einstein whom he had supposed, until today's discovery of the new equation, to be long ago finished. He said that Einstein plays the fiddle interminably and badly and rows with his wife on a small lake, known as Lake Listerine, given him by the millionaire manufacturer of that lotion.

Saturday, 31st December

Such an odd luncheon today with Anthony Chaplin alone at the Berkeley to discuss our mutual plans. A. wanted me to talk to him and find out what precisely was in his mind. The occasion was as happy as could be. Anthony definitely wants A. to divorce him, but he will not marry Rosemary, he assures me. He merely wants to be free: of what, I asked him? Not of A., for he has been free from her ever since he married her? He agrees with me that I would make a great mistake to abandon the Nat. Trust altogether. I told him that A. was depressed by the thought of a divorce. He said this was pure sentiment for, once the divorce was over, he would see as much of A. as before it; and that I must try and make her happy. This should be the first objective of the years that remain to me. We parted in mutual piety.

In the evening she and I went to the theatre and the Savoy. I promised her that if Anthony goes I will live with her and marry her when I get the Church's consent. We went home to her flat before midnight and were together when the New Year came in.

Index

The names and titles of entrants are given as they were in 1948 and 1949. Friends frequently mentioned are cross-referenced under their Christian as well as surname.

The names of properties in CAPITALS are those which today belong to the National Trust. Those in *italics* are under a restrictive covenant with the Trust. Particulars and times of opening (which vary from year to year) may be obtained from the National Trust's 'List of Properties' (circulated to members) and 'Historic Houses, Castles and Gardens in Great Britain and Ireland', which can be bought at most bookshops.

The counties are named as they were before 1969.

Abbey House, Cambridge, 78

Abdy, Lady Diana (Diane), 26, 30, 61, 71–2, 146, 181, **194**

Abdy, Sir Robert, 5th Bt, 71, 73

Aberconway, (Christabel) Lady, 131, 154, 180–1, 186, 220

Aberconway, 2nd Lord, 63, 131, 154, 180–1, 220

Acland, Cuthbert (Cubby), 98, 186–7, 217

Acton, Harold, 159, 181, 188

Adam, Robert, 40, 64, 99

Adam brothers, 28, 49, 219

Adams, C. J., 45

Admiral, *see* Bevir, Rear-Admiral

Agnew, Colin, 115, 201, 211

Aix-en-Provence, 195–6, 197

Albert Hall, London, 33, 123, 135

Alcester church, Warwickshire, 118

ALDERLEY MILL, Cheshire, 49

Alexander of Tunis, General, Viscount, 223

Alexander family, 75

Alexandra, Queen, 193

Alington, (Napier) 3rd Lord, 64

Allies Club, 28, 91, 168, 169, 171, 175, 212

Alvis, Michael, 88, 89

Amberley Castle, Sussex, 73

American Academy, Rome, 157

Amesbury Park, Wilts, 22

Anderson, (Ava) Lady, 18, 28, 31, 135, 144, 151, 165, 167, 182–3, 220

Anderson, Sir John, 182–3

Angeli, (Helen) Mrs, 53, 127, 144

Anglesey, 6th Marquess and Marchioness of, 146

Annan, Noel, 17

Anne, *see* Rosse, Countess of

Ansell, Mr, 165, 193

Apothecaries Hall, London, 48

Arbury Hall, Warwickshire, 127

Arcade Gallery, London, 122

Architectural Review, 137

Arles, Provence, 196

ARLINGTON COURT, Devon, 176–7, 203, 209, 212

Armstrong-Jones, Susan, 46, 78

Arthur, Hon. Prudence (niece), 209–10, 224

Arts Council, 72, 138

Arundel family, 56

ASCOTT, Leighton Buzzard, Beds, 211

Ash, G. Baron, 93

Ashburnham, Lady Catherine, 152

Ashburnham Place, Sussex, 152

Ashcroft, Peggy, 164

Ashley-Cooper family, 64

Ashmolean Museum, Oxford, 33

Ashton, Frederick, 175

Ashton, Sir Leigh, 49, 77, 136, 168, 170, 186, 212

Ashwin, Harry, 119

Aspinall-Oglander, (Joan) Mrs, 35, 48, 49, 71

Asquith, Lady Elizabeth, 228

Asquith, Rt Hon. H. H., 116, 213n.

Assisi, Umbria, 107, 159

Astley, Dr, 169, 207, 208–9, 214, 225

Astley Castle, Warwickshire, 127–8

Astor, Hon. William (Bill), 29, 36

Astor, 2nd Viscount, 29

ATTINGHAM PARK, Shropshire, 38, 68, 82, 119–20, 127, 128, 154, 170, 202–3

Attlee, Rt Hon. Clement, 130

Atwood, Clare (Tony), 192

Audley End, Essex, 29

Augustine, St, 111

Austin, Bunny, 133

Auxerre Cathedral, Yonne, 195

Avignon, Vaucluse, 197

B.B., see Berenson, Bernard

Badbury Hill, Berks, 68

Badger, Colonel, 174

Bailey, Robert (uncle), 88–9

Banbury, Reindeer Inn, Oxon, 51, 166

BANK HOUSE, Wisbech, 58

Barberini Palace, Rome, 105

Barker, Mr, (Office of Works), 154

Barnard, Morogh, 48

BARRINGTON COURT, Somerset, 63

Barry, Sir Charles, 218

Basingstoke, Hants, 54–5, 63

BATEMANS, Sussex, 28

Bath, Somerset, 148, 203, 209

Bath, 6th Marquess of, 89

Batsford, Harry, 35, 60, 74, 124, 144, 208

Batsford's, 74, 85, 99, 144, 163, 187, 208

Battersea House, Battersea, 31

Battersea Park, London, 83

Batoni, Pompeo, 147

Bayley, John, 105, 106, 157

Baynes, Doreen, see Colston-Baynes, Doreen

BBC, 40, 98

Bear, The, Wincanton, 88

Bearsted, (Dorothea) Viscountess, 147

Bearsted, (Heather) Viscountess, 132, 146, 147, 174

Bearsted, Richard, 3rd Viscount, 129, 132, 146, 147, 174

Bearsted, 2nd Viscount, 15, 51, 129, 132, 134

Beaton, Cecil, 26, 131, 144, 163, 183

Beattie, Alex, 149–50, 169, 199

Beatty, Hon. Peter, 66

Beauchamp, Anthony, 133

Beauchamp, Countess, 75–6

Beauchamp, 8th Earl, 75–6

Beaupré Hall, Cambs, 58

Beckett, Lady Marjorie, 67

Beckett, Sir Martyn, 2nd Bt, 37

Beckford, Alderman W., 28

Beckford, William, 56

Bedford, 1st Duke of, 76

Bedford Hotel, Tavistock, Devon, 90

Bedingfeld family, 57

Beerbohm, Max, 161

Beit, Sir Alfred, 2nd Bt, 50

Beit, (Clementine) Lady, 50

Belcher, J. M., 130

Bell, Clive, 171

Bell family, 39

Belvoir Castle, Rutland, 17

Ben, see Nicolson, L. B.

Benmore Forest, Isle of Mull, 127

Benson, E. F., 86

Benthall, Sir Edward, 148

Berenson, Bernard, 93–4, 201

Berkeley, Lennox, 135

Berkeley family, 178
Berners, (Gerald) 14th Lord, 20, 42, 153
Bernhardt, Sarah, 144
Bernini, Gian Lorenzo, 95, 98, 100, 101, 104, 107
Berwick, (Teresa) Lady, 82, 119, 128, 129, 170, 202, 220
Betjeman, John, 170–1
Betjeman, Penelope, Mrs, 42
Bevan, Aneurin, MP, 27
Bevir, Rear-Admiral Oliver, 24, 30, 33, 34, 37, 41, 49, 50, 68, 70–1, 75, 94, 125–6, 165, 172
Bibesco, Prince Antoine, 228
Bibesco, Princess Marthe, 29
Biddlesden Park, Bucks, 174
Bingley, Lord and Lady, 125
Binning, (Katharine) Lady, 124, 134, 163, 178
Birkenhead, (Freddie) 2nd Earl of, 26
Birkett, Sir Norman, 37
Birley, Sir Oswald, 20
Birr Castle, Kings County, Ireland, 40, 46–8
Bisham Abbey, Berks, 75
Blackheath, *32 Dartmouth Row*, 115
Blakiston family, 126, 224
Bletchingley church, Surrey, 86
BLICKLING HALL, Norfolk, 27, 58, 87, 124, 136, 144
BLICKLING TOWER, Norfolk, 61
Blunt, Anthony, 114–15, 154, 165, 183, 215
BOARSTALL TOWER, Bucks, 69
Bodleian Library, Oxford, 137
BODNANT, Denbigh, 180
Bolsover Castle, Derbyshire, 81
Bonham-Carter, (Charlotte) Lady, 135
Bonham-Carter, Sir Edgar, 67
Borromeo, Countess Carlo (Baby), 111
Borromeo, Count Carlo, 110–11, 112
Borromeo, Orietta, Countess, 77, 78, 110, 199, 207
Borromeo family, 111–12
Boughton Court, Kent, 125

Boughton House, Northants, 125
Boulanger, Nadia, 212
Bourlet's (furniture removers), 144
Bouts, Dirk, 177
Bowen, Harold, 53, 60
Bowen, Vera, 53
Bowes-Lyon, Hon. David, 62, 68, 154, 181
Bowes-Lyon family, 33, 41
Bradenham Hall, Norfolk, 57, 182
Bradfield School, Berks, 190
Bradford, Emily (housekeeper), 20, 71, 169, 225
Bradford-on-Avon, Wilts, 91, 92, 113
BRADLEY MANOR, Devon, 21
Bradwell Lodge, Essex, 201
BRAMBER CASTLE, Sussex, 73
Bramham Park, Yorks, 125
Bramshill, Hants, 38, 201
Braybrooke, 9th Lord, 29
Bredon Hill, Worcs, 51, 138
Bretforton Manor, Worcs, 119
Breughel, Pieter, 132
Bridges, Sir Edward, 70
Bridget, *see* Parsons, Lady Bridget
Bridport, 3rd Viscount, 33–4
Brighton Pavilion, Sussex, 73
British Museum, 15, 23, 25, 31, 130, 223
Broadway, Worcs, 75, 83, 92, 137
Brocket, (Ronnie) 2nd Lord, 133, 201
Brocklehurst, Charles, 82, 119–20, 128, 202, 207
Brompton Oratory, London, 31, 200
The Brook, Stamford, London, 115
Brown family (Troutbeck), 186
Buckingham, George Villiers, 1st Duke of, 44
BUCKLAND ABBEY, Devon, 89, 90
Buildwas Abbey, Shropshire, 38
Bullock, Malcolm, MP, 43–4, 69, 78, 124, 131, 137, 145
Burford church, Oxon, 52
Burghley House, Northants, 78
Burlington, 3rd Earl of, 72, 131
Burne-Jones, Sir Edward, 36

Burnet, *see* Pavitt, Burnet
Burnley, Lancs, 217–18
BURROW MUMP, Athelney, Somerset, 22
Burton, Decimus, 30
Burton, Esmond, 44, 190, 191
Bury Farm, Waldenbury, Herts, 41, 45, 62
BUSCOT PARK, Oxon, 49, 68, 215
Buxton, Simon, 65
Byron, Lord (poet), 17, 44, 57, 145
Byron, Robert, 145

Cacciatore, Signora, 157–8
Caffery, Jamie, 178, 211
Cambridge, 57, 78
Cameron, (Rory) Roderick, 153, 155, 195, 196
CAMPDEN MARKET HALL, Glos, 138
Camrose, 1st Viscount and Viscountess, 222
Caprarola Castle, Latium, 104–5, 158
Carlisle, 9th Earl of, 57
Carlyle, Thomas, 165
CARLYLE'S HOUSE, Chelsea, London, 165, 166
Carnegie, Mrs, 25, 189
Caroline of Brunswick, Queen, 31, 57, 112
Carr, (Donna Nennella) Mrs, 168
Carr, Sam, 60, 163, 187
Carr, Tom, 213
Carrington House, London, 35
Carritt, David, 115, 124, 192, 198, 221
Casadesus (violinist), 195
Cassandre (stage decorator), 195
Castel Gandolfo, nr. Rome, 96, 101–4
Castle Bromwich Hall, Warwickshire, 191–2
Castle Howard, Yorks, 43, 216, 217
Cazalet, Thelma, MP, 222
Cecil, Robert, 172
Chafy, H. E., 88
Chair, Somerset de, 144
Chalon-sur-Saône, Saône-et-Loire, 195

Chamberlain, Sir Austen, 25
Champneys, Basil and Mrs, 170–1
Chancellor's Committee, *see* Gowers Committee
Channon, Henry (Chips), 17, 45, 167–8, 171
Channon, Paul, 45
Chantilly, France, 176
Chantrey, Sir Francis, 90, 118
Chantrey Bequest, 153, 155
Chaplin, (Alvilde) Hon. Mrs A., 59, 138, 141, 144, 145–6, 154–212 *passim*, 218, 227, 228, 229–30
Chaplin, Hon. Anthony, 144, 145–6, 155–61, 164, 173–4, 175, 183, 185, 189, 194, 196, 197–8, 207, 208, 210, 211–12, 227, 229–30
Chaplin, Clarissa, 138, 173, 175, 179, 184, 218
Chaplin, 2nd Viscount, 207
Chaplin, Mrs, 192
Chapman, John (architect), 89, 117
CHARLECOTE PARK, Warwickshire, 15, 28, 32, 38, 43, 63, 76, 118, 138, 147–8, 167, 174, 223
Chartres Cathedral, France, 174
CHARTWELL, Kent, 221, 223–4
Chatsworth, Derbyshire, 31, 79–80, 81
Chavchavadze, Prince George, 176, 195, 196, 227–8
CHEDWORTH ROMAN VILLA, Glos, 33, 76, 148, 180
Chenies church, Bucks, 76
Cheyney, Peter, 49
Chicheley Hall, Bucks, 86
Chichester, Colonel John, 209
Chichester, Rosalie Caroline, 176–7, 203, 209
Chichester, Mrs (Pam), 50
Chichester Cathedral, Sussex, 36
Child family, 221–2
Chippendale, Thomas, 119, 120
Chipping Campden, Glos, 59, 66
Chiswick House, Middlesex, 51, 131, 206
Cholmondeley, Lady George, 16
Christ Church, Oxford, 52

Christchurch minster, Hants, 56
Church of England, 212, 226
Churchill, (Clementine) Mrs Winston,
  133, 223
Churchill, Diana, 138
Churchill, Lord Ivor, 151
Churchill, John Spencer-(Johnnie), 84,
  134, 221, 223–4
Churchill, (Mary) Mrs John, 134, 221
Churchill, Sarah, 26, 27, 133
Churchill, Winston, MP, 15–16, 27,
  113, 116, 221, 222, 223–4
Chute, Mr and Mrs Charles, 87
Cimarosa, Domenico, 159, 210
Cirencester, Glos, 65, 148
CLANDON PARK, Surrey, 224
Clark, (Jane) Lady, 168, 184
Clark, Sir Kenneth, 138, 168, 175, 178,
  184, 186, 206, 214
Clark, Mr (Sotheby's), 147
Claydon family, 86
Clayton family, 179
Cleyn, Francis, 81
Clifford, Mr and Mrs (Jenny
  Nicholson), 160
Clifton, Harry, 189
Clifton-Taylor, Alec, 61, 91
CLIVEDEN, Bucks, 29, 36, 84–5
Clouds Hill, Ottley, Bucks, 44
CLUMBER PARK, Notts, 189
Coates, Miss, 89, 117
Coats, Peter, 17, 167–8, 171
Cobb, John (furniture maker), 198
Cobham family, 89
Cockerell, Sir Sydney, 36, 53, 55, 70
Coke, Viscountess, 33
Colefax, (Sibyl) Lady, 17, 18, 28, 31,
  61, 69, 74, 76, 92, 93–4, 114, 124,
  128–9, 141, 144, 146, 153, 163, 170,
  172, 190, 194, 222, 229
COLESHILL HOUSE, Berks, 68, 221
College of Heralds, 134
Coln St Aldwyns, Glos, 179
Colquhoun, Archie, 16
Colston-Baynes, Doreen (pen-name –
  Dormer Creston), 17, 18, 27, 61, 93,
  128, 143, 151, 171, 193

Colt, Maximilian (sculptor), 43
Colville, Lady Cynthia, 116
Colville, John (Jock), 116
Colwall, Old Colwall Manor,
  Herefordshire, 167
communism, 31, 34, 39, 44, 93, 97, 99,
  188
Comper, Ninian, 44
Compton House, Dorset, 63
Compton, Fay, 146
Compton, (Sylvia) Mrs Edward, 171
Compton-Burnett, Ivy, 28, 137, 181,
  199, 200, 209
Connolly, Cyril, 59, 145, 206
Connolly (Lubbock), Lys, 29, 59, 145,
  163
Constable, John (painter), 128, 138
Conway, Field Marshal (Hon. H. S.),
  119
Cook, Ernest, 125, 136–7, 148
Cooper, Lady Diana, 73, 176, 186
Cooper, Duff, 131, 176, 186
Corpus Christi College, Oxford, 83
Corsham Court, Wilts, 67
COTEHELE HOUSE, Cornwall, 21,
  22, 23, 24, 30, 80, 81, 90, 149
Cotswolds, 138, 228–9
Cotta, Baroness Maddalène, 111
Cottrell-Dormer, Thomas, 50
COUGHTON COURT,
  Warwickshire, 39, 128, 167
Country Life, 31, 36, 222
Court House, Chipping Campden,
  Glos, 59
Courtauld, Samuel, 154
Courtauld Institute, 52, 123, 131, 175
Courtauld-Thomson, 1st Lord, 25
Covent Garden, Royal Opera House,
  23, 24, 34–5, 59, 62, 113, 174–5,
  179, 186, 211
Coward, Noël, 143, 157, 167, 176
Cowdray Castle, Sussex, 36
Cowper's Alcove, Olney, Bucks, 32
Craig, Barry, 17
Cranborne Manor, Dorset, 87–8
Cranford, Middx, 178
Crawford, (David) 28th Earl of, 41, 50,

[235]

70–1, 72, 74, 134, 152–3, 156,
165, 172, 220
Creston, Dormer, *see* Colston-Baynes,
Doreen
Crewe, Marchioness of, 122, 124, 133
Crewe, Quentin, 133
Crichel House, Dorset, 64, 73
Cricklade Church, Wilts, 180
Cripps, Sir Stafford, 28, 35, 50, 135,
193
Croome Court, Worcs, 32
Cropper, Theodosia, 17, 20
Cruddas, Hugh, 42
Cumberland, William Augustus,
Duke of (Butcher), 198
Cunard, (Emerald) Lady, 71–3
Cuninghame, Mrs W. J. (Aunt
Deenie), 76, 137, 174, 208, 222, 225,
226, 228

Dalkeith, Francis, Earl of, 28
Dalkeith House, Midlothian, 28
Dalton, Rt Hon. Hugh, 188
Dalton, Mrs Hugh, 117, 188
Dampière, Château de, Aube, 173
d'Arcy, Father M., S. J., 227
Darwin, Robin, 221
Dashwood, Francis, 18, 25, 54
Dashwood, (Helen) Lady, 18, 50, 54,
75, 141, 155, 168, 193
Dashwood, Sir John, 10th Bt, 54, 141,
182
Davenport, Grace, 24
Davison, Hon. Kensington (Ken), 76
Day-Lewis, Cecil, 133
de Courcy, Kenneth, 69
Deenie, *see* Cuninghame, Mrs W. J.
Deepdene, The, Surrey, 215
de Freville, Mrs, 24
De Gasperi, (Italian Prime Minister),
97
De Gaulle, General Charles, 31
Denham, 1st Lord and Lady, 31–2
Denham Place, Bucks, 54
Derwent, 3rd Lord (Peter), 136, 145,
146, 188
Desborough, Lady, 22

Desmond, *see* Shawe-Taylor
Devas, Anthony, 194
Devonshire, 6th Duke of, 79, 81
Dial House, Knowle, Warwickshire,
138
Dillington House, Somerset, 63–4
Disraeli, Benjamin, 113, 182
Ditchley Park, Oxon, 66, 189
Dix, George, 69, 70
Donnington Grove, Newbury, 49
Dorchester Hotel, London, 17, 31, 49,
69, 163, 164, 174, 175, 185
Doria, Orietta, Princess, 115
Doria, Prince and Princess Filippo, 207
DOVER'S HILL, Glos, 137–8
Dower House, Bradford-on-Avon,
Wilts, 92
Downshire, (Mary Sandys)
Marchioness of, 121
Draper, Ruth, 129
Driberg, Tom, MP, 201
Drummond, Lindsay, 61
Drummond, Mrs Lindsay, 192
Dublin, 45, 46, 48
du Cerceau, Jacques Androuet, 69
DUDMASTON, Shropshire, 120–1
Duff, Lady Juliet, 163
Dufferin and Ava, Basil, 4th Marquess
of, and (Maureen) Marchioness of,
26
Dufferin and Ava, Sheridan, 5th
Marquess of, 26
Dugdale, (Carol) Mrs Eric, 89–90, 91,
127, 137
Dugdale, Eric, 70, 89–90, 91, 127
Dumbleton Hills, Glos, 138
Dunbar, Duff, 222
DYRHAM PARK, Glos, 118

Eardley, *see* Knollys, Eardley
East Down Manor, N. Devon, 203
EAST RIDDLESDEN HALL, Yorks,
217
Easton, Hugh, 44
Easton Neston, Northants, 85, 99
Eckington church, Worcs, 52
Eddy, *see* Sackville-West, Edward

Ede, Rt Hon. Chuter, MP, 116
Edensor House, Derbyshire, 79
Edward II, King, 202
Edward VII, King, 76, 162, 193
Edwards, Ralph, 84, 137, 222
Eliot, T. S., 31, 184, 229
Elizabeth, Princess, 116
Elizabeth, Queen, consort of George
    VI, 68, 101, 133, 175
Elizabeth I, Queen, 43, 61, 89, 118, 183
Elliot, Rt Hon. Walter, 176
Emily, *see* Bradford, Emily
Esdaile, Mrs Arundell, 28, 42–3, 50
Esher, (Antoinette) Viscountess, 180,
    202
Esher, 3rd Viscount, 27, 29–30, 34, 35,
    41, 48, 49, 53, 54, 61, 65, 67, 70–1,
    91–2, 94, 125, 126, 127, 137, 141–2,
    151, 152, 153, 154, 163, 165, 166,
    179, 180, 194, 202–3
Eskdale, Low Holme, Cumberland, 84
Eton College, Bucks, 26, 33, 52, 88–9,
    155
Evans, Edith, 163–4, 185
Exeter, 5th Marquess of, 78
Exeter Cathedral, 90, 177
Eyre, Giles, 143, 172

Fairfax-Lucy, Alianore, 118
Fairfax-Lucy, Brian, 147–8
Fairfax-Lucy, Hon. Mrs Brian (Alice),
    32, 147–8
Fairford Park, Glos, 68
Falla, Manuel de, 62
Faringdon House, Bucks, 42, 153
Faringdon, (Gavin) 2nd Lord, 97, 98,
    215
Farmleigh, near Dublin, 45–6
Farnese Palace, Rome, 100
Fedden, (Renée) Mrs Robin, 113, 152
Fedden, Robin, 28, 73, 86, 93, 113, 152,
    168, 178, 224
Fellowes, (Daisy) Hon. Mrs Reginald,
    49, 183
FENTON HOUSE, Hampstead, 124,
    163
Ferdinand, King of Bulgaria, 114

Ferrari, Guido, 96, 97, 223
First World War, 213n.
FitzRoy Nigel, 37, 94
Flagstad, Kirsten, 35, 182–3, 186
Flaxman, John, 43
Fleming, Ian, 35
Fleming, Peter, 35
Fleming, Ronald, 212
Flintham Hall, Notts, 189
Florence, city of, 95, 109–10, 158–9,
    197
Foley, (Edith) Mrs, 50
Fontainebleau, France, 183–4
Fonthill Abbey, Wilts, 56
Ford, Onslow, 134
Forres, 2nd Lady, 130
Fothergill, Colonel, 98, 99, 104–5, 158
Fourment, Hélène, 211
Fowler, John, 24, 43, 90, 122
Fox, Richard, Bishop of Winchester,
    55, 83
Fox, Charles James, 36
Fox, Sir Cyril, 165, 183
Frere, Philip, 127, 137
Frere, (Vera) Mrs, 127
Fry, Charles, 35, 74, 187
Furtwängler, Wilhelm, 33
Fyfe, Mrs D. T., 179

Gainsborough, 5th Earl of, 59
Gallarotti-Scotti, Duchess, 186
Galston, Miss, 64
Gandarillas, Antonio (Tony), 20, 49,
    71, 72–3, 74, 145, 154
Gandarillas, Carmen, 33, 74, 136, 145,
    188, 203, 204
Garda, Lake, Italy, 205, 207
Gardiner, Stephen, Bishop of
    Winchester, 55
Gascoigne, (Midi) Hon. Mrs, 60, 73,
    115, 133, 188, 193, 205, 227
Gathorne-Hardy, Hon. Robert (Bob),
    42, 55, 70, 91, 214, 222
Gaunt, William, 57
GAWTHORPE HALL, Lancs, 217–18
George V, King, 116, 178
Georgian Group, 54, 63, 74, 145

Gesù church, Rome, 96–7
Gibbons, Grinling, 43, 119
Gibbs, Christopher, 49, 125, 154
Gibbs, James (architect), 66, 75, 99, 119
Gielgud, John, 131, 190
Gilbert, Sir Bernard, 34, 70
Gill, Eric, 45
Gillighan, Barbara (artist), 127
Gilmour, Geoffrey, 156
Girouard, (Dick) R. D., 29, 54, 60
Gladstone, William Ewart, 222
Glanusk, (Toby) 3rd Lord, 127
Gleichen, Countess Feodora, 118
Glenconner, (Elizabeth) Lady, 52
Gloucester Cathedral, 202
Glyn, Hon. Lady, 66–7
Godfrey, Walter, 53, 153
Godmanchester Farm Hall, Hunts, 135, 136
Godwin, Edward William, 155
Goldsmiths' Hall, London, 116–17, 175
Goodden, Colonel J. B. H., 63, 87
Goodden, Robert, 63
Goodhart-Rendel, H., 177
Goodwin, Michael, 61, 71
Goodwood House, Sussex, 73
Gordon, Archie, 40, 204
Gosford, (Mildred) Countess of, 53
Gosse, Sir Edmund, 17, 44
Gotch, J. Alfred, 55
Gouray, Gerald du, 149, 199
Gowers, Sir Ernest, 151
Gowers Committee, 135, 136–7, 144, 151, 152, 165, 172, 183, 187, 193, 214
Gowing, Lawrence, 184
Granville, 3rd Countess, 191
Granville family, 118
Graves, Robert, 160
Gray, Effie, 214
GRAY'S MONUMENT, Stoke Poges, Bucks, 33
Great Comberton church, Worcs, 52
GREAT COXWELL BARN, Oxon, 68–9

Green, Henry, *see* Yorke, Henry
Greene, Graham, 157
Grey, Lady Jane, 127–8
Guevara, Madame (Mérode) de, 197
Guinness, Alec, 177
GUNBY HALL, Lincs, 19–20
Gunnis, Rupert, 190
Gurney, Hon. Mrs Avis, 219, 220

Hackness Hall, Yorks, 145
Haddon Hall, Derbyshire, 80
Hake, Sir Henry, 45
Halifax, 1st Earl of, 125
The Hall, Bradford-on-Avon, Wilts, 92
Hall Place, Bexleyheath, Kent, 204–5
HAM HOUSE, Surrey, 33, 84, 137
Hamilton, Hamish, 190
Hamilton, (Yvonne) Mrs Hamish, 186
Hampton Court, Middlesex, 79, 184, 205
Hanford family, 52
Hanworth Manor, Middx, 134
Harcourt-Smith, Simon, 157
HARDWICK HALL, Derbyshire, 80–1
Hardy, Thomas, 21, 70
HARE HILL, Cheshire, 82
Harewood, (George) 7th Earl of, 37
Harewood family, 46
Harewood House, Yorks, 34, 37, 49, 50, 84, 94
Harleyford Manor, Bucks, 179
Harold, *see* Nicolson, Harold
Harris, Henry (Bogey), 144, 201
Harrod, (Billa) Mrs Roy, 50
Harrod, Roy, 24, 66
Hartington, (Andrew) Marquess of, 31, 79–80, 81, 82, 94
Hartington, (Deborah) Marchioness of, 31, 79–80, 81, 82, 94
Hartwell House, Bucks, 69
Harvey, Bishop of Exeter, 90
Harvey, John, 152
Harvington Hall, Worcs, 39
Haslip, Joan, 112
HATCHLANDS, Surrey, 177, 193

Hatfield House, Herts, 61, 130, 136
Hatherop Castle school, Glos, 179
Hayter, Sir George, 31
Heber-Percy family, 23, 42, 153
Heckfield House, Berks, 166, 191
Helpman, Robert, 175
Hendy, Philip, 72
Henham Hall, Suffolk, 221
Henry, Henry, 134
Herbert, Hon. David, 63
Hertford, Hugh, 8th Marquess of, 119
Hesketh, 2nd Lord, 85
Hesketh, Fleetwood- family, 132, 133
Heveningham Hall, Suffolk, 64
Heygate, John, 63
HIDCOTE MANOR, Glos, 66, 91–2,
    138, 167, 181, 223
Higher Bockhampton, Dorset,
    HARDY'S COTTAGE, 21
Hildyard, Myles, 189
Hill, Lady Anne, 223
Hill, Colonel Arthur, see Sandys, 6th
    Lord
Hill, Heywood, 29, 88, 146, 214
Hill, Captain John, 68, 136–7, 182, 221
HILL TOP, Sawrey, Lancs, 186
Hills, Ivan, 163, 204
Hinks, Roger, 97, 99
Hippisley-Cox, Sir Geoffrey, 88
Historic Buildings Committee,
    National Trust, 45, 114, 115, 133,
    152, 170, 212
Hoare, Rennie, 56, 65
Hobhouse, Christopher, 21
Hobhouse family, 142
Hodgson, Major, 142, 148
Hofmannsthal, Lady Elizabeth, 154,
    193
Holkham Hall, Norfolk, 33, 72, 207
Holland, Henry, 119
Holland House, Middlesex, 198
Holland-Martin, Christopher, 52
Holland-Martin, (Ruby) Edward, 52,
    68, 165
Hollyoak, Mr (agent at Charlecote),
    32, 118, 147
Holnest Park, Dorset, 88

Hore-Belisha, Mrs, 69
Hornyold-Strickland, Henry and Hon.
    Mrs, 186–7
HORTON COURT, Glos, 148
Houghton Brown, Geoffrey, 122, 169
Houghton Hall, Norfolk, 19, 135
HOUSESTEADS CAMP,
    Northumberland, 170
Howard, Christian, 216, 217
Howard, George, 43, 152–3, 216, 217
Hudson, Lady, 170, 191
HUGHENDEN MANOR, Bucks,
    84–5, 113, 193, 224
Humphreys, Sir Francis and Lady, 189
Hunt, Leigh, 158
Hussey, (Betty) Mrs Christopher, 68,
    112, 154
Hussey, Christopher, 112, 146, 154,
    215, 222
Hyslop, Geddes (Paul), 15, 65, 115,
    198, 201

Iford Manor, Wilts, 48, 91, 194, 202
Ilchester, 6th Earl and Countess of,
    198
Iraq, Regent of, 198–9
Ireland, 45–7
Ischia, island of, 105–6
Isham, Sir Gyles, 12th Bt, 189
Isle of Wight, 71
Isola Bella, Lake Maggiore, 111–12
Italy, 34, 60, 65, 71, 74, 95–112, 115,
    155–62, 195, 197, 205–7
Iveagh, 2nd Earl and Countess of, 45

Jackson, Canon, 117
James, see Pope-Hennessy, James
James, Henry (novelist), 86, 171
James, Mrs Henry, 84, 86, 130
James, Philip, 72, 138
Jebb, Gladwyn, 77
Jebb, (Cynthia) Mrs Gladwyn, 69, 190
Jenner, Sir Walter, 2nd Bt, 122–3, 142,
    148, 150
Jenyns, Soane, 15
Jersey, Isle of, 40–1, 77
Jersey, (Bianca) Countess of, 27, 40, 77

Jersey, (Grandy) 9th Earl of, 27, 40–1, 77, 122, 221–2
Johnson, Dr Samuel, 165, 222
Johnston, Lawrence, 66, 91–2
Jones, Colin, 167, 180
Jones, Inigo, 16, 19, 79, 80, 94
Jourdain, Margaret, 28, 76, 124, 137, 181, 199, 209, 210, 213, 216
Jouy-en-Josas, Seine et Oise, 172–3, 175, 176, 182, 183, 194–5, 202, 205
Jullian, Philippe, 124

Kaines-Smith, Mr, 43
Kearney, Mary, 142, 146
Keats, John, 104, 133, 157
Keats-Shelley Committee, 122, 124, 133
Kedleston Hall, Derbyshire, 118
Kendrick, Tom (British Museum), 23, 152, 198
Kenilworth Castle, Warwickshire, 192
Kennet, (Kathleen) Lady, 48, 53, 72, 138, 141
Kent, Princess Marina, Duchess of, 73
Kent, William, 16, 33, 51, 94
Ketton-Cremer, Wyndham, 58, 189
Kiftsgate Court, Glos, 223
Kimbolton Castle, Hunts, 85
King, William (Willy) and Viva, 23, 166, 172
King's College Chapel, Cambridge, 57, 108
Kingsley, Hants, 56–7
Kinross, Patrick, 3rd Lord and (Angela) Lady, 21, 36, 63, 84, 123, 135, 136, 145, 220
KNOLE, Kent, 77, 87, 93, 125, 162–3, 183
Knollys, Eardley, 16, 20–2, 27, 28, 33, 42, 55–6, 63–4, 65, 87–8, 90–1, 115, 116, 123, 133, 142, 145, 147–9, 150, 176–7, 180, 198, 203, 209, 212, 213

LACOCK ABBEY, Wilts, 99, 117
Lake District, 186–7
LAMB HOUSE, Rye, Sussex, 84, 86
Lambton, Lady Kitty, 51

Lamington, (Riette) Lady, 16, 48–9, 94, 123, 134, 151
Lancaster, Osbert, 76
Lancret, Nicolas, 194
Lane-Fox, Hon. Mrs, 125
Langley, Batty, 168
Langley Marish church, Bucks, 52
Langley-Taylor, George, 85
Lannerton, Lord, 36
Lansberg, Bertie, 206
Lansel, Dr Pierre, 40, 49, 122, 131, 134, 210, 213
Lascelles, Edward and Mrs, 36
Lawrence, Samuel, 209
Lawrence, T. E., 44
Lawrence, Sir Thomas, 211
Leeper, (Janet) Mrs, 23
Lees-Milne, Dick (brother), 169, 171, 207, 212, 225, 226–7, 228
Lees-Milne, Dorothy (aunt), 68, 219, 220
Lees-Milne, Elaine (sister-in-law), 207, 212, 222–3, 225, 226, 228
Lees-Milne, G. C. (father), 61, 69, 82, 121, 137, 142, 148, 167, 169–70, 171–2, 174, 182, 187, 194, 199, 203, 207, 208–9, 212, 213, 214, 216, 218, 222–3, 225–7, 228, 229
Lees-Milne, Helen (mother), 32, 65, 75, 82, 93, 137, 148, 167, 169–70, 171–2, 182, 191, 194, 197, 203, 207–18 passim, 222, 225–6, 228–9
Leggatt, Harry, 214
Lehmann, John, 155, 157, 172, 228
Leicester, 4th Earl of, 72, 207
Leicester Galleries, London, 126–7
Leigh, Vivien, 26
Lely, Sir Peter, 57
Lennox-Boyd, Alan, 45–6, 149, 198
Lennox-Boyd, Lady Patricia, 45–6
Leslie, John, 158
Levens Castle, Westmorland, 186
Leveson-Gower, William, 88–9
Lindridge, Devon, 148–9
Lindsay, Nancy, 91–2, 223
Lindsay, (Norah) Mrs, 91
Lister, E. G. (Ted), 34, 56, 113–14, 215

Listowel, Freda, Countess of, 198
Little Comberton church, Worcs, 52
LITTLE MORETON HALL,
    Cheshire, 82, 178
Lloyd, (Blanche) Lady, 44
Lloyd, (George) 1st Lord Lloyd of
    Dolobran, 29, 44–5, 124, 171
Lloyd George, Rt Hon. David, 213n.
London, No. 4 St James's Square, 72
London, Bishop of, 116–17
Long, (David) 2nd Viscount, 66–7
Long Crichel House, Dorset, 16, 21,
    22, 54, 55, 56, 63, 64, 87, 142, 150,
    177, 198
Longbridge Deverill church, Wilts,
    215
Longford Castle, Wilts, 201–2
Longleat, Wilts, 89, 117, 146, 154
Lothian, 11th Marquess of, 27
Lothian, 12th Marquess of, 26, 58, 168
Lowinsky, (Ruth) Mrs Thomas, 172
Lowndes, Susan, 167
Lubbock, Lys, see Connolly, Lys
Lucy, Alice, see Fairfax-Lucy, Alice
Lucy, Brian, see Fairfax-Lucy, Brian
Lucy, George, 147
Lucy, Sir Thomas, 15, 223
Lucy family, 43
Luddington family, 58
Lushington, Miss, 53, 56–7
Lutwyche Hall, Shropshire, 38
Lutyens, Sir Edwin, 78
LYME PARK, Cheshire, 82, 207
Lyminge, Robert (architect), 144
Lynn, Olga (Oggy), 95, 136, 175, 186,
    211
LYTES CARY MANOR, Somerset,
    123, 142, 148, 150
Lyttelton, Rosemary, 183, 198, 211,
    229

Macaulay, Rose, 137, 143, 155, 164,
    204, 211–12, 214
MacCarthy, Desmond, 129, 171
Macdonell, Hugh, 172, 194
Macdonell, John, 57
MacGregor, John, 149, 153

McKechnie (dentist), 115, 142–3, 144,
    171
Mackenzie, Compton, 42
McKie, William, 212
Maclagan, Sir Eric, 45
Maclean, Fitzroy, 123
Macmillan, Harold, MP, 222
Madresfield Court, Worcs, 75–6
Malet, Colonel, 24
Mallaby, George, 77
Mander, Sir Geoffrey, 127
Mander, (Rosalie) Lady, 53, 122
Manners, Lord John, 17
Mansard, François, 173
Margaret, Princess, 189
Marlborough, 1st Duke of, 223
Marlborough Club, Pall Mall,
    London, 59, 133
Marsh, (Eddie) Sir Edward, 15–16,
    130, 144, 153, 161, 198
Martineau, Anthony, 18, 125–6
Mary, Princess Royal, 18, 35, 37, 70,
    94
Mary, Queen, consort of George V,
    17, 69–70, 126
Massingberd, Lady Montgomery-,
    19–20
Massingberd, Field Marshal, Sir
    Archibald Montgomery-, 20
Matheson, MacLeod, 68
Matheson, Hilda, 61
Matson House, Glos, 91, 127, 137
Matthews, Dean of St Paul's, 132
Maugham, Somerset (Willie), 129
Maxwell, (Diane) Mrs Terence, 25,
    189–90
Mendelssohn, Félix, 100, 156
Meols Hall, Lancs, 132
MERTON ABBEY WALL, Surrey,
    28
Merton College, Oxford, 137
Messel, Oliver, 126–7, 162, 163, 181
Methuen, Paul, 4th Baron, and
    (Norah) Lady, 65, 67, 141–2
Metternich, Count, 52, 57, 59, 175,
    179
Michelangelo, 106, 110, 200

Middlefield, Cambs, 78
Midi, see Gascoigne, Mrs
Milford, 1st Lord, 146–7
Millais, Sir John Everett, 1st Bt, 214
Millais, Sir Ralph, 5th Bt, 214
Millar, Oliver, 114
Miller-Jones, Keith, 20, 74, 213
Mills, John, 138
Milnes-Gaskell, Lady Constance, 33,
    69–70
Ministry of Planning, 91, 137
Ministry of Works, 29, 33, 34, 38, 84,
    148, 149, 152, 154, 165, 170, 180,
    191, 205
Mitchell, (Clara) Mrs David, 170, 226
Mitford, Hon. Unity (Bobo), 59
Mitford, Nancy (Hon. Mrs Peter
    Rodd), 18, 20, 32, 123, 146, 163,
    196, 205
Mitford, (Tom) Hon. T. D. F., 32, 59,
    150
Monckton, Rt Hon. Walter, 131
Monk Hopton House, Shropshire, 33,
    38, 39, 119
MONTACUTE HOUSE, Somerset,
    20–1, 63, 64, 87, 88, 91, 116, 142,
    149
Montagu, (Venetia) Hon. Mrs Edwin,
    116, 213n.
Montgomery, Field Marshal, 1st
    Viscount, 190–1
Montrose House, Petersham, Surrey,
    63
Moore, (Garrett) Viscount, 33, 168,
    198
Moore, (Joan) Viscountess, 23, 33,
    58–9, 198
Moray, (Barbara) Countess of, 48–9,
    52, 70, 115, 150, 179, 193
Morgan, Hon. John, 219–20
Morland, George, 119
Morris, William, 36, 84
Morrison, Rt Hon. Herbert, 199
Mortimer, Raymond, 16, 22, 115, 142,
    159, 176, 177, 198, 201
Mosley, (Maud) Lady, 68
Motley, (Mary) Mrs Lewis, 38–9

MOTTISFONT ABBEY, Hants, 50
Moulton, Alex, 30, 92
Moulton, Mrs, 92
MOW COP, Cheshire, 82
Mozart, Wolfgang Amadeus, 108,
    161, 173, 175, 176, 195, 200
Muir, (Heather) Mrs Jack, 223
Munday, Mrs, 135
Murat, Princess, 167
Musgrave, Clifford, 73
Mussolini, Benito, 96, 112

Nancy, see Mitford, Nancy
Napoleon I, Emperor, 112, 159, 223
Narni, Latium, Italy, 106–7
National Buildings Record, 45, 174
National Gallery, London, 72, 177–8
National Portrait Gallery, London,
    18–19, 45, 223
National Trust Gardens Committee,
    37
National Trust Gardens Fund, 68
Navarro, Madame de, 192
Neate, Kenneth, 122
Nether Lypiatt Manor, Glos, 180
NEWARK PARK, Glos, 179–80
Newdigate family, 127
Newman, J., 209
Newton, Ivor, 169
Nicolson, (Ben) L. B., 17, 27–8, 30–1,
    45, 48, 84, 114–15, 124, 192, 221,
    222
Nicolson, Hon. Harold, 16, 17, 27,
    30–1, 43–4, 48, 69, 84, 124, 131–2,
    162–3, 185, 190, 220, 222
Nicolson, Nigel, 146
Noel family, 66
Nonesuch House, Surrey, 205
Norman, Hugh, 168
Norman, Ronald C., 168
Normann, Sir Eric de, 34, 205
Norrington Manor, Wilts, 114
Northcliffe, Viscount, 170
Northcote, James, 90

Ockwells Manor, Berks, 178
O'Donovan, Patrick, 93

Ogilvie-Grant, Mark, 69, 84, 137, 188, 194

OLD POST OFFICE, Tintagel, 22

Oliver, Isaac, 223

Oliver, Vic, 27

Olivier, Laurence, 60

Olney, Bucks, 31–2

Ombersley Court, Worcs, 121

Onslow, 6th Earl and Countess of, 224

Osborne, Sir D'Arcy, 98, 100, 101, 104, 106, 156

OSTERLEY PARK, Middlesex, 40–1, 50, 72, 77, 122, 149, 154, 212, 221–2

O'Sullivan, Miss, 27

Overbury Court, Worcs, 52

Oxburgh church, Norfolk, 57

Oxford, 52, 66, 83, 137, 191, 208

PACKWOOD HOUSE, Warwickshire, 32, 138, 167

Paget, Lady Caroline, 183

Palazzo Giraud, Rome, 95

Palazzo Ruccellai, Florence, 95

Palazzo Sacchetti, Rome, 98

Palazzo Venezia, Rome, 99

Palladio, Andrea, 96, 206, 217

Panini, Giovanni Paolo, 157

Parham family, 114

Paris, 95, 112, 161, 172, 173, 183, 194, 205, 175–6

Parish, Woodbine, 28

Parnis, A. E. L., 193, 199

Parsons, Lady Bridget, 20, 26, 33, 37–8, 39, 60, 72, 74, 84, 115, 151, 155, 163, 181, 182, 194, 207

Paterson, Florence, 67, 84–5

Patmore, Coventry, 171

Pavitt, Burnet, 23, 24, 26, 27–8, 33, 34, 41–2, 43, 45, 58, 62, 77, 134, 199

Pavlovsky, Princess Romanovsky (Mamie), 199

Pawson, Tony, 131

Paxton, Sir Joseph, 79

Pearsall Smith, Logan, 55, 214, 222

Pembroke, Mary, wife of 2nd Earl of, 74

Penrose, Alec, 29, 57–8, 123–4, 135, 136, 207

Penrose, Beakers, 57

Penrose, (Frances) Mrs Alec, 58, 123–4

Penshurst Place, Kent, 168

Perugia, Umbria, 107–9, 159

Peruzzi, Baldassare Tommaso, 97

Peterborough Cathedral, 19

Petersham Manor, Surrey, 62, 63

Peto, (Frances) Lady, 25, 91

Peto, Sir Michael, 2nd Bt, 21, 48, 91

Philipps, (Johnnie) Sir John, 3rd Bt, 130, 144, 147

Picton Castle, Pembrokeshire, 147

Piggott, Sir Richard, 50

Pilkington, Vere, 135

Pisa, 159–60

Pisano, G., 159–60

Pissarro, Camille and family, 115

Pitman, Hugo and Mrs, 70, 193

Pius XII, Pope, 98, 100–1, 102–4

Plunkett, (Sheila) Hon. Mrs Randal, 130, 146–7, 164–5

POLESDEN LACEY, Surrey, 73, 86, 177, 185

Polidori, Dr J. W., 44

Pope-Hennessy, James, 16, 17, 27, 30–1, 49, 52, 84, 85, 86–7, 93, 114, 124, 125, 133, 151, 154, 155, 163, 166, 171, 172, 179, 185, 187, 188, 203–4, 209, 211

Pope-Hennessy, John, 52, 204, 214

Pope-Hennessy, Dame Una, 62–3, 203–4

Portsmouth, Louise de Keroualle, Duchess of, 73

Potter, Beatrix, 186

Pratt, Colonel E. Roger, 57

Pratt, Sir Roger, 57

Pratt's Club, Park Place, London, 131

Pre-Raphaelites, 56, 127, 144

Prestbury, nr. Cheltenham, Glos, 65–6

Preston, Stuart, 59, 60, 143

PRIEST'S HOUSE, SMALL-HYTHE, Kent, 192

Pritchett, Victor, 153

Prokofiev, Sergei, 174–5

Provence, France, 195–6, 197, 198
Pryce-Jones, Alan, 21, 29, 31, 46, 60,
    70, 145, 153
Public Records Office, Chancery
    Lane, London, 24, 126, 134, 224
Puleston, Mrs Crawshay (Aunt
    Edith), 51
Pyne, W. H. and family, 203

Quainton church, Bucks, 50, 223
QUEBEC HOUSE, Westerham,
    Kent, 93
Quennell, Peter, 31, 172

Radier Manor, Jersey, 40, 77
Radnor, 7th Earl of, 201
Radziwill, Princess Dolly, 196
Ragley Hall, Warwickshire, 118–19,
    120
Rapallo, Liguria, Italy, 160, 161
Rathbone, (Jack) J. F. W., 125, 162,
    165, 166–7, 177, 188, 201, 214, 222
Rattigan, Terence, 155
Rayner-Wood, A. C., 52, 167
Rea, 2nd Lord, 84
Red Hall, Bourne, Lincs, 19
Redesdale, 2nd Lord, 32, 83
Redfern Gallery, London, 213
Reed, Henry, 63
Revelstoke, 2nd Lord, 70
Reynolds, Graham, 116
Ribbesford House, Worcs, 90, 202
Richardson, Professor A. E., 26–7
Richardson, Ralph, 164, 209
Richmond, Dukes of, 73
Richmond, Sir William, 133
Richmond Lodge, Bath, 148
Rick, see Stewart-Jones, Richard
Rickett, Denis, 123
Rigaud, Hyacinthe, 186
Robert, Duke of Normandy, 202
Roberts, Thomas, 51
Rodd, Hon. Peter, 97, 99
Rodd, (Taffy) Hon. G. G. R., 97–8,
    99
Rolls Museum, Chancery Lane,
    London, 24

Rome, 55, 95–101, 104, 106, 115, 154,
    155–8
Roosevelt, (Eleanor) Mrs, 49
Rose, Sir Francis, 4th Bt, 122
Ross, Alan, 145
Ross, Robert (Robbie), 172
Rosse, (Anne) Countess of, 26, 30, 40,
    46–8, 71, 78, 84, 181, 194
Rosse, (Michael) 6th Earl of, 18, 40,
    46–8, 71, 78, 84, 110, 115, 134, 194
Rothschild, Anthony de, 211
Rothschild, Barbara, Lady, 106–10
Roubiliac, Louis François, 86
Rousham, Oxon, 50–1
Rowley, Joshua, 32, 43, 76
Rowley, Lady Sibell, 181
Rubinstein, Artur, 123
Rufford Abbey, Notts, 189
Ruperra Castle, Monmouthshire, 219
Rupert of the Rhine, Prince, 121
Ruskin, John, 36, 53, 70
Russell, Mrs Alaric, 116
Russell, John, 193–4
Russell, (Maud) Mrs Gilbert, 50
Rutland, 5th Duke of, 17
Rutland, 10th Duke of, 80
Rutland Lodge, Petersham, Surrey, 63
Ryan, Adrian (painter), 213
Ryston Hall, Norfolk, 57

Sackville, (Charles) 4th Lord, 93,
    162–3, 183
Sackville-West, Hon. Edward (Eddy),
    15, 16, 22, 23, 42, 55, 63, 142, 177,
    193, 194
Sackville-West, Hon. Vita, 28, 37, 48,
    61, 84, 114, 124, 129, 133, 185, 188,
    192
St Albans, 12th Duke of, 162
St Clair-Erskine, Hon. Hamish, 23,
    132
St Clere, Kent, 168
St George's Chapel, Windsor, 33
St George's Hall, King's Lynn,
    Norfolk, 29
St Germans, (Nellie) Countess of, 194
St Giles's House, Dorset, 64–5

St James's Palace, London, 84
St John Lateran, Rome, 99
ST JOHN'S, JERUSALEM, Kent, 187
Sta Maria degli Angeli, Rome, 107
St Michael's, Basingstoke, Hants, 63
St Paul's, Waldenbury, Herts, 41, 58, 62, 199
St Paul's Cathedral, London, 126, 132
St Peter's, Rome, 95–6, 101, 104, 156, 158
St Thomas's Hospital, London, 213
Saint-Rémy, Provence, 197
Sale, Frank (singer), 24
Salisbury, 5th Marquess of, 88
Salter, Sir Arthur, 222
Salter, Lady, 170, 222
Salvin, Anthony, 201–2
Sambourne, Linley, 71
San Onofrio, Rome, 96
San Stefano Rotondo, Rome, 100
Sandby, Paul, 132
Sandringham House, Norfolk, 70
Sands, Ethel, 171, 172, 228
Sandys, (Diana) Mrs Duncan, 133
Sandys, Duncan, MP, 223
Sandys, George (poet and traveller), 121
Sandys, 6th Lord, 121
Santa Margherita, Liguria, Italy, 160
Sargent, Malcolm, 135, 227–8
Schwarzkopf, Elizabeth, 108, 113, 122
Scott, Captain R. Falcon, RN, 138, 141
Scott, Geoffrey, 109, 111
Scott, Kathleen, see Kennet, Kathleen
Scott, Peter, 138, 141
SELBORNE HILL, Hants, 200
Selby-Lowndes, Diana, 36
Senago Villa, near Milan, 110–11, 112
Send House, Surrey, 193
Senhouse, Roger, 143, 155
Sens Cathedral, France, 195
Seymour, Lady Helen, 118
Seymour family, 118
Shaftesbury, 1st Earl of and Lady, 64–5

Shakespeare, William, 15, 60, 159, 161, 167, 200
SHALFORD MILL HOUSE, Surrey, 185
Shawe-Taylor, Desmond, 16, 47, 55, 59, 63, 65, 87, 94–6, 97, 98, 99, 100–1, 104–6, 142, 158, 201
Sheafhayne House, Devon, 89
Shearer, Moyra, 167
Shelburne Rooms, Dublin, 48
Shelley, Mary, 56
Shelley, Percy Bysshe, 134, 158
Sherwood, 1st Lord, 49
Shuttleworth, 4th Lord and Lady, 217–18, 219
Sickert, Walter, 223
Sidney, Colonel Henry, 174
Silton Church, Dorset, 43
Silveri, Paolo (singer), 122, 133
Simpson, Sir James, 1st Bt (Dr), 177
SISSINGHURST CASTLE, Kent, 188, 192
Sisson, Marshall, 72, 135–6
Sitwell, (Georgia) Mrs Sacheverell, 31, 86, 145, 153
Sitwell, Sir Osbert, 5th Bt, 59, 81, 181
Sitwell, Reresby, 86
Sitwell, Sacheverell, 17, 24, 85–6, 145, 153
SIZERGH CASTLE, Westmorland, 186–7
SMALLHYTHE PROPERTIES, Kent, 192
Smith, H. Clifford, 124, 134, 152
Smith of Warwick, Francis, 118
Smith, Hubert (chief agent), 29, 49, 71, 75, 94, 125, 131, 154, 180
Smith, Thornton, 67
Smythson, Robert, 78–9, 121, 123, 189, 202
SNOWSHILL MANOR, Glos, 82–3
Soames, Christopher, 223
Soane, Sir John, 57
Soane Museum, London, 59, 69, 71, 124
Society of Antiquaries, 152
Society for the Protection of Ancient

Buildings (SPAB), 35, 36, 48, 127, 151

Somers Cocks, John, 95, 96, 97, 100

South Mimms church, Herts, 44

South Wraxall Manor, Wilts, 66–7

Sparrow, John, 146

Spectator, The, 38, 124, 155

Spello, Umbria, Italy, 107

Spencer, Lord Robert, 36

Spira, Dr Jacques, 210, 213

Spoleto, Umbria, Italy, 107

Stamford, Lincs, 78

Stanhope, Colonel, 17

Stanhope, Lady Hester, 220

Stanley, Hon. Venetia, *see* Montagu, Mrs Edwin

Steegmann, John, 190

Stevens, Alfred, 133

Stevens, Audrey (sister) Mrs, 65, 93, 213, 224–5, 228

Stevens, Dale (niece), 224

Stevenson, Frances, 213n.

STEVENTON PRIORY, Berks, 153

Stewart-Jones, Richard (Rick), 35, 83, 127, 129, 153, 154, 165, 166, 221

Stoke Edith House, Herefordshire, 50

STOKE POGES, GRAY'S MONUMENT, Bucks, 33

STONEACRE, Otham, Kent, 187

STONEHENGE, land at, Wilts, 22

STOURHEAD, Wilts, 16, 22, 28, 33, 42–3, 44, 55–6, 63, 65, 87, 142, 215

Stourton Castle, Worcs, 89

Stow-on-the-Wold, Glos, 208, 222, 228

Stowe, Bucks, 174

Strachey, James, 24

Strachey, Lytton, 24, 172

Stratfield Saye, Hants, 166, 190, 192, 200–1

Stratford-on-Avon, Warwickshire, 32, 147, 167

Stresa, Italy, 111, 112

Stroud, Dorothy, 69

Strutt, (Eny) Hon. Mrs A. C., 17

Stuart, Lady Arabella, 179

Stuart, Hon. David, 179

Stuart family, 186

Subercaseaux, Léon, 48

Subercaseaux, (Paz) Madame, 48–9, 143, 144, 146, 154, 184, 186, 198

Summerson, John, 35, 59, 61, 69, 71, 72, 124, 168

Sutton Scarsdale, Derbyshire, 81–2, 118

Svelode of Russia, Prince, 199

Swakeleys, Middx, 53–4

Sweeny, (Margaret) Mrs Charles, 131

Swell church, Glos, 228

Swinbrook, Oxon, 59

Syon House, Middlesex, 74

Tallents, Sir Stephen, 187

Tanfield family, 52

Tate Gallery, London, 30, 31, 127, 137, 188

Tavistock, Devon, 21–2, 90

Teresa, St, 30

Terry, Ellen, 192

Tewkesbury Abbey, Glos, 202

Thompson, Bruce, 186

Thompson, Francis (librarian at Chatsworth), 79

Thorndike, Sybil, 131

Thornhill, Sir James, 133

Thorpe, John, 69, 71, 123, 124, 202

Throckmorton, Lilian, Lady, 39, 128, 167

Thwaite, Commander, 166

Thynne, Sir John, 117, 215

Tijou, Jean, 80, 205

The Times, 226

TINTAGEL, OLD POST OFFICE, Cornwall, 22

Tisbury church, Wilts, 56

Tivoli, nr. Rome, 99, 156

TOWN END, Troutbeck, Westmorland, 186

Trastevere, Rome, 101

Travellers' Club, Pall Mall, London, 50, 162, 172, 185, 220

Treasury, the, Whitehall, 34, 35, 36, 70–1, 74, 77, 84, 94, 165

Tredegar House, Monmouthshire, 219

Tree, Ronald and Nancy, 66, 128–9, 189
Trelawny, Edward, 158
Trevelyan, Dr G. M., 48, 53
Trevelyan, George, 38, 82, 116, 120
Trevi, Umbria, Italy, 107
Trinity College of Music, 129
Trotter, Philip, 131
TUDOR MERCHANT'S HOUSE, Tenby, 52
Tunnard, Peter, 199
Turf Club, 124
Turner, Blanche (singer), 113
Tussaud, Madame, 228
Tvede, Mogens, 196

University College, Oxford, 134
UPTON HOUSE, Warwickshire, 15, 51, 129, 132, 147, 163, 166–7

Valmarana, Count, 206
Van Nost, John, 43
Vanbrugh, Sir John, 70
Vane, Colonel W. M. Fletcher, 68
Vansittart, 1st Lord, 40
Vardy, John, 16
Vassali, Francesco, 119
Vatican, Rome, 95, 98, 100–1, 158
Vaughan, (Florence) Mrs C. J., 77
Venice, Italy, 206
Verona, Italy, 205
Versailles, France, 174, 175–6, 183
Vesci, (Lois) Viscountess de, 38, 60, 119, 155, 207
Vesci, 5th Viscount de, 38, 39
Vicenza, Italy, 206
Victoria, Queen, 84, 118
Victoria & Albert Museum, London, 45, 49, 116, 212, 221, 222
Vignola, Giacomo Barozzi da, 95, 96–7
Villa Capra, Vicenza, Italy, 206
Villa d'Este, Tivoli, Italy, 156–7
Villa Giulia, Rome, 97
Villa Malcontenta, Venetia, Italy, 206
Villa Maser, Venetia, Italy, 206, 217
Villa Medici, Rome, 106

THE VYNE, Hants, 87

WADDESDON MANOR, Bucks, 50
Wade, Charles, 82–3
Wadham College, Oxford, 137, 191
Wagner, Anthony, 134
Walker, Ethel, 43, 94
WALL MUSEUM, Letocetum, Staffs, 128
Wallace, Carew, 53–4, 122, 178
Wallace Collection, 25, 54, 172
WALLINGTON HALL, Northumberland, 58
Wallraf, Paul, 187
Walpole, Horace, 19, 73, 119
Warde, (Muriel) Mrs R. E., 198
Wardour Castle, Wilts, 56, 202
Wardour Old Castle, Wilts, 121
Warner, Christopher, 144
Warner, Rex, 106–10
Warwick Castle, Warwickshire, 147
Watercolour Society, 203
Waterhouse, Ellis, 45
Watson, Francis, 54
Webb, Philip, 36
Welbeck Abbey, Notts, 189
Wellesbourne church, Warwickshire, 118
Wellington, 1st Duke of, 17, 200–1
Wellington, (Gerry) 7th Duke of, 49, 61, 166, 168, 190, 191, 200–1
WELLINGTON MONUMENT, Somerset, 149
Wells, H. G., 56
Wells Cathedral, Somerset, 203
Wenlock Priory, Shropshire, 38
West, Anthony, 55–6
West, (Kitty) Mrs, 55–6
West, Rebecca, 56
WEST WYCOMBE PARK, Bucks, 25, 54, 75, 168, 182, 193
WESTERHAM, Kent (Wolfe's house), 93
Westminster, 2nd Duke of, 64, 86
Westminster, Loelia, Duchess of, 131, 132, 136, 141, 145, 193

Westminster Abbey, 43, 44, 54, 165, 212
Weston Hall, Northants, 85
Weston-Sub-Edge church, Glos, 51
Weston Underwood Manor, Bucks, 31–2
WESTWOOD MANOR, Wilts, 114, 215
Whitworth family, 51–2
Wickhamford Manor, Worcs, 32, 43, 51, 52, 65, 76, 82, 117, 169, 174, 191, 203, 208, 222, 225, 226–7
WIGHTWICK MANOR, Staffs, 127, 144, 214
WILDERHOPE MANOR, Shropshire, 38
Willersey Hill, Glos, 137
Willingdon, 1st Marquess of, 53
Wilton, (John) 7th Earl of, 28, 32, 188–9
Wilton House, Wilts, 42, 63, 202
Wimborne minster, Dorset, 56
Winant, John (American Ambassador), 66
Wincanton, Somerset, 22, 88
Winchester, St Cross church, Hants, 55
Winchester Cathedral, 16, 55
Windsor Castle, Berks, 33, 49
Wing church, Bucks, 76
Wingfield-Digby, George, 123, 221
Winn, Elizabeth, 116
Winn, Godfrey, 76–7
WINSTER MARKET HOUSE, Derbyshire, 79
Winterbottom, Hiram, 206
Winwood family, 50
Wisbech Museum, Cambs, 58
Wisbech Society, 58, 135
Wolfe, General James, 93

Wollaton Hall, Notts, 78–9, 202
Wolryche-Whitmore, Mr and Mrs G. C., 120–1
Womersley Park, Yorkshire, 78
Woodhouse, Mrs Gordon, 101
WOOLBEDING, Midhurst, Sussex, 36
Woollas Hall, Worcs, 51–2
Woolner, Mrs A. H., 21
Wootton Lodge, Staffs, 218
Worcester Cathedral, 202
Worsley, Lady, 70
Worthington, Lady Diana, 32, 37, 67
Worthington, Greville, 32
Worthington, Hubert, 49
WRAY CASTLE, Windermere, 186
Wren, Sir Christopher, 86, 120
Wrest Park, Beds, 19
Wright, Sir Nathan, 86
Wroxton Church, Oxon, 43
Wyatt, James, 73, 118
Wyattville, Sir Jeffry, 79, 81, 89
Wyndham, John, 116
Wyndham, (Gladys) Hon. Mrs E. S., 127, 129
Wyndham Clark family, 15
Wyndham family, 114

Yarty Farm, Devon, 89–90
Yates, Mr and Mrs (Montacute custodians), 63–4
Yates family, 142
York Minster, 216–17
Yorke, (Dig) Hon. Mrs Henry, 124, 136
Yorke, Henry (Henry Green), 129, 136
Young, Sir Edward Hilton, 141
Young, Hon. Wayland Hilton, 20

Zurich, Switzerland, 205